FIVE ON A TREASURE ISLAND

FIVE ON A TREASURE ISLAND

FIVE ON A TREASURE ISLAND

ENID BLYTON

Illustrated by
Eileen A. Soper

**Hodder
Children's
Books**

a division of Hachette Children's Books

First published in Great Britain in 1942
by Hodder and Stoughton

This edition 1997

39

A catalogue record for this title is available from the
British Library.

ISBN-13: 978 0 340 68106 0

Typeset by Hewer Text (UK) Ltd, Edinburgh
Printed and bound in Great Britain by
Clays Ltd, St Ives plc

Hodder Children's Books
a division of Hachette Children's Books
338 Euston Road, London NW1 3BH
An Hachette UK Company
www.hachette.co.uk

CONTENTS

CONTENTS

CHAPTER ONE

A great surprise

'MOTHER, HAVE you heard about our summer holidays yet?' said Julian, at the breakfast-table. 'Can we go to Polseath as usual?'

'I'm afraid not,' said his mother. 'They are quite full up this year.'

The three children at the breakfast-table looked at one another in great disappointment. They did so love the house at Polseath. The beach was so lovely there, too, and the bathing was fine.

'Cheer up,' said Daddy. 'I dare say we'll find somewhere else just as good for you. And anyway, Mother and I won't be able to go with you this year. Has Mother told you?'

'No!' said Anne. 'Oh, Mother – is it true? Can't you really come with us on our holidays? You always do.'

'Well, this time Daddy wants me to go to Scotland with him,' said Mother. 'All by ourselves! And as you are really getting big enough to look after yourselves now, we thought it would be rather fun for you to have a holiday on your own too. But now that you can't go to Polseath, I don't really quite know where to send you.'

'What about Quentin's?' suddenly said Daddy. Quentin was his brother, the children's uncle. They had only seen him once, and had been rather frightened of him. He was a very tall, frowning man, a clever scientist who spent all his time studying. He lived by the sea – but that was about all that the children knew of him!

'Quentin?' said Mother, pursing her lips. 'Whatever made you think of him? I shouldn't think he'd want the children messing about in his little house.'

'Well,' said Daddy, 'I had to see Quentin's wife in town the other day, about a business matter – and I don't think things are going too well for them. Fanny said that she would be quite glad if she could hear of one or two people to live with her for a while, to bring a little money in. Their house is by the sea, you know. It might be just the thing for the children. Fanny is very nice – she would look after them well.'

'Yes – and she has a child of her own too, hasn't she?' said the children's mother. 'Let me see – what's her name – something funny – yes, Georgina! How old would she be? About eleven, I should think.'

'Same age as me,' said Dick. 'Fancy having a cousin we've never seen! She must be jolly lonely all by herself. I've got Julian and Anne to play with – but Georgina is just one on her own. I should think she'd be glad to see us.'

'Well, your Aunt Fanny said that her Georgina would love a bit of company,' said Daddy. 'You know, I really think that would solve our difficulty, if we telephone to Fanny and arrange for the children to go there. It would

2

help Fanny, I'm sure, and Georgina would love to have someone to play with in the holidays. And we should know that our three were safe.'

The children began to feel rather excited. It would be fun to go to a place they had never been to before, and stay with an unknown cousin.

'Are there cliffs and rocks and sands there?' asked Anne. 'Is it a nice place?'

'I don't remember it very well,' said Daddy. 'But I feel sure it's an exciting kind of place. Anyway, you'll love it! It's called Kirrin Bay. Your Aunt Fanny has lived there all her life, and wouldn't leave it for anything.'

'Oh Daddy, do telephone to Aunt Fanny and ask her if we can go there!' cried Dick. 'I just feel as if it's the right place somehow. It sounds sort of adventurous!'

'Oh, you always say that, wherever you go!' said Daddy, with a laugh. 'All right – I'll ring up now, and see if there's any chance.'

They had all finished their breakfast, and they got up to wait for Daddy to telephone. He went out into the hall, and they heard him dialling.

'I hope it's all right for us!' said Julian. 'I wonder what Georgina's like. Funny name, isn't it? More like a boy's than a girl's. So she's eleven – a year younger than I am – same age as you, Dick – and a year older than you, Anne. She ought to fit in with us all right. The four of us ought to have a fine time together.'

Daddy came back in about ten minutes' time, and the

children knew at once that he had fixed up everything. He smiled round at them.

'Well, that's settled,' he said. 'Your Aunt Fanny is delighted about it. She says it will be awfully good for Georgina to have company, because she's such a lonely little girl, always going off by herself. And she will love looking after you all. Only you'll have to be careful not to disturb your Uncle Quentin. He is working very hard, and he isn't very good-tempered when he is disturbed.'

'We'll be as quiet as mice in the house!' said Dick.

'Honestly we will. Oh, goody, goody – when are we going, Daddy?'

'Next week, if Mother can manage it,' said Daddy.

Mother nodded her head. 'Yes,' she said, 'there's nothing much to get ready for them – just bathing suits and jerseys and jeans. They all wear the same.'

'How lovely it will be to wear jeans again,' said Anne, dancing round. 'I'm tired of wearing school tunics. I want to wear shorts, or a bathing suit, and go bathing and climbing with the boys.'

'Well, you'll soon be doing it,' said Mother, with a laugh. 'Remember to put ready any toys or books you want, won't you? Not many, please, because there won't be a great deal of room.'

'Anne wanted to take all her fifteen dolls with her last year,' said Dick. 'Do you remember, Anne? Weren't you funny?'

4

A GREAT SURPRISE

'No, I wasn't,' said Anne, going red. 'I love my dolls, and I just couldn't choose which to take – so I thought I'd take them all. There's nothing funny about that.'

And do you remember the year before, Anne wanted to take the rocking-horse?' said Dick, with a giggle.

Mother chimed in. 'You know, I remember a little boy called Dick who put aside one teddy bear, three toy dogs, two toy cats and his old monkey to take down to Polseath one year,' she said.

Then it was Dick's turn to go red. He changed the subject at once.

'Daddy, are we going by train or by car?' he asked.

'By car,' said Daddy. 'We can pile everything into the boot. Well – what about Tuesday?'

'That would suit me well,' said Mother. 'Then we could take the children down, come back, and do our own packing at leisure, and start off for Scotland on the Friday. Yes – we'll arrange for Tuesday.'

So Tuesday it was. The children counted the days eagerly, and Anne marked one off the calendar each night. The week seemed a very long time in going. But at last Tuesday did come. Dick and Julian, who shared a room, woke up at about the same moment, and stared out of the nearby window.

'It's a lovely day, hurrah!' cried Julian, leaping out of bed. 'I don't know why, but it always seems very important that it should be sunny on the first day of a holiday. Let's wake Anne.'

Anne slept in the next room. Julian ran in and shook her. 'Wake up! It's Tuesday! And the sun's shining.'

Anne woke up with a jump and stared at Julian joyfully. 'It's come at last!' she said. 'I thought it never would. Oh, isn't it an exciting feeling to go away for a holiday!'

They started soon after breakfast. Their car was a big one, so it held them all very comfortably. Mother sat in front with Daddy, and the three children sat behind, their feet on two suitcases. In the luggage-place at the back of the car were all kinds of odds and ends, and one small trunk. Mother really thought they had remembered everything.

Along the crowded London roads they went, slowly at first, and then, as they left the town behind, more quickly. Soon they were right into the open country, and the car sped along fast. The children sang songs to themselves, as they always did when they were happy.

'Are we picnicking soon?' asked Anne, feeling hungry all of a sudden.

'Yes,' said Mother. 'But not yet. It's only eleven o'clock. We shan't have lunch till at least half-past twelve, Anne.'

'Oh, gracious!' said Anne. 'I know I can't last out till then!'

So her mother handed her some chocolate, and she and the boys munched happily, watching the hills, woods and fields as the car sped by.

The picnic was lovely. They had it on the top of a hill, in a sloping field that looked down into a sunny valley. Anne didn't very much like a big brown cow which came up close and stared at her, but it went away when Daddy told it to. The children ate enormously, and Mother said that instead of having a tea-picnic at half-past four they would have to go to a tea-house somewhere, because they had eaten all the tea sandwiches as well as the lunch ones!

'What time shall we be at Aunt Fanny's?' asked Julian, finishing up the very last sandwich and wishing there were more.

'About six o'clock with luck,' said Daddy. 'Now who wants to stretch their legs a bit? We've another long spell in the car, you know.'

The car seemed to eat up the miles as it purred along. Tea-time came, and then the three children began to feel excited all over again.

'We must watch out for the sea,' said Dick. 'I can smell it somewhere near!'

He was right. The car suddenly topped a hill – and there was the shining blue sea, calm and smooth in the evening sun. The three children gave a yell.

'There it is!'

'Isn't it marvellous!'

'Oh, I want to bathe this very minute!'

'We shan't be more than twenty minutes now, before we're at Kirrin Bay,' said Daddy. 'We've made good time. You'll see the bay soon – it's quite a big one – with a funny sort of island at the entrance of the bay.'

The children looked out for it as they drove along the coast. Then Julian gave a shout.

'There it is – that must be Kirrin Bay. Look, Dick – isn't it lovely and blue?'

'And look at the rocky little island guarding the entrance of the bay,' said Dick. 'I'd like to visit that.'

'Well, I've no doubt you will,' said Mother. 'Now, let's look out for Aunt Fanny's house. It's called Kirrin Cottage.'

They soon came to it. It stood on the low cliff overlooking the bay, and was a very old house indeed. It wasn't really a cottage, but quite a big house, built of old white stone. Roses climbed over the front of it, and the garden was full of flowers.

'Here's Kirrin Cottage,' said Daddy, and he stopped the car in front of it. 'It's supposed to be about three hundred years old! Now – where's Quentin? Hallo, there's Fanny!'

CHAPTER TWO

The strange cousin

THE CHILDREN'S aunt had been watching for the car. She came running out of the old wooden door as soon as she saw it draw up outside. The children liked the look of her at once.

'Welcome to Kirrin!' she cried. 'Hallo, all of you! It's lovely to see you. And what big children!'

There were kisses all round, and then the children went into the house. They liked it. It felt old and rather mysterious somehow, and the furniture was old and very beautiful.

'Where's Georgina?' asked Anne, looking round for her unknown cousin.

'Oh, the naughty girl! I told her to wait in the garden for you,' said her aunt. 'Now she's gone off somewhere. I must tell you, children, you may find George a bit difficult at first – she's always been one on her own, you know, and at first may not like you being here. But you mustn't take any notice of that – she'll be all right in a short time. I was very glad for George's sake that you were able to come. She badly needs other children to play with.'

'Do you call her "George"?' asked Anne, in surprise. 'I thought her name was Georgina.'

9

'So it is,' said her aunt. 'But George hates being a girl, and we have to call her George, as if she were a boy. The naughty girl won't answer if we call her Georgina.'

The children thought that Georgina sounded rather exciting. They wished she would come. But she didn't. Their Uncle Quentin suddenly appeared instead. He was a most extraordinary looking man, very tall, very dark, and with a rather fierce frown on his wide forehead.

'Hallo, Quentin!' said Daddy. 'It's a long time since I've seen you. I hope these three won't disturb you very much in your work.'

'Quentin is working on a very difficult book,' said Aunt Fanny. 'But I've given him a room all to himself on the other side of the house. So I don't expect he will be disturbed.'

Their uncle looked at the three children, and nodded to them. The frown didn't come off his face, and they all felt a little scared, and were glad that he was to work in another part of the house.

'Where's George?' he said, in a deep voice.

'Gone off somewhere again,' said Aunt Fanny, vexed. 'I told her she was to stay here and meet her cousins.'

'She wants a good talking to,' said Uncle Quentin. The children couldn't quite make out whether he was joking or not. 'Well, children, I hope you have a good time here, and maybe you will knock a little common-sense into George!'

There was no room at Kirrin Cottage for Mother and Daddy to stay the night, so after a hurried supper they left to stay at a hotel in the nearest town. They would drive back to London immediately after breakfast the next day. So they said good-bye to the children that night.

Georgina still hadn't appeared. 'I'm sorry we haven't seen Georgina,' said Mother. 'Just give her our love and tell her we hope she'll enjoy playing with Dick, Julian and Anne.'

Then Mother and Daddy went. The children felt a little bit lonely as they saw the big car disappear round the corner of the road, but Aunt Fanny took them upstairs to show them their bedrooms, and they soon forgot to be sad.

The two boys were to sleep together in a room with slanting ceilings at the top of the house. It had a marvellous view of the bay. The boys were really delighted with it. Anne was to sleep with Georgina in a smaller room, whose windows looked over the moors at the back of the house. But one side-window looked over the sea, which pleased Anne very much. It was a nice room, and red roses nodded their heads in at the window.

'I do wish Georgina would come,' Anne said to her aunt. 'I want to see what she's like.'

'Well, she's a funny little girl,' said her aunt. 'She can be very rude and haughty – but she's kind at heart, very loyal and absolutely truthful. Once she makes friends with you, she will always be your friend – but she finds it very difficult indeed to make friends, which is a great pity.'

Anne suddenly yawned. The boys frowned at her, because they knew what would happen next. And it did!

'Poor Anne! How tired you are! You must all go to bed straight away, and have a good night. Then you will wake up quite fresh tomorrow,' said Aunt Fanny.

'Anne, you *are* an idiot,' said Dick, crossly, when his aunt had gone out of the room. 'You know quite well what grown-ups think as soon as we yawn. I did want to go down on the beach for a while.'

'I'm so sorry,' said Anne. 'Somehow I couldn't help it. And anyway, *you're* yawning now, Dick – and Julian too!'

So they were. They were as sleepy as could be with their long drive. Secretly all of them longed to cuddle down into bed and shut their eyes.

'I wonder where Georgina is,' said Anne, when she said good-night to the boys, and went to her own room. 'Isn't she odd – not waiting to welcome us – and not coming in to supper – and not even in yet! After all, she's sleeping in my room – goodness knows what time she'll be in!'

All the three children were fast asleep before Georgina came up to bed! They didn't hear her open Anne's door. They didn't hear her get undressed and clean her teeth. They didn't hear the creak of her bed as she got into it. They were so tired that they heard nothing at all until the sun awoke them in the morning.

When Anne awoke she couldn't at first think where she was. She lay in her little bed and looked up at the slanting ceiling, and at the red roses that nodded at the open window – and suddenly remembered all in a rush where she was! 'I'm at Kirrin Bay – and it's the holidays!' she said to herself, and screwed up her legs with joy.

Then she looked across at the other bed. In it lay the figure of another child, curled up under the bed-clothes. Anne could just see the top of a curly head, and that was all. When the figure stirred a little, Anne spoke.

'I say! Are you Georgina?'

The child in the opposite bed sat up and looked across at Anne. She had very short curly hair, almost as short as a boy's. Her face was burnt a dark-brown with the sun, and her very blue eyes looked as bright as forget-me-nots in her face. But her mouth was rather sulky, and she had a frown like her father's.

'No,' she said. 'I'm not Georgina.'

'Oh!' said Anne, in surprise. 'Then who are you?'

'I'm George,' said the girl. 'I shall only answer if you call me George. I hate being a girl. I won't be. I don't like doing the things that girls do. I like doing the things that boys do. I can climb better than any boy, and swim faster too. I can sail a boat as well as any fisher-boy on this coast. You're to call me George. Then I'll speak to you. But I shan't if you don't.'

'Oh!' said Anne, thinking that her new cousin was most extraordinary. 'All right! I don't care what I call you. George is a nice name, I think. I don't much like Georgina. Anyway, you look like a boy.'

'Do I really?' said George, the frown leaving her face for a moment. 'Mother was awfully cross with me when I cut my hair short. I had hair all round my neck; it was awful.'

The two girls stared at one another for a moment. 'Don't you simply hate being a girl?' asked George.

'No, of course not,' said Anne. 'You see – I do like pretty frocks – and I love my dolls – and you can't do that if you're a boy.'

'Pooh! Fancy bothering about pretty frocks,' said George, in a scornful voice. 'And dolls! Well, you *are* a baby, that's all I can say.'

Anne felt offended. 'You're not very polite,' she said. 'You won't find that my brothers take much notice of you if you act as if you know everything. They're *real* boys, not pretend boys, like you.'

'Well, if they're going to be nasty to me I shan't take any notice of *them*,' said George, jumping out of bed. 'I didn't want any of you to come, anyway. Interfering with my life here! I'm quite happy on my own. Now I've got to put up with a silly girl who likes frocks and dolls, and two stupid boy-cousins!'

Anne felt that they had made a very bad beginning. She said no more, but got dressed herself too. She put on her grey jeans and a red jersey. George put on jeans too, and a boy's jersey. Just as they were ready the boys hammered on their door.

'Aren't you ready? Is Georgina there? Cousin Georgina, come out and see us.'

George flung open the door and marched out with her head high. She took no notice of the two surprised boys at all. She stalked downstairs. The other three children looked at one another.

'She won't answer if you call her Georgina,' explained Anne. 'She's awfully funny, I think. She says she didn't want us to come because we'll interfere with her. She laughed at me, and was rather rude.'

Julian put his arm round Anne, who looked a bit

doleful. 'Cheer up!' he said. 'You've got us to stick up for you. Come on down to breakfast.'

They were all hungry. The smell of bacon and eggs was very good. They ran down the stairs and said good-morning to their aunt. She was just bringing the breakfast to the table. Their uncle was sitting at the head, reading his paper. He nodded at the children. They sat down without a word, wondering if they were allowed to speak at meals. They always were at home, but their Uncle Quentin looked rather fierce.

George was there, buttering a piece of toast. She scowled at the three children.

'Don't look like that, George,' said her mother. 'I hope you've made friends already. It will be fun for you to play together. You must take your cousins to see the bay this morning and show them the best places to bathe.'

'I'm going fishing,' said George.

Her father looked up at once.

'You are not,' he said. 'You are going to show a few good manners for a change, and take your cousins to the bay. Do you hear me?'

'Yes,' said George, with a scowl exactly like her father's.

'Oh, we can go to the bay by ourselves all right, if George is going fishing,' said Anne, at once, thinking that it would be nice not to have George if she was in a bad temper.

'George will do exactly as she's told,' said her father. 'If she doesn't, I shall deal with her.'

16

THE STRANGE COUSIN

So, after breakfast, four children got ready to go down to the beach. An easy path led down to the bay, and they ran down happily. Even George lost her frown as she felt the warmth of the sun and saw the dancing sparkles on the blue sea.

'You go fishing if you want to,' said Anne when they were down on the beach. 'We won't tell tales on you. We don't want to interfere with you, you know. We've got ourselves for company, and if you don't want to be with us, you needn't.'

'But we'd like you, all the same, if you'd like to be with us,' said Julian, generously. He thought George was rude and ill-mannered, but he couldn't help rather liking the look of the straight-backed, short-haired little girl, with her brilliant blue eyes and sulky mouth.

George stared at him. 'I'll see,' she said. 'I don't make friends with people just because they're my cousins, or something silly like that. I only make friends with people if I like them.'

'So do we,' said Julian. 'We may not like *you*, of course.'

'Oh!' said George, as if that thought hadn't occurred to her. 'Well – you may not, of course. Lots of people don't like me, now I come to think of it.'

Anne was staring out over the blue bay. At the entrance to it lay a curious rocky island with what looked like an old ruined castle on the top of it.

'Isn't that a funny place?' she said. 'I wonder what it's called.'

17

'It's called Kirrin Island,' said George, her eyes as blue as the sea as she turned to look at it. 'It's a lovely place to go to. If I like you, I may take you there some day. But I don't promise. The only way to get there is by boat.'

'Who does the funny island belong to?' asked Julian.

George made a most surprising answer. 'It belongs to *me*,' she said. 'At least, it *will* belong to me – some day! It will be my very own island – and my very own castle!'

CHAPTER THREE

A peculiar story – and a new friend

THE THREE children stared at George in the greatest surprise.

George stared back at them.

'What do you mean?' said Dick, at last. 'Kirrin Island can't belong to you. You're just boasting.'

'No, I'm not,' said George. 'You ask Mother. If you're not going to believe what I say I won't tell you another word more. But I don't tell untruths. I think it's being a coward if you don't tell the truth – and I'm not a coward.'

Julian remembered that Aunt Fanny had said that George was absolutely truthful, and he scratched his head and looked at George again. How could she be possibly telling the truth?

'Well, of course we'll believe you if you tell us the truth,' he said. 'But it does sound a bit extraordinary, you know. Really, it does. Children don't usually own islands, even funny little ones like that.'

'It *isn't* a funny little island,' said George, fiercely. 'It's lovely. There are rabbits there, as tame as can be – and the big cormorants sit on the other side – and all kinds of gulls go there. The castle is wonderful too, even if it *is* all in ruins.'

'It sounds fine,' said Dick. 'How does it belong to you, Georgina?'

George glared at him and didn't answer.

'Sorry,' said Dick, hastily. 'I didn't mean to call you Georgina. I meant to call you George.'

'Go on, George – tell us how the island belongs to you,' said Julian, slipping his arm through his sulky little cousin's.

She pulled away from him at once.

'Don't do that,' she said. 'I'm not sure that I want to make friends with you yet.'

'All right, all right,' said Julian, losing patience. 'Be enemies or anything you like. We don't care. But we like your mother awfully, and we don't want her to think we won't make friends with you.'

'Do you like my mother?' said George, her bright blue eyes softening a little. 'Yes – she's a dear, isn't she? Well – all right – I'll tell you how Kirrin Castle belongs to me. Come and sit down here in this corner where nobody can hear us.'

They all sat down in a sandy corner of the beach. George looked across at the little island in the bay.

'It's like this,' she said. 'Years ago my mother's family owned nearly all the land around here. Then they got poor, and had to sell most of it. But they could never sell that little island, because nobody thought it worth anything, especially as the castle has been ruined for years.'

A PECULIAR STORY – AND A NEW FRIEND

'Fancy nobody wanting to buy a dear little island like that!' said Dick. 'I'd buy it at once if I had the money.'

'All that's left of what Mother's family owned is our own house, Kirrin Cottage, and a farm a little way off – and Kirrin Island,' said George. 'Mother says when I'm grown-up it will be mine. She says she doesn't want it now, either, so she's sort of given it to me. It belongs to me. It's my own private island, and I don't let anyone go there unless they get my permission.'

The three children stared at her. They believed every word George said, for it was quite plain that the girl was speaking the truth. Fancy having an island of your very own! They thought she was very lucky indeed.

'Oh, Georgina – I mean George!' said Dick. 'I do think you're lucky. It looks such a nice island. I hope you'll be friends with us and take us there one day soon. You simply can't imagine how we'd love it.'

'Well – I might,' said George, pleased at the interest she had caused. 'I'll see. I never have taken anyone there yet, though some of the boys and girls round here have begged me to. But I don't like them, so I haven't.'

There was a little silence as the four children looked out over the bay to where the island lay in the distance. The tide was going out. It almost looked as if they could wade over to the island. Dick asked if it was possible.

'No,' said George. 'I told you – it's only possible to get to it by boat. It's farther out than it looks – and the water is very, very deep. There are rocks all about too – you have to know exactly where to row a boat, or you bump into them. It's a dangerous bit of coast here. There are a lot of wrecks about.'

'Wrecks!' cried Julian, his eyes shining. 'I say! I've never seen an old wreck. Are there any to see?'

'Not now,' said George. 'They've all been cleared up. Except one, and that's the other side of the island. It's deep down in the water. You can just see the broken mast if you row over it on a calm day and look down into the water. That wreck really belongs to me too.'

This time the children really could hardly believe George. But she nodded her head firmly.

'Yes,' she said, 'it was a ship belonging to one of my great-great-great-grandfathers, or someone like that. He was bringing gold – big bars of gold – back in his ship – and it got wrecked off Kirrin Island.'

'Oooh – what happened to the gold?' asked Anne, her eyes round and big.

'Nobody knows,' said George. 'I expect it was stolen out of the ship. Divers have been down to see, of course, but they couldn't find any gold.'

'Golly – this does sound exciting,' said Julian. 'I wish I could see the wreck.'

'Well – we might perhaps go this afternoon when the tide is right down,' said George. 'The water is so calm and clear today. We could see a bit of it.'

'Oh, how wonderful!' said Anne. 'I do so want to see a real live wreck!'

22

A PECULIAR STORY – AND A NEW FRIEND

The others laughed. 'Well, it won't be very alive,' said Dick. 'I say, George – what about a bathe?'

'I must go and get Timothy first,' said George. She got up.

'Who's Timothy?' said Dick.

'Can you keep a secret?' asked George. 'Nobody must know at home.'

'Well, go on, what's the secret?' asked Julian. 'You can tell us. We're not sneaks.'

'Timothy is my very greatest friend,' said George. 'I couldn't do without him. But Mother and Father don't like him, so I have to keep him in secret. I'll go and fetch him.'

She ran off up the cliff path. The others watched her go. They thought she was the most peculiar girl they had ever known.

'Who in the world can Timothy be?' wondered Julian. 'Some fisher-boy, I suppose, that George's parents don't approve of.'

The children lay back in the soft sand and waited. Soon they heard George's clear voice coming down from the cliff behind them.

'Come on, Timothy! Come on!'

They sat up and looked to see what Timothy was like. They saw no fisher-boy – but instead a big brown mongrel dog with an absurdly long tail and a big wide mouth that really seemed to grin! He was bounding all round George, mad with delight. She came running down to them.

23

'This is Timothy,' she said. 'Don't you think he is simply perfect?'

As a dog, Timothy was far from perfect. He was the wrong shape, his head was too big, his ears were too pricked, his tail was too long and it was quite impossible to say what kind of a dog he was supposed to be. But he was such a mad, friendly, clumsy, laughable creature that every one of the children adored him at once.

A PECULIAR STORY – AND A NEW FRIEND

'Oh, you darling!' said Anne, and got a lick on the nose.

'I say – isn't he grand!' said Dick, and gave Timothy a friendly smack that made the dog bound madly all round him.

'I wish *I* had a dog like this,' said Julian, who really loved dogs, and had always wanted one of his own. 'Oh, George – he's fine. Aren't you proud of him?'

The little girl smiled, and her face altered at once, and became sunny and pretty. She sat down on the sand and her dog cuddled up to her, licking her wherever he could find a bare piece of skin.

'I love him awfully,' she said. 'I found him out on the moors when he was just a pup, a year ago, and I took him home. At first Mother liked him, but when he grew bigger he got terribly naughty.'

'What did he do?' asked Anne.

'Well, he's an awfully chewy kind of dog,' said George. 'He chewed up everything he could – a new rug Mother had bought – her nicest hat – Father's slippers – some of his papers, and things like that. And he barked too. I liked his bark, but Father didn't. He said it nearly drove him mad. He hit Timothy and that made me angry, so I was awfully rude to him.'

'Did you get told off?' said Anne. 'I wouldn't like to be rude to your father. He looks fierce.'

George looked out over the bay. Her face had gone sulky again. 'Well, it doesn't matter what punishment I got,' she said, 'but the worst part of all was when Father

25

said I couldn't keep Timothy any more, and Mother backed Father up and said Tim must go. I cried for days – and I never do cry, you know, because boys don't and I like to be like a boy.'

'Boys do cry sometimes,' began Anne, looking at Dick, who had been a bit of a cry-baby three or four years back. Dick gave her a sharp nudge, and she said no more.

George looked at Anne.

'Boys don't cry,' she said, obstinately. 'Anyway, I've never seen one, and I always try not to cry myself. It's so babyish. But I just couldn't help it when Timothy had to go. He cried too.'

The children looked with great respect at Timothy. They had not known that a dog could cry before.

'Do you mean – he cried real tears?' asked Anne.

'No, not quite,' said George. 'He's too brave for that. He cried with his voice – howled and howled and looked so miserable that he nearly broke my heart. And then I knew I couldn't possibly part with him.'

'What happened then?' asked Julian.

'I went to Alf, a fisher-boy I know,' said George, 'and I asked him if he'd keep Tim for me, if I paid him all the pocket-money I get. He said he would, and so he does. That's why I never have any money to spend – it all has to go on Tim. He seems to eat an awful lot – don't you, Tim?'

'Woof!' said Tim, and rolled over on his back, all his shaggy legs in the air. Julian tickled him.

'How do you manage when you want any sweets or ice-creams?' said Anne, who spent most of her pocket-money on things of that sort.

'I don't manage,' said George. 'I go without, of course.'

This sounded awful to the other children, who loved ice-creams, chocolates and sweets, and had a good many of them. They stared at George.

'Well – I suppose the other children who play on the beach share their sweets and ices with you sometimes, don't they?' asked Julian.

'I don't let them,' said George. 'If I can never give them any myself it's not fair to take them. So I say no.'

The tinkle of an ice-cream man's bell was heard in the distance. Julian felt in his pocket. He jumped up and rushed off, jingling his money. In a few moments he was back again, carrying four fat chocolate ice-cream bars. He gave one to Dick, and one to Anne, and then held out one to George. She looked at it longingly, but shook her head.

'No, thanks,' she said. 'You know what I just said. I haven't any money to buy them, so I can't share mine with you, and I can't take any from you. It's mean to take from people if you can't give even a little back.'

'You can take from us,' said Julian, trying to put the ice into George's brown hand. 'We're your cousins.'

'No, thanks,' said George again. 'Though I do think it's nice of you.'

She looked at Julian out of her blue eyes and the boy frowned as he tried to think of a way to make the obstinate little girl take the ice. Then he smiled.

27

'Listen,' he said, 'you've got something we badly want to share – in fact you've got a lot of things we'd like to share, if only you'd let us. You share those with us, and let us share things like ices with you. See?'

'What things have I got that you want to share?' asked George, in surprise.

'You've got a dog,' said Julian, patting the big brown mongrel. 'We'd love to share him with you, he's such a darling. And you've got a lovely island. We'd be simply thrilled if you'd share it sometimes. And you've got a wreck. We'd like to look at it and share it too. Ices and sweets aren't so good as those things – but it would be nice to make a bargain and share with each other.'

George looked at the brown eyes that gazed steadily into hers. She couldn't help liking Julian. It wasn't her nature to share anything. She had always been an only child, a lonely, rather misunderstood little girl, fierce and hot-tempered. She had never had any friends of her own. Timothy looked up at Julian and saw that he was offering something nice and chocolatey to George. He jumped up and licked the boy with his friendly tongue.

'There you are, you see – Tim wants to be shared,' said Julian, with a laugh. 'It would be nice for him to have three new friends.'

'Yes – it would,' said George, giving in suddenly, and taking the chocolate bar. 'Thank you, Julian. I will share with you. But promise you'll never tell anyone at home that I'm still keeping Timothy?'

A PECULIAR STORY – AND A NEW FRIEND

'Of course we'll promise,' said Julian. 'But I can't imagine that your father or mother would mind, so long as Tim doesn't live in their house. How's the ice? Is it nice?'

'Ooooh – the loveliest one I've ever tasted!' said George nibbling at it. 'It's so cold. I haven't had one this year. It's simply DELICIOUS!'

Timothy tried to nibble it too. George gave him a few crumbs at the end. Then she turned and smiled at the three children.

'You're nice,' she said. 'I'm glad you've come after all. Let's take a boat out this afternoon and row round the island to have a look at the wreck, shall we?'

'Rather!' said all three at once – and even Timothy wagged his tail as if he understood!

CHAPTER FOUR

An exciting afternoon

THEY ALL had a bathe that morning, and the boys found that George was a much better swimmer than they were. She was very strong and very fast, and she could swim under water, too, holding her breath for ages.

'You're jolly good,' said Julian, admiringly. 'It's a pity Anne isn't a bit better. Anne, you'll have to practise your swimming strokes hard, or you'll never be able to swim out as far as we do.'

They were all very hungry at lunch-time. They went back up the cliff-path, hoping there would be lots to eat – and there was! Cold meat and salad, plum-pie and custard, and cheese afterwards. How the children tucked in!

'What are you going to do this afternoon?' asked George's mother.

'George is going to take us out in a boat to see the wreck on the other side of the island,' said Anne. Her aunt looked most surprised.

'*George* is going to take you!' she said. 'Why, George – what's come over you? You've never taken a single person before, though I've asked you to dozens of times!'

George said nothing, but went on eating her plum-pie. She hadn't said a word all through the meal. Her father had not appeared at the table, much to the children's relief.

'Well, George, I must say I'm pleased that you want to try and do what your father said,' began her mother again. But George shook her head.

'I'm not doing it because I've got to,' she said. 'I'm doing it because I want to. I wouldn't have taken anyone to see my wreck, not even the Queen of England, if I didn't like them.'

Her mother laughed. 'Well, it's good news that you like your cousins,' she said. 'I hope they like you!'

'Oh yes!' said Anne, eagerly, anxious to stick up for her strange cousin. 'We do like George – and we like Ti . . .'

She was just about to say that they liked Timothy too, when she got such a kick on her ankle that she cried out in pain and the tears came into her eyes. George glared at her.

'George! Why did you kick Anne like that when she was saying nice things about you?' cried her mother. 'Leave the table at once. I won't have such behaviour.'

George left the table without a word. She went out into the garden. She had just taken a piece of bread and cut herself some cheese. It was all left on her plate. The other three stared at it in distress. Anne was upset. How could she have been so silly as to forget she mustn't mention Tim?

'Oh, please call George back!' she said. 'She didn't mean to kick me. It was an accident.'

But her aunt was very angry with George. 'Finish your meal,' she said to the others. 'I expect George will go into a sulk now. Dear, dear, she *is* such a difficult child!'

The others didn't mind about George going into a sulk. What they did mind was that George might refuse to take them to see the wreck now!

They finished the meal in silence. Their aunt went to see if Uncle Quentin wanted any more pie. He was having his meal in the study by himself. As soon as she had gone out of the room, Anne picked up the bread and cheese from George's plate and went out into the garden.

The boys didn't scold her. They knew that Anne's tongue very often ran away with her – but she always tried to make up for it afterwards. They thought it was very brave of her to go and find George.

George was lying on her back under a big tree in the garden. Anne went up to her. 'I'm sorry I nearly made a mistake, George,' she said. 'Here's your bread and cheese. I've brought it for you. I promise I'll never forget not to mention Tim again.'

George sat up. 'I've a good mind not to take you to see the wreck,' she said. 'Stupid baby!'

Anne's heart sank. This was what she had feared. 'Well,' she said, 'you needn't take me, of course. But you might take the boys, George. After all, they didn't do anything silly. And anyway, you gave me an awful kick. Look at the bruise.'

George looked at it. Then she looked at Anne. 'But wouldn't you be miserable if I took Julian and Dick without you?' she asked.

'Of course,' said Anne. 'But I don't want to make them miss a treat, even if *I* have to.'

Then George did a surprising thing for her. She gave
Anne a hug! Then she immediately looked most ashamed
of herself, for she felt sure that no boy would have done
that! And she always tried to act like a boy.

'It's all right,' she said, gruffly, taking the bread and
cheese. 'You were nearly very silly – and I gave you a

kick – so it's all square. Of course you can come this afternoon.'

Anne sped back to tell the boys that everything was all right – and in fifteen minutes' time four children ran down to the beach. By a boat was a brown-faced fisher-boy, about fourteen years old. He had Timothy with him.

'Boat's all ready, George,' he said with a grin. 'And Tim's ready, too.'

'Thanks,' said George, and told the others to get in. Timothy jumped in, too, his big tail wagging nineteen to the dozen. George pushed the boat off into the surf and then jumped in herself. She took the oars.

She rowed splendidly, and the boat shot along over the blue bay. It was a wonderful afternoon, and the children loved the movement of the boat over the water. Timothy stood at the prow and barked whenever a wave reared its head.

'He's funny on a wild day,' said George, pulling hard. 'He barks madly at the big waves, and gets so angry if they splash him. He's an awfully good swimmer.'

'Isn't it nice to have a dog with us?' said Anne, anxious to make up for her mistake. 'I do so like him.'

'Woof,' said Timothy, in his deep voice and turned round to lick Anne's ear.

'I'm sure he knew what I said,' said Anne in delight.

'Of course he did,' said George. 'He understands every single word.'

'I say – we're getting near to your island now,' said

Julian, in excitement. 'It's bigger than I thought. And isn't the castle exciting?'

They drew near to the island, and the children saw that there were sharp rocks all round about it. Unless anyone knew exactly the way to take, no boat or ship could possibly land on the shore of the rocky little island. In the very middle of it, on a low hill, rose the ruined castle. It had been built of big white stones. Broken archways, tumbledown towers, ruined walls – that was all that was left of a once beautiful castle, proud and strong. Now the jackdaws nested in it and the gulls sat on the topmost stones.

'It looks awfully mysterious,' said Julian. 'How I'd love to land there and have a look at the castle. Wouldn't it be fun to spend a night or two here!'

George stopped rowing. Her face lit up. 'I say!' she said, in delight. 'Do you know, I never thought how lovely that would be! To spend a night on my island! To be there all alone, the four of us. To get our own meals, and pretend we really lived there. Wouldn't it be grand?'

'Yes, rather,' said Dick, looking longingly at the island. 'Do you think – do you suppose your mother would let us?'

'I don't know,' said George. 'She might. You could ask her.'

'Can't we land there this afternoon?' asked Julian.

'No, not if you want to see the wreck,' said George. 'We've got to get back for tea today, and it will take all the time to row round to the other side of Kirrin Island and back.'

'Well – I'd like to see the wreck,' said Julian, torn between the island and the wreck. 'Here, let me take the oars for a bit, George. You can't do all the rowing.'

'I can,' said George. 'But I'd quite enjoy lying back in the boat for a change! Look – I'll just take you by this rocky bit – and then you can take the oars till we come to another awkward piece. Honestly, the rocks around this bay are simply dreadful!'

George and Julian changed places in the boat. Julian rowed well, but not so strongly as George. The boat sped along rocking smoothly. They went right round the island, and saw the castle from the other side. It looked more ruined on the side that faced the sea.

'The strong winds come from the open sea,' explained George. 'There's not really much left of it this side, except piles of stones. But there's a good little harbour in a little cove, for those who know how to find it.'

George took the oars after a while, and rowed steadily out a little beyond the island. Then she stopped and looked back towards the shore.

'How do you know when you are over the wreck?' asked Julian, puzzled. 'I should never know!'

'Well, do you see that church tower on the mainland?' asked George. 'And do you see the tip of that hill over there? Well, when you get them exactly in line with one another, between the two towers of the castle on the island, you are pretty well over the wreck! I found that out ages ago.'

The children saw that the tip of the far-off hill and the church tower were practically in line, when they looked at them between the two old towers of the island castle. They looked eagerly down into the sea to see if they could spy the wreck.

The water was perfectly clear and smooth. There was hardly a wrinkle. Timothy looked down into it too, his head on one side, his ears cocked, just as if he knew what he was looking for! The children laughed at him.

'We're not exactly over it,' said George, looking down too. 'The water's so clear today that we should be able to see quite a long way down. Wait, I'll row a bit to the left.'

'Woof!' said Timothy, suddenly, and wagged his tail – and at the same moment the three children saw something deep down in the water!

'It's the wreck!' said Julian, almost falling out of the boat in his excitement. 'I can see a bit of broken mast. Look, Dick, look!'

All four children and the dog, too, gazed down earnestly into the clear water. After a little while they could make out the outlines of a dark hulk, out of which the broken mast stood.

'It's a bit on one side,' said Julian. 'Poor old ship. How it must hate lying there, gradually falling to pieces. George, I wish I could dive down and get a closer look at it.'

'Well, why don't you?' said George. 'You've got your

swimming trunks on. I've often dived down. I'll come with
you, if you like, if Dick can keep the boat round about
here. There's a current that is trying to take it out to sea.
Dick, you'll have to keep working a bit with this oar to
keep the boat in one spot.'

The girl stripped off her jeans and jersey and Julian did
the same. They both had on bathing costumes underneath.
George took a beautiful header off the end of the boat,
deep down into the water. The others watched her swimming strongly downwards, holding her breath.

After a bit she came up, almost bursting for breath.
'Well, I went almost down to the wreck,' she said. 'It's just
the same as it always is – seaweedy and covered with
limpets and things. I wish I could get right into the ship
itself. But I never have enough breath for that. You go
down now, Julian.'

So down Julian went – but he was not so good at
swimming deep under water as George was, and he
couldn't go down so far. He knew how to open his eyes
under water, so he was able to take a good look at the deck
of the wreck. It looked very forlorn and strange. Julian
didn't really like it very much. It gave him rather a sad sort
of feeling. He was glad to go to the top of the water again,
and take deep breaths of air, and feel the warm sunshine
on his shoulders.

He climbed into the boat. 'Most exciting,' he said.
'Golly, wouldn't I just love to see that wreck properly –
you know – go down under the deck into the cabins and

look around. And oh, suppose we could really find the boxes of gold!'

'That's impossible,' said George. 'I told you proper divers have already gone down and found nothing. What's the time? I say, we'll be late if we don't hurry back now!'

They did hurry back, and managed to be only about five

minutes late for tea. Afterwards they went for a walk over the moors, with Timothy at their heels, and by the time that bedtime came they were all so sleepy that they could hardly keep their eyes open.

'Well, good-night, George,' said Anne, snuggling down into her bed. 'We've had a lovely day – thanks to you!'

'And *I've* had a lovely day, too,' said George, rather gruffly. 'Thanks to *you*. I'm glad you all came. We're going to have fun. And won't you love my castle and my little island!'

'Oooh, yes,' said Anne, and fell asleep to dream of wrecks and castles and islands by the hundred. Oh, when would George take them to her little island?

CHAPTER FIVE

A visit to the island

THE CHILDREN'S aunt arranged a picnic for them the next day, and they all went off to a little cove not far off where they could bathe and paddle to their hearts' content. They had a wonderful day, but secretly Julian, Dick and Anne wished they could have visited George's island. They would rather have done that than anything!

George didn't want to go for the picnic, not because she disliked picnics, but because she couldn't take her dog. Her mother went with the children, and George had to pass a whole day without her beloved Timothy.

'Bad luck!' said Julian, who guessed what she was brooding about. 'I can't think why you don't tell your mother about old Tim. I'm sure she wouldn't mind you letting someone else keep him for you. I know my mother wouldn't mind.'

'I'm not going to tell anybody but you,' said George. 'I get into awful trouble at home always. I dare say it's my fault, but I get a bit tired of it. You see, Daddy doesn't make much money with the learned books he writes, and he's always wanting to give mother and me things he can't afford. So that makes him bad-tempered. He wants to send me away to a good school but he hasn't got the

41

money. I'm glad. I don't want to go away to school. I like being here. I couldn't bear to part with Timothy.'

'You'd like boarding school,' said Anne. 'We all go. It's fun.'

'No, it isn't,' said George obstinately. 'It must be awful to be one of a crowd, and to have other girls all laughing and yelling round you. I should hate it.'

'No, you wouldn't,' said Anne. 'All that is great fun. It would be good for you, George, I should think.'

'If you start telling me what is good for me, I shall hate you,' said George, suddenly looking very fierce. 'Mother and Father are always saying that things are good for me – and they are always the things I don't like.'

'All right, all right,' said Julian, beginning to laugh. 'My goodness, how you do go up in smoke! Honestly, I believe anyone could light a cigarette from the sparks that fly from your eyes!'

That made George laugh, though she didn't want to. It was really impossible to sulk with good-tempered Julian.

They went off to bathe in the sea for the fifth time that day. Soon they were all splashing about happily, and George found time to help Anne to swim. The little girl hadn't got the right stroke, and George felt really proud when she had taught her.

'Oh, thanks,' said Anne, struggling along. 'I'll never be as good as you – but I'd like to be as good as the boys.'

As they were going home, George spoke to Julian. 'Could you say that you want to go and buy a stamp or something?' she said. 'Then I could go with you, and just have a peep at old Tim. He'll be wondering why I haven't taken him out today.'

'Right!' said Julian. 'I don't want stamps, but I *could* do with an ice. Dick and Anne can go home with your mother and carry the things. I'll just go and tell Aunt Fanny.'

He ran up to his aunt. 'Do you mind if I go and buy some ice-creams?' he asked. 'We haven't had one today. I won't be long. Can George go with me?'

'I don't expect she will want to,' said his aunt. 'But you can ask her.'

'George, come with me!' yelled Julian, setting off to the little village at a great pace. George gave a sudden grin and ran after him. She soon caught him up and smiled gratefully at him.

'Thanks,' she said. 'You go and get the ice-creams, and I'll have a look at Tim.'

They parted, Julian bought four ice-creams, and turned to go home. He waited about for George, who came running up after a few minutes. Her face was glowing.

'He's all right,' she said. 'And you can't imagine how pleased he was to see me! He nearly jumped over my head! I say – another ice-cream for me. You really are a sport, Julian. I'll have to share something with you quickly. What about going to my island tomorrow?'

'Golly!' said Julian, his eyes shining. 'That would be marvellous. Will you really take us tomorrow? Come on, let's tell the others!'

The four children sat in the garden eating their ices. Julian told them what George had said. They all felt excited. George was pleased. She had always felt quite important before when she had haughtily refused to take any of the other children to see Kirrin Island – but it felt much nicer somehow to have consented to row her cousins there.

'I used to think it was much, much nicer always to do things on my own,' she thought, as she sucked the last bits of her ice. 'But it's going to be fun doing things with Julian and the others.'

The children were sent to wash themselves and to get tidy before supper. They talked eagerly about the visit to the island next day. Their aunt heard them and smiled.

'Well, I really must say I'm pleased that George is going to share something with you,' she said. 'Would you like to take your dinner there, and spend the day? It's hardly worthwhile rowing all the way there and landing unless you are going to spend some hours there.'

'Oh, Aunt Fanny! It would be marvellous to take our dinner!' cried Anne.

George looked up. 'Are you coming too, Mother?' she asked.

'You don't sound at all as if you want me to,' said her mother, in a hurt tone. 'You looked cross yesterday, too, when you found I was coming. No – I shan't come tomorrow – but I'm sure your cousins must think you are an odd girl never to want your mother to go with you.'

A VISIT TO THE ISLAND

George said nothing. She hardly ever did say a word when she was scolded. The other children said nothing too. They knew perfectly well that it wasn't that George didn't want her mother to go – it was just that she wanted Timothy with her!

'Anyway, I couldn't come,' went on Aunt Fanny. 'I've some gardening to do. You'll be quite safe with George. She can handle a boat like a man.'

The three children looked eagerly at the weather the next day when they got up. The sun was shining, and everything seemed splendid.

'Isn't it a marvellous day?' said Anne to George, as they dressed. 'I'm so looking forward to going to the island.'

'Well, honestly, I think really we oughtn't to go,' said George, unexpectedly.

'Oh, but why?' cried Anne, in dismay.

'I think there's going to be a storm or something,' said George, looking out to the south-west.

'But, George, why do you say that?' said Anne, impatiently. 'Look at the sun – and there's hardly a cloud in the sky!'

'The wind is wrong,' said George. 'And can't you see the little white tops of the waves out there by my island? That's always a bad sign.'

'Oh, George – it will be the biggest disappointment of our lives if we don't go today,' said Anne, who couldn't bear any disappointment, big or small. 'And besides,' she added, artfully, 'if we hang about the house, afraid of a storm, we shan't be able to have dear old Tim with us.'

'Yes, that's true,' said George. 'All right – we'll go. But mind – if a storm does come, you're not to be a baby. You're to try and enjoy it and not be frightened.'

'Well, I don't much like storms,' began Anne, but stopped when she saw George's scornful look. They went down to breakfast, and George asked her mother if they could take their dinner as they had planned.

'Yes,' said her mother. 'You and Anne can help to make the sandwiches. You boys can go into the garden and pick some ripe plums to take with you. Julian, you can go down to the village when you've done that and buy some bottles of lemonade or ginger-beer, whichever you like.'

'Ginger-pop for me, thanks!' said Julian, and everyone else said the same. They all felt very happy. It would be marvellous to visit the strange little island. George felt happy because she would be with Tim all day.

They set off at last, the food in two kit-bags. The first thing they did was to fetch Tim. He was tied up in the fisher-boy's backyard. The boy himself was there, and grinned at George.

''Morning, Master George,' he said. It seemed so funny to the other children to hear Georgina called 'Master George'! 'Tim's been barking his head off for you. I guess he knew you were coming for him today.'

'Of course he did,' said George, untying him. He at once went completely mad, and tore round and round the children, his tail down and his ears flat.

'He'd win any race if only he were a greyhound,' said

A VISIT TO THE ISLAND

Julian, admiringly. 'You can hardly see him for dust. Tim! Hey, Tim! Come and say "Good-morning".'

Tim leapt up and licked Julian's left ear as he passed on his whirlwind way. Then he sobered down and ran lovingly by George as they all made their way to the beach. He licked George's bare legs every now and again, and she pulled at his ears gently.

They got into the boat, and George pushed off. The fisher-boy waved to them. 'You won't be very long, will you?' he called. 'There's a storm blowing up. Bad one it'll be, too.'

'I know,' shouted back George. 'But maybe we'll get back before it begins. It's pretty far off yet.'

George rowed all the way to the island. Tim stood at each end of the boat in turn, barking when the waves reared up at him. The children watched the island coming closer and closer. It looked even more exciting than it had the other day.

'George, where are you going to land?' asked Julian. 'I simply can't imagine how you know your way in and out of these awful rocks. I'm afraid every moment we'll bump into them!'

'I'm going to land at the little cove I told you about the other day,' said George. 'There's only one way to it, but I know it very well. It's hidden away on the east side of the island.'

The girl cleverly worked her boat in and out of the rocks, and suddenly, as it rounded a low wall of sharp rocks, the children saw the cove she had spoken of. It was like a natural little harbour, and was a smooth inlet of water running up to a stretch of sand, sheltered between high rocks. The boat slid into the inlet, and at once stopped rocking, for here the water was like glass, and had hardly a wrinkle.

'I say – this is fine!' said Julian, his eyes shining with delight. George looked at him and her eyes shone too, as bright as the sea itself. It was the first time she had ever taken anyone to her precious island, and she was enjoying it.

They landed on the smooth yellow sand. 'We're really on the island!' said Anne, and she capered about, Tim joining her and looking as mad as she did. The others laughed. George pulled the boat high up on the sand.

'Why so far up?' said Julian, helping her. 'The tide's almost in, isn't it? Surely it won't come as high as this.'

'I told you I thought a storm was coming,' said George. 'If one does, the waves simply tear up this inlet and we don't want to lose our boat, do we?'

'Let's explore the island, let's explore the island!' yelled Anne, who was now at the top of the little natural harbour, climbing up the rocks there. 'Oh do come on!'

They all followed her. It really was a most exciting place. Rabbits were everywhere! They scuttled about as the children appeared, but did not go into their holes.

'Aren't they awfully tame?' said Julian, in surprise.

'Well, nobody ever comes here but me,' said George,

'and I don't frighten them. Tim! Tim, if you go after the rabbits, I'll be furious.'

Tim turned big sorrowful eyes on to George. He and George agreed about every single thing except rabbits. To Tim rabbits were made for one thing – to chase! He never could understand why George wouldn't let him do this. But he held himself in and walked solemnly by the children, his eyes watching the lolloping rabbits longingly.

'I believe they would almost eat out of my hand,' said Julian.

But George shook her head.

'No, I've tried that with them,' she said. 'They won't. Look at those baby ones. Aren't they lovely?'

'Woof!' said Tim, agreeing, and he took a few steps towards them. George made a warning noise in her throat, and Tim walked back, his tail down.

'There's the castle!' said Julian. 'Shall we explore that now? I do want to.'

'Yes, we will,' said George. 'Look – that is where the entrance used to be – through that big broken archway.'

The children gazed at the enormous old archway, now half-broken down. Behind it were ruined stone steps leading towards the centre of the castle.

'It had strong walls all round it, with two towers,' said George. 'One tower is almost gone, as you can see, but the other is not so bad. The jackdaws build in that every year. They've almost filled it up with their sticks!'

As they came near to the better tower of the two the jackdaws circled round them with loud cries of 'Chack, chack, chack!' Tim leapt into the air as if he thought he could get them, but they only called mockingly to him.

'This is the centre of the castle,' said George, as they entered through a ruined doorway into what looked like a great yard, whose stone floor was now overgrown with grass and other weeds. 'Here is where the people used to live. You can see where the rooms were – look, there's one almost whole there. Go through that little door and you'll see it.'

They trooped through a doorway and found themselves in a dark, stone-walled, stone-roofed room, with a space at one end where a fireplace must have been. Two slit-like windows lit the room. It felt very strange and mysterious.

'What a pity it's all broken down,' said Julian, wandering out again. 'That room seems to be the only one quite whole. There are some others here – but all of them seem to have either no roof, or one or other of the walls gone. That room is the only livable one. Was there an upstairs to the castle, George?'

'Of course,' said George. 'But the steps that led up are gone. Look! You can see part of an upstairs room there, by the jackdaw tower. You can't get up to it, though, because I've tried. I nearly broke my neck trying to get up. The stones crumble away so.'

'Were there any dungeons?' asked Dick.

'I don't know,' said George. 'I expect so. But nobody could find them now – everywhere is so overgrown.'

It was indeed overgrown. Big blackberry bushes grew here and there, and a few gorse bushes forced their way into gaps and corners. The coarse green grass sprang everywhere, and pink thrift grew its cushions in holes and crannies.

'Well, I think it's a perfectly lovely place,' said Anne. 'Perfectly and absolutely lovely!'

'Do you really?' said George, pleased. 'I'm so glad.

Look! We're right on the other side of the island now, facing the sea. Do you see those rocks, with those peculiar big birds sitting there?'

The children looked. They saw some rocks sticking up, with great black shining birds sitting on them in strange positions.

'They are cormorants,' said George. 'They've caught plenty of fish for their dinner, and they're sitting there digesting it. Hallo – they're all flying away. I wonder why?'

She soon knew – for, from the south-west there suddenly came an ominous rumble.

'Thunder!' said George. 'That's the storm. It's coming sooner than I thought!'

CHAPTER SIX

What the storm did

THE FOUR children stared out to sea. They had all been so interested in exploring the exciting old castle that not one of them had noticed the sudden change in the weather.

Another rumble came. It sounded like a big dog growling in the sky. Tim heard it and growled back, sounding like a small roll of thunder himself.

'My goodness, we're in for it now,' said George, half-alarmed. 'We can't get back in time, that's certain. It's blowing up at top speed. Did you ever see such a change in the sky?'

The sky had been blue when they started. Now it was overcast, and the clouds seemed to hang very low indeed. They scudded along as if someone was chasing them – and the wind howled round in such a mournful way that Anne felt quite frightened.

'It's beginning to rain,' said Julian, feeling an enormous drop spatter on his outstretched hand. 'We had better shelter, hadn't we, George? We shall get wet through.'

'Yes, we will in a minute,' said George. 'I say, just look at these big waves coming! My word, it really *is* going to be a storm. Golly – what a flash of lightning!'

The waves were certainly beginning to run very high

indeed. It was amazing to see what a change had come
over them. They swelled up, turned over as soon as they
came to rocks, and then rushed up the beach of the island
with a great roar.

'I think we'd better pull our boat up higher still,' said
George suddenly. 'It's going to be a very bad storm
indeed. Sometimes these sudden summer storms are

worse than a winter one.'

She and Julian ran to the other side of the island where they had left the boat. It was a good thing they went, for great waves were already racing right up to it. The two children pulled the boat up almost to the top of the low cliff and George tied it to a stout gorse bush growing there.

By now the rain was simply pelting down, and George and Julian were soaked. 'I hope the others have been sensible enough to shelter in that room that has a roof and walls,' said George.

They were there all right, looking rather cold and scared. It was very dark there, for the only light came through the two slits of windows and the small doorway.

'Could we light a fire to make things a bit more cheerful?' said Julian, looking round. 'I wonder where we can find some nice dry sticks?'

Almost as if they were answering the question a small crowd of jackdaws cried out wildly as they circled in the storm. 'Chack, chack, chack!'

'Of course! There are plenty of sticks on the ground below the tower!' cried Julian. 'You know – where the jackdaws nest. They've dropped lots of sticks there.'

He dashed out into the rain and ran to the tower. He picked up an armful of sticks and ran back.

'Good,' said George. 'We'll be able to make a nice fire with those. Anyone got any paper to start it – or matches?'

'I've got some matches,' said Julian. 'But nobody's got paper.'

'Yes,' said Anne, suddenly. 'The sandwiches are wrapped in paper. Let's undo them, and then we can use the paper for the fire.'

'Good idea,' said George. So they undid the sandwiches, and put them neatly on a broken stone, rubbing it clean first. Then they built up a fire, with the paper underneath and the sticks arranged criss-cross on top.

It was fun when they lit the paper. It flared up and the sticks at once caught fire, for they were very old and dry. Soon there was a fine cracking fire going and the little ruined room was lit by dancing flames. It was very dark outside now, for the clouds hung almost low enough to touch the top of the castle tower! And how they raced by! The wind sent them off to the north-east, roaring behind them with a noise like the sea itself.

'I've never, never heard the sea making such an awful noise,' said Anne. 'Never! It really sounds as if it's shouting at the top of its voice.'

What with the howling of the wind and the crashing of the great waves all round the little island, the children could hardly hear themselves speak! They had to shout at one another.

'Let's have our dinner!' yelled Dick, who was feeling terribly hungry as usual. 'We can't do anything much while this storm lasts.'

WHAT THE STORM DID

'Yes, let's,' said Anne, looking longingly at the ham sandwiches. 'It will be fun to have a picnic round the fire in this dark old room. I wonder how long ago other people had a meal here? I wish I could see them.'

'Well, I don't,' said Dick, looking round half-scared as if he expected to see the old-time people walk in to share their picnic. 'It's quite a strange enough day without wanting things like that to happen.'

They all felt better when they were eating the sandwiches and drinking the ginger-beer. The fire flared up as more and more sticks caught, and gave out quite a pleasant warmth, for now that the wind had got up so strongly, the day had become cold.

'We'll take it in turns to fetch sticks,' said George. But Anne didn't want to go alone. She was trying her best not to show that she was afraid of the storm – but it was more than she could do to go out of the cosy room into the rain and thunder by herself.

Tim didn't seem to like the storm either. He sat close by George, his ears cocked, and growled whenever the thunder rumbled. The children fed him with titbits and he ate them eagerly, for he was hungry too.

All the children had four biscuits each. 'I think I shall give all mine to Tim,' said George. 'I didn't bring him any of his own biscuits, and he does seem so hungry.'

'No, don't do that,' said Julian. 'We'll each give him a biscuit – that will be four for him – and we'll still have three left each. That will be plenty for us.'

'You are really nice,' said George. 'Tim, don't you think they are nice?'

Tim did. He licked everyone and made them laugh. Then he rolled over on his back and let Julian tickle him underneath.

The children fed the fire and finished their picnic. When it came to Julian's turn to get more sticks, he disappeared out of the room into the storm. He stood and looked around, the rain wetting his bare head.

The storm seemed to be right overhead now. The lightning flashed and the thunder crashed at the same moment. Julian was not a bit afraid of storms, but he couldn't help feeling rather over-awed at this one. It was so magnificent. The lightning tore the sky in half almost every minute, and the thunder crashed so loudly that it sounded almost as if mountains were falling down all around!

The sea's voice could be heard as soon as the thunder stopped – and that was magnificent to hear too. The spray flew so high into the air that it wetted Julian as he stood in the centre of the ruined castle.

'I really must see what the waves are like,' thought the boy. 'If the spray flies right over me here, they must be simply enormous!'

He made his way out of the castle and climbed up on to part of the ruined wall that had once run all round the castle. He stood up there, looking out to the open sea. And what a sight met his eyes!

The waves were like great walls of grey-green! They

dashed over the rocks that lay all around the island, and spray flew from them, gleaming white in the stormy sky. They rolled up to the island and dashed themselves against it with such terrific force that Julian could feel the wall beneath his feet tremble with the shock.

The boy looked out to sea, marvelling at the really great sight he saw. For half a moment he wondered if the sea might come right over the island itself! Then he knew that couldn't happen, for it would have happened before. He stared at the great waves coming in – and then he saw something rather strange.

There was something else out on the sea by the rocks besides the waves – something dark, something big, something that seemed to lurch out of the waves and settle down again. What could it be?

'It can't be a ship,' said Julian to himself, his heart beginning to beat fast as he strained his eyes to see through the rain and the spray. 'And yet it looks more like a ship than anything else. I hope it isn't a ship. There wouldn't be anyone saved from it on this dreadful day!'

He stood and watched for a while. The dark shape heaved into sight again and then sank away once more. Julian decided to go and tell the others. He ran back to the firelit room.

'George! Dick! There's something strange out on the rocks beyond the island!' he shouted, at the top of his voice. 'It looks like a ship – and yet it can't possibly be. Come and see!'

The others stared at him in surprise, and jumped to their feet. George hurriedly flung some more sticks on the fire to keep it going, and then she and the others quickly followed Julian out into the rain.

The storm seemed to be passing over a little now. The rain was not pelting down quite so hard. The thunder was rolling a little farther off, and the lightning did not flash so often. Julian led the way to the wall on which he had climbed to watch the sea.

Everyone climbed up to gaze out to sea. They saw a great tumbled, heaving mass of grey-green water, with waves rearing up everywhere. Their tops broke over the rocks and they rushed up to the island as if they would gobble it whole. Anne slipped her arm through Julian's. She felt rather small and scared.

'You're all right, Anne,' said Julian, loudly. 'Now just watch – you'll see something strange in a minute.'

They all watched. At first they saw nothing, for the waves reared up so high that they hid everything a little way out. Then suddenly George saw what Julian meant.

'Gracious!' she shouted. 'It *is* a ship! Yes, it is! Is it being wrecked? It's a big ship – not a sailing-boat, or fishing-smack!'

'Oh, is anyone in it?' wailed Anne.

The four children watched and Tim began to bark as he saw the strange dark shape lurching here and there in the enormous waves. The sea was bringing the ship nearer to shore.

WHAT THE STORM DID

'It will be dashed on to those rocks,' said Julian, suddenly. 'Look – there it goes!'

As he spoke there came a tremendous crashing, splintering sound, and the dark shape of the ship settled down on to the sharp teeth of the dangerous rocks on the southwest side of the island. It stayed there, shifting only slightly as the big waves ran under it and lifted it a little.

'She's stuck there,' said Julian. 'She won't move now. The sea will soon be going down a bit, and then the ship will find herself held by those rocks.'

As he spoke, a ray of pale sunshine came wavering out between a gap in the thinning clouds. It was gone almost at once. 'Good!' said Dick, looking upwards. 'The sun will be out again soon. We can warm ourselves then and get dry – and maybe we can find out what that poor ship is. Oh, Julian – I do so hope there was nobody in it. I hope they've all taken to boats and got safely to land.'

The clouds thinned out a little more. The wind stopped roaring and dropped to a steady breeze. The sun shone out again for a longer time, and the children felt its welcome warmth. They all stared at the ship on the rocks. The sun shone on it and lighted it up.

'There's something odd about it somehow,' said Julian, slowly. 'Something awfully odd. I've never seen a ship quite like it.'

George was staring at it with a strange look in her eyes. She turned to face the three children, and they were astonished to see the bright gleam in her blue eyes. The girl looked almost too excited to speak.

'What is it?' asked Julian, catching hold of her hand.

'Julian – oh, Julian – it's my wreck!' she cried, in a high excited voice. 'Don't you see what's happened? The storm has lifted the ship up from the bottom of the sea, and has lodged it on those rocks. It's my wreck!'

The others saw at once that she was right. It was the old

wrecked ship! No wonder it looked peculiar. No wonder it looked so old and dark, and such a strange shape. It was the wreck, lifted high out of its sleeping-place and put on the rocks nearby.

'George! We shall be able to row out and get into the wreck now!' shouted Julian. 'We shall be able to explore it from end to end. We may find the boxes of gold. Oh, *George*!'

CHAPTER SEVEN

Back to Kirrin Cottage

THE FOUR children were so tremendously surprised and excited that for a minute or two they didn't say a word. They just stared at the dark hulk of the old wreck, imagining what they might find. Then Julian clutched George's arm and pressed it tightly.

'Isn't this wonderful?' he said. 'Oh, George, isn't it an extraordinary thing to happen?'

Still George said nothing, but stared at the wreck, all kinds of thoughts racing through her mind. Then she turned to Julian.

'If only the wreck is still mine now it's thrown up like this!' she said. 'I don't know if wrecks belong to the queen or anyone, like lost treasure does. But after all, the ship did belong to our family. Nobody bothered much about it when it was down under the sea – but do you suppose people will still let me have it for my own now it's thrown up?'

'Well, don't let's tell anyone!' said Dick.

'Don't be silly,' said George. 'One of the fishermen is sure to see it when his ship goes slipping out of the bay. The news will soon be out.'

'Well, then, we'd better explore it thoroughly ourselves

before anyone else does!' said Dick, eagerly. 'No one knows about it yet. Only us. Can't we explore it as soon as the waves go down a bit?'

'We can't wade out to the rocks, if that's what you mean,' said George. 'We might get there by boat – but we couldn't possibly risk it now, while the waves are so big. They won't go down today, that's certain. The wind is still too strong.'

'Well, what about tomorrow morning, early?' said Julian. 'Before anyone has got to know about it? I bet if only *we* can get into the ship first, we can find anything there is to find!'

'Yes, I expect we could,' said George. 'I told you divers had been down and explored the ship as thoroughly as they could – but of course it is difficult to do that properly under water. We might find something they've missed. Oh, this is like a dream. I can't believe it's true that my old wreck has come up from the bottom of the sea like that!'

The sun was now properly out, and the children's wet clothes dried in its hot rays. They steamed in the sun, and even Tim's coat sent up a mist too. He didn't seem to like the wreck at all, and growled deeply at it.

'You are funny, Tim,' said George, patting him. 'It won't hurt you! What do you think it is?'

'He probably thinks it's a whale,' said Anne with a laugh. 'Oh, George – this is the most exciting day of my life! Oh, can't we possibly take the boat and see if we can get to the wreck?'

'No, we can't,' said George. 'I only wish we could. But it's quite impossible, Anne. For one thing, I don't think the wreck has quite settled down on the rocks yet, and maybe it won't till the tide has gone down. I can see it lifting a little still when an extra big wave comes. It would be dangerous to go into it yet. And for another thing I don't want my boat smashed to bits on the rocks, and us thrown into that wild water! That's what would happen. We must wait till tomorrow. It's a good idea to come early. I expect lots of grown-ups will think it's their business to explore it.'

The children watched the old wreck for a little time longer and then went all round the island again. It was certainly not very large, but it really was exciting, with its rocky little coast, its quiet inlet where their boat was, the ruined castle, the circling jackdaws, and the scampering rabbits everywhere.

'I do love it,' said Anne. 'I really do. It's just small enough to *feel* like an island. Most islands are too big to feel like islands. I mean, Britain is an island, but nobody living on it could possibly know it unless they were told. Now this island really *feels* like one because wherever you are you can see to the other side of it. I love it.'

George felt very happy. She had often been on her island before, but always alone except for Tim. She had always vowed that she never, never would take anyone there, because it would spoil her island for her. But it hadn't been spoilt. It had made it much nicer. For the first

66

time George began to understand that sharing pleasures doubles their joy.

'We'll wait till the waves go down a bit then we'll go back home,' she said. 'I rather think there's some more rain coming, and we'll only get soaked through. We shan't be back till tea-time as it is, because we'll have a long pull against the out-going tide.'

All the children felt a little tired after the excitements of the morning. They said very little as they rowed home. Everyone took turns at rowing except Anne, who was not strong enough with the oars to row against the tide. They looked back at the island as they left it. They couldn't see the wreck because that was on the opposite side, facing the open sea.

'It's just as well it's there,' said Julian. 'No one can see it yet. Only when a boat goes out to fish will it be seen. And we shall be there as early as any boat goes out! I vote we get up at dawn.'

'Well, that's pretty early,' said George. 'Can you wake up? I'm often out at dawn, but you're not used to it.'

'Of course we can wake up,' said Julian. 'Well – here we are back at the beach again – and I'm jolly glad. My arms are awfully tired and I'm so hungry I could eat a whole larderful of things.'

'Woof,' said Tim, quite agreeing.

'I'll have to take Tim to Alf,' said George, jumping out of the boat. 'You get the boat in, Julian. I'll join you in a few minutes.'

It wasn't long before all four were sitting down to a good tea. Aunt Fanny had baked new scones for them, and had made a ginger cake with black treacle. It was dark brown and sticky to eat. The children finished it all up and said it was the nicest they had ever tasted.

'Did you have an exciting day?' asked their aunt.

'Oh yes!' said Anne, eagerly. 'The storm was grand. It threw up . . .'

Julian and Dick both kicked her under the table. George couldn't reach her or she would most certainly have kicked her too. Anne stared at the boys angrily, with tears in her eyes.

'Now what's the matter?' asked Aunt Fanny. 'Did somebody kick you, Anne? Well, really, this kicking under the table has got to stop. Poor Anne will be covered with bruises. What did the sea throw up, dear?'

'It threw up the most enormous waves,' said Anne, looking defiantly at the others. She knew they had thought she was going to say that the sea had thrown up the wreck – but they were wrong! They had kicked her for nothing!

'Sorry for kicking you, Anne,' said Julian. 'My foot sort of slipped.'

'So did mine,' said Dick. 'Yes, Aunt Fanny, it was a magnificent sight on the island. The waves raced up that little inlet, and we had to take our boat almost up to the top of the low cliff there.'

'I wasn't really afraid of the storm,' said Anne. 'In fact, I wasn't really as afraid of it as Ti . . .'

BACK TO KIRRIN COTTAGE

Everyone knew perfectly well that Anne was going to mention Timothy, and they all interrupted her at once, speaking very loudly. Julian managed to get a kick in again.

'Oooh!' said Anne.

'The rabbits were so tame,' said Julian, loudly.

'We watched the cormorants,' said Dick and George joined in too, talking at the same time.

'The jackdaws made such a noise, they said "Chack, chack, chack," all the time.'

'Well, really, you sound like jackdaws yourselves, talking all at once like this!' said Aunt Fanny, with a laugh. 'Now, have you all finished? Very well, then, go and wash your sticky hands – yes, George, I know they're sticky, because *I* made that gingerbread, and you've had three slices! Then you had better go and play quietly in the other room, because it's raining, and you can't go out. But don't disturb your father, George. He's very busy.'

The children went to wash. 'Idiot!' said Julian to Anne. 'Nearly gave us away twice!'

'I didn't mean what you thought I meant the first time!' began Anne indignantly.

George interrupted her.

'I'd rather you gave the secret of the wreck away than my secret about Tim,' she said. 'I do think you've got a careless tongue.'

'Yes, I have,' said Anne, sorrowfully. 'I think I'd better not talk at meal-times any more. I love Tim so much I just can't seem to help wanting to talk about him.'

They all went to play in the other room. Julian turned a table upside down with a crash. 'We'll play at wrecks,' he said. 'This is the wreck. Now we're going to explore it.'

The door flew open and an angry, frowning face looked in. It was George's father!

'What was that noise?' he said. 'George! Did you overturn that table?'

'I did,' said Julian. 'I'm sorry. I quite forgot you were working.'

'Any more noise like that and I shall keep you all in tomorrow!' said his uncle Quentin. 'Georgina, keep your cousins quiet.'

The door shut and Uncle Quentin went out. The children looked at one another.

'Your father's awfully fierce, isn't he?' said Julian. 'I'm sorry I made that row. I didn't think.'

'We'd better do something really quiet,' said George. 'Or he'll keep his word – and we'll find ourselves inside tomorrow just when we want to explore the wreck.'

This was a terrible thought. Anne went to get one of her dolls to play with. She had managed to bring quite a number after all. Julian fetched a book. George took up a beautiful little boat she was carving out of a piece of wood. Dick lay back on a chair and thought of the exciting wreck. The rain poured down steadily, and everyone hoped it would have stopped by the morning.

'We'll have to be up most awfully early,' said Dick, yawning. 'What about going to bed in good time tonight? I'm tired with all that rowing.'

In the ordinary way none of the children liked going to bed early – but with such an exciting thing to look forward to, early bed seemed different that night.

'It will make the time go quickly,' said Anne, putting down her doll. 'Shall we go now?'

'Whatever do you suppose Mother would say if we went just after tea?' said George. 'She'd think we were all ill. No, let's go after supper. We'll just say we're tired with rowing – which is perfectly true – and we'll get a good night's sleep, and be ready for our adventure tomorrow morning. And it *is* an adventure, you know. It isn't many people that have the chance of exploring an old, old wreck like that, which has always been at the bottom of the sea!'

So, by eight o'clock, all the children were in bed, rather to Aunt Fanny's surprise. Anne fell asleep at once. Julian and Dick were not long – but George lay awake for some time, thinking of her island, her wreck – and, of course, her beloved dog!

'I must take Tim too,' she thought, as she fell asleep. 'We can't leave old Tim out of this. He shall share in the adventure too!'

CHAPTER EIGHT

Exploring the wreck

JULIAN WOKE first the next morning. He awoke just as the sun was slipping over the horizon in the east, and filling the sky with gold. Julian stared at the ceiling for a moment, and then, in a rush, he remembered all that had happened the day before. He sat up straight in bed and whispered as loudly as he could.

'Dick! Wake up! We're going to see the wreck! Do wake up!'

Dick woke and grinned at Julian. A feeling of happiness crept over him. They were going on an adventure. He leapt out of bed and ran quietly to the girls' room. He opened the door. Both the girls were fast asleep, Anne curled up like a dormouse under the sheet.

Dick shook George and then dug Anne in the back. They awoke and sat up. 'Buck up!' whispered Dick. 'The sun is just rising. We'll have to hurry.'

George's blue eyes shone as she dressed. Anne skipped about quietly, finding her few clothes – just a bathing suit, jeans and jersey – and rubber shoes for her feet. It wasn't many minutes before they were all ready.

'Now, not a creak on the stairs – not a cough or a giggle!' warned Julian, as they stood together on the landing. Anne was a dreadful giggler, and had often given secret plans away by her sudden explosive choke. But this time the little girl was as solemn as the others, and as careful. They crept down the stairs and undid the little front door. Not a sound was made. They shut the door quietly and made their way down the garden path to the gate. The gate always creaked, so they climbed over it instead of opening it.

The sun was now shining brightly, though it was still low in the eastern sky. It felt warm already. The sky was so beautifully blue that Anne couldn't help feeling it had been freshly washed! 'It looks just as if it had come back from the laundry,' she told the others.

They squealed with laughter at her. She did say odd things at times. But they knew what she meant. The day had a lovely new feeling about it – the clouds were so pink in the bright blue sky, and the sea looked so smooth and fresh. It was impossible to imagine that it had been so rough the day before.

George got her boat. Then she went to get Tim, while the boys hauled the boat down to the sea. Alf, the fisher-boy, was surprised to see George so early. He was about to go with his father, fishing. He grinned at George.

'You going fishing, too?' he said to her. 'My, wasn't that a storm yesterday! I thought you'd be caught in it.'

'We were,' said George. 'Come on, Tim! Come on!'

Tim was very pleased to see George so early. He capered round her as she ran back to the others, almost tripping her up as she went. He leapt into the boat as soon as he saw it, and stood at the stern, his red tongue out, his tail wagging violently.

'I wonder his tail keeps on,' said Anne, looking at it. 'One day, Timothy, you'll wag it right off.'

They set off to the island. It was easy to row now, because the sea was so calm. They came to the island, and rowed around it to the other side.

And there was the wreck, piled high on some sharp rocks! It had settled down now and did not stir as waves slid under it. It lay a little to one side, and the broken mast, now shorter than before, stuck out at an angle.

'There she is,' said Julian, in excitement. 'Poor old wreck! I guess she's a bit more battered now. What a noise she made when she went crashing on to those rocks yesterday!'

'How do we get to her?' asked Anne, looking at the mass of ugly, sharp rocks all around. But George was not at all dismayed. She knew almost every inch of the coast around her little island. She pulled steadily at the oars and soon came near to the rocks in which the great wreck rested.

The children looked at the wreck from their boat. It was big, much bigger than they had imagined when they had peered at it from the top of the water. It was encrusted with shellfish of some kind, and strands of brown and green seaweed hung down. It smelt funny. It had great holes in its sides, showing where it had battered against rocks. There were holes in the deck too. Altogether, it looked a sad and forlorn old ship – but to the four children it was the most exciting thing in the whole world.

They rowed to the rocks on which the wreck lay. The tide washed over them. George took a look round.

'We'll tie our boat up to the wreck itself,' she said. 'And we'll get on to the deck quite easily by climbing up the side. Look, Julian! – throw this loop of rope over that broken bit of wood there, sticking out from the side.'

Julian did as he was told. The rope tightened and the boat was held in position. Then George clambered up the side of the wreck like a monkey. She was a marvel at climbing. Julian and Dick followed her, but Anne had to be helped up. Soon all four were standing on the slanting deck. It was slippery with seaweed, and the smell was very strong indeed. Anne didn't like it.

'Well, this was the deck,' said George, 'and that's where the men got up and down.' She pointed to a large hole. They went to it and looked down. The remains of an iron ladder were still there. George looked at it.

'I think it's still strong enough to hold us,' she said. 'I'll go first. Anyone got a torch? It looks pretty dark down there.'

Julian had a torch. He handed it to George. The children became rather quiet. It was mysterious somehow to look down into the dark inside of the big ship. What would they find? George switched on the torch and then swung herself down the ladder. The others followed.

The light from the torch showed a very strange sight. The under-parts of the ship were low-ceilinged, made of thick oak. The children had to bend their heads to get about. It seemed as if there were places that might have been cabins, though it was difficult to tell now, for everything was so battered, sea-drenched and seaweedy. The smell was really horrid, though it was mostly of drying seaweed.

The children slipped about on the seaweed as they went
round the inside of the ship. It didn't seem so big inside
after all. There was a big hold under the cabins, which the
children saw by the light of their torch.

'That's where the boxes of gold would have been kept, I
expect,' said Julian. But there was nothing in the hold
except water and fish! The children couldn't go down
because the water was too deep. One or two barrels
floated in the water, but they had burst open and were
quite empty.

'I expect they were water-barrels, or barrels of pork or
biscuit,' said George. 'Let's go round the other part of the
ship again – where the cabins are. Isn't it strange to see
bunks there that sailors have slept in? – and look at that
old wooden chair. Fancy it still being here after all these
years! Look at the things on those hooks too – they are all
rusty now, and covered with seaweedy stuff – but they
must have been the cook's pans and dishes!'

It was a very weird trip round the old wreck. The
children were all on the look-out for boxes which might
contain bars of gold – but there didn't seem to be one
single box of any kind anywhere!

They came to a rather bigger cabin than the others. It
had a bunk in one corner, in which a large crab rested. An
old bit of furniture looking rather like a table with two
legs, all encrusted with greyish shells, lay against the bunk.
Wooden shelves, festooned with grey-green seaweed, hung
crookedly on the walls of the cabin.

EXPLORING THE WRECK

'This must have been the captain's own cabin,' said Julian. 'It's the biggest one. Look, what's that in the corner?'

'An old cup!' said Anne, picking it up. 'And here's half of a saucer. I expect the captain was sitting here having a cup of tea when the ship went down.'

This made the children feel rather uneasy. It was dark and smelly in the little cabin, and the floor was wet and slippery to their feet. George began to feel that her wreck was really more pleasant sunk under the water than raised above it!

'Let's go,' she said, with a shiver. 'I don't like it much. It *is* exciting, I know – but it's a bit frightening too.'

They turned to go. Julian flashed his torch round the little cabin for the last time. He was about to switch it off and follow the others up to the deck above when he caught sight of something that made him stop. He flashed his torch on to it, and then called to the others.

'I say! Wait a bit. There's a cupboard here in the wall. Let's see if there's anything in it!'

The others turned back and looked. They saw what looked like a small cupboard set in level with the wall of the cabin. What had caught Julian's eye was the keyhole. There was no key there, though.

'There just *might* be something inside,' said Julian. He tried to prise open the wooden door with his fingers, but it wouldn't move. 'It's locked,' he said. 'Of course it would be!'

'I expect the lock is rotten by now,' said George, and she tried too. Then she took out her big strong pocket-knife and inserted it between the cupboard door and the cabin-wall. She forced back the blade – and the lock of the cupboard suddenly snapped! As she had said, it was quite rotten. The door swung open, and the children saw a shelf inside with a few curious things on it.

EXPLORING THE WRECK

There was a wooden box, swollen with the wet sea-water in which it had lain for years. There were two or three things that looked like old, pulpy books. There was some sort of glass drinking-vessel, cracked in half – and two or three funny objects so spoilt by sea-water that no one could possibly say what they were.

'Nothing very interesting – except the box,' said Julian, and he picked it up. 'Anyway, I expect that whatever is inside is ruined. But we may as well try and open it.'

He and George tried their best to force the lock of the old wooden box. On the top of it were stamped initials – H.J.K.

'I expect those were the captain's initials,' said Dick.

'No, they were the initials of my great-great-great-grandfather!' said George, her eyes shining suddenly. 'I've heard all about him. His name was Henry John Kirrin. This was his ship, you know. This must have been his very private box in which he kept his old papers or diaries. Oh – we simply *must* open it!'

But it was quite impossible to force the lid up with the tools they had there. They soon gave it up, and Julian picked up the box to carry it to the boat.

'We'll open it at home,' he said, his voice sounding rather excited. 'We'll get a hammer or something, and get it open somehow. Oh, George – this really is a find!'

They all of them felt that they really had something mysterious in their possession. Was there anything inside the box – and if so, what would it be? They longed to get home and open it!

They went up on deck, climbing the old iron ladder. As soon as they got there they saw that others besides themselves had discovered that the wreck had been thrown up from the bottom of the sea!

'Golly! Half the fishing-smacks of the bay have discovered it!' cried Julian, looking round at the fishing-boats that had come as near as they dared to the wreck. The fishermen were looking at the wreck in wonder. When they saw the children on board they halloo-ed loudly.

'Ahoy there! What's that ship?'

'It's the old wreck!' yelled back Julian. 'She was thrown up yesterday in the storm!'

'Don't say any more,' said George, frowning. 'It's *my* wreck. I don't want sightseers on it!'

So no more was said, and the four children got into their boat and rowed home as fast as they could. It was past their breakfast-time. They might get a good scolding. They might even be sent to bed by George's fierce father – but what did they care? They had explored the wreck – and had come away with a box which *might* contain – well, if not bars of gold, one *small* bar, perhaps!

They did get a scolding. They had to go without half their breakfast, too, because Uncle Quentin said that children who came in so late didn't deserve hot bacon and eggs – only toast and marmalade. It was very sad.

They hid the box under the bed in the boys' room. Tim had been left with the fisher-boy – or rather, had been tied up in his backyard, for Alf had gone out fishing, and was even now gazing from his father's boat at the strange wreck.

'We can make a bit of money taking sightseers out to this wreck,' said Alf. And before the day was out scores of interested people had seen the old wreck from the decks of motor-boats and fishing-smacks.

George was furious about it. But she couldn't do anything. After all, as Julian said, anybody could have a look!

CHAPTER NINE

The box from the wreck

THE FIRST thing that the children did after breakfast was to fetch the precious box and take it out to the tool-shed in the garden. They were simply longing to force it open. All of them secretly felt certain that it would hold treasure of some sort.

Julian looked round for a tool. He found a chisel and decided that would be just the thing to force the box open. He tried, but the tool slipped and jabbed his fingers. Then he tried other things, but the box obstinately refused to open. The children stared at it crossly.

'I know what to do,' said Anne at last. 'Let's take it to the top of the house and throw it down to the ground. It would burst open then, I expect.'

The others thought over the idea. 'It might be worth trying,' said Julian. 'The only thing is it might break or spoil anything inside the box.'

But there didn't seem any other way to open the box, so Julian carried it up to the top of the house. He went to the attic and opened the window there. The others were down below, waiting. Julian hurled the box out of the window as violently as he could. It flew through the air and landed with a terrific crash on the crazy paving below.

THE BOX FROM THE WRECK

At once the french window there opened and their Uncle Quentin came out like a bullet from a gun.

'Whatever are you doing?' he cried. 'Surely you aren't throwing things at each other out of the window? What's this on the ground?'

The children looked at the box. It had burst open and lay on the ground, showing a tin lining that was waterproof. Whatever was in the box would not be spoilt! It would be quite dry!

Dick ran to pick it up.

'I said, what's this on the ground?' shouted his uncle and moved towards him.

'It's – it's something that belongs to us,' said Dick, going red.

'Well, I shall take it away from you,' said his uncle. 'Disturbing me like this! Give it to me. Where did you get it?'

Nobody answered. Uncle Quentin frowned till his glasses nearly fell off. 'Where did you get it?' he barked, glaring at poor Anne, who was nearest.

'Out of the wreck,' stammered the little girl, scared.

'Out of the *wreck*!' said her uncle, in surprise. 'The old wreck that was thrown up yesterday? I heard about that. Do you mean to say you've been in it?'

'Yes,' said Dick. Julian joined them at that moment, looking worried. It would be too awful if his uncle took the box just as they got it open. But that was exactly what he did do!

'Well, this box may contain something important,' he said, and he took it from Dick's hands. 'You've no right to go prying about in that old wreck. You might take something that mattered.'

'Well, it's my wreck,' said George, in a defiant tone. 'Please, Father, let us have the box. We'd just got it opened. We thought it might hold – a gold bar – or something like that!'

86

THE BOX FROM THE WRECK

'A gold bar!' said her father, with a snort. 'What a baby you are! This small box would never hold a thing like that! It's much more likely to contain particulars of what happened to the bars! I have always thought that the gold was safely delivered somewhere – and that the ship, empty of its valuable cargo, got wrecked as it left the bay!'

'Oh, Father – please, please let us have our box,' begged George, almost in tears. She suddenly felt certain that it did contain papers that might tell them what had happened to the gold. But without another word her father turned and went into the house, carrying the box, burst open and cracked, its tin lining showing through under his arm.

Anne burst into tears. 'Don't blame me for telling him we got it from the wreck,' she sobbed. 'Please don't. He glared at me so. I just had to tell him.'

'All right, Baby,' said Julian, putting his arm round Anne. He looked furious. He thought it was very unfair of his uncle to take the box like that. 'Listen – I'm not going to stand this. We'll get hold of that box somehow and look into it. I'm sure your father won't bother himself with it, George – he'll start writing his book again and forget all about it. I'll wait my chance and slip into his study and get it, even if it means a telling off if I'm discovered!'

'Good!' said George. 'We'll all keep a watch and see if Father goes out.'

So they took it in turns to keep watch, but most annoyingly their Uncle Quentin remained in his study all the morning. Aunt Fanny was surprised to see one or two children always about the garden that day, instead of down on the beach.

'Why don't you all keep together and bathe or do something?' she said. 'Have you quarrelled with one another?'

'No,' said Dick. 'Of course not.' But he didn't say why they were in the garden!

'Doesn't your father *ever* go out?' he said to George, when it was her turn to keep watch. 'I don't think he leads a very healthy life.'

'Scientists never do,' said George, as if she knew all about them. 'But I tell you what – he may go to sleep this afternoon! He sometimes does!'

Julian was left behind in the garden that afternoon. He sat down under a tree and opened a book. Soon he heard a curious noise that made him look up. He knew at once what it was!

'That's Uncle Quentin snoring!' he said in excitement. 'It is! Oh – I wonder if I could possibly creep in at the french window and get our box!'

He stole to the windows and looked in. One was a little way open and Julian opened it a little more. He saw his uncle lying back in a comfortable armchair, his mouth a little open, his eyes closed, fast asleep! Every time he took a breath, he snored.

'Well, he really does look sound asleep,' thought the boy. 'And there's the box, just behind him, on that table.

THE BOX FROM THE WRECK

I'll risk it. I bet I'll get an awful telling off if I'm caught, but I can't help that!'

He stole in. His uncle still snored. He tiptoed by him to the table behind his uncle's chair. He took hold of the box.

And then a bit of the broken wood of the box fell to the floor with a thud! His uncle stirred in his chair and opened his eyes. Quick as lightning the boy crouched down behind his uncle's chair, hardly breathing.

'What's that?' he heard his uncle say. Julian didn't move. Then his uncle settled down again and shut his eyes. Soon there was the sound of his rhythmic snoring!

'Hurrah!' thought Julian. 'He's off again!'

Quietly he stood up, holding the box. On tiptoe he crept to the french window. He slipped out and ran softly down the garden path. He didn't think of hiding the box. All he wanted to do was to get to the other children and show them what he had done!

He ran to the beach where the others were lying in the sun. 'Hi!' he yelled. 'Hi! I've got it! I've got it!'

They all sat up with a jerk, thrilled to see the box in Julian's arms. They forgot all about the other people on the beach. Julian dropped down on the sand and grinned.

'Your father went to sleep,' he said to George. 'Tim, don't lick me like that! And George, I went in – and a bit of the box dropped on the floor – and it woke him up!'

'Golly!' said George. 'What happened?'

'I crouched down behind his chair till he went to sleep again,' said Julian. 'Then I fled. Now – let's see what's in here. I don't believe your father's even tried to see!'

He hadn't. The tin lining was intact. It had rusted with the years of lying in the wet, and the lid was so tightly fitted down that it was almost impossible to move it.

But once George began to work at it with her pocket-knife, scraping away the rust, it began to loosen – and in about a quarter of an hour it came off!

The children bent eagerly over it. Inside lay some old papers and a book of some kind with a black cover. Nothing else at all. No bar of gold. No treasure. Everyone felt a little bit disappointed.

'It's all quite dry,' said Julian, surprised. 'Not a bit damp. The tin lining kept everything perfect.'

He picked up the book and opened it. 'It's a diary your great-great-great-grandfather kept of the ship's voyages,' he said. 'I can hardly read the writing. It's so small and funny.'

George picked up one of the papers. It was made of thick parchment, quite yellow with age. She spread it out on the sand and looked at it. The others glanced at it too, but they couldn't make out what it was at all. It seemed to be a kind of map.

'Perhaps it's a map of some place he had to go to,' said Julian. But suddenly George's hands began to shake as she held the map, and her eyes gleamed brilliantly as she looked up at the others. She opened her mouth but didn't speak.

'What's the matter?' said Julian, curiously. 'What's up? Have you lost your tongue?'

George shook her head and then began to speak with a rush. 'Julian! Do you know what this is? It's a map of my old castle – of Kirrin Castle – when it wasn't a ruin. And it shows the dungeons! And look – just look what's written in this corner of the dungeons!'

She put a trembling finger on one part of the map. The others leaned over to see what it was – and, printed in old-fashioned letters was a curious word.

INGOTS

'Ingots!' said Anne, puzzled. 'What does that mean? I've never heard that word before.'

But the two boys had. 'Ingots!' cried Dick. 'Why – that must be the bars of gold. They were called ingots.'

'Most bars of metal are called ingots,' said Julian, going red with excitement. 'But as we know there is gold missing from that ship, then it really looks as if ingots here meant bars of gold. Oh golly! To think they may still be hidden somewhere under Kirrin Castle. George! George! Isn't it terribly, awfully exciting?'

George nodded. She was trembling all over with excitement. 'If only we could find it!' she whispered. 'If only we could!'

'We'll have a jolly good hunt for it,' said Julian. 'It will be awfully difficult because the castle is in ruins now, and so overgrown. But somehow or other we'll find those ingots. What a lovely word. Ingots! Ingots! Ingots!'

It sounded somehow more exciting than the word gold. Nobody spoke about gold any more. They talked about the ingots. Tim couldn't make out what the excitement was at all. He wagged his tail and tried hard to lick first one and then another of the children, but for once not one

THE BOX FROM THE WRECK

of them paid any attention to him! He simply couldn't understand it, and after a while he went and sat down by himself with his back to the children, and his ears down.

'Oh, do look at poor Timothy!' said George. 'He can't understand your excitement. Tim! Tim, darling, it's all right, you're not in disgrace or anything. Oh, Tim, we've got the most wonderful secret in the whole world.'

Tim bounded up, his tail wagging, pleased to be taken notice of once more. He put his big paw on the precious map, and the four children shouted at him at once.

'Golly! We can't have that torn!' said Julian. Then he looked at the others and frowned. 'What are we going to do about the box?' he said. 'I mean – George's father will be sure to miss it, won't he? We'll have to give it back.'

'Well, can't we take out the map and keep it?' said Dick. 'He won't know it was there if he hasn't looked in the box. And it's pretty certain he hasn't. The other things don't matter much – they are only that old diary and a few letters.'

'To be on the safe side, let's take a copy of the map,' said Julian. 'Then we can put the real map back and replace the box.'

They all voted that a very good idea. They went back to Kirrin Cottage and traced out the map carefully. They did it in the tool-shed because they didn't want anyone to see them. It was a strange map. It was in three parts.

'This part shows the dungeons under the castle,' said Julian. 'And this shows a plan of the ground floor of the castle – and this shows the top part. My word, it was a fine place in those days! The dungeons run all under the castle. I bet they were pretty awful places. I wonder how people got down to them.'

'We'll have to study the map a bit more and see,' said George. 'It all looks rather muddled to us at present – but once we take the map over to the castle and study it there, we may be able to make out how to get down to the hidden dungeons. Ooooh! I don't expect any children ever had such an adventure as this.'

Julian put the traced map carefully into his jeans pocket. He didn't mean it to leave him. It was very precious. Then he put the real map back into the box and looked towards the house. 'What about putting it back now?' he said. 'Maybe your father is still asleep, George.'

But he wasn't. He was awake. Luckily he hadn't missed the box! He came into the dining-room to have tea with the family, and Julian took his chance. He muttered an excuse, slipped away from the table, and replaced the box on the table behind his uncle's chair!

He winked at the others when he came back. They felt relieved. They were all scared of Uncle Quentin, and were not at all anxious to be in his bad books. Anne didn't say one word during the whole of the meal. She was so terribly afraid she might give something away, either about Tim or the box. The others spoke very little too. While they were at tea the telephone rang and Aunt Fanny went to answer it.

She soon came back. 'It's for you, Quentin,' she said. 'Apparently the old wreck has caused quite a lot of excitement, and there are men from a London paper who want to ask you questions about it.'

'Tell them I'll see them at six,' said Uncle Quentin. The children looked at one another in alarm. They hoped that their uncle wouldn't show the box to the newspaper men. Then the secret of the hidden gold might come out!

'What a mercy we took a tracing of the map!' said Julian, after tea. 'But I'm jolly sorry now we left the real map in the box. Someone else may guess our secret!'

CHAPTER TEN

An astonishing offer

THE NEXT morning the papers were full of the extraordinary way in which the old wreck had been thrown up out of the sea. The newspaper men had got out of the children's uncle the tale of the wreck and the lost gold, and some of them even managed to land on Kirrin Island and take pictures of the old ruined castle.

George was furious. 'It's *my* castle!' she stormed to her mother. 'It's *my* island. You said it could be mine. You did, you did!'

'I know, George dear,' said her mother. 'But you really must be sensible. It can't hurt the island to be landed on, and it can't hurt the castle to be photographed.'

'But I don't want it to be,' said George, her face dark and sulky. 'It's mine. And the wreck is mine. You said so.'

'Well, I didn't know it was going to be thrown up like that,' said her mother. 'Do be sensible, George. What can it possibly matter if people go to look at the wreck? You can't stop them.'

George couldn't stop them, but that didn't make her any the less angry about it. The children were astonished at the interest that the cast-up wreck caused, and because of that, Kirrin Island became an object of great interest

97

too. Sightseers from the places all around came to see it, and the fishermen managed to find the little inlet and land the people there. George sobbed with rage, and Julian tried to comfort her.

'Listen, George! No one knows our secret yet. We'll wait till this excitement has died down, and then we'll go to Kirrin Castle and find the ingots.'

'If someone doesn't find them first,' said George, drying her eyes. She was furious with herself for crying, but she really couldn't help it.

'How could they?' said Julian. 'No one has seen inside the box yet! I'm going to wait my chance and get that map out before anyone sees it!'

But he didn't have a chance, because something dreadful happened. Uncle Quentin sold the old box to a man who bought antique things! He came out from his study, beaming, a day or two after the excitement began, and told Aunt Fanny and the children.

'I've struck a very good bargain with that man,' he said to his wife. 'You know that old tin-lined box from the wreck? Well, this fellow collects curious things like that, and he gave me a very good price for it. Very good indeed. More even that I could expect for the writing of my book! As soon as he saw the old map there and the old diary he said at once that he would buy the whole collection.'

The children stared at him in horror. The box was sold! Now someone would study that map and perhaps jump to what 'ingots' meant. The story of the lost gold had been put into all the newspapers now. Nobody could fail to know what the map showed if they studied it carefully.

The children did not dare to tell Uncle Quentin what they knew. It was true he was all smiles now, and was promising to buy them new shrimping-nets, and a raft for themselves – but he was such a changeable person. He might fly into a furious temper if he heard that Julian had taken the box and opened it himself, while his uncle was sleeping.

When they were alone the children discussed the whole matter. It seemed very serious indeed to them. They half-wondered if they should let Aunt Fanny into the secret – but it was such a precious secret, and so marvellous, that they felt they didn't want to give it away to anyone at all.

'Now listen!' said Julian, at last. 'We'll ask Aunt Fanny if we can go to Kirrin Island and spend a day or two there – sleep there at night too, I mean. That will give us a little time to poke round and see what we can find. The sightseers won't come after a day or two, I'm sure. Maybe we'll get in before anyone tumbles to our secret. After all, the man who bought the box may not even guess that the map shows Kirrin Castle.'

They felt more cheerful. It was so awful to do nothing. As soon as they had planned to act, they felt better. They decided to ask their aunt the next day if they might go and spend the weekend at the castle. The weather was gloriously fine, and it would be great fun. They could take plenty of food with them.

When they went to ask Aunt Fanny, Uncle Quentin was with her. He was all smiles again, and even clapped Julian on the back. 'Well!' he said. 'What's this deputation for?'

'We just wanted to ask Aunt Fanny something,' said Julian, politely. 'Aunt Fanny, as the weather is so fine, do you think you would let us go for the weekend to Kirrin Castle, please, and spend a day or two there on the island? You can't think how we would love to!'

'Well – what do you think, Quentin?' asked their aunt, turning to her husband.

'If they want to, they can,' said Uncle Quentin. 'They won't have a chance to, soon. My dears, we have had a marvellous offer for Kirrin Island! A man wants to buy it, rebuild the castle as a hotel, and make it into a proper holiday place! What do you think of that?'

All four children stared at the smiling man, shocked and horrified. Somebody was going to buy the island! Had their secret been discovered? Did the man want to buy the castle because he had read the map, and knew there was plenty of gold hidden there?

George gave a curious choke. Her eyes burned as if they were on fire. 'Mother! You can't sell my island! You can't sell my castle! I won't let them be sold.'

Her father frowned. 'Don't be silly, Georgina,' he said. 'It isn't really yours. You know that. It belongs to your mother, and naturally she would like to sell it if she could. We need the money very badly. You will be able to have a great many nice things once we sell the island.'

AN ASTONISHING OFFER

'I don't want nice things!' cried poor George. 'My castle and my island are the nicest things I could ever have. Mother! Mother! You know you said I could have them. You know you did! I believed you.'

'George dear, I did mean you to have them to play on, when I thought they couldn't possibly be worth anything,' said her mother, looking distressed. 'But now things are

101

different. Your father has been offered quite a good sum, far more than we ever thought of getting – and we really can't afford to turn it down.'

'So you only gave me the island when you thought it wasn't worth anything,' said George, her face white and angry. 'As soon as it is worth money you take it away again. I think that's horrid. It – it isn't honourable.'

'That's enough, Georgina,' said her father, angrily. 'Your mother is guided by me. You're only a child. Your mother didn't really mean what she said – it was only to please you. But you know well enough you will share in the money we get and have anything you want.'

'I won't touch a penny!' said George, in a low choking voice. 'You'll be sorry you sold it.'

The girl turned and stumbled out of the room. The others felt very sorry for her. They knew what she was feeling. She took things so very seriously. Julian thought she didn't understand grown-ups very well. It wasn't a bit of good fighting grown-ups. They could do exactly as they liked. If they wanted to take away George's island and castle, they could. If they wanted to sell it, they could! But what Uncle Quentin didn't know was the fact that there might be a store of gold ingots there! Julian stared at his uncle and wondered whether to warn him. Then he decided not to. There was just a chance that the four children could find the gold first!

'When are you selling the island, Uncle?' he asked quietly.

AN ASTONISHING OFFER

'The deeds will be signed in about a week's time,' was the answer. 'So if you really want to spend a day or two there, you'd better do so quickly, for after that you may not get permission from the new owners.'

'Was it the man who bought the old box who wants to buy the island?' asked Julian.

'Yes,' said his uncle. 'I was a little surprised myself, for I thought he was just a buyer of old things. It was astonishing to me that he should get the idea of buying the island to rebuild the castle as a hotel. Still, I dare say there will be big money in running a hotel there – very romantic, staying on a little island like that – people will like it. I'm no businessman myself, and I certainly shouldn't care to invest my money in a place like Kirrin Island. But I should think he knows what he is doing all right.'

'Yes, he certainly does,' thought Julian to himself, as he went out of the room with Dick and Anne. 'He's read that map – and has jumped to the same idea that we did – the store of hidden ingots is somewhere on that island – and he's going to get it! He doesn't want to build a hotel! He's after the treasure! I expect he's offered Uncle Quentin some silly low price that poor old uncle thinks is marvellous! Oh dear – this is a horrible thing to happen.'

He went to find George. She was in the tool-shed, looking quite green. She said she felt sick.

'It's only because you're so upset,' said Julian. He slipped his arm round her. For once George didn't push

103

it away. She felt comforted. Tears came into her eyes, and she angrily tried to blink them away.

'Listen, George!' said Julian. 'We mustn't give up hope. We'll go to Kirrin Island tomorrow, and we'll do our very, very best to get down into the dungeons somehow and find the ingots. We'll jolly well stay there till we do. See? Now cheer up, because we'll want your help in planning everything. Thank goodness we took a tracing of the map.'

George cheered up a little. She still felt angry with her father and mother, but the thought of going to Kirrin Island for a day or two, and taking Timothy too, certainly seemed rather good.

'I do think my father and mother are unkind,' she said.

'Well, they're not really,' said Julian, wisely. 'After all, if they need money badly, they would be silly not to part with something they think is quite useless. And you know, your father did say you could have anything you want. I know what I would ask for, if I were you!'

'What?' asked George.

'Timothy, of course!' said Julian. And that made George smile and cheer up tremendously!

CHAPTER ELEVEN

Off to Kirrin Island

JULIAN AND George went to find Dick and Anne. They were waiting for them in the garden, looking rather upset. They were glad to see Julian and George and ran to meet them.

Anne took George's hands. 'I'm awfully sorry about your island, George,' she said.

'So am I,' said Dick. 'Bad luck, old girl – I mean, old boy!'

George managed to smile. 'I've been behaving like a girl,' she said, half-ashamed. 'But I did get an awful shock.'

Julian told the others what they had planned. 'We'll go tomorrow morning,' he said. 'We'll make out a list of all the things we shall need. Let's begin now.'

He took out a pencil and notebook. The others looked at him.

'Things to eat,' said Dick at once. 'Plenty because we'll be hungry.'

'Something to drink,' said George. 'There's no water on the island – though I believe there was a well or something, years ago, that went right down below the level of the sea, and was fresh water. Anyway, I've never found it.'

'Food,' wrote down Julian, 'and drink.' He looked at the others.

'Spades,' he said solemnly, and scribbled the word down.

Anne stared in surprise.

'What for?' she asked.

'Well, we'll want to dig about when we're hunting for a way down to the dungeons,' said Julian.

'Ropes,' said Dick. 'We may want those too.'

'And torches,' said George. 'It'll be dark in the dungeons.'

'Oooh!' said Anne, feeling a pleasant shiver go down her back at the thought. She had no idea what dungeons were like, but they sounded thrilling.

'Rugs,' said Dick. 'We'll be cold at night if we sleep in that little old room.'

Julian wrote them down. 'Mugs to drink from,' he said. 'And we'll take a few tools too – we may perhaps need them. You never know.'

At the end of half an hour they had quite a nice long list, and everyone felt pleased and excited. George was beginning to recover from her rage and disappointment. If she had been alone, and had brooded over everything, she would have been in an even worse sulk and temper – but somehow the others were so calm and sensible and cheerful. It was impossible to sulk for long if she was with them.

'I think I'd have been much nicer if I hadn't been on my

own so much,' thought George to herself, as she looked at Julian's bent head. 'Talking about things to other people does help a lot. They don't seem so dreadful then; they seem more bearable and ordinary. I like my three cousins awfully. I like them because they talk and laugh and are always cheerful and kind. I wish I were like them. I'm sulky and bad-tempered and fierce, and no wonder Father doesn't like me and scolds me so often. Mother's a dear, but I understand now why she says I am difficult. I'm different from my cousins – they're easy to understand, and everyone likes them. I'm glad they came. They are making me more like I ought to be.'

This was a long thought to think, and George looked very serious while she was thinking it. Julian looked up and caught her blue eyes fixed on him. He smiled.

'Penny for your thoughts!' he said.

'They're not worth a penny,' said George, going red. 'I was just thinking how nice you all are – and how I wished I could be like you.'

'You're an awfully nice person,' said Julian, surprisingly. 'You can't help being an only child. They're always a bit odd, you know, unless they're mighty careful. You're a most interesting person, I think.'

George flushed red again, and felt pleased. 'Let's go and take Timothy for a walk,' she said. 'He'll be wondering what's happened to us today.'

They all went off together, and Timothy greeted them at the top of his voice. They told him all about their plans for the next day, and he wagged his tail and looked up at them out of his soft brown eyes as if he understood every single word they said!

'He must feel pleased to think he's going to be with us for two or three days,' said Anne.

It was very exciting the next morning, setting off in the boat with all their things packed neatly at one end. Julian checked them all by reading out aloud from his list. It didn't seem as if they had forgotten anything.

'Got the map?' said Dick, suddenly.

Julian nodded.

'I put on clean jeans this morning,' he said, 'but you may be sure I remembered to pop the map into my pocket. Here it is!'

He took it out – and the wind at once blew it right out of his hands! It fell into the sea and bobbed there in the wind. All four children gave a cry of utter dismay. Their precious map!

'Quick! Row after it!' cried George, and swung the boat round. But someone was quicker than she was! Tim had seen the paper fly from Julian's hand, and had heard and understood the cries of dismay. With an enormous splash he leapt into the water and swam valiantly after the map.

He could swim well for a dog, for he was strong and powerful. He soon had the map in his mouth and was swimming back to the boat. The children thought he was simply marvellous!

George hauled him into the boat and took the map from his mouth. There was hardly the mark of his teeth on it he had carried it so carefully! It was wet, and the children looked anxiously at it to see if the tracing had been spoilt. But Julian had traced it very strongly, and it was quite all right. He placed it on a seat to dry, and told Dick to hold it there in the sun.

'That was a narrow squeak!' he said, and the others agreed.

George took the oars again, and they set off once more for the island, getting a perfect shower-bath from Timothy when he stood up and shook his wet coat. He was given a big biscuit as a reward, and crunched it up with great enjoyment.

George made her way through the reefs of rocks with a sure hand. It was marvellous to the others how she could slide the boat in between the dangerous rocks and never get a scratch. They thought she was really wonderful. She brought them safely to the little inlet, and they jumped out on to the sand. They pulled the boat high up, in case the tide came far up the tiny cove, and then began to unload their goods.

'We'll carry all the things to that little stone room,' said Julian. 'They will be safe there and won't get wet if it rains. I hope nobody comes to the island while we are here, George.'

'I shouldn't think they would,' said George. 'Father said it would be about a week before the deeds were signed, making over the island to that man. It won't be his till then. We've got a week, anyhow.'

'Well, we don't need to keep a watch in case anyone else arrives then,' said Julian, who had half thought that it would be a good idea to make someone stay on guard at the inlet, to give a warning to the others in case anyone else arrived. 'Come on! You take the spades, Dick. I'll take the food and drink with George. And Anne can take the little things.'

The food and drink were in a big box, for the children did not mean to starve while they were on the island! They had brought loaves of bread, butter, biscuits, jam, tins of fruit, ripe plums, bottles of ginger-beer, a kettle to make tea, and anything else they could think of! George and Julian staggered up the cliff with the heavy box. They had to put it down once or twice to give themselves a rest!

They put everything into the little room. Then they went back to get the collection of blankets and rugs from the boat. They arranged them in the corners of the little room, and thought that it would be most exciting to spend the night there.

'The two girls can sleep together on this pile of rugs,' said Julian. 'And we two boys will have this pile.'

George looked as if she didn't want to be put with Anne, and classed as a girl. But Anne didn't wish to sleep alone in her corner, and she looked so beseechingly at George that the bigger girl smiled at her and made no objection. Anne thought that George was getting nicer and nicer!

'Well, now we'll get down to business,' said Julian, and he pulled out his map. 'We must study this really carefully, and find out exactly under which spot the entrances to the dungeons are. Now – come around and let's do our best to find out! It's up to us to use our brains – and beat that man who's bought the island!'

They all bent over the traced map. It was quite dry now,

and the children looked at it earnestly. It was plain that in the old days the castle had been a very fine place.

'Now look,' said Julian, putting his finger on the plan of the dungeons. 'These seem to run all along under the castle – and here – and – here – are the marks that seem to be meant to represent steps or stairs.'

'Yes,' said George. 'I should think they are. Well, if so, there appear to be two ways of getting down into the dungeons. One lot of steps seems to begin somewhere near this little room – and the other seems to start under the tower there. And what do you suppose this thing is here, Julian?'

She put her finger on a round hole that was shown not only in the plan of the dungeons, but also in the plan of the ground floor of the castle.

'I can imagine what that is,' said Julian, puzzled. 'Oh yes, I know what it might be! You said there was an old well somewhere, do you remember? Well, that may be it, I should think. It would have to be very deep to get fresh water right under the sea – so it probably goes down through the dungeons too. Isn't this thrilling?'

Everyone thought it was. They felt happy and excited. There was something to discover – something they could and must discover within the next day or two.

They looked at one another. 'Well,' said Dick,' what are we going to start on? Shall we try to find the entrance to the dungeons – the one that seems to start round about this little room? For all we know there may be a big stone

112

we can lift that opens above the dungeon steps!'

This was a thrilling thought, and the children jumped up at once. Julian folded up the precious map and put it into his pocket. He looked round. The stone floor of the little room was overgrown with creeping weeds. They must be cleared away before it was possible to see if there were any stones that looked as if they might be moved.

'We'd better set to work,' said Julian, and he picked up a spade. 'Let's clear away these weeds with our spades – scrape them off, look, like this – and then examine every single stone!'

They all picked up spades and soon the little stone room was full of a scraping sound as the four of them chiselled away at the close-growing weeds with their spades. It wasn't very difficult to get the stones clear of them, and the children worked with a will.

Tim got most excited about everything. He hadn't any idea at all what they were doing, but he joined in valiantly. He scraped away at the floor with his four paws, sending earth and plants flying high into the air!

'Hi, Tim!' said Julian, shaking a clod of earth out of his hair. 'You're being a bit too vigorous. My word, you'll send the stones flying into the air too, in a minute. George, isn't Tim marvellous the way he joins in everything?'

How they all worked! How they all longed to find the entrance to the underground dungeons! What a thrill that would be.

CHAPTER TWELVE

Exciting discoveries

SOON THE stones of the little room were clear of earth, sand and weeds. The children saw that they were all the same size – big and square, fitted well together. They went over them carefully with their torches, trying to find one that might move or lift.

'We should probably find one with an iron ring handle sunk into it,' said Julian. But they didn't. All the stones looked exactly the same. It was most disappointing.

Julian tried inserting his spade into the cracks between the various stones, to see if by any chance he could move one. But they couldn't be moved. It seemed as if they were all set in the solid ground. After about three hours' hard work the children sat down to eat a meal.

They were very hungry indeed, and felt glad to think there were so many things to eat. As they ate they discussed the problem they were trying to solve

'It looks as if the entrance to the dungeons was not under this little room after all,' said Julian. 'It's disappointing – but somehow I don't think now that the steps down to the dungeon started from here. Let's measure the map and see if we can make out exactly where the steps do start. It may be, of course, that the measurements aren't correct and won't be any help to us at all. But we can try.'

So they measured as best they could, to try and find out in exactly what place the dungeon steps seemed to begin. It was impossible to tell, for the plans of the three floors seemed to be done to different scales. Julian stared at the map, puzzled. It seemed rather hopeless. Surely they wouldn't have to hunt all over the ground floor of the castle! It would take ages.

'Look,' said George, suddenly, putting her finger on the hole that they all thought must be meant to represent the well. 'The entrance to the dungeons seems to be not very far off the well. If only we could find the well, we could hunt around a bit for the beginning of the dungeon steps. The well is shown in both maps. It seems to be somewhere about the middle of the castle.'

'That's a good idea of yours,' said Julian, pleased. 'Let's go out into the middle of the castle – we can more or less guess where the old well ought to be, because it definitely seems to be about the middle of the old yard out there.'

Out they all went into the sunshine. They felt very important and serious. It was marvellous to be looking for lost ingots of gold. They all felt perfectly certain that they really were somewhere beneath their feet. It didn't occur to any of the children that the treasure might not be there.

They stood in the ruined courtyard that had once been the centre of the castle. They paced out the middle of the yard and then stood there, looking around in vain for anything that might perhaps have been the opening of an old well. It was all so overgrown. Sand had blown in from the shore, and weeds and bushes of all kinds grew there. The stones that had once formed the floor of the big courtyard were now cracked and were no longer lying flat. Most of them were covered with sand or weeds.

'Look! There's a rabbit!' cried Dick, as a big sandy rabbit lolloped slowly across the yard. It disappeared into a hole on the other side. Then another rabbit appeared, sat up and looked at the children, and then vanished too. The children were thrilled. They had never seen such tame rabbits before.

A third rabbit appeared. It was a small one with absurdly big ears, and the tiniest white bob of a tail. It didn't even look at the children. It bounded about in a playful way, and then, to the children's enormous delight, it sat up on its hind legs, and began to wash its big ears, pulling down first one and then the other.

But this was too much for Timothy. He had watched the other two bound across the yard and then disappear without so much as barking at them. But to see this youngster actually sitting there washing its ears under his very nose was really too much for any dog. He gave an excited yelp and rushed full-tilt at the surprised rabbit.

For a moment the little thing didn't move. It had never been frightened or chased before, and it stared with big eyes at the rushing dog. Then it turned itself about and tore off at top speed, its white bobtail going up and down

117

as it bounded away. It disappeared under a gorse bush near the children. Timothy went after it, vanishing under the big bush too.

Then a shower of sand and earth was thrown up as Tim tried to go down the hole after the rabbit and scraped and scrabbled with his strong front paws as fast as he could. He yelped and whined in excitement, not seeming to hear George's voice calling to him. He meant to get that rabbit! He went almost mad as he scraped at the hole, making it bigger and bigger.

'Tim! Do you hear me! Come out of there!' shouted George. 'You're not to chase the rabbits here. You know you mustn't. You're very naughty. Come out!'

But Tim didn't come out. He just went on and on scraping away madly. George went to fetch him. Just as she got up to the gorse bush the scraping suddenly stopped. There came a scared yelp – and no more noise was heard. George peered under the prickly bush in astonishment.

Tim had disappeared! He just simply wasn't there any more. There was the big rabbit-hole, made enormous by Tim – but there was no Tim.

'I say, Julian – Tim's gone,' said George in a scared voice. 'He surely can't have gone down the rabbit's hole, can he? I mean – he's such a big dog!'

The children crowded round the big gorse bush. There came the sound of a muffled whine from somewhere below it. Julian looked astonished.

EXCITING DISCOVERIES

'He *is* down the hole!' he said. 'How funny! I never heard of a dog really going down a rabbit-hole before. How ever are we going to get him out?'

'We'll have to dig up the gorse bush, to begin with,' said George, in a determined voice. She would have dug up the whole of Kirrin Castle to get Tim back, that was certain! 'I can't have poor old Tim whining for help down there and not do what we can to help him.'

The bush was far too big and prickly to creep underneath. Julian was glad they had brought tools of all kinds. He went to fetch an axe. They had brought a small one with them and it would do to chop away the prickly branches and trunk of the gorse bush. The children slashed at it and soon the poor bush began to look a sorry sight.

It took a long time to destroy it, for it was prickly, sturdy and stout. Every child's hands were scratched by the time the bush had been reduced to a mere stump. Then they could see the hole quite well. Julian shone his torch down it.

He gave a shout of surprise. 'I know what's happened! The old well is here! The rabbits had a hole at the side of it – and Tim scraped away to make it bigger and uncovered a bit of the well-hole – and he's fallen down the well!'

'Oh no, oh no,' cried George, in panic. 'Oh Tim, Tim, are you all right?'

A distant whine came to their ears. Evidently Tim was there somewhere. The children looked at one another.

119

'Well, there's only one thing to do,' said Julian. 'We must get out spades now and dig out the hole of the well. Then maybe we can let a rope down or something and get Tim.'

They set to work with their spades. It was not really difficult to uncover the hole, which had been blocked only by the spreading roots of the big gorse bush, some fallen masonry, earth, sand and small stones. Apparently a big slab had fallen from part of the tower across the well-hole, and partly closed it. The weather and the growing gorse bush had done the rest.

It took all the children together to move the slab. Underneath was a very rotten wooden cover, which had plainly been used in the old days to protect the well. It had rotted so much that when Tim's weight had been pressed on it, it had given just there and made a hole for Tim to fall through.

Julian removed the old wooden cover and then the children could see down the well-hole. It was very deep and very dark. They could not possibly see the bottom. Julian took a stone and dropped it down. They all listened for the splash. But there was no splash. Either there was no longer any water there, or the well was too deep even to hear the splash!

'I think it's too deep for us to hear anything,' said Julian. 'Now – where's Tim?'

He shone his torch down – and there was Tim! Many years before a big slab had fallen down the well itself and had stuck a little way down, across the well-hole – and on this old cracked slab sat Tim, his big eyes staring up in fright. He simply could not imagine what had happened to him.

There was an old iron ladder fastened to the side of the well. George was on it before anyone else could get there! Down she went, not caring if the ladder held or not, and reached Tim. Somehow she got him on to her shoulder and, holding him there with one hand, she climbed slowly up again. The other three hauled her out and Tim jumped round her, barking and licking for all he was worth!

'Well, Tim!' said Dick. 'You shouldn't chase rabbits – but you've certainly done us a good turn, because you've found the well for us! Now we've only got to look around a little to find the dungeon entrance!'

They set to work again to hunt for the dungeon entrance. They dug about with their spades under all the bushes. They pulled up crooked stones and dug their spades into the earth below, hoping that they might suddenly find them going through into space! It was really very thrilling.

And then Anne found the entrance! It was quite by accident. She was tired and sat down to rest. She lay on her front and scrabbled about in the sand. Suddenly her fingers touched something hard and cold in the sand. She uncovered it – and lo and behold, it was an iron ring! She gave a shout and the others looked up.

'There's a stone with an iron ring in it here!' yelled Anne, excitedly. They all rushed over to her. Julian dug about with his spade and uncovered the whole stone. Sure enough, it did have a ring in it – and rings are only set into stones that need to be moved! Surely this stone must be the one that covered the dungeon entrance!

All the children took turns at pulling on the iron ring,

but the stone did not move. Then Julian tied two or three turns of rope through it and the four children put out their full strength and pulled for all they were worth.

The stone moved. The children distinctly felt it stir. 'All together again!' cried Julian. And all together they pulled. The stone stirred again and then suddenly gave way. It moved upwards – and the children fell over on top of one another like a row of dominoes suddenly pushed down! Tim darted to the hole and barked madly down it as if all the rabbits of the world lived there!

Julian and George shot to their feet and rushed to the opening that the moved stone had disclosed. They stood there, looking downwards, their faces shining with delight. They *had* found the entrance to the dungeons! A steep flight of steps, cut out of the rock itself, led downwards into deep darkness.

'Come on!' cried Julian, snapping on his torch. 'We've found what we wanted! Now for the dungeons!'

The steps down were slippery. Tim darted down first, lost his footing and rolled down five or six steps, yelping with fright. Julian went after him, then George, then Dick and then Anne. They were all tremendously thrilled. Indeed, they quite expected to see piles of gold and all kinds of treasure everywhere around them!

It was dark down the steep flight of steps, and smelt very musty. Anne choked a little.

'I hope the air down here is all right,' said Julian. 'Sometimes it isn't good in these underground places. If anyone feels a bit funny they'd better say so and we'll go up into the open air again.'

But however funny they might feel, nobody would have said so. It was all far too exciting to worry about feeling strange.

The steps went down a long way. Then they came to an end. Julian stepped down from the last rock-stair and flashed his torch around. It was a weird sight that met his eyes.

The dungeons of Kirrin Castle were made out of the rock itself. Whether there were natural caves here, or whether they had been hollowed out by man the children could not tell. But certainly they were very mysterious, dark and full of echoing sounds. When Julian gave a sigh of excitement it fled into the rocky hollows and swelled out and echoed around as if it were a live thing. It gave all the children a very peculiar feeling.

'Isn't it strange?' said George, in a low voice. At once the echoes took up her words, and multiplied them and made them louder – and all the dungeon caves gave back the girl's words over and over again. 'Isn't it strange, ISN'T IT STRANGE, ISN'T IT STRANGE.'

Anne slipped her hand into Dick's. She felt scared. She didn't like the echoes at all. She knew they *were* only echoes – but they did sound exactly like the voices of scores of people hidden in the caves!

'Where do you suppose the ingots are?' said Dick. And at once the caves threw him back his words. INGOTS! INGOTS ARE! INGOTS ARE! ARE! ARE!

Julian laughed – and his laugh was split up into dozens of different laughs that came out of the dungeons and spun round the listening children. It really was the strangest thing.

'Come on,' said Julian. 'Maybe the echoes won't be so bad a little farther in.'

'FARTHER IN, said the echoes at once. 'FARTHER IN!'

They moved away from the end of the rocky steps and explored the nearby dungeons. They were really only rocky cellars stretching under the castle. Maybe wretched prisoners had been kept there many, many years before, but mostly they had been used for storing things.

'I wonder which dungeon was used for storing the ingots,' said Julian. He stopped and took the map out of his pocket. He flashed his torch on to it. But although it showed him quite plainly the dungeon where INGOTS were marked, he had no idea at all of the right direction.

'I say – look – there's a door here, shutting off the next dungeon!' suddenly cried Dick. 'I bet this is the dungeon we're looking for! I bet there are ingots in here!'

CHAPTER THIRTEEN

Down in the dungeons

FOUR TORCHES were flashed on to the wooden door. It was big and stout, studded with great iron nails. Julian gave a whoop of delight and rushed to it. He felt certain that behind it was the dungeon used for storing things.

But the door was fast shut. No amount of pushing or pulling would open it. It had a great keyhole – but no key there! The four children stared in exasperation at the door. Bother it! Just as they really thought they were near the ingots, this door wouldn't open!

'We'll fetch the axe,' said Julian, suddenly. 'We may be able to chop round the keyhole and smash the lock.'

'That's a good idea!' said George, delighted. 'Come on back!'

They left the big door, and tried to get back the way they had come. But the dungeons were so big and so rambling that they lost their way. They stumbled over old broken barrels, rotting wood, empty bottles and many other things as they tried to find their way back to the big flight of rock-steps.

'This is sickening!' said Julian, at last. 'I simply haven't any idea at all where the entrance is. We keep on going into one dungeon after another, and one passage after

127

another, and they all seem to be exactly the same – dark and smelly and mysterious.'

'Suppose we have to stay here all the rest of our lives!' said Anne, gloomily.

'Idiot!' said Dick, taking her hand. 'We shall soon find the way out. Hallo! – what's this?'

They all stopped. They had come to what looked like a chimney shaft of brick, stretching down from the roof of the dungeon to the floor. Julian flashed his torch on to it. He was puzzled.

'I know what it is!' said George, suddenly. 'It's the well, of course! You remember it was shown in the plan of the dungeons, as well as in the plan of the ground floor. Well, that's the shaft of the well going down and down. I wonder if there's any opening in it just here – so that water could be taken into the dungeons as well as up to the ground floor.'

They went to see. On the other side of the well-shaft was a small opening big enough for one child at a time to put his head and shoulders through and look down. They shone their torches down and up. The well was so deep that it was still impossible to see the bottom of it. Julian dropped a stone down again, but there was no sound of either a thud or a splash. He looked upwards, and could see the faint gleam of daylight that slid round the broken slab of stone lying a little way down the shaft – the slab on which Tim had sat, waiting to be rescued.

'Yes,' he said, 'this is the well all right. Isn't it weird?

128

DOWN IN THE DUNGEONS

Well – now we've found the well we know that the entrance to the dungeons isn't very far off!'

That cheered them all up tremendously. They held hands and hunted around in the dark, their torches making bright beams of light here and there.

Anne gave a screech of excitement. 'Here's the entrance! It must be, because I can see faint daylight coming down!'

The children rounded a corner and sure enough, there was the steep, rocky flight of steps leading upwards. Julian took a quick look round so that he might know the way to go when they came down again. He didn't feel at all certain that he would find the wooden door!

They all went up into the sunshine. It was delicious to feel the warmth on their heads and shoulders after the cold air down in the dungeons. Julian looked at his watch and gave a loud exclamation.

'It's half-past six! *Half-past six!* No wonder I feel hungry. We haven't had any tea. We've been working, and wandering about those dungeons for hours.'

'Well, let's have a kind of tea-supper before we do anything else,' said Dick. 'I don't feel as if I've had anything to eat for about twelve months.'

'Well, considering you ate about twice as much as anyone else at dinner-time,' began Julian, indignantly. Then he grinned. 'I feel the same as you,' he said. 'Come on! – let's get a really good meal. George, what about boiling a kettle and making some cocoa, or something? I feel cold after all that time underground.'

It was fun boiling the kettle on a fire of dry sticks. It was lovely to lie about in the warmth of the evening sun and munch bread and cheese and enjoy cake and biscuits. They all enjoyed themselves thoroughly. Tim had a good meal too. He hadn't very much liked being underground, and had followed the others very closely indeed, his tail well down. He had been very frightened, too, of the curious echoes here and there.

Once he had barked, and it had seemed to Tim as if the whole of the dungeons were full of other dogs, all barking far more loudly than he could. He hadn't even dared to whine after that! But now he was happy again, eating the tit-bits that the children gave him, and licking George whenever he was near her.

It was past eight o'clock by the time that the children had finished their meal and tidied up. Julian looked at the others. The sun was sinking, and the day was no longer so warm.

'Well,' he said, 'I don't know what you feel. But I don't somehow want to go down into those dungeons again today, not even for the sake of smashing in that door with the axe and opening it! I'm tired – and I don't like the thought of losing my way in those dungeons at night.'

The others heartily agreed with him, especially Anne, who had secretly been dreading going down again with the night coming on. The little girl was almost asleep; she was so tired out with hard work and excitement.

'Come on, Anne!' said George, pulling her to her feet.

DOWN IN THE DUNGEONS

'Bed for you. We'll cuddle up together in the rugs on the floor of that little room – and in the morning when we wake we'll be simply thrilled to think of opening that big wooden door.'

All four children, with Tim close behind, went off to the little stone room. They curled up on their piles of rugs, and Tim crept in with George and Anne. He lay down on them, and felt so heavy that Anne had to push him off her legs.

He sat himself down on her again, and she groaned, half-asleep. Tim wagged his tail and thumped it hard against her ankles. Then George pulled him on to her own legs and lay there, feeling him breathe. She was very happy. She was spending the night on her island. They had almost found the ingots, she was sure. She had Tim with her, actually sleeping on her rugs. Perhaps everything would come right after all – somehow.

She fell asleep. The children felt perfectly safe with Tim on guard. They slept peacefully until the morning, when Tim saw a rabbit through the broken archway leading to the little room, and sped away to chase it. He awoke George as he got up from the rugs, and she sat up and rubbed her eyes.

'Wake up!' she cried to the others. 'Wake up, all of you! It's morning! And we're on the island!'

They all awoke. It was really thrilling to sit up and remember everything. Julian thought of the big wooden door at once. He would soon smash it in with his axe, he felt sure. And then what would they find?

131

They had breakfast, and ate just as much as ever. Then Julian picked up the axe they had brought and took everyone to the flight of steps. Tim went too, wagging his tail, but not really feeling very pleased at the thought of going down into the strange places where other dogs seemed to bark, and yet were not to be found. Poor Tim would never understand echoes!

They all went down underground again. And then, of course, they couldn't find the way to the wooden door! It was most tiresome.

'We shall lose our way all over again,' said George, desperately. 'These dungeons are about the most rambling spread-out maze of underground caves I've ever known! We shall lose the entrance again too!'

Julian had a bright idea. He had a piece of white chalk in his pocket, and he took it out. He went back to the steps, and marked the wall there. Then he began to put chalk-marks along the passages as they walked in the musty darkness. They came to the well, and Julian was pleased.

'Now,' he said, 'whenever we come to the well we shall at least be able to find the way back to the steps, because we can follow my chalk-marks. Now the thing is – which is the way next? We'll try and find it and I'll put chalk-marks along the walls here and there – but if we go the wrong way and have to come back, we'll rub out the marks, and start again from the well another way.'

This was really a very good idea. They did go the wrong way, and had to come back, rubbing out Julian's marks.

DOWN IN THE DUNGEONS

They reached the well, and set off in the opposite direction. And this time they did find the wooden door!

There it was, stout and sturdy, its old iron nails rusty and red. The children stared at it in delight. Julian lifted his axe.

Crash! He drove it into the wood and round about the keyhole. But the wood was still strong, and the axe only went in an inch or two. Julian drove it in once more. The axe hit one of the big nails and slipped a little to one side. A big splinter of wood flew out – and struck poor Dick on the cheek!

He gave a yell of pain. Julian jumped in alarm, and turned to look at him. Dick's cheek was pouring with blood!

'Something flew out of the door and hit me,' said poor Dick. 'It's a splinter, or something.'

'Golly!' said Julian, and he shone his torch on to Dick. 'Can you bear it a moment if I pull the splinter out? It's a big one, and it's still sticking into your poor cheek.'

But Dick pulled it out himself. He made a face with the pain, and then turned very white.

'You'd better get up into the open air for a bit,' said Julian. 'And we'll have to bathe your cheek and stop it bleeding somehow. Anne's got a clean hanky. We'll bathe it and dab it with that. We brought some water with us, luckily.'

'I'll go with Dick,' said Anne. 'You stay here with George. There's no need for us all to go.'

133

But Julian thought he would like to see Dick safely up
into the open air first, and then he could leave him with
Anne while he went back to George and went on with the
smashing down of the door. He handed the axe to George.

'You can do a bit of chopping while I'm gone,' he said.
'It will take some time to smash that big door in. You get
on with it – and I'll be down in a few minutes again. We

can easily find the way to the entrance because we've only got to follow my chalk-marks.'

'Right!' said George, and she took the axe. 'Poor old Dick – you do look a sight.'

Leaving George behind with Tim, valiantly attacking the big door, Julian took Dick and Anne up to the open air. Anne dipped her hanky into the kettle of water and dabbed Dick's cheek gently. It was bleeding very much, as cheeks do, but the wound was not really very bad. Dick's colour soon came back, and he wanted to go down into the dungeons again.

'No, you'd better lie down on your back for a little,' said Julian. 'I know that's good for nose-bleeding – and maybe it's good for cheek-bleeding too. What about Anne and you going out on the rocks over there, where you can see the wreck, and staying there for half an hour or so? Come on – I'll take you both there, and leave you for a bit. You'd better not get up till your cheek's stopped bleeding, old boy.'

Julian took the two out of the castle yard and out on to the rocks on the side of the island that faced the open sea. The dark hulk of the old wreck was still there on the rocks. Dick lay down on his back and stared up into the sky, hoping that his cheek would soon stop bleeding. He didn't want to miss any of the fun!

Anne took his hand. She was very upset at the little accident, and although she didn't want to miss the fun either, she meant to stay with Dick till he felt better. Julian sat down beside them for a minute or two. Then he went back to the rocky steps and disappeared down them. He followed his chalk-marks, and soon came to where George was attacking the door.

She had smashed it well round the lock – but it simply would *not* give way. Julian took the axe from her and drove it hard into the wood.

After a blow or two something seemed to happen to the lock. It became loose, and hung a little sideways. Julian put down his axe.

'I think somehow that we can open the door now,' he said, in an excited voice. 'Get out of the way, Tim, old fellow. Now then, push, George!'

They both pushed – and the lock gave way with a grating noise. The big door opened creakingly, and the two children went inside, flashing their torches in excitement.

The room was not much more than a cave, hollowed out of the rock – but in it was something quite different from the old barrels and boxes the children had found before. At the back, in untidy piles, were curious, brick-shaped things of dull yellow-brown metal. Julian picked one up.

'George!' he cried. 'The ingots! These are real gold!' Oh,

DOWN IN THE DUNGEONS

I know they don't look like it – but they are, all the same.
George, oh George, there's a small fortune here in this
cellar – and it's yours! We've found it at last!'

CHAPTER FOURTEEN

Prisoners!

GEORGE COULDN'T say a word. She just stood there, staring at the pile of ingots, holding one in her hands. She could hardly believe that these strange brick-shaped things were really gold. Her heart thumped fast. What a wonderful, marvellous find!

Suddenly Tim began to bark loudly. He stood with his back to the children, his nose towards the door – and how he barked!

'Shut up, Tim!' said Julian. 'What can you hear? Is it the others coming back?'

He went to the door and yelled down the passage outside. 'Dick! Anne! Is it you? Come quickly, because we've found the ingots! We've found them! Hurry! Hurry!'

Tim stopped barking and began to growl. George looked puzzled. 'Whatever *can* be the matter with Tim?' she said. 'He surely can't be growling at Dick and Anne.'

Then both children got a most tremendous shock – for a man's voice came booming down the dark passage, making strange echoes all around.

'Who is here? Who is down here?'

George clutched Julian in fright. Tim went on growling, all the hairs on his neck standing up straight. 'Do be quiet,

Tim!' whispered George, snapping off her torch. But Tim simply would *not* be quiet. He went on growling as if he were a small thunderstorm.

The children saw the beam of a powerful torchlight coming round the corner of the dungeon passage. Then the light picked them out, and the holder of the torch came to a surprised stop.

'Well, well, well!' said a voice. 'Look who's here! Two children in the dungeons of my castle.'

'What do you mean, *your* castle!' cried George.

'Well, my dear little girl, it *is* my castle, because I'm in the process of buying it,' said the voice. Then another voice spoke, more gruffly.

'What are you doing down here? What did you mean when you shouted out "Dick" and "Anne", and said you had found the ingots? What ingots?'

'Don't answer,' whispered Julian to George. But the echoes took his words and made them very loud in the passage. 'DON'T ANSWER! DON'T ANSWER!'

'Oh, so you won't answer,' said the second man, and he stepped towards the children. Tim bared his teeth, but the man didn't seem at all frightened of him. The man went to the door and flashed his torch inside the dungeon. He gave a long whistle of surprise.

'Jake! Look here!' he said. 'You were right. The gold's here all right. And how easy to take away! All in ingots – my word, this is the most amazing thing we've ever struck.'

'This gold is mine,' said George, in a fury. 'This island and the castle belong to my mother – and so does anything found here. This gold was brought here and stored by my great-great-great-grandfather before his ship got wrecked. It's not yours, and never will be. As soon as I get back home I shall tell my father and mother what we've found – and then you may be sure you won't be able to buy the castle or the island! You were very clever, finding out from the map in the old box about the gold – but just not clever enough for us. We found it first!'

The men listened in silence to George's clear and angry voice. One of them laughed. 'You're only a child,' he said. 'You surely don't think you can keep us from getting our way? We're going to buy this island – and everything in it – and we shall take the gold when the deeds are signed. And if by any chance we couldn't buy the island, we'd take the gold just the same. It would be easy enough to bring a ship here and transfer the ingots from here by boat to the ship. Don't worry – we shall get what we want all right.'

'You will not!' said George, and she stepped out of the door. 'I'm going straight home now – and I'll tell my father all you've said.'

'My dear little girl, you are not going home,' said the first man, putting his hands on George and forcing her back into the dungeon. 'And, by the way, unless you want me to shoot this unpleasant dog of yours, call him off, will you?'

George saw, to her dismay, that the man had a shining revolver in his hand. In fright she caught hold of Tim's collar and pulled him to her. 'Be quiet, Tim,' she said. 'It's all right.'

But Tim knew quite well that it wasn't all right. Something was very wrong. He went on growling fiercely.

'Now listen to me,' said the man, after he had had a hurried talk with his companion. 'If you are going to be sensible, nothing unpleasant will happen to you. But if you

141

want to be obstinate, you'll be very sorry. What we are going to do is this – we're going off in our motor-boat, leaving you nicely locked up here – and we're going to get a ship and come back for the gold. We don't think it's worthwhile buying the island now we know where the ingots are.'

'And you are going to write a note to your companions

PRISONERS!

above, telling them you've found the gold and they are to come down and look for it,' said the other man. 'Then we shall lock up all of you in this dungeon, with the ingots to play with, leaving you food and drink till we come back. Now then – here is a pencil. Write a note to Dick and Anne, whoever they are, and send your dog up with it. Come on.'

'I won't,' said George, her face furious. 'I won't. You can't make me do a thing like that. I won't get poor Dick and Anne down here to be made prisoners. And I won't let you have my gold, just when I've discovered it.'

'We shall shoot your dog if you don't do as you're told,' said the first man, suddenly. George's heart sank down and she felt cold and terrified.

'No, no,' she said in a low, desperate voice.

'Well, write the note then,' said the man, offering her a pencil and paper. 'Go on. I'll tell you what to say.'

'I can't!' sobbed George. 'I don't want to get Dick and Anne down here to be made prisoners.'

'All right – I'll shoot the dog then,' said the man, in a cold voice and he levelled his revolver at poor Tim. George threw her arms round her dog and gave a scream.

'No, no! I'll write the note. Don't shoot Tim, don't shoot him!'

The girl took the paper and pencil in a shaking hand and looked at the man. 'Write this,' he ordered. ' "Dear Dick and Anne. We've found the gold. Come on down at once and see it." Then sign your name, whatever it is.'

George wrote what the man had said. Then she signed her name. But instead of writing 'George' she put 'Georgina'. She knew that the others would feel certain she would never sign herself that – and she hoped it would warn them that something odd was up. The man took the note and fastened it to Tim's collar. The dog growled all the time, but George kept telling him not to bite.

'Now tell him to go and find your friends,' said the man.

'Find Dick and Anne,' commanded George. 'Go on, Tim. Find Dick and Anne. Give them the note.'

Tim did not want to leave George, but there was something very urgent in her voice. He took one last look at his mistress, gave her hand a lick and sped off down the passage. He knew the way now. Up the rocky steps he bounded and into the open air. He stopped in the old yard, sniffing. Where were Dick and Anne?

He smelt their footsteps and ran off, his nose to the ground. He soon found the two children out on the rocks. Dick was feeling better now and was sitting up. His cheek had almost stopped bleeding.

'Hallo,' he said in surprise, when he saw Tim. 'Here's Timothy! Why, Tim, old chap, why have you come to see us? Did you get tired of being underground in the dark?'

'Look, Dick – he's got something twisted into his collar,' said Anne, her sharp eyes seeing the paper there. 'It's a note. I expect it's from the others, telling us to go down. Isn't Tim clever to bring it?'

PRISONERS!

Dick took the paper from Tim's collar. He undid it and read it.

'"Dear Dick and Anne,"' he read out aloud. '"We've found the gold. Come on down at once and see it. Georgina."'

'Oooh!' said Anne, her eyes shining. 'They've found it. Oh, Dick – are you well enough to come now? Let's hurry.'

But Dick did not get up from the rocks. He sat and stared at the note, puzzled.

'What's the matter?' said Anne, impatiently.

'Well, don't you think it's funny that George should suddenly sign herself "Georgina"?' said Dick, slowly. 'You know how she hates being a girl, and having a girl's name. You know how she will never answer if anyone calls her Georgina. And yet in this note she signs herself by the name she hates. It does seem a bit funny to me. Almost as if it's a kind of warning that there's something wrong.'

'Oh, don't be so silly, Dick,' said Anne. 'What could be wrong? Do come on.'

'Anne, I'd like to pop over to that inlet of ours to make sure there's no one else come to the island,' said Dick. 'You stay here.'

But Anne didn't want to stay there alone. She ran round the coast with Dick, telling him all the time that she thought he was very silly.

But when they came to the little harbour, they saw that there was another boat there, as well as their own. It was a motor-boat! Someone else *was* on the island!

FIVE ON A TREASURE ISLAND

'Look,' said Dick, in a whisper. 'There *is* someone else
here. And I bet it's the men who want to buy the island. I
bet they've read that old map and know there's gold here.
And they've found George and Julian and want to get us
all together down in the dungeons so that they can keep us
safe till they've stolen the gold. That's why they made
George send us that note – but she signed it with a name
she never uses – to warn us! Now – we must think hard.
What are we going to do?'

CHAPTER FIFTEEN

Dick to the rescue!

DICK CAUGHT hold of Anne's hand and pulled her quickly away from the cove. He was afraid that whoever had come to the island might be somewhere about and see them. The boy took Anne to the little stone room where their things were and they sat down in a corner.

'Whoever has come has discovered Julian and George smashing in that door, I should think,' said Dick, in a whisper. 'I simply can't think what to do. We mustn't go down into the dungeons or we'll most certainly be caught. Hallo – where's Tim off to?'

The dog had kept with them for a while but now he ran off to the entrance of the dungeons. He disappeared down the steps. He meant to get back to George, for he knew she was in danger. Dick and Anne stared after him. They had felt comforted while he was there, and now they were sorry he had gone.

They really didn't know what to do. Then Anne had an idea. 'I know!' she said. 'We'll row back to the land in our boat and get help.'

'I'd thought of that,' said Dick, gloomily. 'But you know perfectly well we'd never know the way in and out of those awful rocks. We'd wreck the boat. I'm sure we're not strong enough either to row all the way back. Oh, dear – I do wish we could think what to do.'

They didn't need to puzzle their brains long. The men came up out of the dungeons and began to hunt for the two children! They had seen Tim when he came back and had found the note gone. So they knew the two children had taken it – and they couldn't imagine why they had not obeyed what George had said in the note, and come down to the dungeons!

Dick heard their voices. He clutched hold of Anne to make her keep quiet. He saw through the broken archway that the men were going in the opposite direction.

'Anne! I know where we can hide!' said the boy, excitedly. 'Down the old well! We can climb down the ladder a little way and hide there. I'm sure no one would ever look there!'

Anne didn't at all want to climb down the well even a little way. But Dick pulled her to her feet and hurried her off to the middle of the old courtyard. The men were hunting around the other side of the castle. There was just time to climb in. Dick slipped aside the old wooden cover of the well and helped Anne down the ladder. She was very scared. Then the boy climbed down himself and slipped the wooden cover back again over his head, as best he could.

The old stone slab that Tim had sat on when he fell down the well was still there. Dick climbed down to it and tested it. It was immovable.

'It's safe for you to sit on, Anne, if you don't want to keep clinging to the ladder,' he whispered. So Anne sat shivering on the stone slab across the well-shaft, waiting to see if they were discovered or not. They kept hearing the voices of the men, now near at hand and now far-off. Then the men began to shout for them.

'Dick! Anne! The others want you! Where are you? We've exciting news for you.'

'Well, why don't they let Julian and George come up and tell us then?' whispered Dick. 'There's something wrong, I know there is. I do wish we could get to Julian and George and find out what has happened.'

The two men came into the courtyard. They were angry. 'Where have those kids got to?' said Jake. 'Their boat is still in the cove, so they haven't got away. They must be hiding somewhere. We can't wait all day for them.'

'Well, let's take some food and drink down to the two we've locked up,' said the other man. 'There's plenty in that little stone room. I suppose it's a store the children brought over. We'll leave half in the room so that the other two kids can have it. And we'll take their boat with us so that they can't escape.'

'Right,' said Jake. 'The thing to do is to get the gold away as quickly as possible, and make sure the children are prisoners here until we've made a safe getaway. We won't bother any more about trying to buy the island. After all, it was only the idea of getting the ingots that put us up to the idea of getting Kirrin Castle and the island.'

'Well – come on,' said his companion. 'We will take the food down now, and not bother about the other kids. You stay here and see if you can spot them while I go down.'

Dick and Anne hardly dared to breathe when they heard all this. How they hoped that the men wouldn't think of looking down the well! They heard one man walk

DICK TO THE RESCUE!

to the little stone room. It was plain that he was getting food and drink to take down to the two prisoners in the dungeons below. The other man stayed in the courtyard, whistling softly.

After what seemed a very long time to the hidden children, the first man came back. Then the two talked together, and at last went off to the cove. Dick heard the motor-boat being started up.

'It's safe to get out now, Anne,' he said. 'Isn't it cold down here? I'll be glad to get out into the sunshine.'

They climbed out and stood warming themselves in the hot summer sunshine. They could see the motor-boat streaking towards the mainland.

'Well, they're gone for the moment,' said Dick. 'And they've not taken our boat, as they said. If only we could rescue Julian and George, we could get help, because George could row us back.'

'Why *can't* we rescue them?' cried Anne, her eyes shining. 'We can go down the steps and unbolt the door, can't we?'

'No – we can't,' said Dick. 'Look!'

Anne looked to where he pointed. She saw that the two men had piled big, heavy slabs of broken stone over the dungeon entrance. It had taken all their strength to put the big stones there. Neither Dick nor Anne could hope to move them.

'It's quite impossible to get down the steps,' said Dick. 'They've made sure we shan't do that! And you know we

151

haven't any idea where the second entrance is. We only know it was somewhere near the tower.'

'Let's see if we can find it,' said Anne eagerly. They set off to the tower on the right of the castle – but it was quite clear that whatever entrance there might have been once, it was gone now! The castle had fallen in very much just there, and there were piles of old broken stones every-where, quite impossible to move. The children soon gave up the search.

'Blow!' said Dick. 'How I do hate to think of poor old Julian and George prisoners down below, and we can't even help them! Oh, Anne – can't *you* think of something to do?'

Anne sat down on a stone and thought hard. She was very worried. Then she brightened up a little and turned to Dick.

'Dick! I suppose – I suppose we couldn't *possibly* climb down the well, could we?' she asked. 'You know it goes past the dungeons – and there's an opening on the dungeon floor from the well-shaft, because don't you remember we were able to put in our heads and shoulders and look right up the well to the top? Could we get past that slab, do you think – the one that I sat on just now, that has fallen across the well?'

Dick thought it all over. He went to the well and peered down it. 'You know, I believe you are right, Anne,' he said at last. 'We might be able to squeeze past that slab. There's just about room. I don't know how far the iron ladder goes down though.'

DICK TO THE RESCUE!

'Oh, Dick – do let's try,' said Anne. 'It's our only chance of rescuing the others!'

'Well,' said Dick, 'I'll try it – but not you, Anne. I'm not going to have you falling down that well. The ladder might be broken half-way down – anything might happen. You must stay up here and I'll see what I can do.'

'You will be careful, won't you?' said Anne, anxiously. 'Take a rope with you, Dick, so that if you need one you won't have to climb all the way up again.'

'Good idea,' said Dick. He went to the little stone room and got one of the ropes they had put there. He wound it round and round his waist. Then he went back to Anne.

'Well, here goes!' he said, in a cheerful voice. 'Don't worry about me. I'll be all right.'

Anne was rather white. She was terribly afraid that Dick might fall right down to the bottom of the well. She watched him climb down the iron ladder to the slab of stone. He tried his best to squeeze by it, but it was very difficult. At last he managed it and after that Anne could see him no more. But she could hear him, for he kept calling up to her.

'Ladder's still going strong, Anne! I'm all right. Can you hear me?'

'Yes,' shouted Anne down the well, hearing her voice echo in a funny hollow manner. 'Take care, Dick. I do hope the ladder goes all the way down.'

'I think it does!' yelled back Dick. Then he gave a loud

exclamation. 'Blow! It's broken just here. Broken right off. Or else it ends. I'll have to use my rope.'

There was a silence as Dick unwound the rope from his waist. He tied it firmly to the last but one rung of the ladder, which seemed quite strong.

'I'm going down the rope now!' he shouted to Anne. 'Don't worry. I'm all right. Here I go!'

Anne couldn't hear what Dick said after that, for the well-shaft made his words go crooked and she couldn't make out what they were. But she was glad to hear him shouting even though she didn't know what he said. She yelled down to him too, hoping he could hear her.

Dick slid down the rope, holding on to it with hands, knees and feet, glad that he was so good at gym at school. He wondered if he was anywhere near the dungeons. He seemed to have gone down a long way. He managed to get out his torch. He put it between his teeth after he had switched it on, so that he might have both hands free for the rope. The light from the torch showed him the walls of the well around him. He couldn't make out if he was above or below the dungeons. He didn't want to go right down to the bottom of the well!

He decided that he must have just passed the opening into the dungeon-caves. He climbed back up the rope a little way and to his delight saw that he was right. The opening on to the dungeons was just by his head. He climbed up till he was level with it and then swung himself to the side of the well where the small opening was. He

DICK TO THE RESCUE!

managed to get hold of the bricked edge, and then tried to scramble through the opening into the dungeon.

It was difficult, but luckily Dick was not very big. He managed it at last and stood up straight with a sigh of relief. He was in the dungeons! He could now follow the chalk-marks to the room or cave where the ingots were – and where he felt sure that George and Julian were imprisoned!

He shone his torch on the wall. Yes – there were the chalk-marks. Good! He put his head into the well-opening and yelled at the top of his voice.

'Anne! I'm in the dungeons! Watch out that the men don't come back!'

Then he began to follow the white chalk-marks, his heart beating fast. After a while he came to the door of the store-room. As he had expected, it was fastened so that George and Julian couldn't get out. Big bolts had been driven home at the top and bottom, and the children inside could not possibly get out. They had tried their hardest to batter down the door, but it was no good at all.

They were sitting inside the store-cave, feeling angry and exhausted. The man had brought them food and drink, but they had not touched it. Tim was with them, lying down with his head on his paws, half-angry with George because she hadn't let him fly at the men as he had so badly wanted to. But George felt certain that Tim would be shot if he tried biting or snapping.

'Anyway, the other two had sense enough not to come down and be made prisoners too,' said George. 'They must have known there was something funny about that note when they saw I had signed myself Georgina instead of George. I wonder what they are doing. They must be hiding.'

Tim suddenly gave a growl. He leapt to his feet and went to the closed door, his head on one side. He had heard something, that was certain.

DICK TO THE RESCUE!

'I hope it's not those men back again already,' said George. Then she looked at Tim in surprise, flashing her torch on to him. He was wagging his tail!

A great bang at the door made them all jump out of their skins! Then came Dick's cheerful voice. 'Hi, Julian! Hi, George! Are you here?'

'Wufffff!' barked Tim joyfully, and scratched at the door.

'Dick! Open the door!' yelled Julian in delight. 'Quick, open the door!'

CHAPTER SIXTEEN

A plan – and a narrow escape

DICK UNBOLTED the door at the top and bottom and flung it open. He rushed in and thumped George and Julian happily on the back.

'Hallo!' he said. 'How does it feel to be rescued?'

'Fine!' cried Julian, and Tim barked madly round them. George grinned at Dick.

'Good work!' she said. 'What happened?'

Dick told them in a few words all that had happened. When he related how he had climbed down the old well, George and Julian could hardly believe their ears. Julian slipped his arm through his younger brother's.

'You're a brick!' he said. 'A real brick! Now quick – what are we going to do?'

'Well, if they've left us our boat I'm going to take us all back to the mainland as quickly as possible,' said George. 'I'm not playing about with men who brandish revolvers all the time. Come on! Up the well we go and find the boat.'

They ran to the well-shaft and squeezed through the small opening one by one. Up the rope they went and soon found the iron ladder. Julian made them go up one by one in case the ladder wouldn't bear the weight of all three at once.

A PLAN – AND A NARROW ESCAPE

It really wasn't very long before they were all up in the open air once more, giving Anne hugs, and hearing her exclaim gladly, with tears in her eyes, how pleased she was to see them all again.

'Now come on!' said George after a minute. 'Off to the boat. Quick! Those men may be back at any time.'

They rushed to the cove. There was their boat, lying

where they had pulled it, out of reach of the waves. But what a shock for them!

'They've taken the oars!' said George, in dismay. 'The beasts! They know we can't row the boat away without oars. They were afraid you and Anne might row off, Dick – so instead of bothering to tow the boat behind them, they just grabbed the oars. Now we're stuck. We can't possibly get away.'

It was a great disappointment. The children were almost ready to cry. After Dick's marvellous rescue of George and Julian, it had seemed as if everything was going right – and now suddenly things were going wrong again.

'We must think this out,' said Julian, sitting down where he could see at once if any boat came in sight. 'The men have gone off – probably to get a ship from somewhere in which they can put the ingots and sail away. They won't be back for some time, I should think, because you can't charter a ship all in a hurry – unless, of course, they've got one of their own.'

'And in the meantime we can't get off the island to get help, because they've got our oars,' said George. 'We can't even signal to any passing fishing-boat because they won't be out just now. The tide's wrong. It seems as if all we've got to do is wait here patiently till the men come back and take my gold! And we can't stop them.'

'You know – I've got a sort of plan coming into my head,' said Julian, slowly. 'Wait a bit – don't interrupt me. I'm thinking.'

A PLAN – AND A NARROW ESCAPE

The others waited in silence while Julian sat and frowned, thinking of his plan. Then he looked at the others with a smile.

'I believe it will work,' he said. 'Listen! We'll wait here in patience till the men come back. What will they do? They'll drag away those stones at the top of the dungeon entrance, and go down the steps. They'll go to the store-room, where they left us – thinking we are still there – and they will go into the room. Well, what about one of us being hidden down there ready to bolt *them* into the room? Then we can either go off in their motor-boat or our own boat if they bring back our oars – and get help.'

Anne thought it was a marvellous idea. But Dick and George did not look so certain. 'We'd have to go down and bolt that door again to make it seem as if we are still prisoners there,' said George. 'And suppose the one who hides down there doesn't manage to bolt the men in? It might be very difficult to do that quickly enough. They will simply catch whoever we plan to leave down there – and come up to look for the rest of us.'

'That's true,' said Julian, thoughtfully. 'Well – we'll suppose that Dick, or whoever goes down, doesn't manage to bolt them in and make them prisoners – and the men come up here again. All right – while they are down below we'll pile big stones over the entrance, just as they did. Then they won't be able to get out.'

'What about Dick down below?' said Anne, at once.

'I could climb up the well again!' said Dick, eagerly. 'I'll be the one to go down and hide. I'll do my best to bolt the men into the room. And if I have to escape I'll climb up the well-shaft again. The men don't know about that. So even if they are not prisoners in the dungeon room, they'll be prisoners underground!'

The children talked over this plan, and decided that it was the best they could think of. Then George said she thought it would be a good thing to have a meal. They were all half-starved and, now that the worry and excitement of being rescued was over, they were feeling very hungry!

They fetched some food from the little room and ate it in the cove, keeping a sharp look-out for the return of the men. After about two hours they saw a big fishing-smack appear in the distance, and heard the chug-chug-chug of a motor-boat too.

'There they are!' said Julian, in excitement, and he jumped to his feet. 'That's the ship they mean to load with the ingots, and sail away in safety – and there's the motor-boat bringing the men back! Quick, Dick, down the well you, go and hide until you hear them in the dungeons!'

Dick shot off. Julian turned to the others. 'We'll have to hide,' he said. 'Now that the tide is out we'll hide over there, behind those uncovered rocks. I don't somehow think the men will do any hunting for Dick and Anne – but they might. Come on! Quick!'

They all hid themselves behind the rocks, and heard the

motor-boat come chugging into the tiny harbour. They could hear men calling to one another. There sounded to be more than two men this time. Then the men left the inlet and went up the low cliff towards the ruined castle.

Julian crept behind the rocks and peeped to see what the men were doing. He felt certain they were pulling away the slabs of stone that had been piled on top of the entrance to prevent Dick and Anne going down to rescue the others.

'George! Come on!' called Julian in a low tone. 'I think the men have gone down the steps into the dungeons now. We must go and try to put those big stones back. Quick!'

George, Julian and Anne ran softly and swiftly to the old courtyard of the castle. They saw that the stones had been pulled away from the entrance to the dungeons. The men had disappeared. They had plainly gone down the steps.

A PLAN – AND A NARROW ESCAPE

The three children did their best to tug at the heavy stones to drag them back. But their strength was not the same as that of the men, and they could not manage to get any very big stones across. They put three smaller ones, and Julian hoped the men would find them too difficult to move from below. 'If only Dick has managed to bolt them into that room!' he said to the others. 'Come on, back to the well now. Dick will have to come up there, because he won't be able to get out of the entrance.'

They all went to the well. Dick had removed the old wooden cover, and it was lying on the ground. The children leaned over the hole of the well and waited anxiously. What was Dick doing? They could hear nothing from the well and they longed to know what was happening.

There was plenty happening down below! The two men, and another, had gone down into the dungeons, expecting, of course, to find Julian, George and the dog still locked up in the store-room with the ingots. They passed the well-shaft not guessing that an excited small boy was hidden there, ready to slip out of the opening as soon as they had passed.

Dick heard them pass. He slipped out of the well-opening and followed behind quietly, his feet making no sound. He could see the beams made by the men's powerful torches, and with his heart thumping loudly he crept along the smelly old passages, between great caves, until the men turned into the wide passage where the store-cave lay.

'Here it is,' Dick heard one of the men say, as he flashed his torch on to the great door. 'The gold's in there – so are the kids!'

The men unbolted the door at top and bottom. Dick was glad that he had slipped along to bolt the door, for if he hadn't done that before the men had come they would have known that Julian and George had escaped, and would have been on their guard.

The man opened the door and stepped inside. The second man followed him. Dick crept as close as he dared, waiting for the third man to go in too. Then he meant to slam the door and bolt it!

The first man swung his torch round and gave a loud exclamation. 'The children are gone! How strange! Where are they?'

Two of the men were now in the cave – and the third stepped in at that moment. Dick darted forward and slammed the door. It made a crash that went echoing round and round the caves and passages. Dick fumbled with the bolts, his hand trembling. They were stiff and rusty. The boy found it hard to shoot them home in their sockets. And meanwhile the men were not idle!

As soon as they heard the door slam they spun round. The third man put his shoulder to the door at once and heaved hard. Dick had just got one of the bolts almost into its socket. Then all three men forced their strength against the door, and the bolt gave way!

A PLAN – AND A NARROW ESCAPE

Dick stared in horror. The door was opening! He turned and fled down the dark passage. The men flashed their torches on and saw him. They went after the boy at top speed.

Dick fled to the well-shaft. Fortunately the opening was on the opposite side, and he could clamber into it without being seen in the light of the torches. The boy only just had

time to squeeze through into the shaft before the three men
came running by. Not one of them guessed that the
runaway was squeezed into the well-shaft they passed!
Indeed, the men did not even know that there was a well
there.

Trembling from head to foot, Dick began to climb the
rope he had left dangling from the rungs of the iron ladder.
He undid it when he reached the ladder itself, for he
thought that perhaps the men might discover the old well
and try to climb up later. They would not be able to do
that if there was no rope dangling down.

The boy climbed up the ladder quickly, and squeezed
round the stone slab near the top. The other children were
there, waiting for him.

They knew at once by the look on Dick's face that he
had failed in what he had tried to do. They pulled him out
quickly. 'It was no good,' said Dick, panting with his
climb. 'I couldn't do it. They burst the door open just as I
was bolting it, and chased me. I got into the shaft just in
time.'

'They're trying to get out of the entrance now!' cried
Anne, suddenly. 'Quick! What shall we do? They'll catch
us all!'

'To the boat!' shouted Julian, and he took Anne's hand
to help her along. 'Come along! It's our only chance. The
men will perhaps be able to move those stones.'

The four children fled down the courtyard. George
darted into the little stone room as they passed it, and

caught up an axe. Dick wondered why she bothered to do that. Tim dashed along with them, barking madly.

They came to the cove. Their own boat lay there without oars. The motor-boat was there too. George jumped into it and gave a yell of delight.

169

'Here are our oars!' she shouted. 'Take them, Julian, I've got a job to do here! Get the boat down to the water, quick!'

Julian and Dick took the oars. Then they dragged their boat down to the water, wondering what George was doing. All kinds of crashing sounds came from the motor-boat!

'George! George! Buck up. The men are out!' suddenly yelled Julian. He had seen the three men running to the cliff that led down to the cove. George leapt out of the motor-boat and joined the others. They pushed their boat out on to the water, and George took the oars at once, pulling for all she was worth.

The three men ran to their motor-boat. Then they paused in the greatest dismay – for George had completely ruined it! She had chopped wildly with her axe at all the machinery she could see – and now the boat could not possibly be started! It was damaged beyond any repair the men could make with the few tools they had.

'You wicked girl!' yelled Jake, shaking his fist at George. 'Wait till I get you!'

'I'll wait!' shouted back George, her blue eyes shining dangerously. 'And you can wait too! You won't be able to leave my island now!'

CHAPTER SEVENTEEN

The end of the great adventure

THE THREE men stood at the edge of the sea, watching George pull away strongly from the shore. They could do nothing. Their boat was quite useless.

'The fishing-smack they've got waiting out there is too big to use in that little inlet,' said George, as she pulled hard at her oars. 'They'll have to stay there till someone goes in with a boat. I guess they're as wild as can be!'

Their boat had to pass fairly near to the big fishing-boat. A man hailed them as they came by.

'Ahoy there! Have you come from Kirrin Island?'

'Don't answer,' said George. 'Don't say a word.' So no one said anything at all, but looked the other way as if they hadn't heard.

'AHOY THERE!' yelled the man, angrily. 'Are you deaf? Have you come from the island?'

Still the children said nothing at all, but looked away while George rowed steadily. The man on the ship gave it up, and looked in a worried manner towards the island. He felt sure the children had come from there – and he knew enough of his comrades' adventures to wonder if everything was right on the island.

'He may put out a boat from the smack and go and see
what's happening, said George. 'Well, he can't do much
except take the men off – with a few ingots! I hardly think
they'll dare to take any of the gold though, now that we've
escaped to tell our tale!'

Julian looked behind at the ship. He saw after a time
that the little boat it carried was being lowered into the sea.

'You're right,' he said to George. 'They're afraid something is up. They're going to rescue those three men. What a pity!'

Their little boat reached land. The children leapt out into the shallow water and dragged it up to the beach. Tim pulled at the rope too, wagging his tail. He loved to join in anything that the children were doing.

'Shall you take Tim to Alf?' asked Dick.

George shook her head. 'No,' she said, 'we haven't any time to waste. We must go and tell everything that has happened. I'll tie Tim up to the fence in the front garden.'

They made their way to Kirrin Cottage at top speed. Aunt Fanny was gardening there. She stared in surprise to see the hurrying children.

'Why,' she said, 'I thought you were not coming back till tomorrow or the next day! Has anything happened? What's the matter with Dick's cheek?'

'Nothing much,' said Dick.

The others chimed in.

'Aunt Fanny, where's Uncle Quentin? We have something important to tell him!'

'Mother, we've had such an adventure!'

'Aunt Fanny, we've an awful lot to tell you! We really have!'

Aunt Fanny looked at the untidy children in amazement. 'Whatever has happened?' she said. Then she turned towards the house and called 'Quentin! Quentin! The children have something to tell us!'

Uncle Quentin came out, looking rather cross, for he was in the middle of his work. 'What's the matter?' he asked.

'Uncle, it's about Kirrin Island,' said Julian, eagerly. 'Those men haven't bought it yet, have they?'

'Well, it's practically sold,' said his uncle. 'I've signed my part, and they are to sign their part tomorrow. Why? What's that to do with you?'

'Uncle, those men won't sign tomorrow,' said Julian. 'Do you know why they wanted to buy the island and the castle? Not because they really wanted to build an hotel or anything like that – but because they knew the lost gold was hidden there!'

'What nonsense are you talking?' said his uncle.

'It isn't nonsense, Father!' cried George indignantly. 'It's all true. The map of the old castle was in that box you sold – and in the map was shown where the ingots were hidden by my great-great-great-grandfather!'

George's father looked amazed and annoyed. He simply didn't believe a word! But his wife saw by the solemn and serious faces of the four children that something important really had happened. And then Anne suddenly burst into loud sobs! The excitement had been too much for her and she couldn't bear to think that her uncle wouldn't believe that everything was true.

'Aunt Fanny, Aunt Fanny, it's all true!' she sobbed. 'Uncle Quentin is horrid not to believe us. Oh, Aunt Fanny, the man had a revolver – and oh, he made Julian

174

and George prisoners in the dungeons – and Dick had to climb down the well to rescue them. And George has smashed up their motor-boat to stop them escaping!'

Her aunt and uncle couldn't make head or tail of this, but Uncle Quentin suddenly seemed to think that the matter was serious and worth looking into. 'Smashed up a motor-boat!' he said. 'Whatever for? Come indoors. I shall have to hear the story from beginning to end. It seems quite unbelievable to me.'

They all trooped indoors. Anne sat on her aunt's knee and listened to George and Julian telling the whole story. They told it well and left nothing out. Aunt Fanny grew quite pale as she listened, especially when she heard about Dick climbing down the well.

'You might have been killed,' she said. 'Oh, Dick! What a brave thing to do!'

Uncle Quentin listened in the utmost amazement. He had never had much liking or admiration for any children – he always thought they were noisy, tiresome, and silly. But now, as he listened to Julian's tale, he changed his mind about these four children at once!

'You've been very clever,' he said. 'And very brave too. I'm proud of you. Yes, I'm very proud of you all. No wonder you didn't want me to sell the island, George, when you knew about the ingots! But why didn't you tell me?'

The four children stared at him and didn't answer. They couldn't very well say, 'Well, firstly, you wouldn't have believed us. Secondly, you are bad-tempered and unjust and we are frightened of you. Thirdly, we didn't trust you enough to do the right thing.'

'Why don't you answer?' said their uncle. His wife answered for them, in a gentle voice.

'Quentin, you scare the children, you know, and I don't expect they liked to go to you. But now that they have, you will be able to take matters into your own hands. The children cannot do any more. You must ring up the police and see what they have to say about all this.'

'Right,' said Uncle Quentin, and he got up at once. He patted Julian on the back. 'You have all done well,' he said. Then he ruffled George's short curly hair. 'And I'm proud of you, too, George,' he said.

'Oh, Father!' said George, going red with surprise and pleasure. She smiled at him and he smiled back. The children noticed that he had a very nice face when he smiled. He and George were really very alike to look at. Both looked ugly when they sulked and frowned – and both were good to look at when they laughed or smiled!

George's father went off to telephone the police and his lawyer too. The children sat and ate biscuits and plums, telling their aunt a great many little details they had forgotten when telling the story before.

As they sat there, there came a loud and angry bark from the front garden. George looked up. 'That's Tim,' she said, with an anxious look at her mother. 'I hadn't time to take him to Alf, who keeps him for me. Mother, Tim was such a comfort to us on the island, you know. I'm sorry he's barking now – but I expect he's hungry.'

'Well, fetch him in,' said her mother, unexpectedly. 'He's quite a hero, too – we must give him a good dinner.'

George smiled in delight. She sped out of the door and went to Tim. She set him free and he came bounding indoors, wagging his long tail. He licked George's mother and cocked his ears at her.

'Good dog,' she said, and actually patted him. 'I'll get you some dinner!'

Tim trotted out to the kitchen with her. Julian grinned at George. 'Well, look at that,' he said. 'Your mother's a brick, isn't she?'

'Yes – but I don't know what Father will say when he sees Tim in the house again,' said George, doubtfully.

Her father came back at that minute, his face grave. 'The police take a serious view of all this,' he said, 'and so does my lawyer. They all agree in thinking that you children have been remarkably clever and brave. And George – my lawyer says that the ingots definitely belong to us. Are there really a lot?'

'Father! There are hundreds!' cried George. 'Simply hundreds – all in a big pile in the dungeon. Oh, Father – shall we be rich now?'

'Yes,' said her father. 'We shall. Rich enough to give you and your mother all the things I've longed to give you for so many years and couldn't. I've worked hard enough for you – but it's not the kind of work that brings in a lot of money, and so I've become irritable and bad-tempered. But now you shall have everything you want!'

'I don't really want anything I haven't already got,' said George. 'But Father, there is one thing I'd like more than anything else in the world – and it won't cost you a penny!'

THE END OF THE GREAT ADVENTURE

'You shall have it, my dear!' said her father, slipping his arm around George, much to her surprise. 'Just say what it is – and even if it costs a hundred pounds you shall have it!'

Just then there came the pattering of big feet down the passage to the room they were in. A big hairy head pushed itself through the door and looked inquiringly at everyone there. It was Tim, of course!

Uncle Quentin stared at him in surprise. 'Why, isn't that Tim?' he asked. 'Hallo, Tim!'

'Father! Tim is the thing I want most in all the world,' said George, squeezing her father's arm. 'You can't think what a friend he was to us on the island – and he wanted to fly at those men and fight them. Oh, Father, I don't want any other present – I only want to keep Tim and have him here for my very own. We could afford to give him a proper kennel to sleep in now, and I'd see that he didn't disturb you, I really would.'

'Well, of course you can have him!' said her father – and Tim came right into the room at once, wagging his tail, looking for all the world as if he had understood every word that had been said. He actually licked Uncle Quentin's hand! Anne thought that was very brave of him.

But Uncle Quentin was quite different now. It seemed as if a great weight had been lifted off his shoulders. They were rich now – George could go to a good school – and his wife could have the things he had so much wanted her to have – and he would be able to go on with the work he loved without feeling that he was not earning enough to keep his family in comfort. He beamed round at everyone, looking as jolly a person as anyone could wish!

George was overjoyed about Tim. She flung her arms round her father's neck and hugged him, a thing she had not done for a long time. He looked astonished but very pleased. 'Well, well,' he said, 'this is all very pleasant. Hallo – is this the police already?'

It was. They came up to the door and had a few words with Uncle Quentin. Then one stayed behind to take down the children's story in his notebook and the others went off to get a boat to the island.

The men had gone from there! The boat from the fishing-smack had fetched them away! – and now both ship and boat had disappeared! The motor-boat was still there, quite unusable. The inspector looked at it with a grin.

'Fierce young lady, isn't she, that Miss Georgina?' he said. 'Done this job pretty well – no one could get away in this boat. We'll have to get it towed into harbour.'

The police brought back with them some of the ingots of gold to show Uncle Quentin. They had sealed up the door of the dungeon so that no one else could get in until the children's uncle was ready to go and fetch the gold. Everything was being done thoroughly and properly – though far too slowly for the children! They had hoped that the men would have been caught and taken to prison – and that the police would bring back the whole of the gold at once!

THE END OF THE GREAT ADVENTURE

They were all very tired that night and didn't make any fuss at all when their aunt said that they must go to bed early. They undressed and then the boys went to eat their supper in the girls' bedroom. Tim was there, ready to lick up any fallen crumbs.

'Well, I must say we've had a wonderful adventure,' said Julian, sleepily. 'In a way I'm sorry it's ended – though at times I didn't enjoy it very much – especially when you and I, George, were prisoners in that dungeon. That was awful.'

George was looking very happy as she nibbled her gingerbread biscuits. She grinned at Julian.

'And to think I hated the idea of you all coming here to stay!' she said. 'I was going to be such a beast to you! I was going to make you wish you were all home again! And now the only thing that makes me sad is the idea of you going away – which you will do, of course, when the holidays end. And then, after having three friends with me, enjoying adventures like this, I'll be all on my own again. I've never been lonely before – but I know I shall be now.'

'No, you won't,' said Anne, suddenly. 'You can do something that will stop you being lonely ever again.'

'What?' said George in surprise.

'You can ask to go to the same boarding-school as I go to,' said Anne. 'It's such a lovely one – and we are allowed to keep our pets, so Tim could come too!'

'Gracious! Could he really?' said George, her eyes shining. 'Well, I'll go then. I always said I wouldn't –

but I will because I see now how much better and happier it is to be with others than all by myself. And if I can have Tim, well that's simply wonderful!'

'You'd better go back to your own bedroom now, boys,' said Aunt Fanny, appearing at the doorway. 'Look at Dick, almost dropping with sleep! Well, you should all have pleasant dreams tonight, for you've had an adventure to be proud of. George – is that Tim under your bed?'

'Well, yes it is, Mother,' said George, pretending to be surprised. 'Dear me! Tim, what are you doing here?'

Tim crawled out and went over to George's mother. He lay flat on his tummy and looked up at her most appealingly out of his soft brown eyes.

'Do you want to sleep in the girls' room tonight?' said George's mother, with a laugh. 'All right – just for once!'

'Mother!' yelled George, overjoyed. 'Oh, thank you, thank you, thank you! How did you guess that I just didn't want to be parted from Tim tonight? Oh, Mother! Tim, you can sleep on the rug over there.'

Four happy children snuggled down into their beds. Their wonderful adventure had come to a happy end. They had plenty of holidays still in front of them – and now that Uncle Quentin was no longer poor, he would give them the little presents he wanted to. George was going to school with Anne – and she had Tim for her own again! The island and castle still belonged to George – everything was marvellous!

182

THE END OF THE GREAT ADVENTURE

'I'm so glad Kirrin Island wasn't sold, George,' said Anne, sleepily. 'I'm so glad it still belongs to you.'

'It belongs to three other people too,' said George. 'It belongs to me – and to you and Julian and Dick. I've discovered that it's fun to share things. So tomorrow I am going to draw up a deed, or whatever it's called, and put in it that I give you and the others a quarter-share each. Kirrin Island and Castle shall belong to us all!'

'Oh, George – how lovely!' said Anne, delighted. 'Won't the boys be pleased? I do feel so ha . . .'

But before she could finish, the little girl was asleep. So was George. In the other room the two boys slept, too, dreaming of ingots and dungeons and all kinds of exciting things.

Only one person was awake – and that was Tim. He had one ear up and was listening to the children's breathing. As soon as he knew they were asleep he got up quietly from his rug. He crept softly over to George's bed. He put his front paws up and sniffed at the sleeping girl.

Then, with a bound he was on the bed, and snuggled himself down into the crook of her legs. He gave a sigh, and shut his eyes. The four children might be happy – but Tim was happiest of all.

'Oh, Tim,' murmured George, half waking up as she felt him against her. 'Oh, Tim, you mustn't – but you do feel so nice. Tim – we'll have other adventures together, the five of us – won't we?'

They will – but that's another story!

h|HODDER *A complete list of the* FAMOUS FIVE
ADVENTURES *by Enid Blyton*

THE
FAMOUS FIVE'S
SURVIVAL GUIDE

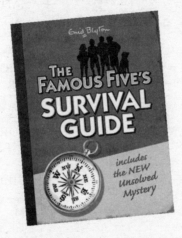

*Packed with useful information on surviving outdoors and solving
mysteries, here is the one mystery that the Famous Five never managed
to solve. See if you can follow the trail to discover the location of the
priceless Royal Dragon of Siam.*

The perfect book for all fans of mystery, adventure and the Famous Five!

ISBN 9780340970836

FIVE GO ADVENTURING AGAIN

FIVE GO ADVENTURING AGAIN

ENID BLYTON

Illustrated by
Eileen A. Soper

Hodder
Children's
Books

a division of Hachette Children's Books

Text copyright © Chorion Rights Ltd
Illustrations copyright © Hodder & Stoughton
Enid Blyton's signature is a Registered Trade Mark of Chorion Rights Ltd

First published in Great Britain in 1942
by Hodder and Stoughton

This edition 1997

The right of Enid Blyton to be identified as the Author of
the Work has been asserted by her in accordance with the
Copyright, Designs and Patents Act 1988.

For further information on Enid Blyton, please contact
www.blyton.com

33

A Catalogue record for this book is available from the
British Library.

ISBN-13: 978 0 340 68107 7

Printed in Great Britain by
Clays Ltd, St Ives plc

The paper and board used in this paperback by Hodder Children's
Books are natural recyclable products made from wood grown
in sustainable forests. The manufacturing processes conform
to the environmental regulations of the country of origin.

Hodder Children's Books
a division of Hachette Children's Books
338 Euston Road, London NW1 3BH
An Hachette UK Company
www.hachette.co.uk

CONTENTS

CHAPTER ONE

Christmas holidays

IT WAS the last week of the Christmas term, and all the girls at Gaylands School were looking forward to the Christmas Holidays. Anne sat down at the breakfast-table and picked up a letter addressed to her.

'Hallo, look at this!' she said to her cousin Georgina, who was sitting beside her. 'A letter from Daddy – and I only had one from him and Mummy yesterday.'

'I hope it's not bad news,' said George. She would not allow anyone to call her Georgina, and now even the mistresses called her George. She really was very like a boy with her short curly hair, and her boyish ways. She looked anxiously at Anne as her cousin read the letter.

'Oh, George – we can't go home for the holidays!' said Anne, with tears in her eyes. 'Mummy's got scarlet fever – and Daddy is in quarantine for it – so they can't have us back. Isn't it just too bad?'

'Oh, I *am* sorry,' said George. She was just as disappointed for herself as for Anne, because Anne's mother had invited George, and her dog Timothy, to stay for the Christmas holidays with them. She had been promised many things she had never seen before – the pantomime,

1

and the circus – and a big party with a fine Christmas tree! Now it wouldn't happen.

'Whatever will the two boys say?' said Anne, thinking of Julian and Dick, her two brothers. 'They won't be able to go home either.'

'Well – what are you going to do for the holidays then?' asked George. 'Won't you come and stay at Kirrin Cottage with *me*? I'm sure my mother would love to have you again. We had such fun when you came to stay for the summer hols.'

'Wait a minute – let me finish the letter and see what Daddy says,' said Anne, picking up the note again. 'Poor Mummy – I do hope she isn't feeling very ill.'

She read a few more lines and then gave such a delighted exclamation that George and the other girls waited impatiently for her to explain.

'George! We *are* to come to you again – but oh blow, blow, blow! – we've got to have a tutor for the hols, partly to look after us so that your mother doesn't have too much bother with us, and partly because both Julian and Dick have been ill with 'flu twice this term and have got behind in their work.'

'A tutor! How sickening! That means I'll have to do lessons too, I'll bet!' said George, in dismay. 'When my mother and father see my report I guess they'll find out how little I know. After all, this is the first time I've ever been to a proper school, and there are heaps of things I don't know.'

CHRISTMAS HOLIDAYS

'What horrid hols they'll be, if we have a tutor running after us all the time,' said Anne, gloomily. 'I expect I'll have quite a good report, because I've done well in the exams – but it won't be any fun for me not doing lessons with you three in the hols. Though, of course, I could go off with Timothy, I suppose. *He* won't be doing lessons!'

'Yes, he will,' said George, at once. She could not bear the idea of her beloved dog Timothy going off each morning with Anne, while she, George, sat and worked hard with Julian and Dick.

'Timothy can't do lessons, don't be silly, George,' said Anne.

'He can sit under my feet while *I'm* doing them,' said George. 'It will be a great help to feel him there. For goodness' sake eat up your sausages, Anne. We've all nearly finished. The bell will be going in a minute and you won't have had any breakfast.'

'I am glad Mummy isn't very bad,' said Anne, hurriedly finishing her letter. 'Daddy says he's written to Dick and Julian – and to your father to ask him to engage a tutor for us. Oh dash – this is an awful disappointment, isn't it? I don't mean I shan't enjoy going to Kirrin Cottage again – and seeing Kirrin Island – but after all there are no pantomimes or circuses or parties to look forward to at Kirrin.'

The end of the term came quickly. Anne and George packed up their trunks, and put on the labels, enjoying the noise and excitement of the last two days. The big school coaches rolled up to the door, and the girls clambered in.

'Off to Kirrin again!' said Anne. 'Come on, Timothy darling, you can sit between me and George.'

Gaylands School allowed the children to keep their own pets, and Timothy, George's big mongrel dog, had been a great success. Except for the time when he had run after the dustman, and dragged the dustbin away from him, all the way up the school grounds and into George's class-room, he had really behaved extremely well.

'I'm sure *you'll* have a good report, Tim,' said George, giving the dog a hug. 'We're going home again. Will you like that?'

'Woof,' said Tim, in his deep voice. He stood up, wagging his tail, and there was a squeal from the seat behind.

'George! Make Tim sit down. He's wagging my hat off!'

It was not very long before the two girls and Timothy were in London, being put into the train for Kirrin.

'I do wish the boys broke up today too,' sighed Anne. 'Then we could all have gone down to Kirrin together. That would have been fun.'

Julian and Dick broke up the next day and were to join the girls then at Kirrin Cottage. Anne was very much looking forward to seeing them again. A term was a long time to be away from one another. She had been glad to have her cousin George with her. The three of them had stayed with George in the summer, and had had some exciting adventures together on the little island off the

4

coast. An old castle stood on the island and in the dungeons the children had made all kinds of wonderful discoveries.

'It will be lovely to go across to Kirrin Island again, George,' said Anne, as the train sped off towards the west.

'We shan't be able to,' said George. 'The sea is terribly rough round the island in the winter. It would be too dangerous to try and row there.'

'Oh, what a pity,' said Anne disappointed. 'I was looking forward to some more adventures there.'

'There won't be any adventures at Kirrin in the winter,' said George. 'It's cold down there – and when it snows we sometimes get frozen up completely – can't even walk to the village because the sea-wind blows the snow-drifts so high.'

'Oooh – that sounds rather exciting!' said Anne.

'Well, it isn't really,' said George. 'It's awfully boring – nothing to do but sit at home all day, or turn out with a spade and dig the snow away.'

It was a long time before the train reached the little station that served Kirrin. But at last it was there pulling in slowly and stopping at the tiny platform. The two girls jumped out eagerly, and looked to see if anyone had met them. Yes – there was George's mother!

'Hallo, George darling – hallo, Anne!' said George's mother, and gave both children a hug. 'Anne, I'm so sorry about your mother, but she's getting on all right, you'll be glad to know.'

'Oh, good!' said Anne. 'It's nice of you to have us, Aunt Fanny. We'll try and be good! What about Uncle Quentin? Will he mind having four children in the house in the winter-time? We won't be able to go out and leave him in peace as often as we did in the summer!'

George's father was a scientist, a very clever man, but rather frightening. He had little patience with children, and the four of them had felt very much afraid of him at times in the summer.

'Oh, your uncle is still working very hard at his book,' said Aunt Fanny. 'You know, he has been working out a secret theory – a secret idea – and putting it all into his book. He says that once it is all explained and finished, he is to take it to some high authority, and then his idea will be used for the good of the country.'

'Oh, Aunt Fanny – it does sound exciting,' said Anne. 'What's the secret?'

'I can't tell you that, silly,' said her aunt, laughing. 'Why, even I myself don't know it. Come along, now – it's cold standing here. Timothy looks very fat and well, George dear.'

'Oh Mother, he's had a marvellous time at school,' said George. 'He really has. He chewed up the cook's old slippers . . .'

'And he chased the cat that lives in the stables every time he saw her,' said Anne.

'And he once got into the larder and ate a whole steak pie,' said George; 'and once . . .'

6

'Good gracious, George, I should think the school will refuse to have Timothy next term,' said her mother, in horror. 'Wasn't he well punished? I hope he was.'

'No – he wasn't,' said George, going rather red. 'You see, Mother, we are responsible for our pets and their behaviour ourselves – so if ever Timothy does anything bad *I'm* punished for it, because I haven't shut him up properly, or something like that.'

'Well, you must have had quite a lot of punishments then,' said her mother, as she drove the little pony-trap along the frosty roads. 'I really think that's rather a good idea!' There was a twinkle in her eyes as she spoke. 'I think I'll keep on with the same idea – punish you every time Timothy misbehaves himself!'

The girls laughed. They felt happy and excited. Holidays were fun. Going back to Kirrin was lovely. Tomorrow the boys would come – and then Christmas would be there!

'Good old Kirrin Cottage!' said Anne, as they came in sight of the pretty old house. 'Oh – look, there's Kirrin Island!' The two looked out to sea, where the old ruined castle stood on the little island of Kirrin – what adventures they had had there in the summer!

The girls went into the house. 'Quentin!' called George's mother. 'Quentin! The girls are here.'

Uncle Quentin came out of his study at the other side of the house. Anne thought he looked taller and darker than ever. 'And frownier!' she said to herself. Uncle Quentin

7

might be very clever, but Anne preferred someone jolly and smiling like her own father. She shook hands with her uncle politely, and watched George kiss him.

'Well!' said Uncle Quentin to Anne. 'I hear I've got to get a tutor for you! At least, for the two boys. My word, you *will* have to behave yourself with a tutor, I can tell you!'

This was meant to be a joke, but it didn't sound very nice to Anne and George. People you had to behave well with were usually very strict and tiresome. Both girls were glad when George's father had gone back into his study.

'Your father has been working far too hard lately,' said George's mother to her. 'He is tired out. Thank goodness his book is nearly finished. He had hoped to finish it by Christmas so that he could join in the fun and games – but now he says he can't.'

'What a pity,' said Anne, politely, though secretly she thought it was a good thing. It wouldn't be much fun having Uncle Quentin to play charades and things like that! 'Oh, Aunt Fanny, I'm so looking forward to seeing Julian and Dick – and won't they be pleased to see Tim and George? Aunt Fanny, nobody calls George Georgina at school, not even our form mistress. I was rather hoping they would, because I wanted to see what would happen when she refused to answer to Georgina! George, you liked school, didn't you?'

'Yes,' said George, 'I did. I thought I'd hate being with a lot of others, but it's fun, after all. But Mother, you won't find my report very good, I'm afraid. There were such a lot of things I was bad at because I'd never done them before.'

'Well, you'd never been to school before!' said her mother. 'I'll explain it to your father if he gets upset. Now go along and get ready for a late tea. You must be very hungry.'

The girls went upstairs to their little room. 'I'm glad I'm not spending my hols by myself,' said George. 'I've had much more fun since I've known you and the boys. Hey, Timothy, where have you gone?'

'He's gone to smell all around the house to make sure it's his proper home!' said Anne, with a giggle. 'He wants to know if the kitchen smells the same – and the bathroom – and his basket. It must be just as exciting for him to come home for the holidays as it is for us!'

Anne was right. Timothy was thrilled to be back again. He ran round George's mother, sniffing at her legs in friendliness, pleased to see her again. He ran into the kitchen but soon came out again because someone new was there – Joanna the cook – a fat, panting person who eyed him with suspicion.

'You can come into this kitchen once a day for your dinner,' said Joanna. 'And that's all. I'm not having meat and sausages and chicken disappearing under my nose if I can help it. I know what dogs are, I do!'

Timothy ran into the scullery and sniffed round there. He ran into the dining-room and the sitting-room, and was pleased to find they had the same old smell. He put his nose to the door of the study where George's father worked, and sniffed very cautiously. He didn't mean to go in. Timothy was just as wary of George's father as the others were!

He ran upstairs to the girl's bedroom again. Where was his basket? Ah, there it was by the window-seat. Good! That meant he was to sleep in the girls' bedroom once more. He curled himself up in his basket, and thumped loudly with his tail.

'Glad to be back,' said his tail, 'glad – to – be – back!'

CHAPTER TWO

All together again

THE NEXT day the boys came back. Anne and George went to meet them with Timothy. George drove the pony-trap, and Tim sat beside her. Anne could hardly wait for the train to stop at the station. She ran along the platform, looking for Julian and Dick in the carriages that passed.

Then she saw them. They were looking out of a window at the back of the train, waving and yelling.

'Anne! Anne! Here we are! Hallo, George! Oh, there's Timothy!'

'Julian! Dick!' yelled Anne. Timothy began to bark and leap about. It was most exciting.

'Oh, Julian! It's lovely to see you both again!' cried Anne, giving her two brothers a hug each. Timothy leapt up and licked them both. He was beside himself with joy. Now he had all the children around him that he loved.

The three children and the dog stood happily together, all talking at once while the porter got the luggage out of the train. Anne suddenly remembered George. She looked round her. She was nowhere to be seen, although she had come on the station platform with Anne.

'Where's old George?' said Julian. 'I saw her here when I waved out of the window.'

11

'She must have gone back to the pony-trap,' said Anne. 'Tell the porter to bring your trunks out to the trap, Julian. Come along! We'll go and find George.'

George was standing by the pony, holding his head. She looked rather gloomy, Anne thought. The boys went up to her.

'Hallo, George, old thing!' cried Julian, and gave her a hug. Dick did the same.

12

ALL TOGETHER AGAIN

'What's up?' asked Anne, wondering at George's sudden silence.

'I believe George felt left-out!' said Julian with a grin. 'Funny old Georgina!'

'*Don't* call me Georgina!' said the little girl fiercely. The boys laughed.

'Ah, it's the same fierce old George, all right,' said Dick, and gave the girl a friendly slap on the shoulder. 'Oh, George – it's good to see you again. Do you remember our marvellous adventures in the summer?'

George felt her awkwardness slipping away from her. She *had* felt left-out when she had seen the great welcome that the two boys gave to their small sister – but no one could sulk for long with Julian and Dick. They just wouldn't let anyone feel left-out or awkward or sulky.

The four children climbed into the trap. The porter heaved in the two trunks. There was only just room for them. Timothy sat on top of the trunks, his tail wagging nineteen to the dozen, and his tongue hanging out because he was panting with delight.

'You two girls were lucky to be able to take Tim to school with you,' said Dick, patting the big dog lovingly. 'No pets are allowed at our school. Awfully hard on those fellows who like live things.'

'Thompson Minor kept white mice,' said Julian. 'And one day they escaped and met Matron round a corner of the passage. She squealed the place down.'

The girls laughed. The boys always had funny tales to tell when they got home.

'And Kennedy keeps snails,' said Dick. 'You know, snails sleep for the winter – but Kennedy kept his in far too warm a place, and they all crawled out of their box and went up the walls. You should have heard how we laughed when the geography master asked Thompson to point out Cape Town on the map – and there was one of the snails in the very place!'

Everyone laughed again. It was so good to be all together once more. They were very much of an age – Julian was twelve. George and Dick were eleven, and Anne was ten. Holidays and Christmas time were in front of them. No wonder they laughed at everything, even the silliest little joke!

'It's good that Mummy is getting on all right, isn't it?' said Dick, as the pony went along the road at a great pace. 'I was disappointed not to go home, I must say – I did want to go to see Aladdin and the Lamp, and the circus – but still, it's good to be back at Kirrin Cottage again. I wish we could have some more exciting adventures. Not a hope of that this time, though.'

'There's one snag about these hols,' said Julian. 'And that's the tutor. I hear we've got to have one because Dick and I missed so much school this term, and we've got to take important exams next summer.'

'Yes,' said Anne. 'I wonder what he'll be like. I do hope he will be a sport. Uncle Quentin is going to choose one today.'

ALL TOGETHER AGAIN

Julian and Dick made faces at one another. They felt sure that any tutor chosen by Uncle Quentin would be anything but a sport. Uncle Quentin's idea of a tutor would be somebody strict and gloomy and forbidding.

Never mind! He wouldn't come for a day or two. And he *might* be fun. The boys cheered up and pulled Timothy's thick coat. The dog pretended to growl and bite. *He* wasn't worried about tutors. Lucky Timothy!

They all arrived at Kirrin Cottage. The boys were really pleased to see their aunt, and rather relieved when she said that their uncle had not yet come back.

'He's gone to see two or three men who have answered the advertisement for a tutor,' she said. 'It won't be long before he's back.'

'Mother, I haven't got to do lessons in the hols too, have I?' asked George. Nothing had yet been said to her about this, and she longed to know.

'Oh yes, George,' said her mother. 'Your father has seen your report, and although it isn't really a bad one, and we certainly didn't expect a marvellous one, still it does show that you are behind your age in some things. A little extra coaching will soon help you along.'

George looked gloomy. She had expected this but it was tiresome all the same. 'Anne's the only one who won't have to do lessons,' she said.

'I'll do some too,' promised Anne. 'Perhaps not always, George, if it's a very fine day, for instance – but sometimes, just to keep you company.'

'Thanks,' said George. 'But you needn't. I shall have Timmy.'

George's mother looked doubtful about this. 'We'll have to see what the tutor says about that,' she said.

'Mother! If the tutor says I can't have Timothy in the room, I jolly well won't do holiday lessons!' began George, fiercely.

Her mother laughed. 'Well, well – here's our fierce, hot-tempered George again!' she said. 'Go along, you two boys, and wash your hands and do your hair. You seem to have collected all the grime on the railway.'

The children and Timothy went upstairs. It was such fun to be five again. They always counted Tim as one of themselves. He went everywhere with them, and really seemed to understand every single word they said.

'I wonder what sort of a tutor Uncle Quentin will choose,' said Dick, as he scrubbed his nails. 'If only he would choose the right kind – someone jolly and full of fun, who knows that holiday lessons are sickening to have, and tries to make up for them by being a sport out of lesson-time. I suppose we'll have to work every morning.'

'Hurry up. I want my tea,' said Julian. 'Come on down, Dick. We'll know about the tutor soon enough!'

They all went down together, and sat round the table. Joanna the cook had made a lovely lot of buns and a great big cake. There was not much left of either by the time the four children had finished!

Uncle Quentin returned just as they were finishing. He

seemed rather pleased with himself. He shook hands with the two boys and asked them if they had had a good term.

'Did you get a tutor, Uncle Quentin?' asked Anne, who could see that everyone was simply bursting to know this.

'Ah – yes, I did,' said her uncle. He sat down, while Aunt Fanny poured him out a cup of tea. 'I interviewed three applicants, and had almost chosen the last one, when another fellow came in, all in a hurry. Said he had only just seen the advertisement, and hoped he wasn't too late.'

'Did you choose him?' asked Dick.

'I did,' said his uncle. 'He seemed a most intelligent fellow. Even knew about me and my work! And he had the most wonderful letters of recommendation.'

'I don't think the children need to know all these details,' murmured Aunt Fanny. 'Anyway – you asked him to come?'

'Oh yes,' said Uncle Quentin. 'He's a good bit older than the others – they were rather young fellows – this one seems very responsible and intelligent. I'm sure you'll like him, Fanny. He'll fit in here very well. I feel I would like to have him to talk to me sometimes in the evening.'

The children couldn't help feeling that the new tutor sounded rather alarming. Their uncle smiled at the gloomy faces.

'You'll like Mr Roland,' he said. 'He knows how to handle youngsters – knows he's got to be very firm, and to see that you know a good bit more at the end of the holidays than you did at the beginning.'

17

This sounded even more alarming. All four children wished heartily that Aunt Fanny had been to choose the tutor, and not Uncle Quentin.

'When is he coming?' asked George.

'Tomorrow,' said her father. 'You can all go to meet him at the station. That will make a nice welcome for him.'

'We *had* thought of taking the bus and going to do a bit of Christmas shopping,' said Julian, seeing Anne looked very disappointed.

'Oh, no, you must certainly go and meet Mr Roland,' said his uncle. 'I told him you would. And mind you, you four – no nonsense with him! You've to do as you're told, and you must work hard with him, because your father is paying very high fees for his coaching. I'm paying a third, because I want him to coach George a little too – so George, you must do your best.'

'I'll try,' said George. 'If he's nice, I'll do my very best.'

'You'll do your best whether you think him nice or not!' said her father, frowning. 'He will arrive by the ten-thirty train. Be sure to be there in time.'

'I do hope he won't be too strict,' said Dick, that evening, when the five of them were alone for a minute or two. 'It's going to spoil the hols, if we have someone down on us all the time. And I do hope he'll like Timothy.'

George looked up at once. 'Like Timothy!' she said. 'Of course he'll like Timothy! How couldn't he?'

'Well – your father didn't like Timothy very much last summer,' said Dick. 'I don't see how anyone could *dislike*

18

darling Tim – but there are people who don't like dogs, you know, George.'

'If Mr Roland doesn't like Timothy, I'll not do a single thing for him,' said George. 'Not one single thing!'

'She's gone all fierce again!' said Dick, with a laugh. 'My word – the sparks will fly if Mr Roland dares to dislike our Timothy!'

CHAPTER THREE

The new tutor

NEXT MORNING the sun was out, all the sea-mist that had hung about for the last two days had disappeared, and Kirrin Island showed plainly at the mouth of Kirrin Bay. The children stared longingly at the ruined castle on it.

'I do wish we could get over to the castle,' said Dick. 'It looks quite calm enough, George.'

'It's very rough by the island,' said George. 'It always is at this time of year. I know Mother wouldn't let us go.'

'It's a lovely island, and it's all our own!' said Anne. 'You said you would share it with us for ever and ever, didn't you, George?'

'Yes, I did,' said George. 'And so I will, dungeons and all. Come on – we must get the trap out. We shall be late meeting the train if we stand here all day looking at the island.'

They got the pony and trap and set off down the hard lanes. Kirrin Island disappeared behind the cliffs as they turned inland to the station.

'Did all this land round about belong to your family once upon a time?' asked Julian.

'Yes, all of it,' said George. 'Now we don't own anything except Kirrin Island, our own house and that farm away over there - Kirrin Farm.'

THE NEW TUTOR

She pointed with her whip. The children saw a fine old farmhouse standing on a hill a good way off, over the heather-clad common.

'Who lives there?' asked Julian.

'Oh, an old farmer and his wife,' said George. 'They were nice to me when I was smaller. We'll go over there one day, if you like. Mother says they don't make the farm pay any more, and in the summertime they take in people who want a holiday.'

'Listen! That's the train whistling in the tunnel!' said Julian, suddenly. 'Buck up, for goodness' sake, George. We shan't be there in time!'

The four children and Timothy looked at the train coming out of the tunnel and drawing in at the station. The pony cantered along swiftly. They would be just in time.

'Who's going on to the platform to meet him?' asked George, as they drew into the little station yard. 'I'm not. I must look after Tim and the pony.'

'I don't want to,' said Anne. 'I'll stay with George.'

'Well, we'd better go, then,' said Julian, and he and Dick leapt out of the trap. They ran on to the platform just as the train pulled up.

Not many people got out. A woman clambered out with a basket. A young man leapt out, whistling, the son of the baker in the village. An old man climbed down with difficulty. The tutor could be none of those!

Then, right at the front of the train, rather an odd-

21

looking man got out. He was short and burly, and he had a beard rather like a sailor. His eyes were piercingly blue, and his thick hair was sprinkled with grey. He glanced up and down the platform, and then beckoned to the porter.

'That must be Mr Roland,' said Julian to Dick.

'Come on – let's ask him. There's no one else it could be.'

The boys went up to the bearded man. 'Are you Mr Roland, sir?' he asked.

'I am,' said the man. 'I suppose you are Julian and Dick?'

'Yes, sir,' answered the boys together. 'We brought the pony-trap for your luggage.'

'Oh, fine,' said Mr Roland. His bright blue eyes looked the boys up and down, and he smiled. Julian and Dick liked him. He seemed sensible and jolly.

'Are the other two here as well?' said Mr Roland, walking down the platform, with the porter trailing behind with his luggage.

'Yes – George and Anne are outside with the trap,' said Julian.

'George and Anne,' said Mr Roland, in a puzzled voice. 'I thought the others were girls. I didn't know there was a third boy.'

'Oh, George is a girl,' said Dick, with a laugh. 'Her real name is Georgina.'

'And a very nice name, too,' said Mr Roland.

'George doesn't think so,' said Julian. 'She won't answer if she's called Georgina. You'd better call her George, sir!'

'Really?' said Mr Roland, in rather a chilly tone. Julian took a glance at him.

'Not quite so jolly as he looks!' thought the boy.

'Tim's out there too,' said Dick.

'Oh – and is Tim a boy or a girl?' inquired Mr Roland, cautiously.

'A dog, sir!' said Dick, with a grin.

Mr Roland seemed rather taken aback. 'A dog?' he said. 'I didn't know there was a dog in the household. Your uncle said nothing to me about a dog.'

'Don't you like dogs?' asked Julian, in surprise.

'No,' said Mr Roland, shortly. 'But I dare say your dog won't worry me much. Hallo, hallo – so here are the little girls! How do you do?'

George was not very pleased at being called a little girl. For one thing she hated to be spoken of as little, and for another thing she always tried to be a boy. She held out her hand to Mr Roland and said nothing. Anne smiled at him, and Mr Roland thought she was much the nicer of the two.

'Tim! Shake hands with Mr Roland!' said Julian to Timothy. This was one of Tim's really good tricks. He could hold out his right paw in a very polite manner. Mr Roland looked down at the big dog, and Tim looked back at him.

Then, very slowly and deliberately, Timothy turned his

back on Mr Roland and climbed up into the pony-trap! Usually he put out his paw at once when told to, and the children stared at him in amazement.

'Timothy! What's come over you?' cried Dick. Tim put his ears down and did not move.

'He doesn't like you,' said George, looking at Mr Roland. 'That's very strange. He usually likes people. But perhaps you don't like dogs?'

'No, I don't, as a matter of fact,' said Mr Roland. 'I was once very badly bitten as a boy, and somehow or other I've never managed to like dogs since. But I dare say your Tim will take to me sooner or later.'

They all got into the trap. It was a tight squeeze. Timothy looked at Mr Roland's ankles as if he would rather like to nibble them. Anne laughed.

'Tim *is* behaving strangely!' she said. 'It's a good thing you haven't come to teach him, Mr Roland!' She smiled up at the tutor, and he smiled back, showing very white teeth. His eyes were as brilliant a blue as George's.

Anne liked him. He joked with the boys as they drove him, and both of them began to feel that their Uncle Quentin hadn't made such a bad choice after all.

Only George said nothing. She sensed that the tutor disliked Timothy, and George was not prepared to like anyone who didn't take to Timothy at first sight. She thought it was very peculiar too, that Tim would not shake paws with the tutor. 'He's a clever dog,' she thought. 'He knows Mr Roland doesn't like him, so he won't shake hands. I don't blame you, Tim darling, I wouldn't shake hands with anyone who didn't like *me*!'

Mr Roland was shown up to his room when he arrived. Aunt Fanny came down and spoke to the children. 'Well! He seems very nice, youngish and jolly.'

'Youngish!' exclaimed Julian. 'Why, he's awfully old! Must be forty at the very least!'

25

Aunt Fanny laughed. 'Does he seem so old to you?' she said. 'Well, old or not, he'll be quite nice to you, I'm sure.'

'Aunt Fanny, we shan't begin lessons until after Christmas, shall we?' asked Julian, anxiously.

'Of course you will!' said his aunt. 'It is almost a week till Christmas – you don't suppose we have asked Mr Roland to come and do nothing till Christmas is over, do you?'

The children groaned. 'We wanted to do some Christmas shopping,' said Anne.

'Well, you can do that in the afternoon,' said her aunt. 'You will only do lessons in the morning, for three hours. That won't hurt any of you!'

The new tutor came downstairs at that moment, and Aunt Fanny took him to see Uncle Quentin. She came out after a while, looking very pleased.

'Mr Roland will be nice company for your uncle,' she said to Julian. 'I think they will get on very well together. Mr Roland seems to understand quite a bit about your uncle's work.'

'Let's hope he spends most of his time with him then!' said George, in a low voice.

'Come on out for a walk,' said Dick. 'It's so fine today. We shan't have lessons this morning, shall we, Aunt Fanny?'

'Oh, no,' said his aunt. 'You'll begin tomorrow. Go for a walk now, all of you – we shan't often get sunny days like this!'

'Let's go over to Kirrin Farm,' said Julian. 'It looks such a nice place. Show us the way, George.'

'Right!' said George. She whistled to Timothy, and he

26

came bounding up. The five of them set off together, going down the lane, and then on to a rough road over the common that led to the farm on the distant hill.

It was lovely walking in the December sun. Their feet rang on the frosty path, and Tim's blunt claws made quite a noise as he pattered up and down, overjoyed at being with his four friends again.

After a good long walk across the common the children came to the farmhouse. It was built of white stone, and stood strong and lovely on the hillside. George opened the farm-gate and went into the farm-yard. She kept her hand on Tim's collar for there were two farm-dogs somewhere about.

Someone clattered round the barn near-by. It was an old man, and George hailed him loudly.

'Hallo, Mr Sanders! How are you?'

'Why, if it isn't Master George!' said the old fellow with a grin. George grinned too. She loved being called Master instead of Miss.

'These are my cousins,' shouted George. She turned to the others. 'He's deaf,' she said. 'You'll have to shout to make him hear.'

'I'm Julian,' said Julian in a loud voice and the others said their names too. The farmer beamed at them.

'You come along in and see the Missis,' he said. 'She'll be rare pleased to see you all. We've known Master George since she was a baby, and we knew her mother when *she* was a baby too, and we knew her granny as well.'

'You must be very, very old,' said Anne.

The farmer smiled down at her.

'As old as my tongue and a little older than my teeth!' he said, chuckling. 'Come away in now.'

They all went into the big, warm farmhouse kitchen, where a little old woman, as lively as a bantam hen, was bustling about. She was just as pleased to see the four children as her husband was.

'Well, there now!' she said. 'I haven't seen you for months, Master George. I did hear that you'd gone away to school.'

'Yes, I did,' said George. 'But I'm home for the holidays now. Does it matter if I let Timothy loose, Mrs Sanders? I think he'll be friendly if your dogs are, too.'

'Yes, you let him loose,' said the old lady. 'He'll have a fine time in the farmyard with Ben and Rikky. Now what would you like to drink? Hot milk? Cocoa? Coffee? And I've some new shortbread baked yesterday. You shall have some of that.'

'Ah, my wife's very busy this week, cooking up all sorts of things,' said the old farmer, as his wife bustled off to the larder. 'We've company this Christmas!'

'Have you?' said George, surprised, for she knew that the old pair had never had any children of their own. 'Who is coming? Anyone I know?'

'Two artists from London Town!' said the old farmer. 'Wrote and asked us to take them for three weeks over Christmas – and offered us good money too. So my old wife's as busy as a bee.'

THE NEW TUTOR

'Are they going to paint pictures?' asked Julian, who rather fancied himself as an artist, too. 'I wonder if I could come and talk to them some day. I'm rather good at pictures myself. They might give me a few hints.'

'You come along whenever you like,' said old Mrs Sanders, making cocoa in a big jug. She set out a plate of most delicious-looking shortbreads, and the children ate them hungrily.

'I should think the two artists will be rather lonely down here, in the depths of the country at Christmastime,' said George. 'Do they know anyone?'

'They say they don't know a soul,' said Mrs Sanders. 'But there – artists can be peculiar folk. I've had some here before. They seemed to like mooning about all alone. These two will be happy enough, I'll be bound.'

'They should be, with all the good things you're cooking up for them,' said her old husband. 'Well, I must be out after the sheep. Good-day to you, youngsters. Come again and see us sometime.'

He went out. Old Mrs Sanders chattered on to the children as she bustled about the big kitchen. Timothy ran in and settled down on the rug by the fire.

He suddenly saw a tabby cat slinking along by the wall, all her hairs on end with fear of the strange dog. He gave a delighted wuff and sprang at the cat. She fled out of the kitchen into the old panelled hall. Tim flew after her, taking no notice at all of George's stern shout.

The cat tried to leap on top of an old grandfather clock

29

in the hall. With a joyous bark Tim sprang too. He flung himself against a polished panel – and then a most extraordinary thing happened!

The panel disappeared – and a dark hole showed in the old wall! George, who had followed Tim out into the hall, gave a loud cry of surprise. 'Look! Mrs Sanders, come and look!'

CHAPTER FOUR

An exciting discovery

OLD MRS Sanders and the other three children rushed out into the hall when they heard George's shout.

'What's up?' cried Julian. 'What's happened?'

'Tim sprang at the cat, missed her, and fell hard against the panelled wall,' said George, 'and the panel moved, and look – there's a hole in the wall!'

'It's a secret panel!' cried Dick, in excitement, peering into the hole. 'Golly! Did you know there was one here, Mrs Sanders?'

'Oh yes,' said the old lady. 'This house is full of funny things like that. I'm very careful when I polish that panel, because if I rub too hard in the top corner, it always slides back.'

'What's behind the panel?' asked Julian. The hole was only about the width of his head, and when he stuck his head inside, he could see only darkness. The wall itself was about eight inches behind the panelling, and was of stone.

'Get a candle, do get a candle!' said Anne, thrilled. 'You haven't got a torch, have you, Mrs Sanders?'

'No,' said the old woman. 'But you can get a candle if you like. There's one on the kitchen mantelpiece.'

Anne shot off to get it. Julian lit it and put it into the

31

hole behind the panel. The others pushed against him to try and peep inside.

'Don't,' said Julian, impatiently. 'Wait your turn, sillies! Let me have a look.'

He had a good look, but there didn't really seem anything to see. It was all darkness behind, and stone wall. He gave the candle to Dick, and then each of the children had a turn at peeping. Old Mrs Sanders had gone back to the kitchen. She was used to the sliding panel!

'She said this house was full of strange things like that,' said Anne. 'What other things are there, do you think? Let's ask her.'

They slid the panel back into place and went to find Mrs Sanders. 'Mrs Sanders, what other funny things are there in Kirrin Farmhouse?' asked Julian.

'There's a cupboard upstairs with a false back,' said Mrs Sanders. 'Don't look so excited! There's nothing in it at all! And there's a big stone over there by the fireplace that pulls up to show a hidey-hole. I suppose in the old days people wanted good hiding-places for things.'

The children ran to the stone she pointed out. It had an iron ring in it, and was easily pulled up. Below was a hollowed-out place, big enough to take a small box. It was empty now, but all the same it looked exciting.

'Where's the cupboard?' asked Julian.

'My old legs are too tired to go traipsing upstairs this morning,' said the farmer's wife. 'But you can go yourselves. Up the stairs, turn to the right, and go into the second door you see. The cupboard is at the farther end. Open the door and feel about at the bottom till you come across a dent in the wood. Press it hard, and the false back slides to the side.'

The four children and Timothy ran upstairs as fast as they could, munching shortbread as they went. This really was a very exciting morning!

They found the cupboard and opened the door. All four went down on hands and knees to press round the bottom of the cupboard to find the dented place. Anne found it.

'I've got it!' she cried. She pressed hard, but her little fingers were not strong enough to work the mechanism of the sliding back. Julian had to help her.

There was a creaking noise, and the children saw the false back of the cupboard sliding sideways. A big space showed behind, large enough to take a fairly thin man.

'A jolly good hiding-place,' said Julian. 'Anyone could hide there and no one would ever know!'

'I'll get in and you shut me up,' said Dick. 'It would be exciting.'

He got into the space. Julian slid the back across, and Dick could no longer be seen!

'Bit of a tight fit!' he called. 'And awfully dark! Let me out again.'

The children all took turns at going into the space behind the back of the cupboard and being shut up. Anne didn't like it very much.

They went down to the warm kitchen again. 'It's a most

exciting cupboard, Mrs Sanders,' said Julian. 'I do wish we lived in a house like this, full of secrets!'

'Can we come and play in that cupboard again?' asked George.

'No, I'm afraid you can't, George,' said Mrs Sanders. 'That room where the cupboard is, is one the two gentlemen are going to have.'

'Oh!' said Julian, disappointed. 'Shall you tell them about the sliding back, Mrs Sanders?'

'I don't expect so,' said the old lady. 'It's only you children that get excited about things like that, bless you. Two gentlemen wouldn't think twice about it.'

'How funny grown-ups are!' said Anne, puzzled. 'I'm quite certain I shall be thrilled to see a sliding panel or a trapdoor even when I'm a hundred.'

'Same here,' said Dick. 'Could I just go and look into the sliding panel in the hall once more, Mrs Sanders? I'll take the candle.'

Dick never knew why he suddenly wanted to have another look. It was just an idea he had. The others didn't bother to go with him, for there really was nothing to see behind the panelling except the old stone wall.

Dick took the candle and went into the hall. He pressed on the panel at the top and it slid back. He put the candle inside and had another good look. There was nothing at all to be seen. Dick took out his head and put in his arm, stretching along the wall as far as his hand would reach. He was just about to take it back when his fingers found a hole in the wall.

34

AN EXCITING DISCOVERY

'Funny!' said Dick. 'Why should there be a hole in the stone wall just there?'

He stuck in his finger and thumb and worked them about. He felt a little ridge inside the wall, rather like a bird's perch, and was able to get hold of it. He wriggled his fingers about the perch, but nothing happened. Then he got a good hold and pulled.

The stone came right out! Dick was so surprised that he let go the heavy stone and it fell to the ground behind the panelling with a crash!

The noise brought the others out into the hall. 'Whatever are you doing, Dick?' said Julian. 'Have you broken something?'

'No,' said Dick, his face reddening with excitement. 'I say – I put my hand in here – and found a hole in one of the stones the wall is made of – and I got hold of a sort of ridge with my finger and thumb and pulled. The stone came right out, and I got such a surprise I let go. It fell, and that's what you heard!'

'Golly!' said Julian, trying to push Dick away from the open panel. 'Let me see.'

'No, Julian,' said Dick, pushing him away. 'This is *my* discovery. Wait till I see if I can feel anything in the hole. It's difficult to get at!'

The others waited impatiently. Julian could hardly prevent himself from pushing Dick right away. Dick put his arm in as far as he could, and curved his hand round to get into the space behind where the stone had been. His fingers felt about and he closed them round something that felt like a book. Cautiously and carefully he brought it out.

'An old book!' he said.

'What's in it?' cried Anne.

They turned the pages carefully. They were so dry and brittle that some of them fell into dust.

'I think it's a book of recipes,' said Anne, as her sharp eyes read a few words in the old brown, faded handwriting. 'Let's take it to Mrs Sanders.'

AN EXCITING DISCOVERY

The children carried the book to the old lady. She laughed at their beaming faces. She took the book and looked at it, not at all excited.

'Yes,' she said. 'It's a book of recipes, that's all it is. See the name in the front – Alice Mary Sanders – that must have been my husband's great-grandmother. She was famous for her medicines, I know. It was said she could cure any ill in man or animal, no matter what it was.'

'It's a pity it's so hard to read her writing,' said Julian, disappointed. 'The whole book is falling to pieces too. It must be very old.'

'Do you think there's anything else in that hidy-hole?' asked Anne. 'Julian, you go and put *your* arm in, it's longer than Dick's.'

'There didn't seem to be anything else at all,' said Dick. 'It's a very small place – just a few inches of hollow space behind that brick or stone that fell down.'

'Well, I'll just put my hand in and see,' said Julian. They all went back into the hall. Julian put his arm into the open panel, and slid it along the wall to where the stone had fallen out. His hand went into the space there, and his long fingers groped about, feeling for anything else that might be there.

There was something else, something soft and flat that felt like leather. Eagerly the boy's fingers closed over it and he drew it out carefully, half afraid that it might fall to pieces with age.

'I've got something!' he said, his eyes gleaming brightly. 'Look – what is it?'

The others crowded round. 'It's rather like Daddy's tobacco pouch,' said Anne, feeling it. 'The same shape. Is there anything inside?'

It was a tobacco pouch, very dark brown, made of soft leather and very much worn. Carefully Julian undid the flap, and unrolled the leather.

A few bits of black tobacco were still in the pouch but there was something else, too! Tightly rolled up in the last bit of pouch was a piece of linen. Julian took it out and unrolled it. He put it flat on the hall-table.

The children stared at it. There were marks and signs on the linen, done in black ink that had hardly faded. But the four of them could not make head or tail of the marks.

'It's not a map,' said Julian. 'It seems a sort of code, or something. I do wonder what it means. I wish we could make it out. It must be some sort of secret.'

The children stared at the piece of linen, very thrilled. It was so old – and contained some kind of secret. Whatever could it be?

They ran to show it to Mrs Sanders. She was studying the old recipe book, and her face glowed with pleasure as she raised it to look at the excited children.

'This book's a wonder!' she said. 'I can hardly read the writing, but here's a recipe for backache. I shall try it myself. My back aches so much at the end of the day. Now, you listen . . .'

But the children didn't want to listen to recipes for

backache. They pushed the piece of linen on to Mrs Sanders's lap.

'Look! What's this about, Mrs Sanders? Do you know? We found it in a kind of tobacco pouch in that place behind the panel.'

Mrs Sanders took off her glasses, polished them, and put them on again. She looked carefully at the piece of linen with its strange marks.

She shook her head. 'No – this doesn't make any sense to me. And what's this now? – it looks like an old tobacco pouch. Ah, my John would like that, I guess. He's got such an old one that it won't hold his tobacco any more! This is old too – but there's a lot of wear in it yet.'

'Mrs Sanders, do you want this piece of linen too?' asked Julian, anxiously. He was longing to take it home and study it. He felt certain there was some kind of exciting secret hidden there, and he could not bear the thought of leaving it with Mrs Sanders.

'You take it, Julian, if you want it,' said Mrs Sanders, with a laugh. 'I'll keep the recipes for myself, and John shall have the pouch. You can have the old rag if you want it, though it beats me why you think it's so fascinating! Ah, here's John!'

She raised her voice and shouted to the deaf old man. 'Hey, John, here's a tobacco pouch for you. The children found it somewhere behind that panel that opens in the hall.'

John took it and fingered it. 'It's a strange one,' he said, 'but better than mine. Well, youngsters, I don't want to hurry you, but it's one o'clock now, and you'd better be going if it's near your dinner-time!'

'Gracious!' said Julian. 'We shall be late! Goodbye, Mrs Sanders, and thanks awfully for the shortbread and this old rag. We'll try our best to make out what's on it and tell you. Hurry, everyone! Where's Tim? Come on, Timothy, we're late!'

The five of them ran off quickly. They really were late, and had to run most of the way, which meant that it was difficult to talk. But they were so excited about their morning that they panted remarks to one another as they went.

'I wonder what this old rag says!' panted Julian. 'I mean to find out. I'm sure it's something mysterious.'

'Shall we tell anyone?' asked Dick.

'No!' said George. 'Let's keep it a secret.'

'If Anne starts to give away anything, kick her under the table, like we did last summer,' said Julian, with a grin. Poor Anne always found it difficult to keep a secret, and often had to be nudged or kicked when she began to give things away.

'I won't say a word,' said Anne, indignantly. 'And don't you dare to kick me. It only makes me cry out and then the grown-ups want to know why.'

'We'll have a good old puzzle over this piece of linen after dinner,' said Julian. 'I bet we'll find out what it says, if we really make up our minds to!'

'Here we are,' said George. 'Not too late. Hallo Mother! We won't be a minute washing our hands! We've had a lovely time.'

CHAPTER FIVE

An unpleasant walk

AFTER DINNER the four children went upstairs to the boys' bedroom and spread out the bit of linen on a table there. There were words here and there, scrawled in rough printing. There was the sign of a compass, with E marked clearly for East. There were eight rough squares, and in one of them, right in the middle, was a cross. It was all very mysterious.

'You know, I believe these words are Latin,' said Julian, trying to make them out. 'But I can't read them properly. And I expect if I *could* read them, I wouldn't know what they meant. I wish we knew someone who could read Latin like this.'

'Could your father, George?' asked Anne.

'I expect so,' said George. But nobody wanted to ask George's father. He might take the curious old rag away. He might forget all about it, he might even burn it. Scientists were such peculiar people.

'What about Mr Roland?' said Dick. 'He's a tutor. He knows Latin.'

'We won't ask him till we know a bit more about him,' said Julian, cautiously. 'He *seems* jolly and nice – but you never know. Oh, blow – I wish we could make this out, I really do.'

'There are two words at the top,' said Dick, and he tried to spell them out. 'VIA OCCULTA.' What do you think they could mean, Julian?'

'Well – the only thing I can think of that they can mean is – Secret Way, or something like that,' said Julian, screwing up his forehead into a frown.

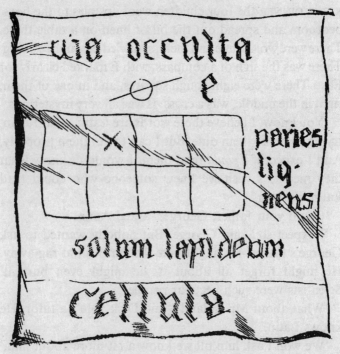

'Secret Way!' said Anne, her eyes shining. 'Oh, I hope it's that! Secret Way! How exciting. What sort of secret way would it be, Julian?'

AN UNPLEASANT WALK

'How do I know, Anne, silly?' said Julian. 'I don't even know that the words are meant to mean "Secret Way". It's really a guess on my part.'

'If they did mean that – the linen might have directions to find the Secret Way, whatever it is,' said Dick. 'Oh Julian, isn't it exasperating that we can't read it? Do, do try. You know more Latin than I do.'

'It's so hard to read the funny old letters,' said Julian, trying again. 'No – it's no good at all. I can't make them out.'

Steps came up the stairs, and the door opened. Mr Roland looked in.

'Hallo, hallo!' he said. 'I wondered where you all were. What about a walk over the cliffs?'

'We'll come,' said Julian, rolling up the old rag.

'What have you got there? Anything interesting?' asked Mr Roland.

'It's a—' began Anne, and at once all the others began to talk, afraid that Anne was going to give the secret away.

'It's a wonderful afternoon for a walk.'

'Come on, let's get our things on!'

'Tim, Tim, where are you?' George gave a piercing whistle. Tim was under the bed and came bounding out. Anne went red as she guessed why all the others had interrupted her so quickly.

'Idiot,' said Julian, under his breath. 'Baby.'

Fortunately Mr Roland said no more about the piece of linen he had seen Julian rolling up. He was looking at Tim.

43

'I suppose he must come,' he said. George stared at him in indignation.

'Of course he must!' she said. 'We never never go anywhere without Timothy.'

Mr Roland went downstairs, and the children got ready to go out. George was scowling. The very idea of leaving Tim behind made her angry.

'You nearly gave our secret away, you silly,' said Dick to Anne.

'I didn't think,' said the little girl, looking ashamed of herself. 'Anyway, Mr Roland seems very nice. I think we might ask him if he could help us to understand those funny words.'

'You leave that to me to decide,' said Julian, crossly. 'Now don't you dare to say a word.'

They all set out, Timothy too. Mr Roland need not have worried about the dog, for Timothy would not go near him. It was very strange, really. He kept away from the tutor, and took not the slightest notice of him even when Mr Roland spoke to him.

'He's not usually like that,' said Dick. 'He's a most friendly dog, really.'

'Well, as I've got to live in the same house with him, I must try and make him friends with me,' said the tutor. 'Hi, Timothy! Come here! I've got a biscuit in my pocket.'

Timothy pricked up his ears at the word 'biscuit', but did not even look towards Mr Roland. He put his tail down and went to George. She patted him.

'If he doesn't like anyone, not even a biscuit or a bone will make him go to them when he is called,' she said.

Mr Roland gave it up. He put the biscuit back into his pocket. 'He's a peculiar-looking dog, isn't he?' he said. 'A terrible mongrel! I must say I prefer well-bred dogs.'

George went purple in the face. 'He's *not* peculiar-looking!' she spluttered. 'He's not nearly so peculiar-

45

looking as you! He's not a terrible mongrel. He's the best dog in the world!'

'I think you are being a little rude,' said Mr Roland, stiffly. 'I don't allow my pupils to be cheeky, Georgina.'

Calling her Georgina made George still more furious. She lagged behind with Tim, looking as black as a thundercloud. The others felt uncomfortable. They knew what tempers George got into, and how difficult she could be. She had been so much better and happier since the summer, when they had come to stay for the first time. They did hope she wasn't going to be silly and get into rows. It would spoil the Christmas holidays.

Mr Roland took no more notice of George. He did not speak to her, but strode on ahead with the others, doing his best to be jolly. He could really be very funny, and the boys began to laugh at him. He took Anne's hand, and the little girl jumped along beside him, enjoying the walk.

Julian felt sorry for George. It wasn't nice to be left out of things, and he knew how George hated anything like that. He wondered if he dared to put in a good word for her. It might make things easier.

'Mr Roland, sir,' he began. 'Could you call my cousin by the name she likes – George – she simply hates Georgina. And she's very fond of Tim. She can't bear anyone to say horrid things about him.'

Mr Roland looked surprised. 'My dear boy, I am sure you mean well,' he said, in rather a dry sort of voice, 'but I

46

hardly think I want your advice about any of my pupils. I shall follow my own wishes in my treatment of Georgina, not yours. I want to be friends with you all, and I am sure we shall be – but Georgina has got to be sensible, as you three are.'

Julian felt rather squashed. He went red and looked at Dick. Dick gave him a squeeze on his arm. The boys knew George could be silly and difficult, especially if anyone didn't like her beloved dog – but they thought Mr Roland might try to be a bit more understanding too. Dick slipped behind and walked with George.

'You needn't walk with me,' said George at once, her blue eyes glinting. 'Walk with your friend Mr Roland.'

'He isn't my friend,' said Dick. 'Don't be silly.'

'I'm not silly,' said George, in a tight sort of voice. 'I heard you all laughing and joking with him. You go on and have a good laugh again. I've got Timothy.'

'George, it's Christmas holidays,' said Dick. 'Do let's all be friends. Do. Don't let's spoil Christmas.'

'I can't like anyone who doesn't like Tim,' said George, obstinately.

'Well, after all, Mr Roland did offer him a biscuit,' said Dick, trying to make peace as hard as he could.

George said nothing. Her small face looked fierce. Dick tried again.

'George! Promise to try and be nice till Christmas is over, anyway. Don't let's spoil Christmas, for goodness' sake! Come on, George.'

'All right,' said George, at last. 'I'll try.'

'Come and walk with us then,' said Dick. So George caught up the others, and tried not to look too sulky. Mr Roland guessed that Dick had been trying to make George behave, and he included her in his talk. He could not make her laugh, but she did at least answer politely.

'Is that Kirrin Farmhouse?' asked Mr Roland, as they came in sight of the farm.

'Yes. Do you know it?' asked Julian, in surprise.

'No, no,' said Mr Roland, at once, 'I've heard of it, and wondered if that was the place.'

'We went there this morning,' said Anne. 'It's an exciting place.' She looked at the others, wondering if they would mind if she said anything about the things they had seen that morning. Julian thought for a moment. After all, it couldn't matter telling him about the stone in the kitchen and the false back to the cupboard. Mrs Sanders would tell anyone that. He could speak about the sliding panel in the hall too, and say they had found an old recipe book there. He did not need to say anything about the old bit of marked linen.

So he told their tutor about the exciting things there had been at the old farmhouse, but said nothing at all about the linen and its strange markings. Mr Roland listened with the greatest interest.

'This is all very remarkable,' he said. 'Very remarkable indeed. Most interesting. You say the old couple live there quite alone?'

'Well, they are having two people to stay over Christmas,' said Dick. 'Artists. Julian thought he would go over and talk to them. He can paint awfully well, you know.'

'Can he really?' said Mr Roland. 'Well, he must show me some of his pictures. But I don't think he'd better go and worry the artists at the farmhouse. They might not like it.'

This remark made Julian feel obstinate. He made up his

mind at once that he *would* go and talk to the two artists when he got the chance!

It was quite a pleasant walk on the whole except that George was quiet, and Timothy would not go anywhere near Mr Roland. When they came to a frozen pond Dick threw sticks on it for Tim to fetch. It was so funny to see him go slithering about on his long legs, trying to run properly!

Everyone threw sticks for the dog, and Tim fetched all the sticks except Mr Roland's. When the tutor threw a stick the dog looked at it and took no more notice. It was almost as if he had said, 'What, *your* stick! No, thank you!'

'Now, home we go,' said Mr Roland, trying not to look annoyed with Tim. 'We shall just be in time for tea!'

CHAPTER SIX

Lessons with Mr Roland

NEXT MORNING the children felt a little gloomy. Lessons! How horrid in the holidays! Still, Mr Roland wasn't so bad. The children had not had him with them in the sitting-room the night before, because he had gone to talk to their uncle. So they were able to get out the mysterious bit of linen again and pore over it.

But it wasn't a bit of good. Nobody could make anything of it at all. Secret Way! What did it mean? Was it really directions for a Secret Way? And where was the way, and why was it secret? It was most exasperating not to be able to find out.

'I really feel we'll have to ask someone soon,' Julian had said with a sigh. 'I can't bear this mystery much longer. I keep on and on thinking of it.'

He had dreamt of it too that night, and now it was morning, with lessons ahead. He wondered what lesson Mr Roland would take – Latin perhaps. Then he could ask him what the words 'VIA OCCULTA' meant.

Mr Roland had seen all their reports and had noted the subjects they were weak in. One was Latin, and another was French. Maths were very weak in both Dick's report and George's. Both children must be helped on in those. Geometry was Julian's weakest spot.

Anne was not supposed to need any coaching. 'But if you like to come along and join us, I'll give you some painting to do,' said Mr Roland, his blue eyes twinkling at her. He liked Anne. She was not difficult and sulky like George.

Anne loved painting. 'Oh, yes,' she said, happily, 'I'd love to do some painting. I can paint flowers, Mr Roland. I'll paint you some red poppies and blue cornflowers out of my head.'

'We will start at half-past nine,' said Mr Roland. 'We are to work in the sitting-room. Take your schoolbooks there, and be ready punctually.'

So all the children were there, sitting round a table, their books in front of them, at half-past nine. Anne had some painting water and her painting-box. The others looked at her enviously. Lucky Anne, to be doing painting while they worked hard at difficult things like Latin and Maths!

'Where's Timothy?' asked Julian in a low voice, as they waited for their tutor to come in.

'Under the table,' said George, defiantly. 'I'm sure he'll lie still. Don't any of you say anything about him. I want him there. I'm not going to do lessons without Tim here.'

'I don't see why he shouldn't be here with us,' said Dick. 'He's very very good. Sh! Here comes Mr Roland.'

The tutor came in, his black beard bristling round his mouth and chin. His eyes looked very piercing in the pale winter sunlight that filtered into the room. He told the children to sit down.

'I'll have a look at your exercise books first,' he said, 'and see what you were doing last term. You come first, Julian.'

Soon the little class were working quietly together. Anne was very busy painting a bright picture of poppies and cornflowers. Mr Roland admired it very much. Anne thought he really was very nice.

Suddenly there was a huge sigh from under the table. It was Tim, tired of lying so still. Mr Roland looked up, surprised. George at once sighed heavily, hoping that Mr Roland would think it was she who had sighed before.

'You sound tired, Georgina,' said Mr Roland. 'You shall all have a little break at eleven.'

George frowned. She hated being called Georgina. She put her foot cautiously on Timothy to warn him not to make any more noises. Tim licked her foot.

After a while, just when the class was at its very quietest, Tim felt a great wish to scratch himself very hard on his back. He got up. He sat down again with a thump, gave a grunt, and began to scratch himself furiously. The children all began to make noises to hide the sounds that Tim was making.

George clattered her feet on the floor. Julian began to cough, and let one of his books slip to the ground. Dick jiggled the table and spoke to Mr Roland.

'Oh dear, this sum is so hard; it really is! I keep doing it and doing it, and it simply *won't* come right!'

'Why all this sudden noise?' said Mr Roland in surprise. 'Stop tapping the floor with your feet, Georgina.'

Tim settled down quietly again. The children gave a sigh of relief. They became quiet, and Mr Roland told Dick to come to him with his Maths book.

The tutor took it, and stretched his legs out under the table, leaning back to speak to Dick. To his enormous surprise his feet struck something soft and warm – and then something nipped him sharply on the ankle! He drew in his feet with a cry of pain.

The children stared at him. He bent down and looked under the table. 'It's that dog,' he said, in disgust. 'The brute snapped at my ankles. He has made a hole in my trousers. Take him out, Georgina.'

Georgina said nothing. She sat as though she had not heard.

'She won't answer if you call her Georgina,' Julian reminded him.

'She'll answer me whatever I call her,' said Mr Roland, in a low and angry voice. 'I won't have that dog in here. If you don't take him out this very minute, Georgina, I will go to your father.'

George looked at him. She knew perfectly well that if she didn't take Tim out, and Mr Roland went to her father, he would order Timothy to live in the garden kennel, and that would be dreadful. There was absolutely nothing to be done but obey. Red in the face, a huge frown almost hiding her eyes, she got up and spoke to Tim.

'Come on, Tim! I'm not surprised you bit him. I would, too, if I were a dog!'

'There is no need to be rude, Georgina,' said Mr Roland, angrily.

The others stared at George. They wondered how she

55

dared to say things like that. When she got fierce it seemed as if she didn't care for anyone at all!

'Come back as soon as you have put the dog out,' said Mr Roland.

George scowled, but came back in a few minutes. She felt caught. Her father was friendly with Mr Roland, and knew how difficult George was – if she behaved as badly as she felt she would like to, it would be Tim who would suffer, for he would certainly be banished from the house. So for Tim's sake George obeyed the tutor – but from that moment she disliked him and resented him bitterly with all her fierce little heart.

The others were sorry for George and Timothy, but they did not share the little girl's intense dislike of the new tutor. He often made them laugh. He was patient with their mistakes. He was willing to show them how to make paper darts and ships, and to do funny little tricks. Julian and Dick thought these were fun, and stored them up to try on the other boys when they went back to school.

After lessons that morning the children went out for half an hour in the frosty sunshine. George called Tim.

'Poor old boy!' she said. 'What a shame to turn you out of the room! Whatever did you snap at Mr Roland for? I think it was a very good idea, Tim – but I really don't know what made you!'

'George, you can't play about with Mr Roland,' said Julian. 'You'll only get into trouble. He's tough. He won't stand much from any of us. But I think he'll be quite a good sport if we get on the right side of him.'

'Well, get on the right side of him if you like,' said George, in rather a sneering voice. 'I'm not going to. If I don't like a person, I don't – and I don't like *him*.'

'Why? Just because he doesn't like Tim?' asked Dick.

'Mostly because of that – but because he makes me feel prickly down my back,' said George. 'I don't like his nasty mouth.'

'But you can't see it,' said Julian. 'It's covered with his moustache and beard.'

'I've seen his lips through them,' said George, obstinately. 'They're thin and cruel. You look and see. I don't like thin-lipped people. They are always spiteful and hard. And I don't like his cold eyes either. You can suck up to him all you like. *I* shan't.'

Julian refused to get angry with the stubborn little girl. He laughed at her. 'We're not going to suck up to him,' he said. 'We're just going to be sensible, that's all. You be sensible too, George, old thing.'

But once George had made up her mind about something nothing would alter her. She cheered up when she heard that they were all to go Christmas shopping on the bus that afternoon – without Mr Roland! He was going to watch an experiment that her father was going to show him.

'I will take you into the nearest town and you shall shop to your hearts' content,' said Aunt Fanny to the children.

57

'Then we will have tea in a tea-shop and catch the six o'clock bus home.'

This was fun. They caught the afternoon bus and rumbled along the deep country lanes till they got to the town. The shops looked very colourful and bright. The children had brought their money with them, and were very busy indeed, buying all kinds of things. There were so many people to get presents for!

'I suppose we'd better get something for Mr Roland, hadn't we?' said Julian.

'I'm going to,' said Anne.

'Fancy buying Mr *Roland* a present!' said George, in her scornful voice.

'Why shouldn't she, George?' asked her mother, in surprise. 'Oh dear, I hope you are going to be sensible about him, and not take a violent dislike to the poor man. I don't want him to complain to your father about you.'

'What are you going to buy for Tim, George?' asked Julian, changing the subject quickly.

'The largest bone the butcher has got,' said George. 'What are *you* going to buy him?'

'I guess if Tim had money, he would buy us each a present,' said Anne, taking hold of the thick hair round Tim's neck, and pulling it lovingly, 'He's the best dog in the world!'

George forgave Anne for saying she would buy Mr Roland a present, when the little girl said that about Tim! She cheered up again and began to plan what she would buy for everyone.

LESSONS WITH MR ROLAND

They had a fine tea, and caught the six o'clock bus back. Aunt Fanny went to see if the cook had given the two men their tea. She came out of the study beaming.

'Really, I've never seen your uncle so jolly,' she said to Julian and Dick. 'He and Mr Roland are getting on like a house on fire. He has been showing your tutor quite a lot of his experiments. It's nice for him to have someone to talk to that knows a little about these things.'

Mr Roland played games with the children that evening. Tim was in the room, and the tutor tried again to make friends with him, but the dog refused to take any notice of him.

'As sulky as his little mistress!' said the tutor, with a laughing look at George, who was watching Tim refuse to go to Mr Roland, and looking rather pleased about it. She gave the tutor a scowl and said nothing.

'Shall we ask him whether "VIA OCCULTA" really does mean "Secret Way" or not, tomorrow?' said Julian to Dick, as they undressed that night. 'I'm just longing to know if it does. What do you think of Mr Roland, Dick?'

'I don't really quite know,' said Dick. 'I like lots of things about him, but then I suddenly don't like him at all. I don't like his eyes. And George is quite right about his lips. They are so thin there's hardly anything of them at all.'

'I think he's all right,' said Julian. 'He won't stand any nonsense, that's all. I wouldn't mind showing him the whole piece of rag and asking him to make out its meaning for us.'

'I thought you said it was to be a proper secret,' said Dick.

'I know – but what's the use of a secret we don't know the meaning of ourselves?' said Julian. 'I'll tell you what we *could* do – ask him to explain the words to us, and not show him the bit of linen.

'But we can't read some of the words ourselves,' said Dick. 'So that's no use. You'd have to show him the whole thing, and tell him where we got it.'

'Well, I'll see,' said Julian, getting into bed.

LESSONS WITH MR ROLAND

The next day there were lessons again from half-past nine to half-past twelve. George appeared without Tim. She was angry at having to do this, but it was no good being defiant and refusing to come to lessons without Tim. Now that he had snapped at Mr Roland, he had definitely put himself in the wrong, and the tutor had every right to refuse to allow him to come. But George looked very sulky indeed.

In the Latin lesson Julian took the chance of asking what he wanted to know. 'Please, Mr Roland,' he said, 'could you tell me what "VIA OCCULTA" means?'

'"VIA OCCULTA"' said Mr Roland, frowning. 'Yes – it means "Secret Path" or, "Secret Road". A hidden way – something like that. Why do you want to know?'

All the children were listening eagerly. Their hearts thumped with excitement. So Julian had been right. That funny bit of rag contained directions for some hidden way, some secret path – but where to! Where did it begin, and end?

'Oh – I just wanted to know,' said Julian. 'Thank you, sir.'

He winked at the others. He was as excited as they were. If only they could make out the rest of the markings, they might be able to solve the mystery. Well – perhaps he would ask Mr Roland in a day or two. The secret must be solved somehow.

'The "Secret Way",' said Julian to himself, as he worked out a problem in geometry. 'The "Secret Way". I'll find it somehow.'

CHAPTER SEVEN

Directions for the Secret Way

FOR THE next day or two the four children did not really have much time to think about the Secret Way, because Christmas was coming near, and there was a good deal to do.

There were Christmas cards to draw and paint for their mothers and fathers and friends. There was the house to decorate. They went out with Mr Roland to find sprays of holly, and came home laden.

'You look like a Christmas card yourselves,' said Aunt Fanny, as they walked up the garden path, carrying the red-berried holly over their shoulders. Mr Roland had found a group of trees with tufts of mistletoe growing from the top branches, and they had brought some of that too. Its berries shone like pale green pearls.

'Mr Roland had to climb the tree to get this,' said Anne. 'He's a good climber – as good as a monkey.'

Everyone laughed except George. She never laughed at anything to do with the tutor. They all dumped their loads down in the porch, and went to wash. They were to decorate the house that evening.

'Is Uncle going to let his study be decorated too?' asked Anne. There were all kinds of strange instruments and glass tubes in the study now, and the children looked at them with wonder whenever they ventured into the study, which was very seldom.

'No, my study is certainly not to be messed about,' said Uncle Quentin, at once. 'I wouldn't hear of it.'

'Uncle, why do you have all these funny things in your study?' asked Anne, looking round with wide eyes.

Uncle Quentin laughed. 'I'm looking for a secret formula!' he said.

'What's that?' said Anne.

'You wouldn't understand,' said her uncle. 'All these "funny things" as you call them, help me in my experiments, and I put down in my book what they tell me – and from all I learn I work out a secret formula, that will be of great use when it is finished.'

'You want to know a secret formula, and we want to know a secret way,' said Anne, quite forgetting that she was not supposed to talk about this.

Julian was standing by the door. He frowned at Anne. Luckily Uncle Quentin was not paying any more attention to the little girl's chatter. Julian pulled her out of the room.

'Anne, the only way to stop you giving away secrets is to sew up your mouth, like Brer Rabbit wanted to do to Mister Dog!' he said.

Joanna the cook was busy baking Christmas cakes. An enormous turkey had been sent over from Kirrin Farm, and was hanging up in the larder. Timothy thought it smelt glorious, and Joanna was always shooing him out of the kitchen.

There were boxes of crackers on the shelf in the sitting-room, and mysterious parcels everywhere. It was very, very Christmassy! The children were happy and excited.

Mr Roland went out and dug up a little spruce fir tree. 'We must have a Christmas tree,' he said. 'Have you any tree-ornaments, children?'

'No,' said Julian, seeing George shake her head.

'I'll go into the town this afternoon and get some for you,' promised the tutor. 'It will be fun dressing the tree. We'll put it in the hall, and light candles on it on Christmas Day after tea. Who's coming with me to get the candles and the ornaments?'

'I am!' cried three children. But the fourth said nothing. That was George. Not even to buy tree-ornaments would the obstinate little girl go with Mr Roland. She had never had a Christmas tree before, and she was very much looking forward to it – but it was spoilt for her because Mr Roland bought the things that made it so beautiful.

Now it stood in the hall, with coloured candles in holders clipped to the branches, and bright shining ornaments hanging from top to bottom. Silver strands of frosted string hung down from the branches like icicles, and Anne had put bits of white cotton-wool here and there to look like snow. It really was a lovely sight to see.

'Beautiful!' said Uncle Quentin, as he passed through the hall, and saw Mr Roland hanging the last ornaments on the tree. 'I say – look at the fairy doll on the top! Who's that for? A good girl?'

Anne secretly hoped that Mr Roland would give her the doll. She was sure it wasn't for George – and anyway, George wouldn't accept it. It was such a pretty doll, with its gauzy frock and silvery wings.

Julian, Dick and Anne had quite accepted the tutor now as teacher and friend. In fact, everyone had, their uncle and aunt too, and even Joanna the cook. George, of course, was the only exception, and she and Timothy kept away from Mr Roland, each looking as sulky as the other whenever the tutor was in the room.

'You know, I never knew a dog could look so sulky!' said Julian, watching Timothy. 'Really, he scowls almost like George.'

'And I always feel as if George puts her tail down like Tim, when Mr Roland is in the room,' giggled Anne.

'Laugh all you like,' said George, in a low tone. 'I think you're beastly to me. I know I'm right about Mr Roland. I've got a feeling about him. And so has Tim.'

'You're silly, George,' said Dick. 'You haven't *really* got a Feeling – it's only that Mr Roland will keep calling you Georgina and putting you in your place, and that he doesn't like Tim. I dare say he can't help disliking dogs. After all, there was once a famous man called Lord Roberts who couldn't bear cats.'

'Oh well, cats are different,' said George. 'If a person doesn't like dogs, especially a dog like our Timothy, then there really *must* be something wrong with him.'

'It's no use arguing with George,' said Julian. 'Once she's made up her mind about something, she won't budge!'

George went out of the room in a huff. The others thought she was behaving rather stupidly.

'I'm surprised really,' said Anne. 'She was so jolly last term at school. Now she's gone all strange, rather like she was when we first knew her last summer.'

DIRECTIONS FOR THE SECRET WAY

'I do think Mr Roland has been decent digging up the Christmas tree and everything,' said Dick. 'I still don't like him awfully much sometimes, but I think he's a sport. What about asking him if he can read that old linen rag for us – I don't think I'd mind him sharing our secret, really.'

'I would *love* him to share it,' said Anne, who was busy doing a marvellous Christmas card for the tutor. 'He's most awfully clever. I'm sure he could tell us what the Secret Way is. Do let's ask him.'

'All right,' said Julian. 'I'll show him the piece of linen. It's Christmas Eve tonight. He will be with us in the sitting-room, because Aunt Fanny is going into the study with Uncle Quentin to wrap up presents for all of us!'

So, that evening, before Mr Roland came in to sit with them, Julian took out the little roll of linen and stroked it out flat on the table. George looked at it in surprise.

'Mr Roland will be here in a minute,' she said. 'You'd better put it away quickly.'

'We're going to ask him if he can tell us what the old Latin words mean,' said Julian.

'You're not!' cried George, in dismay. 'Ask him to share our secret! How ever can you?'

'Well, we want to know what the secret is, don't we?' said Julian. 'We don't need to tell him where we got this or anything about it except that we want to know what the markings mean. We're not exactly sharing the secret with him – only asking him to use his brains to help us.'

'Well, I never thought you'd ask *him*,' said George.

'And he'll want to know simply everything about it, you just see if he won't! He's terribly snoopy.'

'Whatever do you mean?' said Julian, in surprise. 'I don't think he's a bit snoopy.'

'I saw him yesterday snooping round the study when no one was there,' said George. 'He didn't see me outside the window with Tim. He was having a real poke round.'

'You know how interested he is in your father's work,' said Julian. 'Why shouldn't he look at it? Your father likes him too. You're just seeing what horrid things you can find to say about Mr Roland.'

'Oh shut up, you two,' said Dick. 'It's Christmas Eve. Don't let's argue or quarrel or say beastly things.'

Just at that moment the tutor came into the room. 'All as busy as bees?' he said, his mouth smiling beneath its moustache. 'Too busy to have a game of cards, I suppose?'

'Mr Roland, sir,' began Julian, 'could you help us with something? We've got an old bit of linen here with odd markings on it. The words seem to be in some sort of Latin and we can't make them out.'

George gave an angry exclamation as she saw Julian push the piece of linen over towards the tutor. She went out of the room and shut the door with a bang. Tim was with her.

'Our sweet-tempered Georgina doesn't seem to be very friendly tonight,' remarked Mr Roland, pulling the bit of linen towards him. 'Where in the world did you get this? What an odd thing!'

Nobody answered. Mr Roland studied the roll of linen, and then gave an exclamation. 'Ah – I see why you wanted to know the meaning of those Latin words the other day – the ones that meant "hidden path", you remember. They are at the top of this linen roll.'

'Yes,' said Dick. All the children leaned over towards Mr Roland, hoping he would be able to unravel a little of the mystery for them.

'We just want to know the meaning of the words, sir,' said Julian.

'This is really very interesting,' said the tutor, puzzling over the linen. 'Apparently there are directions here for finding the opening or entrance of a secret path or road.'

'That's what we thought!' cried Julian, excitedly. 'That's exactly what we thought. Oh sir, do read the directions and see what you make of them.'

'Well, these eight squares are meant to represent wooden boards or panels, I think,' said the tutor, pointing to the eight rough squares drawn on the linen. 'Wait a minute – I can hardly read some of the words. This is most fascinating. *Solum lapideum – paries ligneus –* and what's this? – *cellula –* yes, *cellula!*'

The children hung on his words. 'Wooden panels!' That must mean panels somewhere at Kirrin Farmhouse.

Mr Roland frowned down at the old printed words. Then he sent Anne to borrow a magnifying glass from her uncle. She came back with it, and the four of them looked through the glass, seeing the words three times as clearly now.

'Well,' said the tutor at last, 'as far as I can make out the directions mean this: a room facing east; eight wooden panels, with an opening somewhere to be found in that marked one; a stone floor – yes, I think that's right, a stone floor, and a cupboard. It all sounds most extraordinary and very thrilling. Where *did* you get this from?'

'We just found it,' said Julian, after a pause. 'Oh

70

Mr Roland, thanks awfully. We could never have made it out by ourselves. I suppose the entrance to the Secret Way is in a room facing east then.'

'It looks like it,' said Mr Roland, poring over the linen roll again. 'Where did you say you found this?'

'We didn't say,' said Dick. 'It's a secret really, you see.'

'I think you might tell me,' said the tutor, looking at Dick with his brilliant blue eyes. 'I can be trusted with secrets. You've no idea how many strange secrets I know.'

'Well,' said Julian, 'I don't really see why you shouldn't know where we found this, Mr Roland. We found it at Kirrin Farmhouse, in an old tobacco pouch. I suppose the Secret Way begins somewhere there! I wonder where and wherever can it lead to?'

'You found it at Kirrin Farmhouse!' exclaimed Mr Roland. 'Well, well – I must say that seems to be an interesting old place. I shall have to go over there one day.'

Julian rolled up the piece of linen and put it into his pocket. 'Well, thank you, sir,' he said. 'You've solved a bit of the mystery for us but set another puzzle! We must look for the entrance of the Secret Way after Christmas, when we can walk over to Kirrin Farmhouse.'

'I'll come with you,' said Mr Roland. 'I may be able to help a little. That is – if you don't mind me having a little share in this exciting secret.'

'Well – you've been such a help in telling us what the words mean,' said Julian, 'we'd like you to come if you want to, sir.'

'Yes, we *would*,' said Anne.

'We'll go and look for the Secret Way, then,' said Mr Roland. 'What fun we shall have, tapping round the panels, waiting for a mysterious dark entrance to appear!'

'I don't suppose George will go,' Dick murmured to Julian. 'You shouldn't have said Mr Roland could go with us, Ju. That means that old George will have to be left out of it. You know how she hates that.'

'I know,' said Julian, feeling uncomfortable. 'Don't let's worry about that now though. George may feel different after Christmas. She can't keep up this kind of behaviour for ever!'

CHAPTER EIGHT

What happened on Christmas night

IT WAS great fun on Christmas morning. The children awoke early and tumbled out of bed to look at the presents that were stacked on chairs near-by. Squeals and yells of delight came from everyone.

'Oh! a railway station! Just what I wanted! Who gave me this marvellous station?'

'A new doll – with eyes that shut! I shall call her Betsy-May. She looks just like a Betsy-May!'

'I say – what a whopping great book – all about aeroplanes. From Aunt Fanny! How decent of her!'

'Timothy! Look what Julian has given you – a collar with big brass studs all round – you *will* be grand. Go and lick him to say thank you!'

'Who's this from? I say, who gave me this? Where's the label? Oh – from Mr Roland. How decent of him! Look, Julian, a pocket-knife with three blades!'

So the cries and exclamations went on, and the four excited children and the equally-excited dog spent a glorious hour before a late Christmas breakfast, opening all kinds and shapes of parcels. The bedrooms were in a fine mess when the children had finished!

'Who gave you that book about dogs, George?' asked

Julian, seeing rather a nice dog-book lying on George's pile.

'Mr Roland,' said George, rather shortly. Julian wondered if George was going to accept it. He rather thought she wouldn't. But the little girl, defiant and obstinate as she was, had made up her mind not to spoil Christmas Day by being 'difficult'. So, when the others thanked the tutor for their things she too added her thanks, though in rather a stiff little voice.

George had not given the tutor anything, but the others had, and Mr Roland thanked them all very heartily, appearing to be very pleased indeed. He told Anne that her Christmas card was the nicest he had ever had, and she beamed at him with joy.

'Well, I must say it's nice to be here for Christmas!' said Mr Roland, when he and the others were sitting round a loaded Christmas table, at the mid-day dinner. 'Shall I carve for you, Mr Quentin? I'm good at that!'

Uncle Quentin handed him the carving knife and fork gladly. 'It's nice to have you here,' he said warmly. 'I must say you've settled in well – I'm sure we all feel as if we've known you for ages!'

It really was a jolly Christmas Day. There were no lessons, of course, and there were to be none the next day either. The children gave themselves up to the enjoyment of eating a great deal, sucking sweets, and looking forward to the lighting of the Christmas tree.

It looked beautiful when the candles were lighted. They

twinkled in the darkness of the hall, and the bright ornaments shone and glowed. Tim sat and looked at it, quite entranced.

'He likes it as much as we do,' said George. And indeed Tim had enjoyed the day just as much as any of them.

They were all tired out when they went to bed. 'I shan't be long before I'm asleep,' yawned Anne. 'Oh, George – it's been fun, hasn't it? I did like the Christmas tree.'

'Yes, it's been lovely,' said George, jumping into bed. 'Here comes Mother to say good-night. Basket, Tim, basket!'

Tim leapt into his basket by the window. He was always there when George's mother came into say good-night to the girls but as soon as she had gone downstairs, the dog took a flying leap and landed on George's bed. There he slept, his head curled round her feet.

'Don't you think Tim ought to sleep downstairs to-night?' said George's mother. 'Joanna says he ate such an enormous meal in the kitchen that she is sure he will be sick.'

'Oh *no*, Mother!' said George, at once. 'Make Tim sleep downstairs on Christmas night? Whatever would he think?'

'Oh, very well,' said her mother, with a laugh. 'I might have known it was useless to suggest it. Now to sleep quickly, Anne and George – it's late and you are all tired.'

She went into the boys' room and said good-night to them too. They were almost asleep.

Two hours later everyone else was in bed. The house was still and dark. George and Anne slept peacefully in their small beds. Timothy slept too, lying heavily on George's feet.

Suddenly George awoke with a jump. Tim was growling softly! He had raised his big shaggy head and George knew that he was listening.

'What is it, Tim?' she whispered. Anne did not wake. Tim went on growling softly. George sat up and put her hand on his collar to stop him. She knew that if he awoke her father, he would be cross.

Timothy stopped growling now that he had roused George. The girl sat and wondered what to do. It wasn't any good waking Anne. The little girl would be frightened. Why was Tim growling? He never did that at night!

'Perhaps I'd better go and see if everything is all right,' thought George. She was quite fearless, and the thought of creeping through the still, dark house did not disturb her at all. Besides she had Tim! Who could be afraid with Tim beside them!

She slipped on her dressing-gown. 'Perhaps a log has fallen out of one of the fire-places and a rug is burning,' she thought, sniffing as she went down the stairs. 'It would be just like Tim to smell it and warn us!'

With her hand on Tim's head to warn him to be quite quiet, George crept softly through the hall to the sitting-room. The fire was quite all right there, just a red glow. In the kitchen all was peace too. Tim's feet made a noise there, as his claws rattled against the linoleum.

A slight sound came from the other side of the house.

Tim growled quite loudly, and the hairs on the back of his neck rose up. George stood still. Could it possibly be burglars?

Suddenly Timothy shook himself free from her fingers and leapt across the hall, down a passage, and into the study beyond! There was the sound of an exclamation, and a noise as if someone was falling over.

'It *is* a burglar!' said George, and she ran to the study. She saw a torch shining on the floor, dropped by someone who was even now struggling with Tim.

George switched on the light, and then looked with the greatest astonishment into the study. Mr Roland was there in his dressing-gown, rolling on the floor, trying to get away from Timothy, who, although not biting him, was holding him firmly by his dressing-gown.

'Oh – it's you, George! Call your beastly dog off!' said Mr Roland, in a low and angry voice. 'Do you want to rouse all the household?'

'Why are you creeping about with a torch?' demanded George.

'I heard a noise down here, and came to see what it was,' said Mr Roland, sitting up and trying to fend off the angry dog. 'For goodness' sake, call your beast off.'

'Why didn't you put on the light?' asked George, not attempting to take Tim away. She was very much enjoying the sight of an angry and frightened Mr Roland.

'I couldn't find it,' said the tutor. 'It's on the wrong side of the door, as you see.'

This was true. The switch was an awkward one to find if you didn't know it. Mr Roland tried to push Tim away again, and the dog suddenly barked.

WHAT HAPPENED ON CHRISTMAS NIGHT

'Well – he'll wake everyone!' said the tutor, angrily. 'I didn't want to rouse the house. I thought I could find out for myself if there was anyone about – a burglar perhaps. Here comes your father!'

George's father appeared, carrying a large poker. He stood still in astonishment when he saw Mr Roland on the ground and Timothy standing over him.

'What's all this?' he exclaimed. Mr Roland tried to get up, but Tim would not let him. George's father called to him sternly.

'Tim! Come here, sir!'

Timothy glanced at George to see if his mistress agreed with her father's command. She said nothing. So Timothy took no notice of the order and merely made a snap at Mr Roland's ankles.

'That dog's mad!' said Mr Roland, from the floor. 'He's already bitten me once before, and now he's trying to do it again!'

'Tim! Will you come here, sir!' shouted George's father. 'George, that dog is really disobedient. Call him off at once.'

'Come here, Tim!' said George, in a low voice. The dog at once came to her, standing by her side with the hairs on his neck still rising up stiffly. He growled softly as if to say, 'Be careful, Mr Roland, be careful!'

The tutor got up. He was very angry indeed. He spoke to George's father.

'I heard some sort of noise and came down with my

79

torch to see what it was,' he said. 'I thought it came from your study, and knowing you kept your valuable books and instruments here, I wondered if some thief was about. I had just got down, and into the room, when that dog appeared from somewhere and got me down on the ground! George came along too, and would not call him off.'

'I can't understand your behaviour, George; I really can't,' said her father, angrily. 'I hope you are not going to behave stupidly, as you used to behave before your cousins came last summer. And what is this I hear about Tim biting Mr Roland before?'

'George had him under the table during lessons,' said Mr Roland. 'I didn't know that, and when I stretched out my legs, they touched Tim, and he bit me. I didn't tell you before, sir, because I didn't want to trouble you. Both George and the dog have tried to annoy me ever since I have been here.'

'Well, Tim must go outside and live in the kennel,' said George's father. 'I won't have him in the house. It will be a punishment for him, and a punishment for you too, George. I will not have this kind of behaviour. Mr Roland has been extremely kind to you all.'

'I won't let Tim live outside,' said George furiously. 'It's such cold weather, and it would simply break his heart.'

'Well, his heart must be broken then,' said her father. 'It will depend entirely on your behaviour from now on whether Tim is allowed in the house at all these holi-

days. I shall ask Mr Roland each day how you have
behaved. If you have a bad report, then Tim stays outside. Now you know! Go back to bed but first apologise to
Mr Roland!'

'I won't!' said George, and choked by feelings of anger
and dismay, she tore out of the room and up the stairs. The
two men stared after her.

'Let her be,' said Mr Roland. 'She's a very difficult child
– and has made up her mind not to like me, that's quite
plain. But I shall be very glad to know that that dog isn't in
the house. I'm not at all certain that Georgina wouldn't set
him on me, if she could!'

'I'm sorry about all this,' said George's father. 'I
wonder what the noise was that you heard? – a log
falling in the grate I expect. Now – what am I to do
about that tiresome dog tonight? Go and take him
outside, I suppose!'

'Leave him tonight,' said Mr Roland. 'I can hear noises
upstairs – the others are awake by now! Don't let's make
any more disturbance tonight.'

'Perhaps you are right,' said George's father, thankfully. He didn't at all want to tackle a defiant little girl and
an angry big dog in the middle of a cold night!

The two men went to bed and slept. George did not
sleep. The others had been awake when she got upstairs,
and she had told them what had happened.

'George! You really are an idiot!' said Dick. 'After all,
why shouldn't Mr Roland go down if he heard a noise!

81

You went down! Now we shan't have darling old Tim in the house this cold weather!'

Anne began to cry. She didn't like hearing that the tutor she liked so much had been knocked down by Tim, and she hated hearing that Tim was to be punished.

'Don't be a baby,' said George. '*I'm* not crying, and it's *my* dog!'

But, when everyone had settled down again in bed, and slept peacefully, George's pillow was very wet indeed. Tim crept up beside her and licked the salt tears off her cheek. He whined softly. Tim was always unhappy when his little mistress was sad.

CHAPTER NINE

A hunt for the Secret Way

THERE WERE no lessons the next day. George looked rather pale, and was very quiet. Tim was already out in the yard-kennel, and the children could hear him whining unhappily. They were all upset to hear him.

'Oh, George, I'm awfully sorry about it all,' said Dick. 'I wish you wouldn't get so fierce about things. You only get yourself into trouble – and poor old Tim.'

George was full of mixed feelings. She disliked Mr Roland so much now that she could hardly bear to look at him – and yet she did not dare to be openly rude and rebellious because she was afraid that if she was, the tutor would give her a bad report, and perhaps she would not be allowed even to *see* Timothy. It was very hard for a defiant nature like hers to force herself to behave properly.

Mr Roland took no notice of her at all. The other children tried to bring George into their talks and plans, but she remained quiet and uninterested.

'George! We're going over to Kirrin Farmhouse today,' said Dick. 'Coming? We're going to try and find the entrance to the Secret Way. It must start somewhere there.'

The children had told George what Mr Roland had said about the piece of marked linen. They had all been thrilled

83

about this, though the excitements of Christmas Day had made them forget about it for a while.

'Yes – of course I'll come,' said George, looking more cheerful. 'Timothy can come too. He wants a walk.'

But when the little girl found that Mr Roland was also going, she changed her mind at once. Not for anything would she go with the tutor! No – she would go for a walk alone with Timothy.

'But, George, think of the excitement we'll have trying to find the Secret Way,' said Julian, taking hold of her arm. George wrenched it away.

'I'm not going if Mr Roland is,' she said, obstinately, and the others knew that it was no good trying to coax her.

'I shall go alone with Tim,' said George. 'You go off together with your dear Mr Roland!'

She set out with Timothy, a lonely little figure going down the garden path. The others stared after her. This was horrid. George was being more and more left out, but what could they do about it?

'Well, children, are you ready?' asked Mr Roland. 'You start off by yourselves, will you? I'll meet you at the farmhouse later. I want to run down to the village first to get something.'

So the three children set off by themselves, wishing that George was with them. She was nowhere to be seen.

Old Mr and Mrs Sanders were pleased to see the three children, and sat them down in the big kitchen to eat ginger buns and drink hot milk.

'Well, have you come to find a few more secret things?' asked Mrs Sanders, with a smile.

'May we try?' asked Julian. 'We're looking for a room that's facing east, with a stone floor, and panelling!'

'All the rooms downstairs have stone floors,' said Mrs Sanders. 'You hunt all you like, my dears. You won't do any damage, I know. But don't go into the room upstairs with the cupboard that has a false back, will you, or the one next to it! Those are the rooms the two artists have.'

'All right,' said Julian, rather sorry that they were unable to fiddle about with the exciting cupboard again. 'Are the artists here, Mrs Sanders? I'd like to talk to them about pictures. I hope one day I'll be an artist too.'

'Dear me, is that so?' said Mrs Sanders. 'Well, well – it's always a marvel to me how people make any money at painting pictures.'

'It isn't making money that artists like, so much as the painting of the pictures,' said Julian, looking rather wise. That seemed to puzzle Mrs Sanders even more. She shook her head and laughed.

'They're peculiar folk!' she said. 'Ah well – you go along and have a hunt for whatever it is you want to find. You can't talk to the two artists today though, Master Julian – they're out.'

The children finished their buns and milk and then stood up, wondering where to begin their search. They must look for a room or rooms facing east. That would be the first thing to do.

'Which side of the house faces east, Mrs Sanders?' asked Julian. 'Do you know?'

'The kitchen faces due north,' said Mrs Sanders. 'So east will be over there,' she pointed to the left.

'Thanks,' said Julian. 'Come on, everyone!' The three children went out of the kitchen, and turned to the left.

A HUNT FOR THE SECRET WAY

There were three rooms there – a kind of scullery, not much used now, a tiny room used as a den by old Mr Sanders, and a room that had once been a drawing-room, but which was now cold and unused.

'They've all got stone floors,' said Julian.

'So we'll have to hunt through all of the three rooms,' said Anne.

'No, we won't,' said Julian. 'We shan't have to look in this scullery, for one thing!'

'Why not?' asked Anne.

'Because the walls are of stone, silly, and we want panelling,' said Julian. 'Use your brains, Anne!'

'Well, that's one room we needn't bother with, then,' said Dick. 'Look – both this little room and the drawing-room have panelling, Julian. We must search in both.'

'There must be some reason for putting *eight* squares of panelling in the directions,' said Julian, looking at the roll of linen again. 'It would be a good idea to see whether there's a place with eight squares only – you know, over a window, or something.'

It was tremendously exciting to look round the two rooms! The children began with the smaller room. It was panelled all the way round in dark oak, but there was no place where only eight panels showed. So the children went into the next room.

The panelling there was different. It did not look so old, and was not so dark. The squares were rather a different size, too. The children tried each panel, tapping and

87

pressing as they went, expecting at any moment to see one slide back as the one in the hall had done.

But they were disappointed. Nothing happened at all. They were still in the middle of trying when they heard footsteps in the hall, and voices. Somebody looked into the drawing-room. It was a man, thin and tall, wearing glasses on his long nose.

'Hallo!' he said. 'Mrs Sanders told me you were treasure-hunting, or something. How are you getting on?'

'Not very well,' said Julian, politely. He looked at the man, and saw behind him another one, younger, with rather screwed-up eyes and a big mouth. 'I suppose you are the two artists?' he asked.

'We are!' said the first man, coming into the room. 'Now, just exactly what are you looking for?'

Julian did not really want to tell him, but it was difficult not to. 'Well – we're just seeing if there's a sliding panel here,' he said at last. 'There's one in the hall, you know. It's exciting to hunt round.'

'Shall we help?' said the first artist, coming into the room. 'What are your names? Mine's Thomas, and my friend's name is Wilton.'

The children talked politely for a minute or two, not at all wanting the two men to help. If there was anything to be found, *they* wanted to find it. It would spoil everything if grown-ups solved the puzzle!

Soon everyone was tap-tap-tapping round the wooden panels. They were in the middle of this when a voice hailed them.

'Hallo! My word, we *are* all busy!'

The children turned, and saw their tutor standing in the doorway, smiling at them. The two artists looked at him.

'Is this a friend of yours?' asked Mr Thomas.

'Yes – he's our tutor, and he's very nice!' said Anne, running to Mr Roland and putting her hand in his.

89

'Perhaps you will introduce me, Anne,' said Mr Roland, smiling at the little girl.

Anne knew how to introduce people. She had often seen her mother doing it. 'This is Mr Roland,' she said to the two artists. Then she turned to Mr Roland. 'This is Mr Thomas,' she said, waving her hand towards him, 'and the other one is Mr Wilton.'

The men half-bowed to one another and nodded. 'Are you staying here?' asked Mr Roland. 'A very nice old farmhouse, isn't it?'

'It isn't time to go yet, is it?' asked Julian, hearing a clock strike.

'Yes, I'm afraid it is,' said Mr Roland. 'I'm later meeting you than I expected. We must go in about five minutes – no later. I'll just give you a hand in trying to find this mysterious secret way!'

But no matter how any one of them pressed and tapped around the panels in either of the two rooms, they could not find anything exciting. It really was most disappointing.

'Well, we really must go now,' said Mr Roland. 'Come and say good-bye to Mrs Sanders.'

They all went into the warm kitchen, where Mrs Sanders was cooking something that smelt most delicious.

'Something for our lunch, Mrs Sanders?' said Mr Wilton. 'My word, you really are a wonderful cook!'

Mrs Sanders smiled. She turned to the children. 'Well, dearies, did you find what you wanted?' she asked.

'No,' said Mr Roland, answering for them. 'We haven't been able to find the secret way, after all!'

'The secret way?' said Mrs Sanders, in surprise. 'What do you know about that now? I thought it had all been forgotten – in fact, I haven't believed in that secret way for many a year!'

'Oh, Mrs Sanders – do you know about it?' cried Julian. 'Where is it?'

'I don't know, dear – the secret of it has been lost for many a day,' said the old lady. 'I remember my old grandmother telling me something about it when I was smaller than any of you. But I wasn't interested in things like that when I was little. I was all for cows and hens and sheep.'

'Oh, Mrs Sanders – do, do try and remember something!' begged Dick. 'What *was* the secret way?'

'Well, it was supposed to be a hidden way from Kirrin Farmhouse to somewhere else,' said Mrs Sanders. 'I don't know where, I'm sure. It was used in the olden days when people wanted to hide from enemies.'

It was disappointing that Mrs Sanders knew so little. The children said good-bye and went off with their tutor, feeling that their morning had been wasted.

George was indoors when they got to Kirrin Cottage. Her cheeks were not so pale, now, and she greeted the children eagerly.

'Did you discover anything? Tell me all about it!' she said.

'There's nothing to tell,' said Dick, rather gloomily. 'We found three rooms facing east, with stone floors, but only two of them had wooden panelling, so we hunted round those, tapping and punching – but there wasn't anything to be discovered at all.'

'We saw the two artists,' said Anne. 'One was tall and thin and had a long nose with glasses on. He was called Mr Thomas. The other was younger, with little piggy eyes and an enormous mouth.'

'I met them out this morning,' said George. 'It must have been them. Mr Roland was with them, and they were all talking together. They didn't see me.'

'Oh, it couldn't have been the artists you saw,' said Anne, at once. 'Mr Roland didn't know them, I had to introduce them.'

'Well, I'm sure I heard Mr Roland call one of them Wilton,' said George, puzzled. 'He *must* have known them.'

'It couldn't have been the artists,' said Anne, again. 'They really didn't know Mr Roland. Mr Thomas asked if he was a friend of ours.'

'I'm sure I'm not mistaken,' said George, looking obstinate. 'If Mr Roland said he didn't know the two artists, he was telling lies.'

'Oh, you're always making out that he is doing something horrid!' cried Anne, indignantly. 'You just make up things about him!'

'Sh!' said Julian. 'Here he is.'

A HUNT FOR THE SECRET WAY

The door opened and the tutor came in. 'Well,' he said, 'it *was* disappointing that we couldn't find the secret way, wasn't it? Anyway, we were rather foolish to hunt about that drawing-room as we did – the panelling there wasn't really old – it must have been put in years after the other.'

'Oh – well, it's no good looking there again,' said Julian, disappointed. 'And I'm pretty sure there's nothing to be found in that other little room. We went all over it so thoroughly. Isn't it disappointing?'

'It is,' said Mr Roland. 'Well, Julian, how did you like the two artists? I was pleased to meet them – they seemed nice fellows, and I shall like to know them.'

George looked at the tutor. Could he possibly be telling untruths in such a truthful voice? The little girl was very puzzled. She felt sure it was the artists she had seen him with. But why should he pretend he didn't know them? She must be mistaken. But all the same, she felt uncomfortable about it, and made up her mind to find out the truth, if she could.

CHAPTER TEN

A shock for George and Tim

NEXT MORNING there were lessons again – and no Timothy under the table! George felt very much inclined to refuse to work, but what would be the good of that? Grown-ups were so powerful, and could dole out all kinds of punishments. She didn't care how much she was punished herself but she couldn't bear to think that Timothy might have to share in the punishments too.

So, pale and sullen, the little girl sat down at the table with the others. Anne was eager to join in the lessons – in fact she was eager to do anything to please Mr Roland, because he had given her the fairy doll from the top of the Christmas tree! Anne thought it was the prettiest doll she had ever seen.

George had scowled at the doll when Anne showed it to her. She didn't like dolls, and she certainly wasn't going to like one that Mr Roland had chosen, and given to Anne! But Anne loved it, and had made up her mind to do lessons with the others, and work as well as she could.

George did as little as she could without getting into trouble. Mr Roland took no interest in her or in her work. He praised the others, and took a lot of trouble to show Julian something he found difficult.

The children heard Tim whining outside as they worked. This troubled them very much, for Timothy was such a companion, and so dear to them all. They could not bear to think of him left out of everything, cold and miserable in the yard-kennel. When the ten minutes' break came, and Mr Roland went out of the room for a few minutes, Julian spoke to George.

'George! It's awful for us to hear poor old Tim whining out there in the cold. And I'm sure I heard him cough. Let me speak to Mr Roland about him. You must feel simply dreadful knowing that Tim is out there.'

'I thought I heard him cough, too,' said George, looking worried. 'I hope he won't get a cold. He simply doesn't understand why I have to put him there. He thinks I'm terribly unkind.'

The little girl turned her head away, afraid that tears might come into her eyes. She always boasted that she never cried – but it was very difficult to keep the tears away when she thought of Timothy out there in the cold.

Dick took her arm. 'Listen, George – you just hate Mr Roland, and I suppose you can't help it. But we can none of us bear Timothy being out there all alone – and it looks like snow today, which would be awful for him. Could you be awfully, awfully good today, and forget your dislike, so that when your father asks Mr Roland for your report, he can say you were very good – and then we'll ask Mr Roland if he wouldn't let Timmy come back into the house.'

A SHOCK FOR GEORGE AND TIM

'See?'

Timothy coughed again, out in the yard, and George's heart went cold. Suppose he got that awful illness called pneumonia – and she couldn't nurse him because he had to live in the kennel? She would die of unhappiness! She turned to Julian and Dick.

'All right,' she said. 'I do hate Mr Roland – but I love Timothy more than I hate the tutor – so for Tim's sake I'll pretend to be good and sweet and hard-working. And then you can beg him to let Timothy come back.'

'Good girl!' said Julian. 'Now here he comes – so do your best.'

To the tutor's enormous surprise, George gave him a smile when he came into the room. This was so unexpected that it puzzled him. He was even more puzzled to find that George worked harder than anyone for the rest of the morning, and she answered politely and cheerfully when he spoke to her. He gave her a word of praise.

'Well done, Georgina! I can see you've got brains.'

'Thank you,' said George, and gave him another wan smile – a very watery, poor affair, compared with the happy smiles the others had been used to – but still, it *was* a smile!

At dinner-time George looked after Mr Roland most politely – passed him the salt, offered him more bread, got up to fill his glass when it was empty! The others looked at her in admiration. George had plenty of pluck. She must be finding it very difficult to behave as if Mr Roland was a great friend, when she really disliked him so much!

Mr Roland seemed very pleased, and appeared to be quite willing to respond to George's friendliness. He made a little joke with her, and offered to lend her a book he had about a dog. George's mother was delighted to find that her difficult daughter seemed to be turning over a new leaf. Altogether things were very much happier that day.

'George, you go out of the room before your father comes in to ask Mr Roland about your behaviour tonight,' said Julian. 'Then, when the tutor gives you a splendid report, we will all ask if Timothy can come back. It will be easier if you are not there.'

'All right,' said George. She was longing for this difficult day to be over. It was very hard for her to pretend to be friendly, when she was not. She could never never do it, if it wasn't for Timothy's sake!

George disappeared out of the room just before six o'clock, when she heard her father coming. He walked into the room and nodded to Mr Roland.

'Well? Have your pupils worked well today?' he asked.

'Very well indeed,' said Mr Roland. 'Julian has really mastered something he didn't understand today. Dick has done well in Latin. Anne has written out a French exercise without a single mistake!'

'And what about George?' asked Uncle Quentin.

'I was coming to Georgina,' said Mr Roland, looking round and seeing that she was gone. 'She has worked better than anyone else today! I am really pleased with her.

She has tried hard – and she has really been polite and friendly. I feel she is trying to turn over a new leaf.'

'She's been a brick today,' said Julian, warmly. 'Uncle Quentin, she has tried awfully hard, she really has. And, you know, she's terribly unhappy.'

'Why?' asked Uncle Quentin in surprise.

'Because of Timothy,' said Julian. 'He's out in the cold, you see. And he's got a dreadful cough.'

'Oh, Uncle Quentin, please do let poor Timmy come indoors,' begged Anne.

'Yes, please do,' said Dick. 'Not only for George's sake, because she loves him so, but for us too. We hate to hear him whining outside. And George does deserve a reward, Uncle – she's been marvellous today.'

'Well,' said Uncle Quentin, looking doubtfully at the three eager faces before him, 'well – I hardly know what to say. If George is going to be sensible – and the weather gets colder – well . . .'

He looked at Mr Roland, expecting to hear him say something in favour of Timothy. But the tutor said nothing. He looked annoyed.

'What do you think, Mr Roland?' asked Uncle Quentin.

'I think you should keep to what you said and let the dog stay outside,' said the tutor. 'George is spoilt, and needs firm handling. You should really keep to your decision about the dog. There is no reason to give way about it just because she tried to be good for once!'

The three children stared at Mr Roland in surprise and

dismay. It had never entered their heads that he would not back them up!

'Oh, Mr Roland, you *are* horrid!' cried Anne. 'Oh do, do say you'll have Timothy back.'

A SHOCK FOR GEORGE AND TIM

The tutor did not look at Anne. He pursed up his mouth beneath its thick moustache and looked straight at Uncle Quentin.

'Well,' said Uncle Quentin, 'perhaps we had better see how George behaves for a whole week. After all – just one day isn't much.'

The children stared at him in disgust. They thought he was weak and unkind. Mr Roland nodded his head.

'Yes,' he said, 'a week will be a better test. If Georgina behaves well for a whole week, we'll have another word about the dog. But at present I feel it would be better to keep him outside.'

'Very well,' said Uncle Quentin, and went out of the room. He paused to look back. 'Come along into my study sometime,' he said. 'I've got a bit further with my formula. It's at a very interesting stage.'

The three children looked at one another but said nothing. How mean of the tutor to stop Uncle Quentin from having Timothy indoors again! They all felt disappointed in him. The tutor saw their faces.

'I'm sorry to disappoint you,' he said. 'But I think if you'd been bitten by Timothy once and snapped at all over when he got you on the floor, you would not be very keen on having him in either!'

He went out of the room. The children wondered what to say to George. She came in a moment later, her face eager. But when she saw the gloomy looks of the other three, she stopped short.

'Isn't Tim to come in?' she asked, quickly. 'What's happened? Tell me!'

They told her. The little girl's face grew dark and angry when she heard how the tutor had put his foot down about Timothy, even when her father had himself suggested that the dog might come indoors.

'Oh, what a beast he is!' she cried. 'How I do hate him! I'll pay him back for this. I will, I will, I will!'

She rushed out of the room. They heard her fumbling in the hall, and then the front door banged.

'She's gone out into the dark,' said Julian. 'I bet she's gone to Timmy. Poor old George. Now she'll be worse than ever!'

That night George could not sleep. She lay and tossed in her bed, listening for Timothy. She heard him cough. She heard him whine. He was cold, she knew he was. She had put plenty of fresh straw into his kennel and had turned it away from the cold north wind – but he must feel the bitter night terribly, after sleeping for so long on her bed!

Timothy gave such a hollow cough that George could bear it no longer. She must, she simply must, get up and go down to him. 'I shall bring him into the house for a little while and rub his chest with some of that stuff Mother uses for herself when she's got a cold on her chest,' thought the girl. 'Perhaps that will do him good.'

She quickly put a few clothes on and crept downstairs. The whole house was quiet. She slipped out into the yard and undid Tim's chain. He was delighted to see her and licked her hands and face lovingly.

'Come along into the warm for a little while,' whispered the little girl. 'I'll rub your poor chest with some oil I've got.'

Timmy pattered behind her into the house. She took him to the kitchen – but the fire was out and the room was cold. George went to look at the other rooms.

There was quite a nice fire still in her father's study. She and Tim went in there. She did not put on the light, because the firelight was fairly bright. She had with her the little bottle of oil from the bathroom cupboard. She put it down by the fire to warm.

Then she rubbed the dog's hairy chest with the oil, hoping it would do him good. 'Don't cough now if you can help it, Tim,' she whispered. 'If you do, someone may hear you. Lie down here by the fire, darling, and get nice and warm. Your cold will soon be better.'

Timothy lay down on the rug. He was glad to be out of his kennel and with his beloved mistress. He put his head on her knee. She stroked him and whispered to him.

The firelight glinted on the curious instruments and glass tubes that stood around on shelves in her father's study. A log shifted a little in the fire and settled lower, sending up a cloud of sparks. It was warm and peaceful there.

The little girl almost fell asleep. The big dog closed his eyes too, and rested peacefully, happy and warm. George settled down with her head on his neck.

She awoke to hear the study clock striking six! The room was cold now, and she shivered. Goodness! Six o'clock! Joanna the cook would soon be awake. She must not find Timmy and George in the study!

'Tim darling! Wake up! We must put you back into your kennel,' whispered George. 'I'm sure your cold is better, because you haven't coughed once since you've been indoors. Get up – and don't make a noise. Sh!'

A SHOCK FOR GEORGE AND TIM

Tim stood up and shook himself. He licked George's hand. He understood perfectly that he must be quite quiet. The two of them slipped out of the study, went into the hall and out of the front door.

In a minute or two Timothy was on the chain, and in his kennel, cuddled down among the straw. George wished she could cuddle there with him. She gave him a pat and slipped back indoors again.

She went up to bed, sleepy and cold. She forgot that she was partly dressed and got into bed just as she was. She was asleep in a moment!

In the morning Anne was most amazed to find that George had on vest, knickers, jeans and jersey, when she got out of bed to dress.

'Look!' she said. 'You're half-dressed! But I *saw* you undressing last night.'

'Be quiet,' said George. 'I went down and let Tim in last night. We sat in front of the study fire and I rubbed him with oil. Now don't you dare to say a word to anyone! Promise!'

Anne promised – and she faithfully kept her word. Well, well – to think that George dared to roam about like that all night – what an extraordinary girl she was!

CHAPTER ELEVEN

Stolen papers

'GEORGE, DON'T behave fiercely today, will you?' said Julian, after breakfast. 'It won't do you or Timothy any good at all.'

'Do you suppose I'm going to behave well when I know perfectly well that Mr Roland will never let me have Tim indoors all these holidays?' said George.

'Well – they said a week,' said Dick. 'Can't you try for a week?'

'No. At the end of a week Mr Roland will say I must try for another week,' said George. 'He's got a real dislike for poor Tim. And for me too. I'm not surprised at that, because I know that when I try to be horrid, I really *am* horrid. But he shouldn't hate poor Timmy.'

'Oh George – you'll spoil the whole hols if you are silly, and keep getting into trouble,' said Anne.

'Well, I'll spoil them then,' said George, the sulky look coming back on her face.

'I don't see why you have to spoil them for us, as well as for yourself,' said Julian.

'They don't need to be spoilt for you,' said George. 'You can have all the fun you want – go for walks with your dear Mr Roland, play games with him in the evening, and laugh and talk as much as you like. You don't need to take any notice of me.'

'You are a funny girl, George,' said Julian, with a sigh. 'We like you, and we hate you to be unhappy – so how can we have fun if we know you're miserable – and Timmy too?'

'Don't worry about *me*,' said George, in rather a choky voice. 'I'm going out to Tim. I'm not coming in to lessons today.'

'George! But you must!' said Dick and Julian together.

'There's no "must" about it,' said George. 'I'm just not coming. I won't work with Mr Roland till he says I can have Timothy indoors again.'

'But you know you can't do things like that – you'll be told off or something,' said Dick.

'I shall run away if things get too bad,' said George, in a shaky voice. 'I shall run away with Tim.'

She went out of the room and shut the door with a bang. The others stared after her. What could you do with a person like George? Anyone could rule her with kindness and understanding – but as soon as she came up against anyone who disliked her, or whom she disliked, she shied away like a frightened horse – and kicked like a frightened horse, too!

Mr Roland came into the sitting-room, his books in his hand. He smiled at the three children.

'Well? All ready for me, I see. Where's Georgina?'

Nobody answered. Nobody was going to give George away!

'Don't you know where she is?' asked Mr Roland in surprise. He looked at Julian.

'No, sir,' said Julian, truthfully. 'I've no idea where she is.'

'Well – perhaps she will come along in a few minutes,' said Mr Roland. 'Gone to feed that dog of hers, I suppose.'

They all settled down to work. The time went on and George did not come in. Mr Roland glanced at the clock and made an impatient clicking noise with his tongue.

'Really, it's too bad of Georgina to be so late! Anne, go and see if you can find her.'

Anne went. She looked in the bedroom. There was no George there. She looked in the kitchen. Joanna was there, making cakes. She gave the little girl a hot piece to eat. She had no idea where George was.

Anne couldn't find her anywhere. She went back and told Mr Roland. He looked angry.

'I shall have to report this to her father,' he said. 'I have never had to deal with such a rebellious child before. She seems to do everything she possibly can to get herself into trouble.'

Lessons went on. Break came, and still George did not appear. Julian slipped out and saw that the yard-kennel was empty. So George had gone out with Timmy! What a row she would get into when she got back!

No sooner had the children settled down after break to do the rest of the morning's lessons, than a big disturbance came.

Uncle Quentin burst in looking upset and worried.

'Have any of you children been into my study?' he asked.

'No, Uncle Quentin,' they all answered.

'You said we weren't to,' said Julian.

'Why? Has something been broken?' asked Mr Roland.

'Yes – the test-tubes I set yesterday for an experiment have been broken – and what is worse, three most important pages of my book have gone,' said Uncle Quentin. 'I can write them out again, but only after a great deal of work. I can't understand it. Are you *sure*, children, that none of you has been meddling with things in my study?'

'Quite sure,' they answered. Anne went very red – she suddenly remembered what George had told her. George said she had taken Timmy into Uncle Quentin's study last night, and rubbed his chest with oil! But George couldn't possibly have broken the test-tubes, and taken pages from her father's book!

Mr Roland noticed that Anne had gone red.

'Do you know anything about this, Anne?' he asked.

'No, Mr Roland,' said Anne, blushing even redder, and looking very uncomfortable indeed.

'Where's George?' suddenly said Uncle Quentin.

The children said nothing, and it was Mr Roland who answered:

'We don't know. She didn't come to lessons this morning.'

'Didn't come to lessons! Why not?' demanded Uncle Quentin, beginning to frown.

'She didn't say,' said Mr Roland dryly. 'I imagine she was upset because we were firm about Timothy last night, and this is her way of being defiant.'

'The naughty girl!' said George's father, angrily. 'I don't know what's come over her lately. Fanny! Come here! Did you know that George hasn't been in to her lessons today?'

STOLEN PAPERS

Aunt Fanny came into the room. She looked very worried. She had a little bottle in her hand. The children wondered what it was.

'Didn't come in to lessons!' repeated Aunt Fanny. 'How extraordinary! Then where is she?'

'I don't think you need to worry about her,' said Mr Roland, smoothly. 'She's probably gone off with Timothy in a fit of temper. What is very much more important, is the fact that your work appears to have been spoilt by someone. I only hope it is not George, who has been spiteful enough to get back at you for not allowing her to have her dog in the house.'

'Of *course* it wasn't George!' cried Dick, angry that anyone should even think such a thing of his cousin.

'George would never, never do a thing like that,' said Julian.

'No, she never would,' said Anne, sticking up valiantly for her cousin, although a horrid doubt was in her mind. After all – George *had* been in the study last night!

'Quentin, I am sure George would not even *think* of such a thing,' said Aunt Fanny. 'You will find those pages somewhere – and as for the test-tubes that were broken, well, perhaps the wind blew the curtain against them, or something! When did you last see those pages?'

'Last night,' said Uncle Quentin. 'I read them over again, and checked my figures to make sure they were right. Those pages contain the very heart of my formula! If they got into anyone else's hands, they could use my secret. This is a terrible thing for me! I *must* know what has happened to them.'

'I found this in your study, Quentin,' said Aunt Fanny, and she held up the little bottle she carried. 'Did you put it there? It was in the fender.'

Uncle Quentin took the bottle and stared at it. 'Camphorated oil!' he said. 'Of course I didn't take it there. Why should I?'

'Well – who took it there, then?' asked Aunt Fanny, puzzled. 'None of the children has a cold – and anyway, they wouldn't think of the camphorated oil, and take it into the study to use! It's most extraordinary!'

Everyone was astonished. Why should a bottle of camphorated oil appear in the study fender?

Only one person could think why. It suddenly came into Anne's mind in a flash. George had said she had taken Timmy into the study, and rubbed him with oil! He had had a cough, that was why. And she had left the oil in the study. Oh dear, oh dear – now what would happen? What a pity George had forgotten the oil!

Anne went very red again as she looked at the oil. Mr Roland, whose eyes seemed very sharp this morning, looked hard at the little girl.

'Anne! You know something about that oil!' he said suddenly. 'What do you know? Did you put it there?'

'No,' said Anne. 'I haven't been into the study. I said I hadn't.'

STOLEN PAPERS

'Do you know anything about the oil?' said Mr Roland, again. 'You *do* know something.'

Everyone stared at Anne. She stared back. This was simply dreadful. She could not give George away. She could *not*. George was in quite enough trouble as it was, without getting into any more. She pursed up her little mouth and did not answer.

'Anne!' said Mr Roland, sternly. 'Answer when you are spoken to.'

Anne said nothing. The two boys stared at her, guessing that it was something to do with George. They did not know that George had brought Timothy in the night before.

'Anne, dear,' said her aunt, gently. 'Tell us if you know something. It might help us to find out what has happened to Uncle Quentin's papers. It is very, very, important.'

Still Anne said nothing. Her eyes filled with tears. Julian squeezed her arm.

'Don't bother Anne,' he said to the grown-ups. 'If she thinks she can't tell you, she's got some very good reason.'

'I think she's shielding George,' said Mr Roland. 'Is that it, Anne?'

Anne burst into tears. Julian put his arms round his little sister, and spoke again to the three grown-ups.

'*Don't* bother Anne! Can't you see she's upset?'

'We'll let George speak for herself, when she thinks she will come in,' said Mr Roland. 'I'm sure she knows how that bottle got there – and if she put it there herself she must have been into the study – and she's the only person that *has* been there.'

The boys could not think for one moment that George would do such a thing as spoil her father's work. Anne feared it, and it upset her. She sobbed in Julian's arms.

'When George comes in, send her to me in my study,' said Uncle Quentin, irritably. 'How can a man work when these upsets go on? I was always against having children in the house.'

He stamped out, tall, cross and frowning. The children were glad to see him go. Mr Roland shut the books on the table with a snap.

'We can't do any more lessons this morning,' he said. 'Put on your things and go out for a walk till dinner-time.'

'Yes, do,' said Aunt Fanny, looking white and worried. 'That's a good idea.'

Mr Roland and their aunt went out of the room. 'I don't know if Mr Roland thinks he's coming out with us,' said Julian, in a low voice, 'but we've got to get out first and give him the slip. We've got to find George and warn her what's up.'

'Right!' said Dick. 'Dry your eyes, Anne darling. Hurry and get your things. We'll slip out of the garden door before Mr Roland comes down. I bet George has gone for her favourite walk over the cliffs. We'll meet her!' The three children threw on their outdoor things and crept out of the garden door quietly. They raced down the garden path, and out of the gate before Mr Roland even knew they were gone! They made their way to the cliffs, and looked to see if George was coming.

'There she is – and Timothy, too!' cried Julian, pointing. 'George! George! Quick, we've got something to tell you!'

CHAPTER TWELVE

George in trouble

'WHAT'S THE matter?' asked George, as the three children tore up to her. 'Has something happened?'

'Yes, George. Someone has taken three most important pages out of your father's book!' panted Julian. 'And broken the test-tubes he was making an experiment with. Mr Roland thinks you might have had something to do with it!'

'The beast!' said George, her blue eyes deepening with anger. 'As if I'd do a thing like that! Why should he think it's me, anyway?'

'Well, George, you left that bottle of oil in the study fender,' said Anne. 'I haven't told anyone at all what you told me happened last night – but somehow Mr Roland guessed you had something to do with the bottle of oil.'

'Didn't you tell the boys how I got Timmy indoors?' asked George. 'Well, there's nothing much to tell, Julian. I just heard poor old Tim coughing in the night, and I half-dressed, went down, and took him into the study, where there was a fire. Mother keeps a bottle of oil that she used to rub her chest with when she has a cough – so I thought it might do Timmy's cold good, too. I got the oil and rubbed him well – and we both fell asleep by the

116

fire till six o'clock. I was sleepy when I woke up, and forgot the oil. That's all.'

'And you didn't take any pages from the book Uncle Quentin is writing, and you didn't break anything in the study, did you?' said Anne.

'Of course not, silly,' said George, indignantly. 'How can you ask me a thing like that? You must be mad.'

George never told a lie, and the others always believed her, whatever she said. They stared at her, and she stared back.

'I wonder who could have taken those pages then?' said Julian. 'Maybe your father will come across them, after all. I expect he put them into some safe place and then forgot all about them. And the test-tubes might easily have over-balanced and broken themselves. Some of them look very shaky to me.'

'I suppose I shall get into trouble now for taking Tim into the study,' said George.

'And for not coming into lessons this morning,' said Dick. 'You really are an idiot, George. I never knew anyone like you for walking right into trouble.'

'Hadn't you better stay out a bit longer, till everyone has calmed down a bit?' said Anne.

'No,' said George at once. 'If I'm going to get into a row, I'll get into it now! I'm not afraid!'

She marched over the cliff path, with Timmy running round her as usual. The others followed. It wasn't nice to think that George was going to get into such trouble.

They came to the house and went up the path.

Mr Roland saw them from the window and opened the door. He glanced at George.

'Your father wants to see you in the study,' said the tutor. Then he turned to the others, looking annoyed.

'Why did you go out without me? I meant to go with you.'

'Oh did you, sir? I'm sorry,' said Julian, politely, not looking at Mr Roland. 'We just went out on the cliff a little way.'

'Georgina, did you go into the study last night?' asked Mr Roland, watching George as she took off her hat and coat.

'I'll answer my father's questions, not yours,' said George.

'What you want is a good telling off,' said Mr Roland. 'And if I were your father I'd give it to you!'

'You're not my father,' answered George. She went to the study door and opened it. There was no one there.

'Father isn't here,' said George.

'He'll be there in a minute,' said Mr Roland. 'Go in and wait. And you others, go up and wash for lunch.'

The other three children felt almost as if they were deserting George as they went up the stairs. They could hear Timmy whining from the yard outside. He knew his little mistress was in trouble, and he wanted to be with her.

George sat down on a chair, and gazed at the fire, remembering how she had sat on the rug there with Tim last night, rubbing his hairy chest. How silly of her to have forgotten the bottle of oil!

Her father came into the room, frowning and angry. He looked sternly at George.

'Were you in here last night, George?' he asked.

'Yes, I was,' answered George at once.

'What were you doing in here?' asked her father. 'You know you children are forbidden to come into my study.'

'I know,' said George. 'But you see Timmy had a dreadful cough, and I couldn't bear it. So I crept down about one o'clock and let him in. This was the only room that was really warm, so I sat here and rubbed his chest with the oil Mother uses when she has a cold.'

'Rubbed the dog's chest with camphorated oil!' exclaimed her father, in amazement. 'What a mad thing to do! As if it would do him any good.'

'It didn't seem mad to me,' said George. 'It seemed sensible. And Timmy's cough is much better today. I'm sorry for coming into the study. I didn't touch a thing, of course.'

'George, something very serious has happened,' said her father, looking gravely at her. 'Some of my test-tubes with which I was doing an important experiment, have been broken – and, worse than that, three pages of my book have gone. Tell me on your honour that you know nothing of these things.'

'I know nothing of them,' said George, looking her father straight in the eyes. Her own eyes shone very blue and clear as she gazed at him. He felt quite certain that George was speaking the truth. She could know nothing of the damage done. Then where were those pages?

'George, last night when I went to bed at eleven o'clock,

everything was in order,' he said. 'I read over those three important pages and checked them once more myself. This morning they are gone.'

'Then they must have been taken between eleven o'clock and one o'clock,' said George. 'I was here from that time until six.'

'But *who* could have taken them?' said her father. 'The window was fastened, as far as I know. And nobody knows that those three pages were so important but myself. It is most extraordinary.'

'Mr Roland probably knew,' said George, slowly.

'Don't be absurd,' said her father. 'Even if he did realise they were important, he would not have taken them. He's a very decent fellow. And that reminds me – why were you not at lessons this morning, George?'

'I'm not going to do lessons any more with Mr Roland,' said George. 'I simply hate him!'

'George! I will *not* have you talking like this!' said her father. 'Do you want me to say you are to lose Tim altogether?'

'No,' said George, feeling shaky about the knees. 'And I don't think it's fair to keep trying to force me to do things by threatening me with losing Timothy. If – if – you do a thing like that – I'll – I'll run away or something!'

There were no tears in George's eyes. She sat bolt upright on her chair, gazing defiantly at her father. How difficult she was! Her father sighed, and remembered that he too in his own childhood had been called 'difficult'. Perhaps George took after him. She could be so good and sweet – and here she was being perfectly impossible!

Her father did not know what to do with George. He thought he had better have a word with his wife. He got up and went to the door.

'Stay here. I shall be back in a moment. I want to speak to your mother about you.'

'Don't speak to Mr Roland about me, will you?' said George, who felt quite certain that the tutor would urge terrible punishments for her and Timmy. 'Oh, Father, if only Timothy had been in the house last night, sleeping in my room as usual, he would have heard whoever it was that stole your secret – and he would have barked and roused the house!'

Her father said nothing, but he knew that what George had said was true. Timmy wouldn't have let anyone get into the study. It was funny he hadn't barked in the night, if anyone from outside had climbed in at the study window. Still, it was the other side of the house. Maybe he had heard nothing.

The door closed. George sat still on her chair, gazing up at the mantelpiece, where a clock ticked away the time. She felt very miserable. Everything was going wrong, every single thing!

As she gazed at the panelled overmantel, she counted the wooden panels. There were eight. Now, where had she heard of eight panels before? Of course – in that Secret Way. There were eight panels marked on the roll of linen.

What a pity there had not been eight panels in a wooden overmantel at Kirrin Farmhouse!

George glanced out of the window, and wondered if it faced east. She looked to see where the sun was – it was not shining into the room – but it did in the early morning – so it must face east. Fancy – here was a room facing east and with eight wooden panels. She wondered if it had a stone floor.

The floor was covered with a large thick carpet. George got up and went to the wall. She pulled up the edge of the carpet there – and saw that the floor underneath was made of large flat stones. The study had a stone floor too!

She sat down again and gazed at the wooden panels, trying to remember which one in the roll of linen was marked with a cross. But of course it couldn't be a room in Kirrin Cottage – it must be in Kirrin Farmhouse where the Secret Way began.

But just suppose it *was* Kirrin Cottage! Certainly the directions had been found in Kirrin Farmhouse – but that was not to say that the Secret Way had to begin there, even though Mrs Sanders seemed to think it did.

George was feeling excited. 'I must tap round about those eight panels and try to find the one that is marked on the linen roll,' she thought. 'It may slide back or something, and I shall suddenly see the entrance opening!'

She got up to try her luck – but at that moment the door opened again and her father came in looking very grave.

'I have been talking to your mother,' he said. 'She agrees

123

with me that you have been very disobedient, rude and defiant. We can't let behaviour like that pass, George. You will have to be punished.'

George looked anxiously at her father. If only her punishment had nothing to do with Timothy! But, of course, it had.

'You will go to bed for the rest of the day, and you will not see Timothy for three days,' said her father. 'I will get Julian to feed him and take him for a walk. If you persist in being defiant, Timothy will have to go away altogether. I am afraid, strange as it may seem, that that dog has a bad influence on you.'

'He hasn't, he hasn't!' cried George. 'Oh, he'll be so miserable if I don't see him for three whole days.'

'There's nothing more to be said,' said her father. 'Go straight upstairs to bed, and think over all I have said to you, George. I am very disappointed in your behaviour these holidays. I really did think the influence of your three cousins had made you into a normal, sensible girl. Now you are worse then you have ever been.'

He held open the door and George walked out, holding her head high. She heard the others having their dinner in the dining-room. She went straight upstairs and undressed. She got into bed and thought miserably of not seeing Tim for three days. She couldn't bear it! Nobody could possibly know how much she loved Timothy!

Joanna came up with a tray of dinner. 'Well, it's a pity

to see you in bed,' she said cheerfully. 'Now you be a sensible girl and behave properly and you'll soon be downstairs again.'

George picked at her dinner. She did not feel at all hungry. She lay back on the bed, thinking of Tim and thinking of the eight panels over the mantelpiece. Could they possibly be the ones shown in the Secret Way directions? She gazed out of the window and thought hard.

'Golly, it's snowing!' she said suddenly, sitting up. 'I thought it would when I saw that leaden sky this morning. It's snowing hard! It will be quite thick by tonight – inches deep. Oh, poor Timothy. I hope Julian will see that his kennel is kept clear of the drifting snow.'

George had plenty of time to think as she lay in bed. Joanna came and took the tray away. No one else came to see her. George felt sure the other children had been forbidden to go up and speak to her. She felt lonely and left-out.

She thought of her father's lost pages. Could Mr Roland have taken them? After all, he was very interested in her father's work and seemed to understand it. The thief must have been someone who knew which were the important pages. Surely Timothy would have barked if a thief had come in from outside, even though the study was the other side of the house. Timmy had such sharp ears.

'I think it must have been someone *in*side the house,' said George. 'None of us children, that's certain – and not Mother or Joanna. So that only leaves Mr Roland. And I did find him in the study that other night when Timmy woke me by growling.'

She sat up in bed suddenly. 'I believe Mr Roland had Timothy put out of the house because he wanted to go poking round the study again and was afraid Tim would bark!' she thought. 'He was so very insistent that Tim should go out of doors – even when everyone else begged for me to have him indoors. I believe – I really do believe – that Mr Roland is the thief!'

The little girl felt very excited. Could it be that the tutor had stolen the pages – and broken those important test-tubes? How she wished that the others would come and see her, so that she could talk things over with them!

CHAPTER THIRTEEN

Julian has a surprise

THE THREE children downstairs felt very sorry for George. Uncle Quentin had forbidden them to go up and see her.

'A little time for thinking out things all alone may do George good,' he said.

'Poor old George,' said Julian. 'It's too bad, isn't it? I say – look at the snow!'

The snow was falling very thickly. Julian went to the window and looked out. 'I shall have to go and see that Timmy's kennel is all right,' he said. 'We don't want the poor old fellow to be snowed up! I expect he is wondering what the snow is!'

Timothy was certainly very puzzled to see everywhere covered with soft white stuff. He sat in his kennel and stared out at the falling flakes, his big brown eyes following them as they fell to the ground. He was puzzled and unhappy. Why was he living out here by himself in the cold? Why didn't George come to him? Didn't she love him any more? The big dog was very miserable, as miserable as George!

He was delighted to see Julian. He jumped up at the boy and licked his face. 'Good old Tim!' said Julian. 'Are you all right? Let me sweep away some of this snow and swing your kennel round a bit so that no flakes fly inside. There – that's better. No, we're not going for a walk, old thing – not now.'

The boy patted the dog and fussed him a bit, then went indoors. The others met him at the sitting-room door.

'Julian! Mr Roland is going out for a walk by himself. Aunt Fanny is lying down, and Uncle Quentin is in his study. Can't we go up and see George?'

'We were forbidden to,' said Julian, doubtfully.

'I know,' said Dick. 'But I don't mind risking it for the sake of making George feel a bit happier. It must be so awful for her, lying up there all alone, knowing she can't see Tim for days.'

'Well – let me go up, as I'm the eldest,' said Julian. 'You two stay down here in the sitting-room and talk. Then Uncle Quentin will think we're all here. I'll slip up and see George for a few minutes.'

'All right,' said Dick. 'Give her our love and tell her we'll look after Timmy.'

Julian slipped quietly up the stairs. He opened George's door and crept inside. He shut the door, and saw George sitting up in bed, looking at him in delight.

'Sh!' said Julian. 'I'm not supposed to be here!'

'Oh Julian!' said George joyfully. 'How good of you to come. I was so lonely. Come this side of the bed. Then if anyone comes in suddenly, you can duck down and hide.'

Julian went to the other side of the bed. George began to pour out to him all she had been thinking of.

'I believe Mr Roland is the thief, I really do!' she said. 'I'm not saying that because I hate him, Julian, really I'm not. After all, I *did* find him snooping round the study one afternoon – and again in the middle of the night. He may have got to hear of my father's work, and come to see if he could steal it. It was just lucky for him that we needed a

130

tutor. I'm sure he stole those pages, and I'm sure he wanted Timmy out of the house so that he could do his stealing without Tim hearing him and growling.'

'Oh, George – I don't think so,' said Julian, who really could not approve of the idea of the tutor doing such a thing. 'It all sounds so far-fetched and unbelievable.'

'Lots of unbelievable things happen,' said George. 'Lots. And this is one of them.'

'Well, if Mr Roland *did* steal the pages, they must be somewhere in the house,' said Julian. 'He hasn't been out all day. They must be somewhere in his bedroom.'

'Of course!' said George, looking thrilled. 'I wish he'd go out! Then I'd search his room.'

'George, you can't do things like that,' said Julian, quite shocked.

'You simply don't know what things I can do, if I really want to,' said George, setting her mouth in a firm line. 'Oh – what's that noise?'

There was the bang of a door. Julian went cautiously to the window and peeped out. The snow had stopped falling for a time, and Mr Roland had taken the chance of going out.

'It's Mr Roland,' said Julian.

'Oooh – I could search his room now, if you'll keep watch at the window and tell me if he comes back,' said George, throwing back the bedclothes at once.

'No, George, don't,' said Julian. 'Honestly and truly, it's awful to search somebody's room like that. And

131

anyway, I dare say he's got the pages with him. He may even be going to give them to somebody!'

'I never thought of that,' said George, and she looked at Julian with wide eyes. 'Isn't that sickening? Of course he may be doing that. He knows those two artists at Kirrin Farmhouse, for instance. They may be in the plot too.'

'Oh, George, don't be silly,' said Julian. 'You are making a mountain out of a mole-hill, talking of plots and goodness knows what! Anyone would think we were in the middle of a big adventure.'

'Well, I think we are,' said George, unexpectedly, and she looked rather solemn. 'I sort of feel it all round me – a Big Adventure!'

Julian stared at his cousin thoughtfully. Could there possibly be anything in what she said?

'Julian, will you do something for me?' said George.

'Of course,' said the boy, at once.

'Go out and follow Mr Roland,' said George. 'Don't let him see you. There's a white macintosh in the hall cupboard. Put it on and you won't be easily seen against the snow. Follow him and see if he meets anyone and gives them anything that looks like the pages of my father's book – you know those big pages he writes on. They're very large.'

'All right,' said Julian. 'But if I do, promise you won't go and search his room. You can't do things like that, George.'

'I can,' said George. 'But I won't, if you'll just follow

JULIAN HAS A SURPRISE

Mr Roland for me. I'm sure he's going to hand over what he has stolen to others who are in the plot! And I bet those others will be the two artists at Kirrin Farmhouse that he pretended not to know!'

'You'll find you're quite wrong,' said Julian, going to the door. 'I'm sure I shan't be able to follow Mr Roland, anyway – he's been gone five minutes now!'

'Yes, you will, silly – he'll have left his footmarks in the snow,' said George. 'And oh, Julian – I quite forgot to tell you something else exciting. Oh dear, there isn't time now. I'll tell you when you come back, if you can come up again then. It's about the Secret Way.'

'Really?' said Julian, in delight. It had been a great disappointment to him that all their hunting and searching had come to nothing. 'All right – I'll try and creep up again later. If I don't come, you'll know I can't, and you must wait till bed-time.'

He disappeared and shut the door quietly. He slipped downstairs, popped his head into the sitting-room and whispered to the others that he was going out after the tutor.

'Tell you why, later,' he said. He put the white macintosh around him and went out into the garden. Snow was beginning to fall again, but not yet heavily enough to hide Mr Roland's deep footsteps. He had had big wellington boots on, and the footmarks showed up well in the six-inch-deep snow.

The boy followed them quickly. The countryside was

133

very wintry-looking now. The sky was low and leaden, and he could see there was much more snow to come. He hurried on after Mr Roland, though he could not see a sign of the tutor.

Down the lane and over the path that led across the common went the double row of footmarks. Julian stumbled on, his eyes glued to the foot-prints. Suddenly he heard the sound of voices and stopped. A big gorse bush lay to the right and the voices came from there. The boy went nearer to the bush. He heard his tutor's voice, talking in low tones. He could not hear a word that was said.

'Whoever can he be talking to?' he wondered. He crept up closer to the bush. There was a hollow space inside. Julian thought he could creep right into it, though it would be very prickly, and peer out of the other side. Carefully the boy crept into the prickly hollow, where the branches were bare and brown.

He parted the prickly branches slowly and cautiously – and to his amazement he saw Mr Roland talking to the two artists from Kirrin Farmhouse – Mr Thomas and Mr Wilton! So George was right. The tutor had met them – and, as Julian watched, Mr Roland handed over to Mr Thomas a doubled-up sheaf of papers.

'They look just like pages from Uncle Quentin's book,' said Julian to himself. 'I say – this is mighty strange. It does begin to look like a plot – with Mr Roland at the centre of it!'

JULIAN HAS A SURPRISE

Mr Thomas put the papers into the pocket of his overcoat. The men muttered a few more words, which even Julian's sharp ears could not catch, and then parted.

The artists went off towards Kirrin Farmhouse, and Mr Roland took the path back over the common. Julian crouched down in the hollow of the prickly gorse bush, hoping the tutor would not turn and see him. Luckily he didn't. He went straight on and disappeared into the snow, which was now falling thickly. It was also beginning to get dark and Julian, unable to see the path very clearly, hurried after Mr Roland, half-afraid of being lost in the snowstorm.

Mr Roland was not anxious to be out longer than he could help, either. He almost ran back to Kirrin Cottage. He came to the gate at last, and Julian watched him go into the house. He gave him a little time to take off his things and then, giving Timothy a pat as he went by, he went to the garden door. He took off his macintosh, changed his boots, and slipped into the sitting-room before Mr Roland had come down from his bedroom.

'What's happened?' asked Dick and Anne, seeing that Julian was in a great state of excitement. But he could not tell them, for just then Joanna came in to lay the tea.

Much to Julian's disappointment, he could not say a word to the others all that evening, because one or other of the grown-ups was always in the room. Neither could he go up to see George. He could hardly wait to tell his news, but it was no good, he had to.

'Is it still snowing, Aunt Fanny?' asked Anne.

Her aunt went to the front door and looked out. The snow was piled high against the step!

136

JULIAN HAS A SURPRISE

'Yes,' she said, when she came back. 'It is snowing fast and thickly. If it goes on like this we shall be completely snowed up, as we were two winters ago! We couldn't get out of the house for five days then. The milkman couldn't get to us, nor the baker. Fortunately we had plenty of tinned milk, and I can bake my own bread. You poor children, you will not be able to go out tomorrow – the snow will be too thick!'

'Will Kirrin Farmhouse be snowed up too?' asked Mr Roland.

'Oh yes – worse than we shall be,' said Aunt Fanny. 'But they won't mind! They have plenty of food there. They will be prisoners just as much, and more, as we shall.'

Julian wondered why Mr Roland had asked that question. Was he afraid that his friends would not be able to send those pages away by the post – or take them anywhere by bus or car? The boy felt certain this was the reason for the question. How he longed to be able to talk over everything with the others.

'I'm tired!' he said, about eight o'clock. 'Let's go to bed.'

Dick and Anne stared at him in astonishment. Usually, as he was the eldest, he went to bed last of all. Tonight he was actually *asking* to go! Julian winked quickly at them, and they backed him up at once.

Dick yawned widely, and so did Anne. Their aunt put down the sewing she was doing. 'You *do* sound tired!' she said. 'I think you'd better all go to bed.'

'Could I just go out and see if Timmy is all right?' asked

137

Julian. His aunt nodded. The boy put on his rubber boots and coat, and slipped out through the garden door into the yard. It was very deep in snow, too. Tim's kennel was half-hidden in it. The dog had trampled a space in front of the kennel door, and stood there, looking for Julian as he came out of the house.

'Poor old boy, out here in the snow all alone,' said Julian. He patted the dog, and Timmy whined. He was asking to go back with the boy.

'I wish I *could* take you back with me,' said Julian. 'Never mind, Timothy. I'll come and see you tomorrow.'

He went indoors again. The children said good-night to their aunt and Mr Roland, and went upstairs.

'Undress quickly, put on dressing-gowns and meet in George's room,' whispered Julian to the others. 'Don't make a sound or we'll have Aunt Fanny up. Quick now!'

In less than three minutes the children were undressed, and were sitting on George's bed. She was very pleased to see them. Anne slipped into bed with her, because her feet were cold.

'Julian! Did you follow Mr Roland all right?' whispered George.

'Why did he follow him?' asked Dick, who had been dying to know.

Julian told them everything as quickly as he could – all that George suspected – and how he had followed the tutor – and what he had seen. When George heard how Julian had watched him giving a sheaf of papers to the two artists, her eyes gleamed angrily.

'The thief! They must have been the lost pages! And to think my father has been so friendly to him. Oh, what can we do? Those men will get the papers away as quickly as they can, and the secret Father has been working on for ages will be used by someone else – for some other country, probably!'

'They can't get the papers away,' said Julian. 'You've no idea how thick the snow is now, George. We shall be prisoners here for a few days, if this snow goes on, and so will the people in Kirrin Farmhouse. If they want to hide the papers, they will have to hide them in the farmhouse! If only we could get over there and hunt round!'

'Well, we can't,' said Dick. 'That's quite certain. We'd be up to our necks in snow!'

The four children looked gloomily at one another. Dick and Anne could hardly believe that the jolly Mr Roland was a thief – a spy perhaps, trying to steal a valuable secret from a friendly scientist. And they couldn't stop it.

'We'd better tell your father,' said Julian at last.

'No,' said Anne. 'He wouldn't believe it, would he, George?'

'He'd laugh at us and go straight and tell Mr Roland,' said George. 'That would warn him, and he mustn't be warned. He mustn't know that we guess anything.'

'Sh! Aunt Fanny's coming!' whispered Dick, suddenly. The boys slipped out of the room and into bed. Anne hopped across to her own little bed. All was peace and quiet when the children's aunt came into the bedroom.

She said good-night and tucked them up. As soon as she had gone down, the four children met together again in George's room.

'George, tell me now what you were going to say about the Secret Way,' said Julian.

'Oh, yes,' said George. 'Well, there may be nothing in my idea at all – but in the study downstairs, there are eight wooden panels over the mantelpiece – and the floor is of stone – and the room faces east! A bit odd, isn't it? Just what the directions said.'

'Is there a cupboard there too?' asked Julian.

'No. But there is everything else,' said George. 'And I was just wondering if by any chance the entrance to the Secret Way is in this house, not in the farmhouse. After all, they both belonged to my family at one time, you know. The people living in the farmhouse years ago must have known all about this cottage.'

'Golly, George – suppose the entrance *was* here!' said Dick. 'Wouldn't it be simply marvellous! Let's go straight down and look!'

'Don't be silly,' said Julian. 'Go down to the study when Uncle Quentin is there? I'd rather meet twenty lions than face Uncle! Especially after what has happened!'

'Well, we simply MUST find out if George's idea is right; we simply must,' said Dick, forgetting to whisper.

'Shut up, idiot!' said Julian, giving him a punch. 'Do you want to bring the whole household up here?'

JULIAN HAS A SURPRISE

'Sorry!' said Dick. 'But, oh golly, this *is* exciting. It's an Adventure again.'

'Just what I said,' said George, eagerly. 'Listen, shall we wait till midnight, and then creep down to the study when everyone is asleep, and try our luck? There may be nothing in my idea at all – but we'll have to find out now. I don't believe I could go to sleep till I've tried each one of those panels over the mantelpiece to see if something happens.'

'Well, I know I can't sleep a wink either,' said Dick. 'Listen – is that someone coming up? We'd better go. Come on, Julian! We'll meet in George's room at midnight – and creep down and try out George's idea!'

The two boys went off to their own room. Neither of them could sleep a wink. Nor could George. She lay awake, and went over and over in her mind all that had happened those holidays. 'It's like a jigsaw puzzle,' she thought. 'I couldn't understand a lot of things at first – but now they are fitting together, and making a picture.'

Anne was fast asleep. She had to be awakened at midnight. 'Come on!' whispered Julian, shaking her. 'Don't you want to share in this adventure?'

CHAPTER FOURTEEN

The Secret Way at last!

THE FOUR children crept downstairs through the dark and silent night. Nobody made a sound at all. They made their way to the study. George softly closed the door and then switched on the light.

The children stared at the eight panels over the mantelpiece. Yes – there were exactly eight, four in one row and four in the row above. Julian spread the linen roll out on the table, and the children pored over it.

'The cross is in the middle of the second panel in the top row,' said Julian in a low voice. 'I'll try pressing it. Watch, all of you!'

He went to the fireplace. The others followed him, their hearts beating fast with excitement. Julian stood on tiptoe and began to press hard in the middle of the second panel. Nothing happened.

'Press harder! Tap it!' said Dick.

'I daren't make too much noise,' said Julian, feeling all over the panel to see if there was any roughness that might tell of a hidden spring or lever.

Suddenly, under his hands, the panel slid silently back, just as the one had done at Kirrin Farmhouse in the hall! The children stared at the space behind, thrilled.

THE SECRET WAY AT LAST!

'It's not big enough to get into,' said George. 'It can't be the entrance to the Secret Way.'

Julian got out his torch from his dressing-gown pocket. He put it inside the opening, and gave a low exclamation.

'There's a sort of handle here – with strong wire or something attached to it. I'll pull it and see what happens.'

He pulled – but he was not strong enough to move the handle that seemed to be embedded in the wall. Dick put his hand in and the two boys then pulled together.

'It's moving – it's giving way a bit,' panted Julian. 'Go on, Dick, pull hard!'

The handle suddenly came away from the wall, and behind it came thick wire, rusty and old. At the same time a curious grating noise came from below the hearthrug in front of the fireplace, and Anne almost fell.

'Julian! Something is moving under the rug!' she said, frightened. 'I felt it. Under the rug, quick!'

The handle could not be pulled out any farther. The boys let go, and looked down. To the right of the fireplace, under the rug, something had moved. There was no doubt of that. The rug sagged down instead of being flat and straight.

'A stone has moved in the floor,' said Julian, his voice shaking with excitement. 'This handle works a lever, which is attached to this wire. Quick – pull up the rug, and roll back the carpet.'

With trembling hands the children pulled back the rug and the carpet – and then stood staring at a very strange thing. A big flat stone laid in the floor had slipped downwards, pulled in some manner by the wire attached to the handle hidden behind the panel! There was now a black space where the stone had been.

'Look at that!' said George, in a thrilling whisper.

'The entrance to the Secret Way!'

THE SECRET WAY AT LAST!

'It's here after all!' said Julian.

'Let's go down!' said Dick.

'No!' said Anne, shivering at the thought of disappearing into the black hole.

Julian flashed his torch into the black space. The stone had slid down and then sideways. Below was a space just big enough to take a man, bending down.

'I expect there's a passage or something leading from here, under the house, and out,' said Julian. 'Golly, I wonder where it leads to?'

'We simply must find out,' said George.

'Not now,' said Dick. 'It's dark and cold. I don't fancy going along the Secret Way at midnight. I don't mind just hopping down to see what it's like – but don't let's go along any passage till tomorrow.'

'Uncle Quentin will be working here tomorrow,' said Julian.

'He said he was going to sweep the snow away from the front door in the morning,' said George. 'We could slip into the study then. It's Saturday. There may be no lessons.'

'All right,' said Julian, who badly wanted to explore everything then and there. 'But for goodness' sake let's have a look and see if there *is* a passage down there. At present all we can see is a hole!'

'I'll help you down,' said Dick. So he gave his brother a hand and the boy dropped lightly down into the black space, holding his torch. He gave a loud exclamation.

It's the entrance to the Secret Way all right! There's a passage leading from here under the house – awfully low and narrow – but I can see it's a passage. I do wonder where it leads to!'

THE SECRET WAY AT LAST!

He shivered. It was cold and damp down there. 'Give me a hand up, Dick,' he said. He was soon out of the hole and in the warm study again.

The children looked at one another in the greatest joy and excitement. This *was* an Adventure, a real Adventure. It was a pity they couldn't go on with it now.

'We'll try and take Timmy with us tomorrow,' said George. 'Oh, I say – how are we going to shut the entrance up?'

'We can't leave the rug and carpet sagging over that hole,' said Dick. 'Nor can we leave the panel open.'

'We'll see if we can get the stone back,' said Julian. He stood on tiptoe and felt about inside the panel. His hand closed on a kind of knob, set deep in a stone. He pulled it, and at once the handle slid back, pulled by the wire. At the same time the sunk stone glided to the surface of the floor again, making a slight grating sound as it did so.

'Well, it's like magic!' said Dick. 'It really is! Fancy the mechanism working so smoothly after years of not being used. This is the most exciting thing I've ever seen!'

There was a noise in the bedroom above. The children stood still and listened.

'It's Mr Roland!' whispered Dick. 'He's heard us. Quick, slip upstairs before he comes down.'

They switched out the light and opened the study door softly. Up the stairs they fled, as quietly as church mice, their hearts thumping so loudly that it seemed as if everyone in the house must hear the beat.

147

The girls got safely to their rooms and Dick was able to slip into his. But Julian was seen by Mr Roland as he came out of his room with a torch.

'What are you doing, Julian!' asked the tutor, in surprise. 'Did you hear a noise downstairs? I thought I did.'

'Yes – I heard quite a lot of noise downstairs,' said Julian, truthfully. 'But perhaps it's snow falling off the roof, landing with a plop in the ground, sir. Do you think that's it?'

'I don't know,' said the tutor doubtfully. 'We'll go down and see.'

They went down, but of course there was nothing to be seen. Julian was glad they had been able to shut the panel and make the stone come back to its proper place again. Mr Roland was the very last person he wanted to tell his secret to.

They went upstairs and Julian slipped into his room. 'Is it all right?' whispered Dick.

'Yes,' said Julian. 'Don't let's talk. Mr Roland's awake, and I don't want him to suspect anything.'

The boys fell asleep. When they awoke in the morning, there was a completely white world outside. Snow covered everything and covered it deeply. Timothy's kennel could not be seen! But there were footmarks round about it.

George gave a squeal when she saw how deep the snow was. 'Poor Timothy! I'm going to get him in. I don't care what anyone says! I won't let him be buried in the snow!'

She dressed and tore downstairs. She went out to the

kennel, floundering knee deep in the snow. But there was no Timmy there!

A loud bark from the kitchen made her jump. Joanna the cook knocked on the kitchen window. 'It's all right! I couldn't bear the dog out there in the snow, so I fetched him in, poor thing. Your mother says I can have him in the kitchen but you're not to come and see him.'

'Oh, good – Timmy's in the warmth!' said George, gladly. She yelled to Joanna, 'Thanks awfully! You *are* kind!'

She went indoors and told the others. They were very glad. 'And *I've* got a bit of news for *you*,' said Dick. 'Mr Roland is in bed with a bad cold, so there are to be no lessons today. Cheers!'

'Golly, that *is* good news,' said George, cheering up tremendously. 'Timmy in the warm kitchen and Mr Roland kept in bed. I do feel pleased!'

'We shall be able to explore the Secret Way safely now,' said Julian. 'Aunt Fanny is going to do something in the kitchen this morning with Joanna, and Uncle is going to tackle the snow. I vote we say we'll do lessons by ourselves in the sitting-room, and then, when everything is safe, we'll explore the Secret Way!'

'But why must we do lessons?' asked George in dismay.

'Because if we don't, silly, we'll have to help your father dig away the snow,' said Julian.

So, to his uncle's surprise, Julian suggested that the four children should do lessons by themselves in the sitting-room. 'Well, I thought you'd like to come and help dig away the snow,' said Uncle Quentin. 'But perhaps you had better get on with your work.'

The children sat themselves down as good as gold in the sitting-room, their books before them. They heard Mr Roland coughing in his room. They heard their aunt go into the kitchen and talk to Joanna. They heard Timmy scratching at the kitchen door – then paws pattering down the passage – then a big, inquiring nose came round the door, and there was old Timmy, looking anxiously for his beloved mistress!

'Timmy!' squealed George, and ran to him. She flung her arms round his neck and hugged him.

'You act as if you hadn't seen Tim for a year,' said Julian.

'It seems like a year,' said George. 'I say, there's my father digging away like mad. Can't we go to the study now? We ought to be safe for a good while.'

They left the sitting-room and went to the study. Julian was soon pulling the handle behind the secret panel. George had already turned back the rug and the carpet. The stone slid downward and sideways. The Secret Way was open!

'Come on!' said Julian. 'Hurry!'

He jumped down into the hole. Dick followed, then Anne, then George. Julian pushed them all into the narrow, low passage. Then he looked up. Perhaps he had better pull the carpet and rug over the hole, in case anyone came into the room and looked around. It took him a few seconds to do it. Then he bent down and joined the others in the passage. They were going to explore the Secret Way at last!

CHAPTER FIFTEEN

An exciting journey and hunt

TIMOTHY HAD leapt down into the hole when George had jumped. He now ran ahead of the children, puzzled at their wanting to explore such a cold, dark place. Both Julian and Dick had torches, which threw broad beams before them.

There was not much to be seen. The Secret Way under the old house was narrow and low, so that the children were forced to go in single file, and to stoop almost double. It was a great relief to them when the passage became a little wider, and the room a little higher. It was very tiring to stoop all the time.

'Have you any idea where the Secret Way is going?' Dick asked Julian. 'I mean – is it going towards the sea, or away from it?'

'Oh, not towards the sea!' said Julian, who had a very good sense of direction. 'As far as I can make out the passage is going towards the common. Look at the walls – they are rather sandy in places, and we know the common has sandy soil. I hope we shan't find that the passage has fallen in anywhere.'

They went on and on. The Secret Way was very straight, though occasionally it would round a rocky part in a curve.

AN EXCITING JOURNEY AND HUNT

'Isn't it dark and cold?' said Anne, shivering. 'I wish I had put on a coat. How many miles have we come, Julian?'

'Not even one, silly!' said Julian. 'Hallo – look here – the passage has fallen in a bit there!'

Two bright torches shone in front of them and the children saw that the sandy roof had fallen in. Julian kicked at the pile of sandy soil with his foot.

'It's all right,' he said. 'We can force our way through easily. It isn't much of a fall, and it's mostly sand. I'll do a bit of kicking!'

After some trampling and kicking, the roof-fall no longer blocked the way. There was now enough room for the children to climb over it, bending their heads low to avoid knocking them against the top of the passage. Julian shone his torch forward, and saw that the way was clear.

'The Secret Way is very wide just here!' he said suddenly, and flashed his torch around to show the others.

'It's been widened out to make a sort of little room,' said George. 'Look, there's a kind of bench at the back, made out of the rock. I believe it's a resting-place.'

George was right. It was very tiring to creep along the narrow passage for so long. The little wide place with its rocky bench made a very good resting-place. The four tired children, cold but excited, huddled together on the funny seat and took a welcome rest. Timmy put his head on George's knee. He was delighted to be with her again.

'Well, come on,' said Julian, after a few minutes. 'I'm

getting awfully cold. I do wonder where this passage comes out!'

'Julian – do you think it could come out at Kirrin Farmhouse?' asked George, suddenly. 'You know what Mrs Sanders said – that there was a secret passage leading from the farmhouse somewhere. Well, this may be the one – and it leads to Kirrin Cottage!'

'George, I believe you're right!' said Julian. 'Yes – the two houses belonged to your family years ago! And in the old days there were often secret passages joining houses, so it's quite plain this secret way joins them up together! Why didn't I think of that before?'

'I say!' squealed Anne, in a high, excited voice, 'I say! I've thought of something too!'

'What?' asked everyone.

'Well – if those two artists have got Uncle's papers, we may be able to get them away before the men can send them off by post, or take them away themselves!' squeaked Anne, so thrilled with her idea that she could hardly get the words out quickly enough. 'They're prisoners at the farmhouse because of the snow, just as we were at the cottage.'

'*Anne*! You're right!' said Julian.

'Clever girl!' said Dick.

'I *say* – if we *could* get those papers again – how wonderful it would be!' said George. Timmy joined in the general excitement, and jumped up and down in joy. Something had pleased the children, so he was pleased too!

AN EXCITING JOURNEY AND HUNT

'Come on!' said Julian, taking Anne's hand. 'This is thrilling. If George is right, and this Secret Way comes out at Kirrin Farmhouse somewhere, we'll somehow hunt through those men's rooms and find the papers.'

'You said that searching people's rooms was a shocking thing to do,' said George.

'Well, I didn't know then all I know now,' said Julian. 'We're doing this for your father – and maybe for our country too, if his secret formula is valuable. We've got to set our wits to work now, to outwit dangerous enemies.'

'Do you really think they are dangerous?' asked Anne rather afraid.

'Yes, I should think so,' said Julian. 'But you needn't worry, Anne, you've got me and Dick and Tim to protect you.'

'I can protect her too,' said George, indignantly.

'You're fiercer than any boy I know!' said Dick.

'Come on,' said Julian, impatiently. 'I'm longing to get to the end of this passage.'

They all went on again, Anne following behind Julian, and Dick behind George. Timmy ran up and down the line, squeezing by them whenever he wanted to. He thought it was a very peculiar way to spend a morning!

Julian stopped suddenly, after they had gone a good way. 'What's up?' asked Dick, from the back. 'Not another roof-fall, I hope!'

'No – but I think we've come to the end of the passage!' said Julian, thrilled. The others crowded as close to him as they could. The passage certainly had come to an end. There was a rocky wall in front of them, and set firmly in it were iron staples intended for footholds. These went up the wall and when Julian turned his torch upwards, the children saw that there was a square opening in the roof of the passage.

'We have to climb up this rocky wall now,' said Julian, 'go through that dark hole there, keep on climbing – and goodness knows where we come out! I'll go first. You wait here, everyone, and I'll come back and tell you what I've seen.'

The boy put his torch between his teeth, and then pulled himself up by the iron staples set in the wall. He set his feet on them, and then climbed up through the square dark hole, feeling for the staples as he went.

He went up for a good way. It was almost like going up a chimney shaft, he thought. It was cold and smelt musty.

Suddenly he came to a ledge, and he stepped on to it. He took his torch from his teeth and flashed it around him.

There was a stone wall behind him, at the side of him and stone above him. The black hole up which he had come, yawned by his feet. Julian shone his torch in front of him, and a shock of surprise went through him.

There was no stone wall in front of him, but a big wooden door, made of black oak. A handle was set about waist-high; Julian turned it with trembling fingers. What was he going to see?

The door opened outwards, over the ledge, and it was

difficult to get round it without falling back into the hole. Julian managed to open it wide, squeezed round it without losing his footing, and stepped beyond it, expecting to find himself in a room.

But his hand felt more wood in front of him! He shone his torch round, and found that he was up against what looked like yet another door. Under his searching fingers it suddenly moved sideways, and slid silently away!

And then Julian knew where he was! 'I'm in the cupboard at Kirrin Farmhouse – the one that has a false back!' he thought. 'The Secret Way comes up behind it! How clever! Little did we know when we played about in this cupboard that not only did it have a sliding back, but that it was the entrance to the Secret Way, hidden behind it!'

The cupboard was now full of clothes belonging to the artists. Julian stood and listened. There was no sound of anyone in the room. Should he just take a quick look round, and see if those lost papers were anywhere about?

Then he remembered the other four, waiting patiently below in the cold. He had better go and tell them what had happened. They could all come and help in the search.

He stepped into the space behind the sliding back. The sliding door slipped across again, and Julian was left standing on the narrow ledge, with the old oak door wide open to one side of him. He did not bother to shut it. He felt about his feet, and found the iron staples in the hole below him. Down he went, clinging with his hands and feet, his torch in his teeth again.

'Julian! What a time you've been! Quick, tell us all about it!' cried George.

'It's most terribly thrilling,' said Julian. 'Absolutely super! Where do you suppose all this leads to? Into the cupboard at Kirrin Farmhouse – the one that's got a false back!'

'Golly!' said Dick.

'I *say*!' said George.

'Did you go into the room?' cried Anne.

'I climbed as far as I could and came to a big oak door,' said Julian. 'It has a handle this side, so I swung it wide open. Then I saw another wooden door in front of me – at least, I thought it was a door, I didn't know it was just the false back of that cupboard. It was quite easy to slide back and I stepped through, and found myself among a whole lot of clothes hanging in the cupboard! Then I hurried back to tell you.'

'Julian! We can hunt for those papers now,' said George, eagerly. 'Was there anyone in the room?'

'I couldn't *hear* anyone,' said Julian. 'Now what I propose is this – we'll all go up, and have a hunt round those two rooms. The men have the room next to the cupboard one too.'

'Oh good!' said Dick, thrilled at the thought of such an adventure. 'Let's go now. You go first, Ju. Then Anne, then George and then me.'

'What about Tim?' asked George.

'He can't climb, silly,' said Julian. 'He's a simply

marvellous dog, but he certainly can't climb, George.
We'll have to leave him down here.'

'He won't like that,' said George.

'Well, we can't carry him up,' said Dick. 'You won't mind staying here for a bit, will you, Tim, old fellow?'

Tim wagged his tail. But, as he saw the four children mysteriously disappearing up the wall, he put his big tail down at once. What! Going without him? How could they?

He jumped up at the wall, and fell back. He jumped again and whined. George called down in a low voice.

'Be quiet, Tim dear! We shan't be long.'

Tim stopped whining. He lay down at the bottom of the wall, his ears well-cocked. This adventure was becoming more and more peculiar!

Soon the children were on the narrow ledge. The old oak door was still wide open. Julian shone his torch and the others saw the false back of the cupboard. Julian put his hands on it and it slid silently sideways. Then the torch shone on coats and dressing-gowns!

The children stood quite still, listening. There was no sound from the room. 'I'll open the cupboard door and peep into the room,' whispered Julian. 'Don't make a sound!'

The boy pushed between the clothes and felt for the outer cupboard door with his hand. He found it, and pushed it slightly. It opened a little and a shaft of daylight came into the cupboard. He peeped cautiously into the room.

There was no one there at all. That was good. 'Come on!' he whispered to the others. 'The room's empty!'

AN EXCITING JOURNEY AND HUNT

One by one the children crept out of the clothes cupboard and into the room. There was a big bed there, a wash-stand, chest of drawers, small table and two chairs. Nothing else. It would be easy to search the whole room.

'Look, Julian, there's a door between the two rooms,' said George, suddenly. 'Two of us can go and hunt there and two here – and we can lock the doors that lead on to the landing, so that no one can come in and catch us!'

'Good idea!' said Julian, who was afraid that at any moment someone might come in and catch them in their search. 'Anne and I will go into the next room, and you and Dick can search this one. Lock the door that opens on to the landing, Dick, and I'll lock the one in the other room. We'll leave the connecting-door open, so that we can whisper to one another.'

Quietly the boy and girl slipped through the connecting-door into the second room, which was very like the first. That was empty too. Julian went over to the door that led to the landing, and turned the key in the lock. He heard Dick doing the same to the door in the other room. He heaved a big sigh. Now he felt safe!

'Anne, turn up the rugs and see if any papers are hidden there,' he said. 'Then look under the chair-cushions and strip the bed to see if anything is hidden under the mattress.'

Anne set to work, and Julian began to hunt too. He started on the chest of drawers, which he thought would be a very likely place to hide things in. The children's hands were shaking, as they felt here and there for the lost papers. It was so terribly exciting.

They wondered where the two men were. Down in the warm kitchen, perhaps. It was cold up here in the bed-rooms, and they would not want to be away from the warmth. They could not go out because the snow was piled in great drifts round Kirrin Farmhouse!

Dick and George were searching hard in the other room. They looked in every drawer. They stripped the bed. They turned up rugs and carpet. They even put their hands up the big chimney-place!

'Julian? Have you found anything?' asked Dick in a low voice, appearing at the door between the two rooms.

'Not a thing,' said Julian, rather gloomily. 'They've hidden the papers well! I only hope they haven't got them on them – in their pockets, or something!'

Dick stared at him in dismay. He hadn't thought of that. 'That *would* be sickening!' he said.

'You go back and hunt *everywhere* – simply *everywhere!*' ordered Julian. 'Punch the pillows to see if they've stuck them under the pillow-case!'

Dick disappeared. Rather a lot of noise came from his room. It sounded as if he were doing a good deal of punching!

Anne and Julian went on hunting too. There was simply nowhere that they did not look. They even turned the pictures round to see if the papers had been stuck behind

162

one of them. But there was nothing to be found. It was bitterly disappointing.

'We can't go without finding them,' said Julian, in desperation. 'It was such a bit of luck to get here like this, down the Secret Way – right into the bedrooms! We simply *must* find those papers!'

'I say,' said Dick, appearing again, 'I can hear voices! Listen!'

All four children listened. Yes – there were men's voices – just outside the bedroom doors!

CHAPTER SIXTEEN

The children are discovered

'WHAT SHALL we do?' whispered George. They had all tiptoed to the first room, and were standing together, listening.

'We'd better go down the Secret Way again,' said Julian.

'Oh no, we . . .' began George, when she heard the handle of the door being turned. Whoever was trying to get in, could not open the door. There was an angry exclamation, and then the children heard Mr Wilton's voice. 'My door seems to have stuck. Do you mind If I come through your bedroom and see what's the matter with this handle?'

'Come right along!' came the voice of Mr Thomas. There was the sound of footsteps going to the outer door of the second room. Then there was the noise of a handle being turned and shaken.

'What's this!' said Mr Wilton, in exasperation. 'This won't open, either. Can the doors be locked?'

'It looks like it!' said Mr Thomas.

There was a pause. Then the children distinctly heard a few words uttered in a low voice. 'Are the papers safe? Is anyone after them?'

'They're in your room, aren't they?' said Mr Thomas.

THE CHILDREN ARE DISCOVERED

There was another pause. The children looked at one another. So the men *had* got the papers – and what was more, they *were* in the room! The very room the children stood in! They looked round it eagerly, racking their brains to think of some place they had not yet explored.

'Quick! Hunt round again while we've time,' whispered Julian. 'Don't make a noise.'

On tiptoe the children began a thorough hunt once more. How they searched! They even opened the pages of the books on the table, thinking that the papers might have been slipped in there. But they could find nothing.

'Hi, Mrs Sanders!' came Mr Wilton's voice. 'Have you by any chance locked these two doors? We can't get in!'

'Dear me!' said the voice of Mrs Sanders from the stairs. 'I'll come along and see. I certainly haven't locked any doors!'

Once again the handles were turned, but the doors would not open. The men began to get very impatient.

'Do you suppose anyone is in our rooms?' Mr Wilton asked Mrs Sanders.

She laughed.

'Well now, who would be in your rooms? There's only me and Mr Sanders in the house, and you know as well as I do that no one can come in from outside, for we're quite snowed up. I don't understand it – the locks of the doors must have slipped.'

Anne was lifting up the wash-stand jug to look underneath, at that moment. It was heavier than she thought, and she had to let it down again suddenly. It struck the marble wash-stand with a crash, and water slopped out all over the place!

Everyone outside the door heard the noise. Mr Wilton banged on the door and rattled the handle.

THE CHILDREN ARE DISCOVERED

'Who's there? Let us in or you'll be sorry! What are you doing in there?'

'Idiot, Anne!' said Dick. 'Now they'll break the door down!'

That was exactly what the two men intended to do! Afraid that someone was mysteriously in their room, trying to find the stolen papers, they went quite mad, and began to put their shoulders to the door, and heave hard. The door shook and creaked.

'Now you be careful what you're doing!' cried the indignant voice of Mrs Sanders. The men took no notice. There came a crash as they both tried out their double strength on the door.

'Quick! We must go!' said Julian. 'We mustn't let the men know how we got here, or we shan't be able to come and hunt another time. Anne, George, Dick – get back to the cupboard quickly!'

The children raced for the clothes cupboard. 'I'll go first and help you down,' said Julian. He got out on to the narrow ledge and found the iron foot-holds with his feet. Down he went, torch held between his teeth as usual.

'Anne, come next,' he called. 'And Dick, you come third, and give a hand to Anne if she wants it. George is a good climber – she can easily get down herself.'

Anne was slow at climbing down. She was terribly excited, rather frightened, and so afraid of falling that she hardly dared to feel for each iron staple as she went down.

'Buck up, Anne!' whispered Dick, above her. 'The men have almost got the door down!'

There were tremendous sounds coming from the bedroom door. At any moment now it might break down, and the men would come racing in. Dick was thankful when he could begin to climb down the wall! Once they were all out, George could shut the big oak door, and they would be safe.

George was hidden among the clothes in the cupboard, waiting her turn to climb down. As she stood there, trying in vain to go over any likely hiding-place in her mind, her hands felt something rustly in the pocket of a coat she was standing against. It was a macintosh coat, with big pockets. The little girl's heart gave a leap.

Suppose the papers had been left in the pocket of the coat the man had on when he took them from Mr Roland? That was the only place the children had not searched – the pockets of the coats in the cupboard! With trembling fingers the girl felt in the pocket where the rustling was.

She drew out a sheaf of papers. It was dark in the cupboard, and she could not see if they were the ones she was hunting for, or not – but how she hoped they were! She stuffed them up the front of her jersey, for she had no big pocket, and whispered to Dick:

'Can I come now?'

CRASH! The door fell in with a terrific noise, and the two men leapt into the room. They looked round. It was empty! But there was the water spilt on the wash-stand

168

and on the floor. Someone must be there somewhere!

'Look in the cupboard!' said Mr Thomas.

George crept out of the clothes cupboard and on to the narrow ledge, beyond the place where the false back of the cupboard used to be. It was still hidden sideways in the wall. The girl climbed down the hole a few steps and then shut the oak door which was now above her head. She had not enough strength to close it completely, but she hoped that now she was safe!

The men went to the cupboard and felt about in the clothes for anyone who might possibly be hiding there. Mr Wilton gave a loud cry.

'The papers are gone! They were in this pocket! There's not a sign of them. Quick, we must find the thief and get them back!'

The men did not notice that the cupboard seemed to go farther back than usual. They stepped away from it now that they were sure no one was there, and began to hunt round the room.

By now all the children except George were at the bottom of the hole, standing in the Secret Way, waiting impatiently for George to come down. Poor George was in such a hurry to get down that she caught her clothing on one of the staples, and had to stand in a very dangerous position trying to disentangle it.

'Come on, George, for goodness' sake!' said Julian.

Timothy jumped up at the wall. He could feel the fear and excitement of the waiting children, and it upset him.

He wanted George. Why didn't she come? Why was she up that dark hole? Tim was unhappy about her.

He threw back his head and gave such a loud and mournful howl that all the children jumped violently.

'Shut up, Tim!' said Julian.

Tim howled again, and the weird sound echoed round and about in a strange manner. Anne was terrified, and she began to cry. Timothy howled again and again. Once he began to howl it was difficult to stop him.

The men in the bedroom above heard the extraordinary noise, and stopped in amazement.

'Whatever's that?' said one.

'Sounds like a dog howling in the depths of the earth,' said the other.

'Funny!' said Mr Wilton. 'It seems to be coming from the direction of that cupboard.'

He went over to it and opened the door. Tim chose that moment to give a specially mournful howl, and Mr Wilton jumped. He got into the cupboard and felt about at the back. The oak door there gave way beneath his hand, and he felt it open.

'There's something weird here,' called Mr Wilton. 'Bring my torch off the table.'

Tim howled again and the noise made Mr Wilton shiver! Tim had a peculiarly horrible howl. It came echoing up the hole, and burst out into the cupboard.

Mr Thomas got the torch. The men shone it at the back of the cupboard, and gave an exclamation.

THE CHILDREN ARE DISCOVERED

'Look at that! There's a door here! Where does it lead to?'

Mrs Sanders, who had been watching everything in surprise and indignation, angry that her door should have been broken down, came up to the cupboard.

'My!' she said. 'I knew there was a false back to that cupboard – but I didn't know there was another door behind it too! That must be the entrance to the Secret Way that people used in the old days.'

'Where does it lead to?' rapped out Mr Wilton.

'Goodness knows!' said Mrs Sanders. 'I never took much interest in such things.'

'Come on, we must go down,' said Mr Wilton, shining his torch into the square black hole, and seeing the iron foot-holds set in the stone. 'This is where the thief went. He can't have got far. We'll go after him. We've got to get those papers back!'

It was not long before the two men had swung themselves over the narrow ledge and down into the hole, feeling with their feet for the iron staples. Down they went and down, wondering where they were coming to. There was no sound below them. Clearly the thief had got away!

George had got down at last. Tim almost knocked her over in his joy. She put her hand on his head. 'You old silly!' she said. 'I believe you've given our secret away! Quick, Ju – we must go, because those men will be after us in a minute. They could easily hear Tim's howling!'

Julian took Anne's hand. 'Come along, Anne,' he said. 'You must run as fast as you can. Hurry now! Dick, keep with George.'

The four of them hurried down the dark, narrow passage. What a long way they had to go home! If only the passage wasn't such a long one! The children's hearts were beating painfully as they made haste, stumbling as they went.

Julian shone his light steadily in front of him, and Dick shone his at the back. Half-leading, half-dragging Anne, Julian hurried along. Behind them they heard a shout.

'Look! There's a light ahead! That's the thief! Come on, we'll soon get him!'

CHAPTER SEVENTEEN

Good old Tim!

'HURRY, ANNE. Do hurry!' shouted Dick, who was just behind.

Poor Anne was finding it very difficult to get along quickly. Pulled by Julian and pushed by Dick, she almost fell two or three times. Her breath came in loud pants, and she felt as if she would burst.

'Let me have a rest!' she panted. But there was no time for that, with the two men hurrying after them! They came to the piece that was widened out, where the rocky bench was, and Anne looked longingly at it. But the boys hurried her on.

Suddenly the little girl caught her foot on a stone and fell heavily, almost dragging Julian down with her. She tried to get up, and began to cry.

'I've hurt my foot! I've twisted it! Oh, Julian, it hurts me to walk.'

'Well, you've just *got* to come along, darling,' said Julian, sorry for his little sister, but knowing that they would all be caught if he was not firm. 'Hurry as much as you can.'

But now it was impossible for Anne to go fast. She cried with pain as her foot hurt her, and hobbled along so slowly that Dick almost fell over her. Dick cast a look behind him and saw the light of the men's torches coming nearer and nearer. Whatever were they to do?

'I'll stay here with Tim and keep them off,' said George, suddenly. 'Here, take these papers, Dick! I believe they're the ones we want, but I'm not sure till we get a good light to see them. I found them in a pocket of one of the coats in the cupboard.'

'Golly!' said Dick, surprised. He took the sheaf of papers and stuffed them up his jersey, just as George had stuffed them up hers. They were too big to go into his trouser pockets. 'I'll stay with you, George, and let the other two go on ahead.'

'No. I want the papers taken to safety, in case they are my father's,' said George. 'Go on, Dick! I'll be all right here with Tim. I shall stay here just where the passage curves round this rocky bit. I'll make Tim bark like mad.'

'Suppose the men have got revolvers?' said Dick doubtfully. 'They might shoot him.'

'I bet they haven't,' said George. '*Do* go, Dick! The men are almost here. There's the light of their torch.'

Dick sped after the stumbling Anne. He told Julian what George had suggested. 'Good for George!' said Julian. 'She really is marvellous – not afraid of anything! She will keep the men off till I get poor old Anne back.'

George was crouching behind the rocky bit, her hand on Tim's collar, waiting. 'Now, Tim!' she whispered. 'Bark your loudest. Now!'

Timothy had been growling up till now, but at George's command he opened his big mouth and barked. How he barked! He had a simply enormous voice, and the barks went echoing all down the dark and narrow passage. The hurrying men, who were near the rocky piece of the passage, stopped.

'If you come round this bend, I'll set my dog on you!' cried George.

'It's a child shouting,' said one man to another. 'Only a child! Come on!'

Timothy barked again, and pulled at his collar. He was longing to get at the men. The light of their torch shone round the bend. George let Tim go, and the big dog sprang joyfully round the curve to meet his enemies.

They suddenly saw him by the light of their torch, and he was a very terrifying sight! To begin with, he was a big dog, and now that he was angry all the hairs on the back of his neck had risen up, making him look even more enormous. His teeth were bared and glinted in the torch-light.

The men did not like the look of him at all. 'If you move one step nearer I'll tell my dog to fly at you!' shouted George. 'Wait, Tim, wait! Stand there till I give the word.'

The dog stood in the light of the torch, growling deeply. He looked an extremely fierce animal. The men looked at him doubtfully. One man took a step forward and George heard him. At once she shouted to Tim.

'Go for him, Tim, go for him!'

Tim leapt at the man's throat. He took him completely by surprise and the man fell to the ground with a thud, trying to beat off the dog. The other man helped.

'Call off your dog or we'll hurt him!' cried the second man.

'It's much more likely he'll hurt *you*!' said George, coming out from behind the rock and enjoying the fun. 'Tim, come off.'

Tim came away from the man he was worrying, looking up at his mistress as if to say, 'I was having *such* a good time! Why did you spoil it?'

'Who are you?' said the man on the ground.

'I'm not answering any of your questions,' said George. 'Go back to Kirrin Farmhouse, that's my advice to you. If you dare to come along this passage I'll set my dog on to you again – and next time he'll do more damage.'

The men turned and went back the way they had come. They neither of them wanted to face Tim again. George waited until she could no longer see the light of their torch, then she bent down and patted Timothy.

'Brave, good dog!' she said. 'I love you, darling Tim, and you don't know how proud I am of you! Come along – we'll hurry after the others now. I expect those two men will explore this passage some time tonight, and won't they get a shock when they find out where it leads to, and see who is waiting for them!'

George hurried along the rest of the long passage, with Tim running beside her. She had Dick's torch, and it did not take her long to catch the others up. She panted out to them what had happened, and even poor Anne chuckled in delight when she heard how Tim had flung Mr Wilton to the ground.

'Here we are,' said Julian, as the passage came to a stop below the hole in the study floor. 'Hallo – what's this?'

A bright light was shining down the hole, and the rug and carpet, so carefully pulled over the hole by Julian, were now pulled back again. The children gazed up in surprise.

GOOD OLD TIM!

Uncle Quentin was there, and Aunt Fanny, and when they saw the children's faces looking up at them from the hole, they were so astonished that they very nearly fell down the hole too!

'Julian! Anne! What in the wide world are you doing down there?' cried Uncle Quentin. He gave them each a hand up, and the four children and Timothy were at last safe in the warm study. How good it was to feel warm again! They got as near the fire as they could.

'Children – what *is* the meaning of this?' asked Aunt Fanny. She looked white and worried. 'I came into the study to do some dusting, and when I stood on that bit of the rug, it seemed to give way beneath me. When I pulled it up and turned back the carpet, I saw that hole – and the hole in the panelling too! And then I found that all of you had disappeared, and went to fetch your uncle. What *has* been happening – and where does that hole lead to?'

Dick took the sheaf of papers from under his jersey and gave them to George. She took them and handed them to her father. 'Are these the missing pages?' she asked.

Her father fell on them as if they had been worth more than a hundred times their weight in gold. 'Yes! Yes! They're the pages – all three of them! Thank goodness they're back. They took me three years to bring to perfection, and contained the heart of my secret formula. George, where did you get them?'

'It's a very long story,' said George. 'You tell it all, Julian, I feel tired.'

Julian began to tell the tale. He left out nothing. He told how George had found Mr Roland snooping about the study – how she had felt sure that the tutor had not wanted Timmy in the house because the dog gave warning of his movements at night – how George had seen him talking to the two artists, although he had said he did not know them. As the tale went on, Uncle Quentin and Aunt Fanny looked more and more amazed. They simply could not believe it all.

But after all, there were the missing papers, safely back. That was marvellous. Uncle Quentin hugged the papers as if they were a precious baby. He would not put them down for a moment.

George told the bit about Timmy keeping the men off the escaping children. 'So you see, although you made poor Tim live out in the cold, away from me, he really saved us all, and your papers too,' she said to her father, fixing her brilliant blue eyes on him.

Her father looked most uncomfortable. He felt very guilty for having punished George and Timothy. They had been right about Mr Roland and he had been wrong.

'Poor George,' he said, 'and poor Timmy. I'm sorry about all that.'

George did not bear malice once anyone had owned themselves to be in the wrong. She smiled at her father.

'It's all right,' she said. 'But don't you think that as I was punished unfairly, Mr Roland might be punished well and truly? He deserves it!'

'Oh, he shall be, certainly he shall be,' promised her father. 'He's up in bed with a cold, as you know. I hope he doesn't hear any of this, or he may try to escape.'

'He can't,' said George. 'We're snowed up. You could ring up the police, and arrange for them to come here as soon as ever they can manage it, when the snow has cleared. And I rather think those other two men will try to explore the Secret Way as soon as possible, to get the papers back. Could we catch them when they arrive, do you think?'

'Rather!' said Uncle Quentin, though Aunt Fanny looked as if she didn't want any more exciting things to happen! 'Now look here, you seem really frozen all of you, and you must be hungry too, because it's almost lunch-time. Go into the dining-room and sit by the fire, and Joanna shall bring us all a hot lunch. Then we'll tal' about what to do.'

Nobody said a word to Mr Roland, of course. He lay in bed, coughing now and then. George had slipped up and locked his door. She wasn't going to have him wandering out and overhearing anything!

They all enjoyed their hot lunch, and became warm and cosy. It was nice to sit there together, talking over their adventure, and planning what to do.

'I will telephone to the police, of course,' said Uncle Quentin. 'And tonight we will put Timmy into the study to give the two artists a good welcome if they arrive!'

Mr Roland was most annoyed to find his door locked

that afternoon when he took it into his head to dress and go downstairs. He banged on it indignantly. George grinned and went upstairs. She had told the other children how she had locked the door.

'What's the matter, Mr Roland?' she asked, in a polite voice.

'Oh, it's you, George, is it?' said the tutor. 'See what's the matter with my door, will you? I can't open it.'

George had pocketed the key when she had locked the door. She answered Mr Roland in a cheerful voice.

'Oh Mr Roland, there's no key in your door, so I can't unlock it. I'll see if I can find it!'

Mr Roland was angry and puzzled. He couldn't understand why his door was locked and the key gone. He did not guess that everyone knew about him now. Uncle Quentin laughed when George went down and told him about the locked door.

'He may as well be kept a prisoner,' he said. 'He can't escape now.'

'That night, everyone went to bed early, and Timmy was left in the study, guarding the hole. Mr Roland had become more and more angry and puzzled when his door was not unlocked. He had shouted for Uncle Quentin, but only George had come. He could not understand it. George, of course, was enjoying herself. She made Timothy bark outside Mr Roland's door, and this puzzled him too, for he knew that George was not supposed to see Timmy for three days. Wild thoughts raced through his head. Had that fierce, impossible

182

child locked up her father and mother and Joanna, as well as himself? He could not imagine what had happened.

In the middle of the night Timmy awoke everyone by barking madly. Uncle Quentin and the children hurried downstairs, followed by Aunt Fanny, and the amazed Joanna. A fine sight met their eyes!

Mr Wilton and Mr Thomas were in the study crouching behind the sofa, terrified of Timothy, who was barking for all he was worth! Timmy was standing by the hole in the stone floor, so that the two men could not escape down there. Artful Timmy! He had waited in silence until the men had crept up the hole into the study, and were exploring it, wondering where they were – and then the dog had leapt to the hole to guard it, preventing the men from escaping.

'Good evening, Mr Wilton, good evening, Mr Thomas,' said George, in a polite voice. 'Have you come to see our tutor Mr Roland?'

'So this is where he lives!' said Mr Wilton. 'Was it you in the passage today?'

'Yes – and my cousins,' said George. 'Have you come to look for the papers you stole from my father?'

The two men were silent. They knew they were caught. Mr Wilton spoke after a moment.

'Where's Mr Roland?'

'Shall we take these men to Mr Roland, Uncle?' asked Julian, winking at George. 'Although it's in the middle of the night I'm sure he would love to see them.'

'Yes,' said his uncle, jumping at once to what the boy meant to do. 'Take them up. Timmy, you go too.'

The men followed Julian upstairs, Timmy close at their heels. George followed too, grinning. She handed Julian the key. He unlocked the door and the men went in, just as Julian switched on the light. Mr Roland was wide awake and gave an exclamation of complete amazement when he saw his friends.

Before they had time to say a word Julian locked the door again and threw the key to George.

'A nice little bag of prisoners,' he said. 'We will leave old Tim outside the door to guard them. It's impossible to get out of that window, and anyway, we're snowed up if they could escape that way.'

Everyone went to bed again, but the children found it difficult to sleep after such an exciting time. Anne and George whispered together and so did Julian and Dick. There was such a lot to talk about.

Next day there was a surprise for everyone. The police did arrive after all! The snow did not stop them, for somewhere or other they had got skis and had come skimming along valiantly to see the prisoners! It was a great excitement for everyone.

'We won't take the men away, sir, till the snow has gone,' said the Inspector. 'We'll just put the handcuffs on them, so that they don't try any funny tricks. You keep the door locked too, and that dog outside. They'll be safe there for a day or two. We've taken them enough food till we come back again. If they go a bit short, it will serve them right!'

The snow melted two days later, and the police took away Mr Roland and the others. The children watched.

'No more lessons *these* hols!' said Anne gleefully.

'No more shutting Timothy out of the house,' said George.

'You were right and we were wrong, George,' said Julian. 'You were fierce, weren't you? – but it's a jolly good thing you were!'

'She is fierce, isn't she?' said Dick, giving the girl a sudden hug. 'But I rather like her when she's fierce, don't you, Julian? Oh George, we do have marvellous adventures with you! I wonder if we'll have any more?'

They will – there isn't a doubt of that!

FIVE RUN AWAY TOGETHER

FIVE RUN AWAY TOGETHER

ENID BLYTON

Illustrated by
Eileen A. Soper

Hodder
Children's
Books

a division of Hachette Children's Books

CONTENTS

CHAPTER ONE

Summer holidays

'GEORGE DEAR, do settle down and do something,' said George's mother. 'You keep wandering in and out with Timothy, and I am trying to have a rest.'

'Sorry, Mother,' said Georgina, taking hold of Timothy's collar. 'But I feel lonely without the others. Oh I do wish tomorrow would come. I've been without them for three whole weeks already.'

Georgina went to boarding-school with her cousin Anne, and in the holidays she and Anne, and Anne's two brothers, Julian and Dick, usually joined up together and had plenty of fun. Now it was the summer holidays, and already three weeks had gone by. Anne, Dick and Julian had gone away with their father and mother, but Georgina's parents had wanted their little girl with them, so she had not gone.

Now her three cousins were coming the next day to spend the rest of the summer holidays with her at her old home, Kirrin Cottage.

'It will be lovely when they are here,' said George, as she was always called, to Timothy her dog. 'Simply lovely, Timothy. Don't you think so?'

'Woof,' said Timothy and licked George's hand.

FIVE RUN AWAY TOGETHER

George was dressed, as usual, exactly like a boy, in jeans and jersey. She had always wanted to be a boy, and would never answer if she was called Georgina. So everyone called her George. She had missed her cousins very much during the first weeks of the summer holidays.

'I used to think I liked best to be alone,' George said to Timothy, who always seemed to understand every word she said. 'But now I know that was silly. It's nice to be with others and share things, and make friends.'

Timothy thumped his tail on the ground. He certainly liked being with the other children too. He was longing to see Julian, Anne and Dick again.

George took Timothy down to the beach. She shaded her eyes with her hand, and looked out to the entrance of the bay. In the middle of it, almost as if it were guarding it, lay a small, rocky island, on which rose the ruins of an old castle.

'We'll visit you again this summer, Kirrin Island,' said George softly. 'I haven't been able to go to you yet this summer, because my boat was being mended – but it will be ready soon, then I'll come to you. And I'll look all round the old castle again. Oh Tim – do you remember the adventures we had on Kirrin Island last summer?'

Tim remembered quite well, because he himself had shared in the thrilling adventures. He had been down in the dungeons of the castle with the others; he had helped to find treasure there, and had had just as grand a time as the four children he loved. He gave a little bark.

'You're remembering, aren't you, Tim?' said George, patting him. 'Won't it be fun to go there again? We'll go down into the dungeons again, shall we? And oh! – do you remember how Dick climbed down the deep well-shaft to rescue us?'

It was exciting, remembering all the things that had happened last year. It made George long all the more for the next day, when her three friends would arrive.

'I wish Mother would let us go and live on the island for a week,' thought George. 'That would be the greatest fun we could have. To live on my very own island!'

It *was* George's island. It really belonged to her mother,

but she had said, two or three years back, that George could have it, and George now thought of it as really her own. She felt that all the rabbits on it belonged to her, all the wild birds and other creatures.

'I'll suggest that we go there for a week, when the others come,' she thought, excitedly. 'We'll take our food and everything, and live there quite by ourselves. We shall feel like Robinson Crusoe.'

She went to meet her cousins the next day, driving the pony and trap by herself. Her mother wanted to come, but she said she did not feel very well. George felt a bit worried about her. So often lately her mother had said she didn't feel very well. Perhaps it was the heat of the summer. The weather had been so very hot lately. Day after day had brought nothing but blue sky and sunshine. George had been burnt a dark-brown, and her eyes were startlingly blue in her sunburnt face. She had had her hair cut even shorter than usual, and it really was difficult to know whether she was a boy or a girl.

The train came in. Three hands waved madly from a window, and George shouted in delight.

'Julian! Dick! Anne! You're here at last.'

The three children tumbled pell-mell out of their carriage. Julian yelled to a porter.

'Our bags are in the guard's van. Hallo, George! How are you? Golly, you've grown.'

They all had. They were all a year older and a year bigger than when they had had their exciting adventures on Kirrin

Island. Even Anne, the youngest, didn't look such a small girl now. She flung herself on George, almost knocking her over, and then went down on her knees beside Timothy, who was quite mad with joy to see his three friends.

There was a terrific noise. They all shouted their news at once, and Timothy barked without stopping.

'We thought the train would never get here!'

'Oh Timothy, you darling, you're just the same as ever!'

'Woof, woof, woof!'

'Mother's sorry she couldn't come and meet you too.'

'George, how brown you are! I say, aren't we going to have fun.'

'WOOF, WOOF!'

'Shut up, Tim darling, and do get down; you've bitten my tie almost in half. Oh, you dear old dog, it's grand to see you!'

'WOOF!'

The porter wheeled up their luggage, and soon it was in the pony-cart. George clicked to the waiting pony, and it cantered off. The five in the little cart all talked at once at the top of their voices, Tim far more loudly than anyone else, for his doggy voice was strong and powerful.

'I hope your mother isn't ill?' said Julian, who was fond of his Aunt Fanny. She was gentle and kind, and loved having them all.

'I think it must be the heat,' said George.

'What about Uncle Quentin?' asked Anne. 'Is he all right?'

5

FIVE RUN AWAY TOGETHER

The three children did not very much like George's father because he could get into very fierce tempers, and although he welcomed the three cousins to his house, he did not really care for children. So they always felt a little awkward with him, and were glad when he was not there.

'Father's all right,' said George, cheerfully. 'Only he's worried about Mother. He doesn't seem to notice her much when she's well and cheerful, but he gets awfully upset if anything goes wrong with her. So be a bit careful of him at the moment. You know what he's like when he's worried.'

The children did know. Uncle Quentin was best avoided when things went wrong. But not even the thought of a cross uncle could damp them today. They were on holiday; they were going to Kirrin Cottage; they were by the sea, and there was dear old Timothy beside them, and fun of all kinds in store for them.

'Shall we go to Kirrin Island, George?' asked Anne. 'Do let's! We haven't been there since last summer. The weather was too bad in the winter and Easter holidays. Now it's gorgeous.'

'Of course we'll go,' said George, her blue eyes shining. 'Do you know what I thought? I thought it would be marvellous to go and stay there for a whole week by ourselves! We are older now, and I'm sure Mother would let us.'

'Go and stay on your island for a week!' cried Anne. 'Oh! That would be too good to be true.'

'Our island,' said George, happily. 'Don't you remember I said I would divide it into four, and we'd all share it? Well, I meant it, you know. It's ours, not mine.'

'What about Timothy?' said Anne. 'Oughtn't he to have a share as well? Can't we make it five bits, one for him too?'

'He can share mine,' said George. She drew the pony to a stop, and the four children and the dog gazed out across the blue bay. 'There's Kirrin Island,' said George. 'Dear little island. I can hardly wait to get to it now. I haven't been able to go there yet, because my boat wasn't mended.'

'Then we can all go together,' said Dick. 'I wonder if the rabbits are just as tame as ever.'

'Woof!' said Timothy at once. He had only to hear the word 'rabbits' to get excited.

'It's no good your thinking about the rabbits on Kirrin,' said George. 'You know I don't allow you to chase them, Tim.'

Timothy's tail dropped and he looked mournfully at George. It was the only thing on which he and George did not agree. Tim was firmly convinced that rabbits were meant for him to chase, and George was just as firmly convinced that they were not.

'Get on!' said George to the pony, and jerked the reins. The little creature trotted on towards Kirrin Cottage, and very soon they were all opposite the front gate.

A sour-faced woman came out from the back door to

help them down with their luggage. The children did not know her.

'Who's she?' they whispered to George.

'The new cook,' said George. 'Joanna had to go and look after her mother, who broke her leg. Then Mother got this cook – Mrs Stick her name is.'

'Good name for her,' grinned Julian. 'She looks a real old stick! But all the same I hope she doesn't stick here for long. I hope Joanna comes back. I liked old fat Joanna, and she was nice to Timmy.'

'Mrs Stick has a dog too,' said George. 'A dreadful animal, smaller than Tim, all sort of mangy and moth-eaten. Tim can't bear it.'

SUMMER HOLIDAYS

'Where is it?' asked Anne, looking round.

'It's kept in the kitchen, and Tim isn't allowed near it,' said George. 'Good thing too, because I'm sure he'd eat it! He can't think what's in the kitchen, and goes sniffing round the shut door till Mrs Stick nearly goes mad.'

The others laughed. They had all climbed down from the pony-cart now, and were ready to go indoors. Julian had helped Mrs Stick in with all the bags. George took the pony-cart away, and the other three went in to say hello to their uncle and aunt.

'Well, dears,' said Aunt Fanny, smiling at them from the sofa where she was lying down. 'How are you all? I'm sorry I could not come to meet you. Uncle Quentin is out for a walk. You had better go upstairs, and wash and change. Then come down for tea.'

The boys went up to their old bedroom, with its funny slanting roof, and its window looking out over the bay. Anne went to the little room she shared with George. How good it was to be back again at Kirrin! What fun they would have these holidays with George and dear old Timmy!

CHAPTER TWO

The Stick family

IT WAS lovely to wake up the next morning at Kirrin Cottage and see the sun shining in at the windows, and to hear the far-off plash-plash-plash of the sea. It was gorgeous to leap out of bed and rush to see how blue the sea was, and how lovely Kirrin Island looked at the entrance of the bay.

'I'm going for a bathe before breakfast,' said Julian, and snatched up his bathing trunks. 'Coming, Dick?'

'You bet!' said Dick. 'Call the girls. We'll all go.'

So down they went, the four of them, with Tim galloping behind them, his tail wagging nineteen to the dozen, and his long pink tongue hanging out of his mouth. He went into the water with the others, and swam all round them. They were all good swimmers, but Julian and George were the best.

They put towels round themselves, rubbed their bodies dry and pulled on jeans and jerseys. Then back to breakfast they went, as hungry as hunters. Anne noticed a boy in the back garden and stared in surprise.

'Who's that?' she said.

'Oh, that's Edgar, Mrs Stick's boy,' said George. 'I don't like him. He does silly things, like putting out his tongue and calling rude names.'

THE STICK FAMILY

Edgar appeared to be singing when the others went in at the gate. Anne stopped to listen.

'Georgie-porgie, pudding and pie!' sang Edgar, a silly look on his face. He seemed about thirteen or fourteen, a stupid, yet sly-looking youth. 'Georgie-porgie pudding and pie!'

George went red. 'He's always singing that,' she said, furiously. 'Just because I'm called "George", I suppose. He thinks he's clever. I can't bear him.'

Julian called out to Edgar. 'You shut up! You're not funny, only jolly silly!'

'Georgie-porgie,' began Edgar again, a silly smile on his wide red face. Julian made a step towards him, and he at once disappeared into the house.

'Shan't stand much of *him*,' said Julian, in a decided voice. 'I wonder *you* do, George. I wonder you haven't slapped his face, stamped on his foot, bitten his ears off and done a few other things! You used to be so fierce.'

'Well – I am still, really,' said George. 'I *feel* frightfully fierce down inside me when I hear Edgar singing silly songs at me like that and calling out names – but you see, Mother really hasn't been well, and I know jolly well if I go for Edgar, Mrs Stick will leave, and poor old Mother would have to do all the work, and she really isn't fit to at present. So I just hold myself in, and hope that Timmy will do the same.'

'Good for *you* old thing!' said Julian, admiringly, for he

11

knew how hard it was for George to keep her temper at times.

'I think I'll just go up to Mother's room and see if she'd like breakfast in bed,' said George. 'Hang on to old Timmy a moment, will you? If Edgar appears again, he might go for him.'

Julian hung on to Timmy's collar. Timmy had growled when Edgar had been in the garden, now he stood stock still, his nose twitching as if he were trying to trace some smell.

Suddenly a mangy-looking dog appeared out of the kitchen door. It had a dirty white coat, out of which patches seemed to have been bitten, and its tail was well between its legs.

'Wooooof!' said Timmy, joyfully, and leapt at the dog. He pulled Julian over, for he was a big dog, and the boy let go his hold of the dog's collar. Timmy pounced excitedly on the other dog, who gave a fearful whine and tried to go into the kitchen door again.

'Timmy! Come here!' yelled Julian. But Timmy didn't hear. He was busy trying to snap off the other dog's ears – or at least, that is what he appeared to be doing. The other dog yelled for help, and Mrs Stick appeared at the kitchen door, a saucepan in her hand.

'Call off that dog!' she screeched. She hit out at Timmy with the saucepan, but he dodged and it hit her own dog instead, making it yelp all the more.

'Don't hit out with that!' said Julian. 'You'll hurt the dogs. Hi, Timmy, TIMMY!'

12

Edgar now appeared, looking very scared. He picked up a stone and seemed to be watching his chance to hurl it at Timmy. Anne shrieked.

'You're not to throw that stone; you're not to! You bad wicked boy!'

In the middle of all this turmoil Uncle Quentin appeared, looking angry and irritable.

'Good heavens! What is all this going on? I never heard such a row in my life.'

Then George appeared, flying out of the door like the wind, to rescue her beloved Timothy. She rushed to the two dogs and tried to pull Timmy away. Her father yelled at her.

'Come away, you little idiot! Don't you know better than to separate two fighting dogs with your bare hands? Where's the garden hose?'

It was fixed to a tap nearby. Julian ran to it and turned on the tap. He picked up the hose and turned it on the two dogs. At once the jet of water spurted out at them, and they leapt apart in surprise. Julian saw Edgar standing near, and couldn't resist swinging the hose a little so that the boy was soaked. He gave a scream and ran in at once.

'What did you do that for?' said Uncle Quentin, annoyed. 'George, tie Timothy up at once. Mrs Stick, didn't I tell you not to let your dog out of the kitchen unless you had him on a lead? I won't have this kind of thing happening. Where's the breakfast? Late as usual!'

THE STICK FAMILY

Mrs Stick disappeared into the kitchen, muttering and grumbling, taking her drenched dog with her. George, looking sulky, tied Timothy up. He lay down in his kennel, looking beseechingly at his mistress.

'I've told you not to take any notice of that mangy-looking dog,' said George, severely. 'Now you see what happens! You put Father into a bad temper for the rest of the day, and Mrs Stick will be so angry she won't make any cakes for tea!'

Timmy gave a whine, and put his head down on his paws. He licked a few hairs from the corner of his mouth. It was sad to be tied up – but anyhow he had bitten a bit off the tip of one of that dreadful dog's ears!

They all went in to breakfast. 'Sorry I let Timmy go,' said Julian to George. 'But he nearly tore my arm off. I couldn't possibly hold him! He's grown into an awfully powerful dog, hasn't he?'

'Yes,' said George, proudly. 'He has. He could eat Mrs Stick's dog up in a mouthful if we'd let him. And Edgar too.'

'And Mrs Stick,' said Anne. 'All of them. I don't like any of them.'

Breakfast was rather a subdued meal, as Aunt Fanny was not there, but Uncle Quentin was – and Uncle Quentin in a bad temper was not a very cheerful person to have at the breakfast-table. He snapped at George and glared at the others. Anne almost wished they hadn't come to Kirrin Cottage! But her spirits rose when she thought of

15

the rest of the day – they would take their dinner out, perhaps, and have it on the beach – or maybe even go out to Kirrin Island. Uncle Quentin wouldn't be with them to spoil things.

Mrs Stick appeared to take away the porridge plates and bring in the bacon. She banged the plates down on the table.

'No need to do that,' said Uncle Quentin, irritably. Mrs Stick said nothing. She was scared of Uncle Quentin, and no wonder! She put the next lot of plates down quietly.

'What are you going to do today?' asked Uncle Quentin, towards the end of breakfast. He was feeling a little better by that time, and didn't like to see such subdued faces round him.

'We thought we might go out for a picnic,' said George, eagerly. 'I asked Mother. She said we might, if Mrs Stick will make us sandwiches.'

'Well, I shouldn't think she'll try very hard,' said Uncle Quentin, trying to make a little joke. They all smiled politely. 'But you can ask her.'

There was a silence. Nobody liked the idea of asking Mrs Stick for sandwiches.

'I do wish she hadn't brought Stinker,' said George, gloomily. 'Everything would be easier if he wasn't here.'

'Is that the name of her son?' asked Uncle Quentin, startled.

George grinned. 'Oh no. Though it wouldn't be a bad

name for him, because he hardly ever has a bath, and he's jolly smelly. It's her dog I mean. She calls him Tinker, but I call him Stinker, because he really does smell awful.'

'I don't think it's a very nice name,' said her father, in the midst of the others' giggles.

'No, it isn't,' said George, 'but then, he isn't a very nice dog.'

In the end it was Aunt Fanny who saw Mrs Stick and arranged about the sandwiches. Mrs Stick went up to see Aunt Fanny, who was having breakfast in bed, and agreed to make sandwiches, though with a very bad grace.

'I didn't bargain for three more children to come traipsing along,' she said, sulkily.

'I told you they were coming, Mrs Stick,' said Aunt Fanny, patiently. 'I didn't know I should be feeling so ill myself when they came. If I had been well I could have made their sandwiches and done many more things. I can only ask you to help as much as you can till I feel better. I may be all right tomorrow. Let the children have a good time for a week or so, and then, if I still feel ill, I am sure they will all turn to and help a bit. But let them have a good time first.'

The children took their packets of sandwiches and set off. On the way they met Edgar, looking as stupid and sly as usual. 'Why don't you let me come along with you?' he said. 'Let's go to that island. I know a lot about it, I do.'

'No, you don't,' said George, in a flash. 'You don't know anything about it. And I'd never take *you*. It's *my* island, see? Well, *ours*. It belongs to all four of us and Timmy, too. We should never allow you to go.'

''Tisn't your island,' said Edgar. 'That's a lie, that is!'

'You don't know what you're talking about,' said George, scornfully. 'Come on, you others! We can't waste time talking to Edgar.'

They left him, looking sulky and angry. As soon as they were at a safe distance he lifted up his voice:

> *'Georgie-porgie, pudding and pie,*
> *She knows how to tell a lie,*
> *Georgie-porgie, pudding and pie!'*

Julian started to go back after the rude Edgar, but George pulled him on. 'He'll only go and tell tales to his mother, and she'll walk out and there'll be no one to help Mother,' she said. 'I'll just have to put up with it. We'll try and think of some way to get our own back, though. Nasty creature! I hate his pimply nose and screwed-up eyes.'

'Woof!' said Timmy, feelingly.

'Timmy says he hates Stinker's miserable tail and silly little ears,' explained George, and they all laughed. That made them feel better. They were soon out of hearing of Edgar's silly song, and forgot all about him.

'Let's go and see if your boat is ready,' said Julian. 'Then maybe we could row out to the dear old island.'

CHAPTER THREE

A nasty shock

GEORGE'S BOAT was almost ready, but not quite. It was having a last coat of paint on it. It looked very nice, for George had chosen a bright red paint, and the oars were painted red too.

'Oh, can't we possibly have it this afternoon?' said George to Jim the boatman.

He shook his head.

'No, Master George,' he said, 'not unless you all want to be messed up with red paint. It'll be dry tomorrow, but not before.'

It always made the others smile to hear the boatmen and fishermen call Georgina 'Master George'. The local people all knew how badly she wanted to be a boy, and they knew, too, how plucky and straightforward she was, so they laughed to one another and said: 'Well, they reckoned she behaved like a boy, and if she wanted to be called "Master George" instead of "Miss Georgina", she deserved it!'

So Georgina was Master George, and enjoyed strutting about in her jeans and jersey on the beach, using her boat as well as any fisher-boy, and swimming faster than them all.

'We'll go to the island tomorrow then,' said Julian. 'We'll just picnic on the beach today. Then we'll go for a walk.'

So they picnicked on the sands with Timothy sharing more than half their lunch. The sandwiches were not very nice. The bread was too stale; there was not enough butter inside, and they were far too thick. But Timothy didn't mind. He gobbled up as many as he could, his tail wagging so hard that it sent sand over everyone.

'Timothy, do take your tail out of the sand if you want to wag it,' said Julian, getting sand all over his hair for the fourth time. Timmy wagged his tail hard again, and sent another shower over him. Everyone laughed.

'Let's go for a walk now,' said Dick, jumping up. 'My legs could do with some good exercise. Where shall we go?'

'We'll walk along the cliff-top, where we can see the

island all the time, shall we?' said Anne. 'George, is the old wreck still there?'

George nodded. The children had once had a most exciting time with an old wreck that had lain at the bottom of the sea. A great storm had lifted it up and set it firmly on the rocks. They had been able to explore the wreck then, and had found a map of the castle in it, with instructions as to where hidden treasure was to be found.

'Do you remember how we found that old map in the wreck, and how we looked for the ingots of gold and found them?' said Julian, his eyes gleaming as he remembered it all. 'Isn't the wreck battered to pieces yet, George?'

'No,' said George. 'I don't think so. It's on the rocks on the other side of the island, you remember, so we can't see it from here. But we might have a look at it when we go on the island tomorrow.'

'Yes, let's,' said Anne. 'Poor old wreck! I guess it won't last many winters now.'

They walked along the cliff-top with Timothy capering ahead of them. They could see the island easily and the ruined castle rising up from the middle.

'There's the jackdaw tower,' said Anne, looking. 'The other tower's fallen down, hasn't it? Look at the jackdaws circling round and round the tower, George!'

'Yes. They build in it every year,' said George. 'Don't you remember the masses of sticks round about the tower that the jackdaws dropped when they built their nests? We picked some up and made a fire with them once.'

'I'd like to do that again,' said Anne. 'I would really. Let's do it each night if we stay a week on the island. George, did you ask your mother?'

'Oh yes,' said George. 'She said she thought we might, but she would see.'

'I don't like it when grown-ups say they'll see,' said Anne. 'It so often means they won't let you do something after all, but they don't like to tell you at the time.'

'Well, I expect she will let us,' said George. 'After all, we're much older than last year. Why, Julian is in his teens already, and I soon shall be and so will Dick. Only Anne is small.'

'I'm not,' said Anne, indignantly. 'I'm as strong as you are. I can't help being younger.'

'Hush, hush, baby!' said Julian, patting his little sister on the back and laughing at her furious face. 'Hallo – look! What's that over there on the island?'

He had caught sight of something as he was teasing Anne. Everyone swung round and gazed at Kirrin. George gave an exclamation.

'Golly – a spire of smoke! Surely it's smoke! Someone's on my island.'

'On *our* island,' corrected Dick. 'It can't be! That smoke must come from a steamer out beyond the island. We can't see it, that's all. But I bet the smoke comes from a steamer. We know no one can get to the island but us. They don't know the way.'

'If anyone's on my island,' began George, looking very

22

fierce and angry, 'if anyone's on my island, I'll – I'll – I'll . . .'

'You'll explode and go up in smoke!' said Dick. 'There – it's gone now. I'm sure it was only a steamer letting off steam or smoking hard, whatever they do.'

They watched Kirrin Island for some time after that, but they could see no more smoke. 'If only my boat was ready!' said George, restlessly. 'I'd go over this afternoon. I've a good mind to go and get my boat, even if the paint *is* wet.'

'Don't be an idiot!' said Julian. 'You know what an awful row we'd get into if we go home with all our things bright red. Have a bit of sense, George.'

George gave up the idea. She watched for a steamer to appear at one side of the island or another, to come into the bay, but none came.

'Probably anchored out there,' said Dick. 'Come on! Are we going to stand rooted to this spot for the rest of the day?'

'We'd better get back home,' said Julian, looking at his wrist-watch. 'It's almost tea-time. I hope your mother is up, George. It's much nicer when she's at meals.'

'Oh, I expect she will be,' said George. 'Come on then, let's go back!'

They turned to go back. They watched Kirrin Island as they walked, but all they could see were jackdaws or gulls in the sky above it. No more spires of smoke appeared. It must have been a steamer!

'All the same, I'm going over tomorrow to have a look,' said George, firmly. 'If any trippers are visiting my island I'll turn them off.'

'*Our* island,' said Dick. 'George, I wish you'd remember you said you'd share it with us.'

'Well – I did share it out with you,' said George, 'but I can't help feeling it's still my island. Come on! I'm getting hungry.'

They came back at last to Kirrin Cottage. They went into the hall, and then into the sitting-room. To their great surprise Edgar was there, reading one of Julian's books.

'What are you doing here?' said Julian. 'And who told you you could borrow my book?'

'I'm not doing any harm,' said Edgar. 'If I want to have a quiet read, why shouldn't I?'

'You wait till my father comes in and finds you lolling about here,' said George. 'My goodness, if you'd gone into his study, you'd have been sorry.'

'I've been in there,' said Edgar, surprisingly. 'I've seen those funny instruments he's working with.'

'How *dare* you!' said George, going white with rage. 'Why, even *we* are not allowed to go into my father's study. As for touching his things – well!'

Julian eyed Edgar curiously. He could not imagine why the boy should suddenly be so insolent.

'Where's your father, George?' he said. 'I think we had better get him to deal with Edgar. He must be mad.'

'Call him if you like,' said Edgar, still lolling in the chair, and flicking over the pages of Julian's book in a most irritating way. 'He won't come.'

'What do you mean?' said George, feeling suddenly scared. 'Where's my mother?'

'Call her too, if you like,' said the boy, looking sly. 'Go on! Call her.'

The children suddenly felt afraid. What did Edgar mean? George flew upstairs to her mother's room, shouting loudly.

'Mother! Mother! Where are you?'

But her mother's bed was empty. It had not been made – but it was empty. George flew into all the other bedrooms, shouting desperately: 'Mother! Mother! Father! Where are you?'

But there was no answer. George ran downstairs, her face very white. Edgar grinned up at her.

'What did I tell you?' he said. 'I said you could call all you liked, but they wouldn't come.'

'Where are they?' demanded George. 'Tell me at once!'

'Find out yourself,' said Edgar.

There was a resounding slap, and Edgar leapt to his feet, holding his left cheek with his hand. George had flown at him and dealt him the hardest smack she could. Edgar lifted his hand to slap her back, but Julian stood in front.

'You're not fighting George,' he said. 'She's a girl. If you want a fight, I'll take you on.'

'I won't be a girl; I'm a boy!' shouted George, trying to push Julian away. 'I'll fight Edgar, and I'll beat him, you see if I don't.'

But Julian kept her off. Edgar began to edge towards the doorway, but he found Dick there.

'One minute,' said Dick. 'Before you go – where are our uncle and aunt?'

'Gr-r-r-r-r-r,' suddenly said Timothy, in such a threatening voice that Edgar stared at him in fright. The dog

26

had bared his great teeth, and had put up the hackles on his neck. He looked very frightening.

'Hold that dog!' said Edgar, his voice trembling. 'He looks as if he's going to spring at me.'

Julian put his hand on Tim's collar. 'Quiet, Tim!' he said. 'Now, Edgar, tell us what we want to know, and tell us quickly, or you'll be sorry.'

'Well, there isn't much to tell,' said Edgar, keeping his eye on Timothy. He shot a look at George and went on. 'Your mother was suddenly taken very ill – with a terrible pain *here* – and they got the doctor and they've taken her away to hospital, and your father went with her. That's all!'

George sat down on the sofa, looking paler still and rather sick.

'Oh!' she said. 'Poor Mother! I wish I hadn't gone out today. Oh dear – how can we find out what's happened?'

Edgar had slipped out of the room, shutting the door behind him so that Timmy should not follow. The kitchen door was slammed, too. The children stared at one another, feeling sorry and dismayed. Poor George! Poor Aunt Fanny!

'There must be a note somewhere,' said Julian, and looked round the room. He saw a letter stuck into the rim of the big mirror there, addressed to George. He gave it to her. It was from George's father.

'Read it, quickly,' said Anne. 'Oh dear – this is really a horrid beginning to our holidays here!'

CHAPTER FOUR

A few little upsets

GEORGE READ the letter out loud. It was not very long, and had evidently been written in a great hurry.

DEAR GEORGE,

Your mother has been taken very ill. I am going with her to the hospital. I shall not leave her till she is getting better. That may be in a few days' time, or in a week's time. I will telephone to you each day at nine o'clock in the morning to tell you how she is. Mrs Stick will look after you all. Try to manage all right till I come back.

Your loving
FATHER

'Oh dear!' said Anne, knowing how dreadful George must feel. George loved her mother dearly, and for once the girl had tears in her eyes. George never cried – but it was terrible to come home and find her mother gone like this. And Father too! No one there but Mrs Stick and Edgar.

'I can't bear Mother going like this,' sobbed George, suddenly, and buried her head in a cushion. 'She – she might never come back.'

'Don't be silly, George,' said Julian, sitting down and putting his arm round her. 'Of course she will. Why shouldn't she? Didn't your father say he was staying with her till she was getting better – and that would be probably in a few days' time. Cheer up, George! It isn't like you to give way like this.'

'But I didn't say good-bye,' sobbed poor George. 'And I made her ask Mrs Stick for the sandwiches, instead of me. I want to go and find Mother and see how she is myself.'

'You don't know where they've taken her, and if you did, they wouldn't let you in,' said Dick, gently. 'Let's have some tea. We shall all feel better after that.'

'I couldn't eat *any*thing,' said George, fiercely. Timothy pushed his nose into her hands, and tried to lick them. They were under her buried face. The dog whined a little.

'Poor Timmy! He can't understand,' said Anne. 'He's awfully upset because you are unhappy, George.'

That made George sit up. She rubbed her hands over her eyes, and let Timmy lick the wet tears off them. He looked surprised at the salty taste. He tried to get on to George's knee.

'Silly Timmy!' said George, in a more ordinary voice. 'Don't be upset. I just got a shock, that's all! I'm better now, Timmy. Don't whine like that, silly! I'm all right. I'm not hurt.'

But Timothy felt certain George was really hurt or injured in some way to cry like that, and he kept whining, and pawing at George, and trying to get on to her knee.

29

Julian opened the door. 'I'm going to tell Mrs Stick we want our tea,' he said, and went out. The others thought he was rather brave to face Mrs Stick.

Julian went to the kitchen door and opened it. Edgar was sitting there, one side of his face scarlet, where George had slapped it. Mrs Stick was there, looking grim.

'If that girl slaps my Edgar again, I'll be after her,' she said, threateningly.

'Edgar deserved what he got,' said Julian. 'Can we have some tea, please?'

'I've a good mind to get you none,' said Mrs Stick. Her dog started up from its corner and growled at Julian. 'That's right, Tinker! You growl at folks that slap Edgar,' said Mrs Stick.

Julian was not in the least afraid of Tinker. 'If you are not going to get us any tea, I'll get it myself,' said the boy. 'Where is the bread, and where are the cakes?'

Mrs Stick stared at Julian, and the boy looked back at her steadfastly. He thought she was a most unpleasant woman, and he certainly was not going to allow her to get the better of him. He wished he could tell her to go – but he had a feeling that she wouldn't, so it would be a waste of his breath.

Mrs Stick dropped her eyes first. 'I'll get your tea,' she said, 'but if I have any nonsense from you I'll get you no other meals.'

'And if I have any nonsense from you I shall go to the police,' said Julian, unexpectedly. He hadn't meant to say that. It came out quite suddenly, but it had a surprising effect on Mrs Stick. She looked startled and alarmed.

'Now, there's no call to be nasty,' she said in a much more polite voice. 'We've all had a bit of a shock, and we're upset, like – I'll get you your tea right now.'

Julian went out. He wondered why his sudden threat of going to the police had made Mrs Stick so much more polite. Perhaps she was afraid the police would get on to his Uncle Quentin and he would come tearing back. Uncle Quentin wouldn't care for a hundred Mrs Sticks!

He went back to the others. 'Tea's coming,' he said. 'So cheer up, everyone!'

It wasn't a very cheerful company that sat down to the tea Mrs Stick brought in. George was now feeling ashamed of her tears. Anne was still upset. Dick tried to make a few silly jokes to cheer everyone up, but they fell so flat that he soon gave it up. Julian was grave and helpful, suddenly very grown-up.

Timothy sat close beside George, his head on her knee. 'I do wish I had a dog who loved me like that,' thought Anne. Timmy kept gazing up at George out of big brown devoted eyes. He had no eyes or ears for anyone but his little mistress now she was sad.

Nobody noticed what they had for tea, but all the same it did them good, and they felt better after it. They didn't like to go out to the beach afterwards in case the telephone bell rang, and there was news of George's mother. So they

31

sat about in the garden, keeping an ear open for the telephone.

From the kitchen came a song.

> *'Georgie-porgie, pudding and pie,*
> *Sat herself down and had a good cry,*
> *Georgie-porgie . . .'*

Julian got up. He went to the kitchen window and looked in. Edgar was there alone.

'Come on out here, Edgar!' said Julian, in a grim voice. 'I'll teach you to sing another song. Come along!'

Edgar didn't stir. 'Can't I sing if I want to?' he said.

'Oh yes,' said Julian, 'but not that song. I'll teach you another. Come along out!'

'No fear,' said Edgar. 'You want to fight me.'

'Yes, I do,' said Julian. 'I think a little bit of good honest fighting would be better for you than sitting singing nasty little songs about a girl who is miserable. Are you coming out? Or shall I come in and fetch you?'

'Ma!' called Edgar, suddenly feeling panicky. 'Ma! Where are you?'

Julian suddenly reached a long arm in at the window, caught hold of Edgar's over-long nose, and pulled it so hard that Edgar yelled in pain.

'Led go! Led go! You're hurding me! Led go by dose!'

Mrs Stick came hurrying into the kitchen. She gave a scream when she saw what Julian was doing. She flew at

32

him. Julian withdrew his arm, and stood outside the window.

'How dare you!' yelled Mrs Stick. 'First that girl slaps Edgar, and then you pull his nose! What's the matter with you all?'

'Nothing,' said Julian, pleasantly, 'but there's an awful lot wrong with Edgar, Mrs Stick. We feel we just *must* put it right. It should be your job, of course, but you don't seem to have done it.'

'You're down right insolent,' said Mrs Stick, outraged and furious.

'Yes, I dare say I am,' said Julian. 'It's just the effect Edgar has on me. Stinker has the same effect.'

'Stinker!' cried Mrs Stick, getting angrier still. 'That's not my dog's name, and well you know it.'

'Well, it really ought to be,' said Julian, strolling off. 'Give him a bath, and maybe we'll call him Tinker instead.'

Leaving Mrs Stick muttering in fury, he went back to the others. They stared at him curiously. He somehow seemed a different Julian – a grim and determined Julian, a very grown-up Julian, a rather frightening Julian.

'I'm afraid the fat's in the fire now,' said Julian, sitting down on the grass. 'I pulled old Edgar's nose nearly off his fat face, and Ma saw me doing it. I guess it's open warfare now! We shan't have a very merry time from now on. I doubt if we'll get any meals.'

'We'll get them ourselves then,' said George. 'I hate Mrs Stick. I wish Joanna would come back. I hate that horrid Edgar too, and that awful Stinker.'

'Look – there *is* Stinker!' suddenly said Dick, putting out his hand to catch Timothy, who had risen with a growl. But Timmy shook off his hand and leapt across the grass at once. Stinker gave a woeful howl and tried to escape. But Timothy had him by the neck and was shaking him like a rat.

Mrs Stick appeared with a stick and lashed out, not seeming to mind which dog she hit. Julian rushed for the hose again. Edgar skipped indoors at once, remembering what had happened to him before.

The water gushed out, and Timothy gave a gasp and let go the howling mongrel he held in his teeth. Stinker at once hurled himself on Mrs Stick, and tried to hide in her skirts, trembling with terror.

'I'll poison that dog of yours!' said Mrs Stick, furiously, to George. 'Always setting on to mine. You look out or I'll poison him.'

She disappeared indoors, and the four children went and sat down again. George looked really alarmed. 'Do you suppose she really *might* try to poison Timmy?' she asked Julian, in a scared voice.

'She's a nasty bit of work,' said Julian, in a low tone. 'I think it would be just as well to keep old Timmy close by us, day and night, and only to feed him ourselves, from our own plates.'

George pulled Timothy to her, horrified at the thought that anyone might want to poison him. But Mrs Stick really was awful – she might do anything like that, George thought. How she wished her father and mother were back! It was horrid to be on their own, like this.

The telephone bell suddenly shrilled out and made everyone jump. They all leapt to their feet and Timmy growled. George flew indoors and lifted the receiver. She heard her father's voice, and her heart began to beat fast.

'Is that you, George?' said her father. 'Are you all right? I haven't time to stay and tell you everything.'

'Father – what about Mother? Tell me quick – how is she?' said George.

'We shan't know till the day after next,' said her father. 'I'll telephone tomorrow morning and then the next morning too. I shan't come back till I know she's better.'

'Oh Father – it's awful without you and Mother,' said poor George. 'Mrs Stick is so horrid.'

'Now, George,' said her father, rather impatiently, 'surely you children can see to yourselves and make do with Mrs Stick till I get back! Don't worry me about such things now. I've enough worry as it is.'

'When will you be back, do you think?' said George. 'Can I come and see Mother?'

'No,' said her father. 'Not for at least two weeks, they say. I'll be back as soon as I can. But I'm not going to leave your Mother now. She needs me. Goodbye and be good, all of you.'

George put back the receiver. She turned to face the others. 'Shan't know about Mother till the day after next,' she said. 'And we've got to put up with Mrs Stick till Father comes back – and goodness knows when that will be! It's awful, isn't it?'

CHAPTER FIVE

In the middle of the night

MRS STICK was in such a bad temper that evening that there was no supper at all. Julian went to ask about some, but he found the kitchen door locked.

He went back to the others with a gloomy face, for they were all hungry. 'She's locked the door,' he said. 'She really is a dreadful creature. I don't believe we'll get any supper tonight.'

'We'll have to wait till she goes to bed,' said George. 'We'll go down and hunt in the larder then, and see what we can find.'

They went to bed hungry. Julian listened for Mrs Stick and Edgar to go to bed, too. When he heard them going upstairs, and was sure their doors had shut, he slipped down into the kitchen. It was dark there, and Julian was just about to put on the light when he heard the sound of someone breathing heavily. He wondered who it could be. Was it Stinker? No – it couldn't be the dog. It sounded like a human being.

Julian stood there, his hand over the light switch, puzzled and a little scared. It couldn't be a burglar, because burglars don't go to sleep in the house they have come to rob. It couldn't be Mrs Stick or Edgar. Then who was it?

He snapped on the light. The kitchen was flooded with radiance, and Julian's eyes fastened on the figure of a small man lying on the sofa. He was fast asleep, his mouth wide open.

He was not a very pleasant sight. He had not shaved for some days, and his cheeks and chin were bluish-black. He didn't seem to have washed for even longer than that, for his hands were black, and so were his fingernails. He had untidy hair and a nose exactly like Edgar's.

'Must be dear Edgar's father,' thought Julian to himself. 'What a sight! Well, poor Edgar hadn't much chance to be decent with a father and mother like his.'

The man snored. Julian wondered what to do. He badly wanted to go to the larder, but on the other hand he didn't particularly want to wake up the man and have a row. He didn't see how he could turn him out – for all he knew his aunt and uncle might have agreed to Mrs Stick's husband coming there now and again, though he hardly thought so.

Julian was very hungry. The thought of the good things in the larder made him snap off the light again and creep towards the larder door in the dark. He opened the door. He felt along the shelves. Good! – that felt like a pie of some sort. He lifted it up and sniffed. It smelt of meat. A meat-pie – good!

He felt along the shelf again and came to a plate on which were what he thought must be jam-tarts, for they were round and flat, and had something sticky in the

38

middle. Well, a meat-pie and jam-tarts ought to be all right for four hungry children!

Julian picked up the meat-pie and the dish of tarts, and made his way carefully out of the larder. He pushed the door to with his foot. Then he turned to go out of the room.

But in the dark he went the wrong way, and by bad luck walked straight into the sofa! The dish of tarts got a sudden jerk and one of them fell off. It landed on the open mouth of the sleeping man, and woke him up with a start.

'Blow!' said Julian to himself, and began to back away quietly, hoping that the man would turn over and go to sleep again. But the sticky jam-tart sliding down his chin had startled the man, and he sat up with a jerk.

'Who's there? That you, Edgar? What are you doing down here?'

Julian said nothing but sidled towards what he hoped was the door. The man leapt up and lurched over to where he thought the light switch was. He found it and switched it on. He stared in the greatest astonishment at Julian.

'What are you doing here?' he demanded.

'Just what I was about to ask *you*,' said Julian, coolly. 'What do you think *you're* doing here, sleeping in my uncle's kitchen?'

'I've a right to be here,' said the man, in a rude voice. 'My wife's cook here, isn't she? My ship's in and I'm on leave. Your uncle arranged with my wife I could come here then, see?'

Julian had feared as much. How awful to have a Mr Stick as well as a Mrs and Master Stick in the house! It would be quite unbearable.

'I can ask my uncle about it when he telephones in the morning,' said Julian. 'Now get out of my way, please, I want to go upstairs.'

'Ho!' said Mr Stick, eyeing the meat-pie and jam-tarts that Julian was carrying. 'Ho! Stealing out of the larder, I see! Nice goings-on I must say.'

Julian was not going to argue with Mr Stick, who evidently felt that he was top-dog. 'Get out of my way,' he said. 'I will talk to you in the morning after my uncle has telephoned.'

IN THE MIDDLE OF THE NIGHT

Mr Stick didn't seem as if he was going to get out of the way at all. He stood there, a nasty little man, not much taller than Julian, a sarcastic smile on his unshaven face.

Julian pursed his lips and whistled. There came a bump on the floor above. That was Timothy jumping off George's bed! Then there came the pattering of feet down the stairs and up the kitchen passage. Timmy was coming!

He smelt Mr Stick in the doorway, put up his hackles, bared his teeth and growled. Mr Stick hastily removed himself from the doorway and then neatly banged the door in the dog's face. He grinned at Julian.

'Now what are you going to do?' he said.

'Shall I tell you?' said Julian, his temper suddenly rising. 'I'm going to hurl this nice juicy meat-pie straight into your grinning face!'

He raised his arms, and Mr Stick ducked.

'Now don't you do that,' he said. 'I'm only pulling your leg, see? Don't you waste that nice meat-pie. You can go upstairs if you want to.'

He moved away to the sofa. Julian opened the door and Timothy bounded in growling. Mr Stick eyed him uncomfortably.

'Don't you let that nasty great dog come near me,' he said. 'I don't like dogs.'

'Then I wonder you don't get rid of Stinker,' said Julian. 'Come here, Timmy! Leave him alone. He's not worth growling at.'

Julian went upstairs with Timothy close at his heels. The

41

others crowded round him, wondering what had happened, for they had heard the voices downstairs. They laughed when Julian told them how he had nearly thrown the meat-pie at Mr Stick.

'It would have served him right,' said Anne, 'though it would have been a great pity, because we shouldn't have been able to eat it. Well, Mrs Stick may be simply horrible, but she *can* cook. This pie is gorgeous.'

The children finished all the pie and the tarts, too. Julian told them all about Mr Stick coming on leave from his ship.

'Three Sticks are a lot too much,' said Dick thoughtfully. 'Pity we can't get rid of them all and manage for ourselves. George, can't you possibly persuade your father tomorrow to let us get rid of the Sticks and look after ourselves?'

'I'll try,' said George. 'But you know what he is – awfully difficult to argue with. But I'll try. Golly, I'm sleepy now. Come on, Timmy, let's get to bed! Lie on my feet. I'm hardly going to let you out of my sight now, in case those awful Sticks poison you!'

Soon the four children, now no longer hungry, were sleeping peacefully. They did not fear the Sticks coming up to their rooms, for they knew that Timmy would wake and warn them at once. Timmy was the best guard they could have.

In the morning Mrs Stick actually produced some sort of breakfast, which surprised the children very much.

IN THE MIDDLE OF THE NIGHT

'Guess she knows your father will telephone, George,' said Julian, 'and she wants to keep herself in the right. When did he say he would 'phone? Nine o'clock, wasn't it? Well, it's half-past eight now. Let's go for a quick run down to the beach and back.'

So off they went, the five of them, ignoring Edgar, who stood in the back garden ready to make some of his silly faces at them. The children couldn't help thinking he must be a bit mad. He didn't behave at all like a boy of Julian's age.

When they came back it was about ten minutes to nine. 'We'll sit in the sitting-room till the telephone rings,' said Julian. 'We don't want Mrs Stick to answer it first.'

But to their great dismay, as they reached the house, they heard Mrs Stick using the telephone in the hall!

'Yes,' they heard her say, 'everything is quite all right. I can manage the children, even if they do make things a bit difficult. Yes, of course. Well it's lucky my husband is home on leave from his ship, because he can help me round, like, and it makes things easier. Don't you worry about anything, and don't you bother to come back till you're ready. I'll manage everything.'

George flew into the hall like a wild thing, and snatched the receiver out of Mrs Stick's hand.

'Father! It's me, George! How's Mother? Tell me quick!'

'No worse, George,' said her father's voice. 'But we shan't know anything definite till tomorrow morning. I'm glad to hear from Mrs Stick that everything is all right. I'm very upset and worried, and I'm glad to feel I can tell your mother that you are all right, and everything is going smoothly at Kirrin Cottage.'

'But it isn't,' said George, wildly. 'It isn't. It's all horrid. Can't the Sticks go and let us manage things by ourselves?'

'Good gracious me, of course not,' said her father's voice, surprised and annoyed. 'What can you be thinking of? I did hope, George, that you would be sensible and helpful. I must say . . .'

'*You* talk to him, Julian,' said George, helplessly, and thrust the receiver into Julian's hand. The boy put it to his ear and spoke into the telephone in his clear voice.

'Good morning. This is Julian! I'm glad my aunt is no worse.'

'Well, she will be if she thinks things are going wrong at Kirrin Cottage,' said Uncle Quentin, in an exasperated voice. 'Can't you manage George and make her see reason? Good gracious, can't she put up with the Sticks for a week or two? I tell you frankly, Julian, I am not going to sack the Sticks in my absence – I want the house ready for me to bring back your aunt. If you can't put up with them, you had better find out from your own parents if they can take you back for the rest of the holidays. But George is not to go with you. She is to stay at Kirrin Cottage. That's my last word on the subject.'

'But . . .' began Julian, wondering how in the world he could deal properly with his hot-tempered uncle, 'I must tell you that . . .'

44

IN THE MIDDLE OF THE NIGHT

There was a click at the other end of the 'phone. Uncle Quentin had put down his receiver and gone. There was no more to be said. Blow! Julian pursed up his mouth and looked round at the others, frowning.

'He's gone!' he said. 'Cut me off just as I was trying to reason with him!'

'Serves you right!' said Mrs Stick's harsh voice from the end of the hall. 'Now you know where you stand. I'm here and I'm staying here, on your uncle's orders. And you're all going to behave yourselves, or it'll be the worse for you.'

CHAPTER SIX

Julian defeats the Sticks

THERE WAS a slam. The kitchen door shut, and Mrs Stick could be heard telling the news triumphantly to Edgar and Mr Stick. The children went into the sitting-room, sat down and stared at one another gloomily.

'Father's awful!' said George, furiously. 'He never will listen to anything.'

'Well, after all, he is very upset,' said Dick, reasonably. 'It was a great pity that he rang before nine, so that Mrs Stick got her say in first.'

'What did Father say to you?' said George. 'Tell us exactly.'

'He said that if we couldn't put up with the Sticks, Anne and Dick and I were to go back to our own parents,' said Julian. 'But you were to stay here.'

George stared at Julian. 'Well,' she said at last, 'you *can't* put up with the Sticks, so you'd better all go back. I can look after myself.'

'Don't be an idiot!' said Julian, giving her arm a friendly shake. 'You know we wouldn't desert you. I can't say I look forward to the idea of being under the thumb of the amiable Sticks for a week or two, but there are worse things than that. We'll "stick" it together.'

But the feeble little joke didn't raise a smile, even from Anne. The idea of being under the Sticks' three thumbs was a most unpleasant prospect. Timothy put his head on George's knee. She patted him and looked round.

'You go back home,' she said to the others. 'I've got a plan of my own, and you're not in it. I've got Timmy, and he'll look after me. Telephone to your parents and go home tomorrow.'

George stared round defiantly. Her head was up, and there was no doubt but that she had made a plan of some sort.

Julian felt uneasy.

'Don't be silly,' he said. 'I tell you we all stand together in this. If you've got a plan, we'll come into it. But we're staying here with you, whatever happens.'

'Stay if you like,' said George, 'but my plan goes on, and you'll find you'll have to go home in the end. Come on, Timothy! Let's go to Jim and see if my boat is ready.'

'We'll go with you,' said Dick. He was sorry for George. He could see below her defiance, and he knew she was very unhappy, worried about her mother, angry with her father, and upset because she felt the others were staying on because of her, when they could go back home and have a lovely time.

It was not a happy day. George was very stand-offish, and kept on insisting that the others should go back home and leave her. She grew quite angry when they were as insistent that they would not.

'You're spoiling my plan,' she said at last. 'You *should* go back, you really should. I tell you, you're spoiling my plan completely.'

'Well, what *is* your plan?' said Julian impatiently. 'I can't help feeling you're just *pretending* you've got a plan, so that we'll go.'

'I'm *not* pretending,' said George, losing her temper. 'Do I ever pretend? You know I don't! If I say I've got a plan, I *have* got a plan. But I'm not giving it away, so it's no good asking me. It's my own secret, private plan.'

'Well, I really do think you might tell us,' said Dick, quite hurt. 'After all, we're your best friends, aren't we? And we're going to stick by you, plan or no plan – yes, even if we spoil your plan, as you say, we shall still stay here with you.'

'I shan't *let* you spoil my plan,' said George, her eyes flashing. 'You're mean. You're against me, just like the Sticks are.'

'Oh, George, don't,' said Anne, almost in tears. 'Don't let's quarrel. It's bad enough quarrelling with those awful Sticks, without *us* quarrelling too.'

George's temper died down as quickly as it had risen. She looked ashamed.

'Sorry!' she said. 'I'm an idiot. I won't quarrel. But I do mean what I say. I shall go on with my plan, and I shan't tell you what it is, because if I do, it will spoil the holidays for you. Please believe me.'

'Let's take our dinner out with us again,' said Julian,

getting up. 'We'll all feel better away from this house today. I'll go and tackle the old Stick.'

'Dear old Ju, isn't he brave!' said Anne, who would rather have died than go and face Mrs Stick at that moment.

Mrs Stick proved very difficult. She felt rather victorious at the time, and was also very annoyed to find that her beautiful meat-pie and jam-tarts had disappeared. Mr Stick was in the middle of telling her where they had gone when Julian appeared.

'How you can expect sandwiches for a picnic when you've stolen my meat-pie and jam-tarts, I *don't* know!' she began, indignantly. 'You can have dry bread and jam for your picnic, and that's all. And what's more, I wouldn't give you that either except that I'm glad to be rid of you.'

'Good riddance to bad rubbish,' murmured Edgar to himself. He was lying sprawled on the sofa, reading some kind of highly-coloured comic.

'If you've anything to say to me, Edgar, come outside and say it,' said Julian, dangerously.

'You leave Edgar alone,' said Mrs Stick, at once.

'There's nothing I should like better,' said Julian, scornfully. 'Who wants to be with him? Cowardly little spotty-face!'

'Now, now, look 'ere!' began Mr Stick, from his corner.

'I don't want to look at you,' said Julian at once.

'Now, look *'ere*,' said Mr Stick, angrily, standing up.

49

'I've told you I don't want to,' said Julian. 'You're not a pleasant sight.'

'*Insolence!*' said Mrs Stick, rapidly losing her temper.

'No, not insolence – just the plain truth,' said Julian, airily. Mrs Stick glared at him. Julian defeated her. He had such a ready tongue, and he said everything so politely. The ruder his words were, the more politely he spoke. Mrs Stick didn't understand people like Julian. She felt that they were too clever for her. She hated the boy, and banged a saucepan viciously down on the sink, wishing that it was Julian's head under the saucepan instead of the sink.

Stinker jumped up and growled at the sudden noise.

'Hallo, Stinker!' said Julian. 'Had a bath yet? Alas, no! – as smelly as ever, aren't you?'

'You know that dog's name isn't Stinker,' said Mrs Stick, angrily. 'You get out of my kitchen.'

'Right!' said Julian. 'Pleased to go. Don't bother about the dry bread and jam. I'll manage something a bit better than that.'

He went out, whistling. Stinker growled, and Edgar repeated loudly what he had said before: 'Good riddance to bad rubbish!'

'What did you say?' said Julian, suddenly poking his head in at the kitchen door again. But Edgar did not dare to repeat it, so off went Julian again, whistling merrily, but not feeling nearly as merry as his whistle. He was worried. After all, if Mrs Stick was going to make meals as difficult as this, life was not going to be very pleasant at Kirrin Cottage.

'Anyone feel inclined to have dry bread and jam for lunch?' inquired Julian, when he returned to the others. 'No? I rather thought so, so I turned down Mrs Stick's kind offer. I vote we go and buy something decent. That shop in the village has good sausage-rolls.'

George was very silent all that day. She was worrying about her mother, the others knew. She was probably thinking about her plan too, they thought, and wondered whatever it could be.

'Shall we go over to Kirrin Island today?' asked Julian, thinking that it would take George's mind off her worries, if they went to her beloved island.

George shook her head.

'No,' she said. 'I don't feel like it. The boat's all ready, I know – but I just don't feel like it. You see, till I know Mother is going to get better, I don't feel I want to be out of reach of the house. If a telephone message came from Father, the Sticks could always send Edgar to look for me – and if I was on the island, he couldn't find me.'

The children messed about that day, doing nothing at all. They went back to tea, and Mrs Stick provided them with bread and butter and jam, but no cake. The milk was sour too, and everyone had to have tea without milk, which they all disliked.

As they ate their tea, the children heard Edgar outside

the window. He held a tin bowl in his hand, and put it down on the grass outside.

'Your dog's dinner,' he yelled.

'He looks like a dog's dinner himself,' said Dick, in disgust. 'Messy creature!'

That made everyone laugh. 'Edgar, the Dog's Dinner!' said Anne. 'Any biscuits in that tin on the sideboard, do you think, George?'

George got up to see. Timothy slipped out of doors and went to the dish put down for him. He sniffed at it. George, coming back from the sideboard, looked out of the window as she passed and saw him. At once the thought of poison came back to her mind and she yelled to Timothy, making the others jump out of their skins.

'TIM! TIM! Don't touch it!'

Timothy wagged his tail as if to say he didn't mean to touch it, anyway. George rushed out of doors, and picked up the mess of raw meat. She sniffed at it.

'You haven't touched it, have you, Timothy?' she said, anxiously.

Dick leaned out of the window.

'No, he didn't eat any. I watched him. He sniffed all round and about it, but he wouldn't touch it. I bet it's been dosed with rat-poison or something.'

George was very white. 'Oh Timmy!' she said. 'You're such a sensible dog. You wouldn't touch poisoned stuff, would you?'

52

JULIAN DEFEATS THE STICKS

'Woof!' said Timmy, decidedly. Stinker heard the bark and put his nose out of the kitchen door.

George called to him in a loud voice:

'Stinker, Stinker, come here! Timmy doesn't want his dinner. You can have it. Come along, Stinker, here it is!'

Edgar came rushing out behind Stinker. 'Don't you give that to him,' he said.

'Why not?' asked George. 'Go on, Edgar – tell me why not.'

'He doesn't eat raw meat,' said Edgar, after a pause. 'He only eats dog biscuits.'

'That's a lie!' said George, flaming up. 'I saw him eating meat yesterday. Here, Stinker – you come and eat this.'

Edgar snatched the bowl from George, almost snarling at her, and ran indoors at top speed. George was about to go after him, but Julian, who had jumped out of the window when Edgar came up, stopped her.

'No good, old thing!' he said. 'You won't get anything out of him. The meat's probably at the back of the kitchen fire by now. From now on, we feed Timothy ourselves with meat bought from the butcher with our own money. Don't be afraid that he'll eat poisoned stuff. He's too wise a dog for that.'

'He might, if he was terribly, awfully hungry, Julian,' said George, looking rather green now. She felt sick inside. 'I wasn't going to let Stinker eat that poisoned stuff, of course, but I guessed that if it *was* poisoned, one of the Sticks would come rushing out and stop Stinker eating it. And Edgar did. So it proves it was poisoned, doesn't it?'

'I rather think it does,' said Julian. 'But don't worry,
George. Timmy won't be poisoned.'

'But he might, he might,' said George, putting her hand

on the big dog's head. 'Oh, I can't bear the thought of it, Julian. I can't, I really can't.'

'Don't think about it then,' said Julian, taking her indoors again. 'Here, have a biscuit!'

'You don't think the Sticks would poison *us*, do you?' said Anne, looking suddenly scared and gazing at her biscuit as if it might bite her.

'No, idiot. They only want to get Timmy out of the way because he guards us so well,' said Julian. 'Don't look so scared. All this will settle down in a day or two, and we'll have a grand time after all. You'll see!'

But Julian only said this to comfort his little sister. Secretly he was very worried. He wished he could take Anne, Dick and George back to his own home. But he knew George wouldn't come. And how could they leave her to the Sticks? It was quite impossible. Friends must stick together, and somehow they must face things until Aunt Fanny and Uncle Quentin came back.

CHAPTER SEVEN

Better news

'DO YOU think we'd better slip down after the Sticks have gone to bed and get some food out of the larder again?' said Dick, when no supper appeared that evening.

Julian didn't feel inclined to sneak down and confront Mr Stick again. Not that he was afraid of him, but the whole thing was so unpleasant. This was their house, the food was theirs – so why should they have to beg for it, or take it on the sly? It was ridiculous.

'Come here, Timothy!' said Julian. The dog left George's side and went to Julian, looking up at the boy inquiringly. 'You're going to come with me and persuade dear kind Mrs Stick to give us the best things out of the larder!' said Julian, with a grin.

The others laughed, cheering up at once.

'Good idea!' said Dick. 'Can we all come and see the fun.'

'Better not,' said Julian. 'I can manage fine by myself.'

He went down the passage to the kitchen. The radio was going inside, so no one in the kitchen heard Julian till he was actually standing inside the door. Then Edgar looked up and saw Timothy as well as Julian.

Edgar was scared of the big dog, who was now growling

fiercely. He went behind the kitchen sofa and stayed there, eyeing Timmy fearfully.

'What do you want?' said Mrs Stick, turning off the radio.

'Supper,' said Julian, pleasantly. 'Supper! The best things out of the larder – bought with my uncle's money, cooked on my aunt's stove with gas she pays for – yes, supper! Open the larder door and let's see what there is in there.'

'Well, of all the nerve!' began Mr Stick, in amazement.

'You can have a loaf of bread and some cheese,' said Mrs Stick, 'and that's my last word.'

'Well, it isn't my last word,' said Julian, and he went to the larder door. 'Timmy, keep to heel! Growl all you like, but don't bite anybody – yet!'

Timmy's growls were really frightful. Even Mr Stick put himself at the other end of the room. As for Stinker, he was nowhere to be seen. He had gone into the scullery at the very first growl, and was now shivering behind the wringer.

Mrs Stick's mouth went into a hard straight line. 'You take the bread and cheese and clear out,' she said

Julian opened the larder door, whistling softly which annoyed Mrs Stick more than anything else. 'My word!' said Julian, admiringly. 'You do know how to stock a larder, I must say, Mrs Stick. A roast chicken! I thought I smelt one cooking. I suppose Mr Stick killed one of our chickens today. I thought I heard a lot of squawking. And what fine tomatoes! Best to be got from the village, I've no doubt. And oh, Mrs Stick – what a perfectly *marvellous* treacle tart! I must say you're a good cook, I really must.'

Julian picked up the chicken, the dish of tomatoes and then balanced the plate with the treacle tart on the top.

Mrs Stick yelled at him.

'You leave those things alone! That's our supper! You leave them there.'

'You've made a little mistake,' said Julian, politely. 'It's *our* supper! We've had very little to eat today, and we could do with a good supper. Thanks awfully!'

'Now look 'ere!' began Mr Stick, angrily, furious at seeing his lovely supper walking away.

'You surely don't want me to look at you *again*,' said Julian, in a tone of amazement. 'What for? Have you shaved yet – or washed? I'm afraid not. So, if you don't mind I think I'd rather *not* look at you.'

Mr Stick was speechless. He was not ready with his tongue at any time, and a boy like Julian took his breath away, and left him with nothing to say except his favourite 'Now, look 'ere!'

'Put those things down,' said Mrs Stick sharply. 'What do you think we're going to have for *our* supper if you walk off with them? You tell me that!'

'Easy!' said Julian. 'Let me offer you *our* supper – bread and cheese, Mrs Stick, bread and cheese!'

Mrs Stick made an angry noise, and started to go after Julian with her hand raised. But Timothy immediately

58

leapt at her, and his teeth snapped together with a loud click.

'Oh!' howled Mrs Stick. 'That dog of yours nearly took my hand off! The brute! I'll do for him one day, you see if I don't.'

'You had a good try today, didn't you?' said Julian, in a quiet voice, fixing his eyes straight on the woman's face. 'That's a matter for the police, isn't it? Be careful, Mrs Stick. I've a good mind to go to the police tomorrow.'

Just as before, the mention of the police seemed to frighten Mrs Stick. She cast a look at her husband and took a step backwards. Julian wondered if the man had done something wrong and was hiding from the police. He never seemed to put a foot out of doors.

The boy went up the passage triumphantly. Timmy followed at his heels, disappointed that he hadn't been able to get a nibble at Stinker. Julian marched into the sitting-room, and set the dishes carefully down on the table.

'What ho!' he said. 'Look what *I've* got – the Sticks' own supper!' Then he told the others all that had happened, and they laughed loudly.

'How do you think of all those things to say?' said Anne, admiringly. 'I don't wonder you make them feel wild, Ju. It's a good thing we've got Timmy to back us up.'

'Yes, I shouldn't feel nearly so bold without Timmy,' said Julian.

It was a very good supper. There were knives and forks in the sideboard, and the children made do with fruit plates from the sideboard too, rather than go and get plates from the kitchen. There was bread over from their tea, so they were able to make a very good meal. They enjoyed it thoroughly.

'Sorry we can't give you the chicken bones, Tim,' said George, 'but they might splinter inside you and injure you. You can have all the scraps. See you don't leave any for Stinker!'

Timmy didn't. With two or three great gulps he cleared his plate, and then sat waiting for any scraps of treacle tart that might descend his way.

BETTER NEWS

The children felt cheerful after such a good meal. They had completely eaten the chicken. Nothing was left except a pile of bones. They had eaten all the tomatoes too, finished the bread, and enjoyed every scrap of the treacle tart.

It was late, Anne yawned, and then George yawned too. 'Let's go to bed,' she said. 'I don't feel like having a game of cards or anything.'

So they went to bed, and as usual Timothy lay heavily on George's feet. He lay there awake for some time, his ears cocked to hear noises from below. He heard the Sticks go up to bed. He heard doors closing. He heard a whine from Stinker. Then all was silence. Timmy dropped his head on to his paws and slept – but he kept one ear cocked for danger. Timothy didn't trust the Sticks any more than the children did!

The children awoke very early in the morning. Julian awoke first. It was a marvellous day. Julian went to the window and looked out. The sky was a very pale blue, and rosy-pink clouds floated about it. The sea was a clear blue too, smooth and calm. Julian remembered what Anne often said – she said that the world in the early morning always looked as if it had come back fresh from the laundry – so clean and new and fresh!

The children all bathed before breakfast, and this time they were back at half-past eight, afraid that George's father might telephone early again. Julian saw Mrs Stick on the stairs and called to her.

'Has my uncle telephoned yet?'

'No,' said the woman, in a surly tone. She had been hoping that the telephone would ring while the children were out, then, as she had done the day before, she could answer it, and get a few words in first.

'We'll have breakfast now, please,' said Julian. 'A *good* breakfast, Mrs Stick. My uncle *might* ask us what we'd had for breakfast, mightn't he? You never know.'

Mrs Stick evidently thought that Julian might tell his uncle if she gave them only bread and butter for breakfast, so very soon the children smelt a delicious smell of bacon frying. Mrs Stick brought in a dish of it garnished with tomatoes. She banged it down on the table with the plates. Edgar arrived with a pot of tea and a tray of cups and saucers.

'Ah, here is dear Edgar!' said Julian, in a tone of amiable surprise. 'Dear old spotty-face!'

'Garn!' said Edgar, and banged down the teapot. Timmy growled, and Edgar fled for his life.

George didn't want any breakfast. Julian put hers back in the warm dish and put a plate over it. He knew that she was waiting for news. If only the telephone would ring – then she would know if her mother was really better or not.

It did ring as they were half-way through the meal. George was there before the bell had stopped pealing. She put the receiver to her ear. 'Father! Yes, it's George. How's Mother?'

BETTER NEWS

There was a pause as George listened. All the children stopped eating and listened in silence, waiting for George to speak. They would know by her next words if the news was good or not.

'Oh – oh, I'm so glad!' they heard George say. 'Did she have the operation yesterday? Oh, you never told me! But it's all right now, is it? Poor Mother! Give her my love. I do want to see her. Oh Father, can't I come?'

Evidently the answer was no. George listened for a while then spoke a few more words and said goodbye.

She ran into the sitting-room. 'You heard, didn't you?' she said, joyfully. 'Mother's better. She'll get all right now, and will be back home soon – in about ten days. Father won't come back till he brings her home. It's good news about Mother – but I'm afraid we can't get rid of the Sticks.'

CHAPTER EIGHT

George's plan

MRS STICK had overheard the conversation on the telephone – at least, she had heard George's side of it. She knew that George's mother was better and that her father would not return till her mother could be brought home. That would be in about ten days! The Sticks could have a fine time till then, no doubt about that!

George suddenly found that her appetite had come back. She ate her bacon hungrily, and scraped the dish round with a piece of bread. She had three cups of tea, and then sat back contentedly.

'I feel better,' she said. Anne slipped her hand in hers. She was very glad that her aunt was going to be all right. If it wasn't for those awful Sticks they could have a lovely time. Then George said something that made Julian cross.

'Well, now that I know Mother is going to be better, I can stand up to the Sticks all right by myself with Timmy. So I want you three to go back home and finish the hols without me. I shall be all right.'

'Shut up, George,' said Julian. 'We've argued this all out before. I've made up my mind – and I don't change it, any more than *you* do, when I've made it up. You make me cross.'

GEORGE'S PLAN

'Well,' said George, 'I told you I'd got a plan – and you don't come into it, I'm afraid – and you'll find you'll have to go back home whether you mean to or not.'

'Don't be so mysterious, George!' said Julian, impatiently. 'What is this strange plan? You'd better tell us, even if we're not in it. Can't you trust us?'

'Yes, of course. But you might try to stop me,' said George, looking sulky.

'Then you'd certainly better tell us,' said Julian feeling uneasy. George could be so reckless once she got ideas into her head. Goodness knows what she might do!

But George wouldn't say another word. Julian gave it up at last, but secretly made up his mind not to let George out of his sight that day. If she was going to carry out some wild plan, then she would have to do it under his, Julian's, eye!

But George didn't seem to be carrying out any wild plan. She bathed again with the others, went out for a walk with them, and went for a row on the sea. She didn't want to go to Kirrin Island, so the others didn't press her, thinking that she didn't want to be out of sight of the beach in case Edgar came with a message from her father.

It was quite a pleasant day. The children bought sausage rolls again, and fruit, and picnicked on the beach. Timmy had a large and juicy bone from the butcher's.

'I've got a bit of shopping to do,' said George, about tea-time. 'You others go and see if Mrs Stick is getting some tea for us, and I'll fly down to the shops and get what I want.'

Julian pricked up his ears at once. Was George sending them off so that she could be alone to carry out this mysterious plan of hers?

'I'll come with you,' said Julian, getting up. 'Dick can tackle Mrs Stick for once, and take Timmy with him.'

'No, you go,' said George. 'I won't be long.'

But Julian was determined not to go. In the end they all went with George, for Dick did not want to face Mrs Stick without Julian or George.

George went into the little general shop and got a new battery for her torch. She bought two boxes of matches, and a bottle of methylated spirit.

GEORGE'S PLAN

'Whatever do you want that for?' said Anne in surprise.

'Oh, it might come in useful,' said George, and said no more.

They all went back to Kirrin Cottage. Tea was actually on the table! True, it was not a thrilling tea, being merely bread and jam and a pot of hot tea – still it was there, and was edible.

It rained that evening. The children sat round the table and played cards. Their hearts were lighter now that they had had good news of George's mother. In the middle of the game Julian got up and rang the bell. The others stared at him in the greatest surprise.

'What are you ringing the bell for?' asked George, her eyes wide with astonishment.

'To tell Mrs Stick to bring some supper,' said Julian, with a grin. But no one answered the bell. So Julian rang again and then again.

The kitchen door opened at last and Mrs Stick came up the passage, evidently in a bad temper. She came into the sitting-room.

'You stop ringing that bell!' she said, angrily. 'I'm not answering any bells rung by you.'

'I rang it to tell you that we wanted some supper,' said Julian. 'And to say that if you would rather I came and got it myself from the larder – with Timmy – as I did last night, I'll come with pleasure. But if not, you can bring a decent supper to us yourself.'

'If you come stealing things out of my larder again, I'll – I'll . . .' began Mrs Stick.

'You'll call in the police!' Julian finished for her. 'Do. That would please us very much. I can see our local policeman taking down all the details in his note book. I could give him quite a few.'

Mrs Stick muttered something rude under her breath, glared at Julian as if she could kill him, and went off down the passage again. By the sound of the clattering and crashing of crockery in the kitchen it was plain that Mrs Stick was getting some sort of supper for them, and Julian grinned to himself as he dealt out the cards.

Supper was not as good as the night before, but it was not bad. It was a little cold ham, cheese and the remains of a milk pudding. There was also a plate of cooked meat for Timmy.

George looked at it sharply. 'Take that away,' she said. 'I bet you've poisoned it again. Take it away!'

'No. On the contrary, leave it here,' said Julian. 'I'll take it down to the local chemist tomorrow and get him to test it. If, as George thinks, it's poisoned, the chemist might have a lot of interesting things to tell us.'

Mrs Stick took the meat away without a word. 'Horrible woman!' said George, pulling Timothy close to her. 'How I hate her! I feel so afraid for Timmy.'

Somehow that spoilt the evening. As it grew dark the children became sleepy. 'It's ten o'clock,' said Julian. 'Bed, I think, everyone! Anne ought to have gone long ago. She isn't nearly old enough to stay up as late as this.'

GEORGE'S PLAN

'*Well*!' began Anne, indignantly. 'I'm nearly as old as George, aren't I? I can't help being younger, can I?'

'All right, all right!' said Julian laughing. 'I shan't make you go off to bed by yourself, don't worry. We all keep together in this house while the Sticks are about. Come on! We'll go now, shall we?'

The children were tired. They had swum, walked and rowed that day. Julian tried to keep awake a little while, but he too fell asleep very quickly.

He awoke with a jump, thinking that he had heard a noise. But everything was quiet. What could the noise have been? Was it one of the Sticks creeping about? No – it couldn't be that, or Tim would have barked the house down. Then what was it? *Something* must have woken him.

'I suppose it's not old George doing anything about that plan of hers!' thought Julian, suddenly. He sat up. He felt about for his dressing-gown and put it on. Without waking Dick he crept to the girls' room, and switched on his torch to see that they were all right.

Anne was in her bed, sleeping peacefully. But George's bed was empty. George's clothes were gone!

'Blow!' said Julian, under his breath. 'Where has she gone? I bet she's run away to find where her mother is!'

His torch picked out a white envelope pinned to George's pillow. He stepped softly over to it.

It had his name printed on it in bold letters. 'JULIAN.' Julian ripped it open and read it.

FIVE RUN AWAY TOGETHER

'DEAR JULIAN,' said the note,

'Don't be angry with me, please. I daren't stay in Kirrin Cottage any longer in case the Sticks somehow poison Timmy. You know that would break my heart. So I've gone to live by myself on our island till Mother and Father come back. Please leave a note for Father and tell him to ask Jim to sail near Kirrin Island with his little red flag flying from the mast as soon as they are back. Then I'll come home. You and Dick and Anne must go back to your own parents now I've gone. It would be silly to stay at Kirrin Cottage with the Sticks now I'm not there.

Love from
GEORGE.'

Julian read the note through. 'Well, why didn't I *guess* that was her plan!' he said to himself. 'That's why we didn't come into it! She meant to go off by herself with Timmy. I can't let her do that. She can't live all by herself on Kirrin Island for so long. She might fall ill. She might slip on a rock and hurt herself, and no one would ever know!'

The boy was really worried about the determined little girl. He wondered what to do. That noise he heard must have been made by George. So she couldn't have got a very long start really. If he tore down to the beach, George might still be there, and he could stop her.

So, in his dressing-gown, he ran down the front path,

out of the gate, and took the road to the beach. The rain had stopped, and the stars were out. But it was not at all a light night.

'How can George expect to get through those rocks in the dark,' he thought. 'She's mad! She'll strike her boat on a rock, and sink.'

He tore on in the darkness, talking aloud to himself. 'No wonder she wanted a new battery for her torch, and matches – and I suppose the methylated spirit was for her little cooking stove! Why ever couldn't she tell us? It would have been fun to go with her.'

He came to the beach. He saw the light of a torch where George kept her boat. He ran to it, his feet sinking in the soft wet sand.

'George! Idiot! You're not to go off like this all alone, in the dead of night!' called Julian.

George was pushing her boat out into the water. She jumped when she heard Julian's voice. 'You can't stop me!' she said. 'I'm just off!'

But Julian caught hold of the boat, as he waded up to his waist in the water. 'George, listen to me! You can't go like this. You'll strike a rock. Come back!'

'No,' said George, getting cross. 'You can go back to your own home, Julian. I shall be all right. Let go my boat!'

'George, why didn't you tell me your plan?' said Julian, almost swept off his feet by a wave. 'Dash these waves! I shall have to get into the boat.'

He climbed in. He could not see George, but he felt quite certain she was glaring at him. Timmy licked his wet legs.

'You're spoiling everything,' said George, with a break

in her voice that meant she was upset.

'I'm not, silly!' said Julian, in a gentle voice. 'Listen! – you come back to Kirrin Cottage with me now, George, and I'll faithfully promise you something. Tomorrow we'll *all* go to the island with you. See? The whole lot of us. Why shouldn't we? Your mother said we could spend a week there, anyway, didn't she? We shall be out of the reach of those horrible Sticks. We shall enjoy ourselves, and have a marvellous time. So will you come back now, George, and let us go together tomorrow?'

CHAPTER NINE

An exciting night

THERE WAS a silence, except for the waves splashing round the boat. Then George's voice came out of the darkness, lifted joyfully.

'Oh Julian – do you really mean it? Will you really come with me? I was afraid I'd get into trouble for doing this, because Father said I must stay at Kirrin Cottage till he came back – and you know how he hates disobedience. But I knew if I stayed there, you would too – and I didn't want you to be miserable with those horrid Sticks – so I thought I'd come away. I didn't think you'd come too, because of getting into trouble! I never even thought of asking you.'

'You're a very stupid person sometimes, aren't you, George?' said Julian. 'As if we'd care about getting into trouble, so long as we were all together, sticking by one another! Of course we'll come with you – and I'll take all the responsibility for this escape, and tell your father it's my fault.'

'Oh no you won't,' said George, quickly. 'I shall say it was my idea. If I do wrong, I'm not afraid to own up to it. You know that.'

'Well, we won't argue that now,' said Julian. 'We shall

have at least a week or ten days on Kirrin Island to do all the arguing we want to. The thing is – let's get back now, wake up the others for a bit, and have a nice quiet talk in the dead of night about this plan of yours. I must say it's a very, very good idea!'

George was overjoyed. 'I feel as if I could hug you, Julian,' she said. 'Where are the oars? Oh, here they are! The boat's floated quite a long way out.'

She rowed strongly back to the shore. Julian jumped out and pulled the boat up the beach, with George's help. He shone his torch into the boat and gave an exclamation.

'You've quite a nice little store of things here,' he said. 'Bread and ham and butter and stuff. How did you manage to get them without old Mr Stick seeing you tonight? I suppose you slipped down and got them out of the larder?'

'Yes, I did,' said George. 'But there was no one in the kitchen tonight. Perhaps Mr Stick has gone to sleep upstairs. Or maybe he has gone back to his ship. Anyway, there was no one there when I crept down, not even Stinker.'

'We'd better leave them here,' said Julian. 'Stuff them into that locker and shut down the lid. No one will guess there's anything there. We'll have to bring down a lot more stuff if we're all going to live on the island. Golly, this is going to be fun!'

The children made their way back to the house, feeling thrilled and excited. Julian's wet dressing-gown flapped round his legs, and he pulled it up high to be out of the way. Timothy gambolled round, not seeming at all surprised at the night's doings.

When they got back to the house they woke the other two, who listened in astonishment to what had happened that night. Anne was so excited to think that they were all going to live on the island that she raised her voice in joy.

'Oh! That's the loveliest thing that could happen! Oh, I do think . . .'

'Shut up!' said three furious voices in loud whispers. 'You'll wake the Sticks!'

'Sorry!' whispered Anne. 'But oh – it's so terribly, awfully exciting.'

They began to discuss the plans. 'If we go for a week or ten days, we must take plenty of stores,' said Julian.

'The thing is – can we possibly find food enough for so long? Even if we entirely empty the larder I doubt if that would be enough for a week or so. We all seem such hungry people, somehow.'

'Julian,' said George, suddenly remembering something, '*I* know what we'll do! Mother has a store-cupboard in her room. She keeps dozens and dozens of tins of food there, in case we ever get snowed up in the winter, and can't go to the village. That has happened once or twice, you know. And I know where Mother keeps the key! Can't we open the cupboard and get out some tins?'

'Of course!' said Julian, delighted. 'I know Aunt Fanny wouldn't mind. And anyway, we can make a list of what we take and replace them for her, if she does mind. It will be my birthday soon, and I am sure to get money then.'

'Where's the key?' whispered Dick.

'Let's go into Mother's room, and I'll show you where she keeps it,' said George. 'I only hope she hasn't taken it with her.'

But George's mother had felt far too ill when she left home to think of cupboard keys. George fumbled at the back of a drawer in the dressing-table and brought out two or three keys tied together with thin string. She fitted first one and then another into a cupboard set in the wall. The second one opened the door.

Julian shone his torch into the cupboard. It was filled with tins of food of all kinds, neatly arranged on the shelves.

'Golly!' said Dick, his eyes gleaming. 'Soup – tins of meat – tins of fruit – tinned milk – sardines – tinned butter – biscuits – tinned vegetables! There's everything we want here!'

'Yes,' said Julian, pleased. 'It's fine. We'll take all we can carry. Is there a sack or two anywhere about, George, do you know?'

Soon the tins were quietly packed into two sacks. The cupboard door was shut and locked again. The children stole to their own rooms once more.

'Well, that's the biggest problem solved – food,' said Julian. 'We'll raid the larder too, and take what bread there is – and cake. What about water, George? Is there any on the island?'

'Well, I suppose there is some in that old well,' said George, thinking, 'but as there's no bucket or anything, we can't get any. I was taking a big container of fresh water with me – but we'd better fill two or three more now you are all coming! I know where there are some, quite clean and new.'

So they filled some containers with fresh water, and put them with the sacks, ready to take to the boat. It was so exciting doing all these things in the middle of the night! Anne could hardly keep her voice down to a whisper, and it was a wonder that Timothy didn't bark for he sensed the excitement of the others.

AN EXCITING NIGHT

There was a tin of cakes in the larder, freshly made, so those were added to the heap that was forming in the front garden. There was a large joint of meat too, and George wrapped it in a cloth and put that with the heap, telling Timmy in a fierce voice that if he so much as sniffed at it she would leave him behind!

'I've got my little stove for boiling water on, or heating up anything,' whispered George. 'It's in the boat. That's what I bought the methylated spirit for, of course. You didn't guess, did you? And the matches for lighting it. I say – what about candles? We can't use our torches all the time, the batteries would soon run out.'

They found a packet of candles in the kitchen cupboard, a kettle, a saucepan, some old knives and forks and spoons, and a good many other things they thought they might possibly want. They also came across some small bottles of ginger-beer, evidently stored for their own use by the Sticks.

'All bought out of my mother's money!' said George. 'Well, we'll take the ginger-beer too. It will be nice to drink it on a hot day.'

'Where are we going to sleep at night?' said Julian. 'In that ruined part of the old castle, where there is just one room with a roof left, and walls?'

'That's where I planned to sleep,' said George. 'I was going to make my bed of some of the heather that grows on the island, covered by a rug or two, which I've got down in the boat.'

'We'll take all the rugs we can find,' said Julian. 'And some cushions for pillows. I say, isn't this simply thrilling? I don't know when I've felt so excited. I feel like a prisoner escaping to freedom! Won't the Sticks be amazed when they find us gone!'

'Yes – we'll have to decide what to say to them,' said George, rather soberly. 'We don't want them sending people after us to the island, making us come back. I don't think they should know we've gone there.'

'We'll discuss that later,' said Dick. 'The thing is to get everything to the boat while it's dark. It will soon be dawn.'

'How are we going to get all this down to George's boat?' said Anne, looking at the enormous pile of goods by the light of her torch. 'We'll never be able to carry them all!'

Certainly it looked a great pile. Julian had an idea, as usual. 'Are there any barrows in the shed?' he asked George. 'If we could pile the things into a couple of barrows, we could easily take everything in one journey. We could wheel the barrows along on the sandy side of the road so that we don't make any noise.'

'Oh, good idea!' said George, delighted. 'I wish I'd thought of that before. I had to make about five journeys to and from the boat when I took my own things. There are two barrows in the shed. We'll get them. One has a squeaky wheel, but we'll hope no one hears it.'

Stinker heard the squeak, as he lay in a corner of

AN EXCITING NIGHT

Mrs Stick's room. He pricked up his ears and growled softly. He did not dare to bark, for he was afraid of bringing Timothy up. Mrs Stick did not hear the growl. She slept soundly, not even stirring. She had no idea what was going on downstairs.

The things were all stowed into the boat. The children didn't like leaving them there unguarded. In the end they decided to leave Dick there, sleeping on the rugs. They stood thinking for a moment before they went back without Dick.

'I do hope we've remembered all we shall want,' said George, wrinkling up her forehead. 'Golly – I know! We haven't remembered a tin-opener – nor a thing to take off the tops of the ginger-beer bottles. They've got those little tin lids that have to be forced off by an opener.'

'We'll put those in our pockets when we get back to the house and find them,' said Julian. 'I remember seeing some in the sideboard drawer. Goodbye, Dick. We'll be down very early to row off. We must get some bread at the baker's as soon as he opens, because we've got hardly any, and we'll see if we can pick up a very large bone at the butcher's for Timmy. George has got a bag of biscuits in the boat for him too.'

The three of them set off back to the house with Timmy, leaving Dick curled up comfortably on the rugs. He soon fell asleep again, his face upturned to the stars that would soon fade from the sky.

The others talked about what to tell the Sticks. 'I think

we won't tell them anything,' said Julian, at last. 'I don't particularly want to tell them deliberate lies, and I'm certainly not going to tell them the truth. I know what we'll do – there is a train that leaves the station about eight o'clock, which would be the one we'd catch if we were going back to our own home. We'll find a time-table, leave it open on the dining-room table, as if we'd been looking up a train, and then we'll all set off across the moor at the back of the house, as if we were going to the station.'

'Oh yes – then the Sticks will think we've run away, and gone to catch the train back home,' said Anne. 'They will never guess we've gone to the island.'

'That's a good idea,' said George, pleased. 'But how shall we know when Father and Mother get back?'

'Is there anyone you could leave a message with – somebody you could really trust?' asked Julian.

George thought hard. 'There's Alf the fisher-boy,' she said at last. 'He used to look after Tim for me when I wasn't allowed to have him in the house. I know he'd not give us away.'

'We'll call on Alf before we go then,' said Julian. 'Now, let's look for that timetable and lay it open on the table at the right place.'

They hunted for the timetable, found the right page, and underlined the train they hoped that the Sticks would think they were catching. They found the tin and bottle openers and put them into their pockets. Julian found two or three more boxes of matches too. He thought two would not last long enough.

By this time dawn had come and the house was being flooded with early sunshine. 'I wonder if the baker is open,' said Julian. 'We might as well go and see. It's about six o'clock.'

They went to the baker. He was not open, but the new loaves had already been made. The baker was outside, sunning himself. He had baked his bread at night, ready to sell it new-made in the morning. He grinned at the children.

'Up early today,' he said. 'What, you want some of my loaves – how many? Six! Good gracious, whatever for?'

'To eat,' said George, grinning. Julian paid for six enormous loaves, and they went to the butcher's. His shop was not open either, but the butcher himself was sweeping the path outside. 'Could we buy a very big bone for Timmy, please?' asked George. She got an enormous one, and Timmy looked at it longingly. Such a bone would last him for days, he knew!

'Now,' said Julian, as they set off to the boat, 'we'll pack these things into the boat, then go back to the house, and make a noise so that the Sticks know we're there. Then we'll set off across the moors, and hope the Sticks will think we are making for the train.'

They woke Dick, who was still sleeping peacefully in the boat, and packed in the bread and bone.

'Take the boat into the next cove,' said George. 'Can

you do that? We shall be hidden there from anyone on the beach then. The fishermen are all out in their boats, fishing. We shan't be seen, if we set off in about an hour's time. We'll be back by then.'

They went back to the house and made a noise as if they were just getting up. George whistled to Timmy, and Julian sang at the top of his voice. Then, with a great banging of doors, they set out down the path and cut across the moors, in full sight of the kitchen window.

'Hope the Sticks won't notice Dick isn't with us,' said Julian, seeing Edgar staring out of the window. 'I expect they'll think he's gone ahead.'

They kept to the path until they came to a dip, where they were hidden from any watcher at Kirrin Cottage. Then they took another path that led them, unseen, to the cove where Dick had taken the boat. He was there, waiting anxiously for them.

'Ahoy there!' yelled Julian, in excitement. 'The adventure is about to begin.'

CHAPTER TEN

Kirrin Island once more!

THEY ALL clambered into the boat. Timothy leapt in lightly and ran to the prow, where he always stood. His tongue hung out in excitement. He knew quite well that something was up – and he was in it! No wonder he panted and wagged his tail hard.

'Off we go!' said Julian, taking the oars. 'Sit over there a bit, Anne. The luggage is weighing down the boat awfully the other end. Dick, sit by Anne to keep the balance better. That's right. Off we go!'

And off they went in George's boat, rocking up and down on the waves. The sea was fairly calm, but a good breeze blew through their hair. The water splashed round the boat and made a nice gurgly, friendly noise. The children all felt very happy. They were on their own. They were escaping from the horrid Sticks. They were going to stay on Kirrin Island, with the rabbits and gulls and jackdaws.

'Doesn't that new-made bread smell awfully good?' said Dick, feeling very hungry as usual. 'Can we just grab a bit, do you think?'

'Yes, let's,' said George. So they broke off bits of the warm brown crust, handed some to Julian, who was rowing, and chewed the delicious new-made bread. Timmy got a bit too, but his was gone as soon as it went into his mouth.

'Timmy's funny,' said Anne. 'He never eats his food as we do – he seems to *drink* it – just takes it into his mouth and swallows it, as if it was water!'

The others laughed. 'He doesn't drink his bones,' said George. 'He always eats those all right – chews on them for hours and hours. Don't you, Timothy?'

'Woof!' said Timmy, agreeing. He eyed the place where that enormous bone was, wishing he could have it now. But the children wouldn't let him. They were afraid it might go overboard, and that would be a pity.

'I don't believe anyone has noticed us going,' said Julian. 'Except Alf the fisher-boy, of course. We told him about going to the island, Dick, but nobody else.'

They had called at Alf's house on their way to the cove. Alf was alone in the yard at the back. His mother was away and his father was out fishing. They had told him their secret, and Alf had nodded his tousled head and promised faithfully to tell nobody at all. He was evidently very proud at being trusted.

'If my mother and father come back, you must let us know,' said George. 'Sail as near the island as you dare, and hail us. You can get nearer to it than anyone else.'

'I'll do that,' promised Alf, wishing he could go with them.

'So, you see, Dick,' said Julian, as he rowed out to the

island, 'if by any chance Aunt Fanny does return sooner than we expect, we shall know at once and come back. I think we've planned everything very well.'

'Yes, we have,' said Dick. He turned and faced the island, which was coming nearer. 'We shall soon be there. Isn't George going to take the oars and guide the boat in?'

'Yes,' said George. 'We've come to the difficult bit now, where we've got to weave our way in and out of the different rocks that keep sticking up. Give me the oars, Ju.'

She took the oars, and the others watched in admiration as the girl guided the big boat skilfully in and out of the hidden rocks. She certainly was very clever. They felt perfectly safe with her.

The boat slid into the little cove. It was a natural harbour, with the water running up to a stretch of sand. High rocks sheltered it. The children jumped out eagerly, and four pairs of willing hands tugged the boat quickly up the sand.

'Higher up still,' panted George. 'You know what awful storms suddenly blow up in this bay. We want to be sure the boat is quite safe, no matter how high the seas run.'

The boat soon lay on one side, high up the stretch of sand. The children sat down, puffing and blowing. 'Let's have breakfast here,' said Julian. 'I don't feel like unloading all those heavy things at the moment. We'll get what we want for breakfast, and have it here on this warm bit of sand.'

They got a loaf of new bread, some cold ham, a few tomatoes and a pot of jam. Anne found knives and forks and plates. Julian opened two bottles of ginger-beer.

'Funny sort of breakfast,' he said, setting the bottles down on the sand, 'but simply gorgeous when anyone is as hungry as we are.'

They ate everything except about a third of the loaf. Timmy was given his bone and some of his own biscuits. He crunched up the biscuits at once, and then sat down contentedly to gnaw the fine bone.

'How nice to be Timmy – with no plate or knife or fork or cup to bother about,' said Anne, lying on her back in the sun, feeling that she really couldn't eat anything more. 'Oh, if we are always going to have mixed-up meals like this on the island, I shall never want to go back. Who would have thought that ham and jam and ginger-beer would go so well together?'

Timmy was thirsty. He sat with his tongue hanging out wishing that George would give him a drink. He didn't like ginger-beer.

George eyed him lazily.

'Oh Timmy – are you thirsty?' she said. 'Oh dear, I feel as if I really can't get up! You'll have to wait a few minutes, then I'll go to the boat and empty out some water for you.'

But Timothy couldn't wait. He went off to some nearby rocks, which were out of reach of the sea. In a hole in one of them he found some rain-water, and he lapped it up eagerly. The children heard him lapping it, and laughed.

'Isn't Timmy clever?' murmured Anne. 'I should never have thought of that.'

The children had been up half the night, and now they were full of good things, and were very sleepy. One by one they fell asleep on the warm sand. Timothy eyed them in astonishment. It wasn't night-time! Yet here were all the children sleeping tightly. Well, well – a dog could always go to sleep too at any time! So Timothy threw himself down beside George, put his head right on her middle, and closed his eyes.

The sun was high when the little company awoke. Julian awoke first, then Dick, feeling very hot indeed, for the sun was blazing down. They sat up, yawning.

'Goodness!' said Dick, looking at his arms. 'The sun has caught me properly. I shall be terribly sore by tonight. Did we bring any cream, Julian?'

'No. We never thought of it,' said Julian. 'Cheer up! You'll be burnt much more by the time this day ends. The sun's going to be hot – there's not a cloud in the sky!'

They woke up the girls. George pushed Timmy's head off her tummy. 'You give me nightmares when you put your heavy head there,' she complained. 'Oh, I say – we're on the island, aren't we? For a moment I thought I was back in bed at Kirrin Cottage!'

'Isn't it gorgeous? – here we are for ages, all by ourselves, with tons of nice things to eat, able to do just what we like!' said Anne, contentedly.

'I guess the old Sticks are glad we've gone.' said Dick. 'Spotty Face will be able to loll in the sitting-room and read all our books, if he wants to.'

'And Stinker-dog will be able to wander all over the house and lie on anybody's bed without being afraid that Timothy will eat him whole,' said George. 'Well, let him. I don't care about anything now that I've escaped.'

It was fun to lie there and talk about everything. But soon Julian, who could never rest for long, once he was awake, got up and stretched himself.

'Come on!' he said to the others. 'There is work to do, Lazy-Bones! Come along!'

'Work to do? What do you mean?' said George in astonishment.

'Well, we've got to unload the boat and pack everything somewhere where it won't get spoilt if the rain happens to come,' said Julian. 'And we've got to decide exactly where we're going to sleep, and get the heather for our beds and pile the rugs on them. There's plenty to do!'

'Oh, don't let's do it yet,' said Anne, not at all wanting to get up out of the warm sand. But the others pulled her up, and together they all set to work to unload the boat.

'Let's go and have a look at the castle,' said Julian. 'And find the little room where we'll sleep. It's the only one left whole, so it will have to be that one.'

They went right to the top of the inlet, climbed up on to the rocks and made their way towards the old ruined castle, whose walls rose up from the middle of the little island. They stopped to gaze at it.

'It's a fine old ruin,' said Dick. 'Aren't we lucky to have an island and castle of our own! Fancy, this is all ours!'

They gazed through a big broken-down archway, to old steps beyond. The castle had once had two fine towers, but now one was almost gone. The other rose high in the air, half-ruined. The black jackdaws collected there, talking loudly. 'Chack, chack, chack! Chack, chack, chack!'

'Nice birds,' said Dick. 'I like them. See the grey patch at the back of their heads, Anne? I wonder if they ever stop talking.'

'I don't think so,' said George. 'Oh, look at the rabbits – tamer than ever!'

The courtyard was full of big rabbits, who eyed them as they came near. It really seemed as if it would be possible to pat them, they were so tame – but one by one they edged away as the children approached.

FIVE RUN AWAY TOGETHER

Timothy was in a great state of excitement, and his tail quivered from end to end. Oh those rabbits! Why couldn't he chase them? Why was George so difficult about rabbits? Why couldn't he make them run a bit?

But George had her hand on his collar, and gave him a stern glance. 'Now, Timothy, don't you *dare* to chase even the smallest of these rabbits. They're mine, every one of them.'

'Ours!' corrected Anne at once. She wanted to share in the rabbits, as well as in the castle and the island.

'Ours!' said George. 'Let's go and have a look at the little dark room where we'll spend the nights.'

They made their way to where the castle did not seem to be quite so ruined. They came to a doorway and looked inside.

'Here it is!' said Julian, peeping in. 'I shall have to use my torch. The windows are only slits here, and it's quite dark.'

He turned on his torch – and the children all gazed into the old room where they proposed to store their goods and sleep.

George gave a loud exclamation. 'Golly! We can't use this room! The roof has fallen in since last summer.'

So it had. Julian's torch shone on to a heap of fallen stones, scattered all over the floor. It was quite impossible to use the old room now. In any case it might be dangerous to do so, for it looked as if more stones might fall at any moment.

'Blow!' said Julian. 'What shall we do about this? We shall have to find somewhere else for a storing and sleeping-place!'

CHAPTER ELEVEN

On the old wreck

IT WAS quite a shock to have their plans spoilt. They knew there was no other room in the ruined castle that was sufficiently whole to shelter them. And they must find some sort of shelter, for although the weather was fine at the moment, it might rain hard any day – or a storm might blow up.

'And storms round about Kirrin are so very violent,' said Julian, remembering one or two. 'Do you remember the storm that tossed your wreck up from the bottom of the sea, George?'

'Oh yes,' said George and Anne, together, and Anne added eagerly: 'Let's go and see the wreck today if we can. I'd love to see if it's still balanced on those rocks, as it was last year, when we explored it.'

'Well, first we must make up our minds where we are going to sleep,' said Julian, firmly. 'I don't know if you realise it, but it's about three o'clock in the afternoon! We slept for hours on the sand – tired out with our exciting night, I suppose. We really must find some safe place and put our things there at once, and make our beds.'

'Well, but where shall we go?' said Dick. 'There's no other place in the old castle.'

'There's the dungeon below,' said Anne, shivering. 'But I don't want to go there. It's so dark and mysterious.'

Nobody wanted to sleep down in the dungeons! Dick frowned and thought hard. 'What about the wreck?' he said. 'Any chance of living there?'

'We might go and see,' said Julian. 'I don't somehow fancy living on a damp old rotting wreck – but if it's still high on the rocks, maybe the sun will have dried it, and it might be possible to have our beds and stores there.'

'Let's go and see now,' said George. So they made their way from the ruined castle to the old wall that ran round it. From there they would be able to see the wreck. It had been cast up the year before, and had settled firmly on some rocks.

They stood on the wall and looked for the wreck, but it was not where they had expected it. 'It's moved,' said Julian, in surprise. 'There it is, look, on those rocks – nearer to the shore than it was before. Poor old wreck! It's been battered about a good bit this last winter, hasn't it? It looks much more of a real wreck than it did last summer.'

'I don't believe we shall be able to sleep there,' said Dick. 'It's dreadfully battered. We might be able to store food there, though. Do you know, I believe we could get to it from those rocks that run out from the island!'

'Yes, I believe we could,' said George. 'We could only reach it safely by boat last summer – but when the tide is down, I think we *could* climb out over the line of rocks, right to the wreck itself.'

ON THE OLD WRECK

'We'll try in about an hour,' said Julian, feeling excited. 'The tide will be off the rocks by then.'

'Let's go and have a look at the old well,' said Dick, and they made their way back to the courtyard of the castle. Here, the summer before, they had found the entrance to the well-shaft that ran deep down through the rock, past the dungeons below, lower than the level of the sea, to fresh water.

The children looked about for the well, and came to the old wooden cover. They drew it back.

'There are the rungs of the old iron ladder I went down last year,' said Dick, peering in. 'Now let's find the entrance to the dungeon. The steps down into it are somewhere near here.'

They found the entrance, but to their surprise some enormous stones had been pulled across it. 'Who did that?' said George, frowning. 'We didn't. Someone has been here!'

'Trippers, I suppose,' said Julian. 'Do you remember that we thought we saw a spire of smoke here the other day? I bet it was trippers. You know, the story of Kirrin Island, and its old castle and dungeons, and the treasure we found in it last year, was all in the newspapers. I expect one of the fishermen has been making money by taking trippers and landing them on *our* island.'

'How dare they?' said George, looking very fierce. 'I shall put up a board that says "Trespassers will be sent to prison". I won't have strangers on our island.'

'Well, don't worry about the stones pulled across the dungeon entrance,' said Julian. 'I don't think any of us want to go down there. Look at poor old Timmy! He's gazing at those rabbits most unhappily. Isn't he funny?'

Timothy was sitting down behind the children, looking most mournfully at the ring of rabbits all round the weed-grown courtyard. He looked at the rabbits and then he looked at George, then he looked back at the rabbits.

'No good, Timmy,' said George, firmly. 'I'm not going to change my mind about rabbits. You're not to chase them on our island.'

'I expect he thinks you're most unfair to him,' said Anne. 'After all, you said he might share your quarter of the island with you – and so he thinks he ought to have his share of your rabbits too!'

96

ON THE OLD WRECK

Everyone laughed. Timmy wagged his tail and looked hopefully at George. They all walked across the courtyard – and then Julian suddenly came to a stop.

'Look!' he said in surprise, pointing to something on the ground. 'Look! Someone *has* been here! This is where they built a fire!'

Everyone gazed at the ground. There was a heap of wood-ash there, quite evidently left from a fire. Stamped into the ground was a cigarette end, too. There was absolutely no doubt about it – someone had been on the island!

'If trippers come here I'll set Timmy on to them!' cried George, in a fury. 'This is our own place, it doesn't belong to anybody else at all. Timothy, you mustn't chase rabbits here, but you can chase anybody on two legs, except us! See?'

Timmy wagged his tail at once. 'Woof!' he said, quite agreeing. He looked all round as if he hoped to see some-body appearing that he could chase. But there was no one.

'I should think the tide is about off those rocks by now,' said Julian. 'Let's go and see. If it is we'll climb along them and see if we can get to the wreck. Anne had better not come. She might slip and fall, and the sea is raging all round the rocks.'

'Of course I'm coming!' cried Anne, indignantly. 'You're just as likely to fall as I am.'

'Well, I'll see if it looks too dangerous,' said Julian. They made their way over the castle wall, down to the line of rocks that ran out seawards, towards the wreck. Big

97

waves did wash over the rocks occasionally, but it seemed fairly safe.

'If you keep between me and Dick, you can come, Anne,' said Julian. 'But you must let us help you over difficult parts, and not make a fuss. We don't want you to fall in and get washed away.'

They began to make their way along the line of rugged, slippery rocks. The tide went down even farther as they got nearer to the wreck, and soon there was very little danger of being washed off the rocks. It was possible now to get right to the wreck across the rocks – a thing they had not been able to do the summer before.

'Here we are!' said Julian at last, and he put his hand on the side of the old wreck. She was a big ship now that they were near to her. She towered above them, thick with shellfish and seaweed, smelling musty and old. The water washed round the bottom part of her, but the top part was right out of the water, even when the tide was at its highest.

'She's been thrown about a bit last winter,' said George, looking at her. 'There are a lot more new holes in her side, aren't there? And part of her old mast is gone, and some of the deck. How can we get up to her?'

'I've got a rope,' said Julian, and he undid a rope that he had wound round his waist. 'Half a minute – I'll make a loop and see if I can throw it round that post sticking out up there.'

He threw the rope two or three times, but could not get the loop round the post. George took it from him impatiently. At the first throw she got it round the post. She was very good indeed at things like that – better than a boy in some things, Anne thought admiringly.

She was up the rope like a monkey, and soon stood on the sloping slippery deck. She almost slipped, but caught at a broken piece of deck just in time. Julian helped Anne to go up, and then the two boys followed.

'It's a horrid smell, isn't it?' said Anne, wrinkling up her nose. 'Do all wrecks smell like this? I don't think I'll go and look down in the cabins like we did last time. The smell would be worse there.'

So the others left Anne up on the half-rotten deck while they went to explore a bit. They went down to the smelly, seaweed-hung cabins, and into the captain's old cabin, the biggest of the lot. But it was quite plain that not only could they not sleep there, but they could certainly not hope to store anything there, either. The whole place was damp and rotten. Julian was half afraid his foot would go through the planking at any moment.

'Let's go up to the deck,' he said. 'It's nasty down here – awfully dark too.'

They were just going up, when they heard a shout from Anne. 'I say! Come here, quick! I've found something!'

They hurried up as fast as they could, slipping and sliding on the sloping deck. Anne was standing where they had left her, her eyes shining brightly. She was pointing to something on the opposite side of the ship.

'What is it?' said George. 'What's the matter?'

'Look – that wasn't here when we came here before, surely!' said Anne, still pointing. The others looked where she pointed. They saw an open locker at the other side of the deck, and stuffed into it was a small black trunk! How extraordinary!

'A little black trunk!' said Julian, in surprise. 'No – that wasn't there before. It's not been there long either – it's quite dry and new! Whoever does it belong to? And why should it be here?'

CHAPTER TWELVE

The cave in the cliff

CAUTIOUSLY the children made their way down the slippery deck towards the locker. The door of this had evidently been shut on the trunk but had come open, so that the trunk was not hidden, as had been intended.

Julian pulled out the little black trunk. All the children were amazed. *Why* should anyone put a trunk there?

'Smugglers, do you think?' said Dick, his eyes gleaming.

'Yes – it might be,' said Julian, thoughtfully, trying to undo the straps of the trunk. 'This would be a very good place for smugglers. Ships that knew the way could put in, cast off a boat with smuggled goods, leave them here, and go on their way, knowing that people could come and collect the goods at their leisure.'

'Do you think there are smuggled goods inside the trunk?' asked Anne, in excitement. 'What would there be? Diamonds? Silks?'

'Anything that has a duty to be paid on it before it can get into the country,' said Julian. 'Blow these straps! I can't undo them.'

'Let *me* try,' said Anne, who had very deft little fingers. She began to work at the buckles, and in a short time had the straps undone. But a further disappointment awaited them. The trunk was well and truly locked! There were two good locks, and no keys!

'Blow!' said George. 'How sickening! How can we get the trunk open now?'

'We can't,' said Julian. 'And we mustn't smash it open, because it would warn whoever it belongs to that the goods had been found. We don't want to warn the smugglers that we have discovered their little game. We want to try and catch them!'

'Ooooh!' said Anne, going red with excitement. 'Catch the smugglers! Oh Julian! Do you really think we could?'

'Why not?' said Julian. 'No one knows we are here. If we hid whenever we saw a ship approaching the island, we might see a boat coming to it, and we could watch and find out what is happening. I should think that the smugglers are using this island as a sort of dropping-place for goods. I wonder who comes and fetches them? Someone from Kirrin Village or the nearby places, I should think.'

'This is going to be awfully exciting,' said Dick. 'We always seem to have adventures when we come to Kirrin. It's absolutely *full* of them. This will be the third one we have had.'

'I think we ought to be getting back over the rocks,' said Julian, suddenly looking over the side of the ship and seeing that the tide had turned. 'Come on – we don't want to be caught by the tide and have to stay here for hours and hours! I'll go down the rope first. Then you come, Anne.'

THE CAVE IN THE CLIFF

They were soon climbing over the rocks again, feeling very excited. Just as they reached the last stretch of rocks leading to the rocky cliff of the island itself, Dick stopped.

'What's up?' said George, pushing behind him. 'Do get on!'

'Isn't that a cave, just beyond that big rock there?' said Dick, pointing. 'It looks awfully like one to me. If it was, it would be a simply lovely place to store our things in, and even to sleep in, if it was out of reach of the sea.'

'There aren't any caves on Kirrin,' began George, and then she stopped short. What Dick was pointing at really did look like a cave. It was worthwhile seeing if it was one. After all, George had never explored this line of rocks, and so had never been able to catch sight of the cave that lay just beyond. It could not possibly be seen from the land.

'We'll go and see,' she said. So they changed their direction, and instead of climbing back the way they had come, they cut across the mass of rock and made their way towards a jutting-out part of the cliff, in which the cave seemed to be.

They came to it at last. Steep rocks guarded the entrance, and half hid it. Except from where Dick had seen it, it was really impossible to catch sight of it, it was so well-hidden.

'It *is* a cave!' said Dick, in delight, stepping into it. 'And my, what a fine one!'

It really was a beauty. Its floor was spread with fine white sand, as soft as powder, and perfectly dry, for the

103

cave was clearly higher than the tide reached, except, possibly, in a bad winter storm. Round one side of it ran a stone ledge.

'Exactly like a shelf made for us!' cried Anne, in joy. 'We can put all our things here. How lovely! Let's come and live here and sleep here. And look, Julian we've even got a skylight in the roof!'

The little girl pointed upwards, and the others saw that the roof of the cave was open in one part, giving on to the cliff-top itself. It was plain that somewhere on the heathery cliff above was a hole that looked down to the cave, making what Anne called a 'skylight'.

'We could drop all our things down through that hole,' said Julian, quickly making plans. 'We would have an awful time bringing them over the rocks. If we can find that hole up there when we are out on the cliff again, we can let down everything on a rope. It's not a very high "skylight", as Anne calls it, for the cliffs are low just here. I believe we could swing ourselves down a rope easily, so that we needn't have the bother of clambering over the rocks to the seaward entrance we have just come in by!'

This was a grand discovery. 'Our island is even more exciting than we thought,' said Anne, happily. 'We've got a beautiful cave to share now!'

The next thing to do, of course, was to go up on the cliff and find the hole that led to the roof of the cave. So out they all went, Timmy too. Timmy was funny on the slippery rocks. His feet slithered about, and two or three times he fell into the water. But he just swam across the pools he fell into, clambered out and went on again with his slithering.

'He's like George!' said Anne, with a laugh. 'He never gives up, whatever happens to him!'

They climbed up to the top of the cliff. It was easy to find the hole once they knew it was there.

'Pretty dangerous, really,' said Julian, when he had found it, and was peering down. 'Any one of us might have run on this cliff and popped down the hole by accident. See, it's all criss-crossed with blackberry brambles.'

They scratched their hands, trying to free the hole from the brambles. Once they had cleared the hole, they could look right down into the cave quite easily.

'It's not very far down,' said Anne. 'It looks almost as if we could jump down, if we let ourselves slide down this hole.'

'Don't you do anything of the sort,' said Julian. 'You'd break your leg. Wait till we get a rope fixed up, hanging down into the cave. Then we can manage to get in and out easily.'

They went back to the boat, and began unloading it. They took everything across to the seaward side of the island, where the cave was. Julian took a strong rope and knotted it thickly at intervals.

'To give our feet a hold as we go down,' he explained. 'If we drop down too quickly, we'll hurt our hands. These knots will stop us slipping and help us to climb up.'

'Let me go down first, and then you can lower all our things to me,' said George. So down she went, hand over hand, her feet easily finding the thick knots, feeling for one after another. It was a good way to go down.

'How shall we get Timmy down?' said Julian. But Timothy, who had been whining anxiously at the edge of the hole, watching George sliding away from him, solved the difficulty himself.

He jumped into the hole and disappeared down it! There came a shriek from below.

'Oh! My goodness, what's this? Oh *Timmy*! Have you hurt yourself?'

The sand was very soft, like a velvet cushion, and Tim had not hurt himself at all. He gave himself a shake and then barked joyfully. He was with George again! He wasn't going to have his mistress disappearing down mysterious holes without following her at once. Not Timmy!

Then followed the business of lowering down all the goods. Anne and Dick tied the things together in rugs, and Julian lowered them carefully. George untied the rope as soon as it reached her, took out the goods, and then back went the rope again to be tied round another bundle.

'Last one!' called Julian, after a long spell of really hard work. 'Then down we come too, and I don't mind telling you that before we make our beds or anything, our next job is to have a jolly good meal! It's hours and hours since we had a meal, and I'm starving.'

Soon they were all sitting on the warm soft floor of the

cave. They opened a tin of meat, cut huge slices of bread and made sandwiches. Then they opened a tin of pineapple chunks and ate those, spooning them out of the tin, full of sweetness and juice. After that they still felt hungry, so they opened two tins of sardines and dug them out with biscuits. It made a really grand meal.

'Ginger-pop to finish up with, please,' said Dick. 'My word, why don't people always have meals like this?'

'We'd better hurry up or we shan't be able to get heather for our beds,' said George, sleepily.

'Who wants heather?' said Dick. '*I* don't! This lovely soft sand is all *I* shall want – and a cushion and a rug or two. I shall sleep better here than ever I did in bed!'

So the rugs and cushions were spread out on the sandy floor of the cave. A candle was lit as it grew dark, and the four sleepy children looked at one another. Timmy, as usual, was with George.

'Goodnight,' said George. 'I can't keep awake another minute. Goodnight, ev . . . ery . . . body . . . good . . . night!

CHAPTER THIRTEEN

A day on the island

THE CHILDREN hardly knew where they were the next day when they woke up. The sun was pouring into the cave entrance, and fell first of all on George's sleeping face. It awoke her and she lay half-dozing, wondering why her bed felt rather less soft than usual.

'But I'm not in my bed – I'm on Kirrin Island, of course!' she thought suddenly to herself. She sat up and gave Anne a punch. 'Wake up, sleepy-head! We're on the island!'

Soon they were all awake rubbing the sleep from their eyes. 'I think I'm going to get heather today for my bed, after all,' said Anne. 'The sand feels soft at first, but it gets hard after a bit.'

The others agreed that they would all get heather for their beds, set on the sand, with rugs for covering. Then they would have really fine beds.

'It's fun to live in a cave,' said Dick. 'Fancy having a fine cave like this on our island, as well as a castle and dungeons! We are really very lucky.'

'I feel sticky and dirty,' said Julian. 'Let's go and have a bathe before we have breakfast. Then cold ham, bread, pickles and marmalade for me!'

'We shall be cold after our bathe,' said George. 'We'd better light my little stove and put the kettle on to boil while we're bathing. Then we can make some hot cocoa when we come back shivering!'

'Oh yes,' said Anne, who had never boiled anything on such a tiny stove before. 'Do let's. I'll fill the kettle with water from one of the containers. What shall we do for milk?'

'There's a tin of milk somewhere in the pile,' said Julian. 'We can open that. Where's the tin-opener?'

It was not to be found, which was most exasperating. But at last Julian discovered it in his pocket, so all was well.

The little stove was filled with methylated spirit, and lit. The kettle was filled and set on top. Then the children went off to bathe.

'Look! There's a simply marvellous pool in the middle of those rocks over there!' called Julian, pointing. 'We've never spotted it before. Golly, it's like a small swimming pool, made specially for us!'

'Kirrin Swimming Pool, twenty pence a dip!' said Dick. 'Free to the owners, though! Come on – it looks gorgeous! And see how the waves keep washing over the top of the rocks and splashing into the pool. Couldn't be better!'

It really was a lovely rock-pool, deep, clear and not too cold. The children enjoyed themselves thoroughly, splashing about and swimming and floating. George tried a dive off one of the rocks, and went in beautifully.

A DAY ON THE ISLAND

'George can do anything in the water,' said Anne, admiringly. 'I wish I could dive and swim like George. But I never shall.'

'We can see the old wreck nicely from here,' said Julian, coming out of the water. 'Blow! We didn't bring any towels.'

'We'll use one of the rugs, turn and turn about,' said Dick. 'I'll go and fetch the thinnest one. I say – do you remember that trunk we saw in the wreck yesterday? Odd, wasn't it?'

'Yes, very odd,' said Julian. 'I don't understand it. We'll have to keep a watch on the wreck and see who comes to collect the trunk.'

'I suppose the smugglers – if they are smugglers – will come slinking round this side of the island and quietly send off a boat to the wreck,' said George, drying herself vigorously. 'Well, we'd better keep a strict look-out, and see if anything appears on the sea out there in the way of a small steamer, boat or ship.'

'Yes. We don't want them to spot us,' said Dick. 'We shan't find out anything if they see us and are warned. They'd at once give up coming to the island. I vote we each of us take turns at keeping a look-out, so that we can spot anything at once and get under cover.'

'Good idea!' said Julian. 'Well, I'm dry, but not very warm. Let's race to the cave, and get that hot drink. And breakfast – golly, I could eat a whole chicken and probably a duck as well, to say nothing of a turkey.'

The others laughed. They all felt the same. They raced off to the cave, running over the sand and climbing over a few rocks, then down to the cave-beach and into the big entrance, still splashed with sunshine.

The kettle was boiling away merrily, sending a cloud of steam up from its tin spout. 'Get the ham out and a loaf of bread, and that jar of pickles we brought,' ordered Julian. 'I'll open the tin of milk. George, you take the tin of cocoa and that jug, and make enough for all of us.'

'I'm so terribly happy,' said Anne, as she sat at the entrance to the cave, eating her breakfast. 'It's a lovely feeling. It's simply gorgeous being on our island like this, all by ourselves, able to do what we like.'

They all felt the same. It was such a lovely day too, and the sky and sea were so blue. They sat eating and drinking, gazing out to sea, watching the waves break into spray over the rocks beyond the old wreck. It certainly was a very rocky coast.

'Let's arrange everything very nicely in the cave,' said Anne, who was the tidiest of the four, and always liked to play at 'houses' if she could. 'This shall be our house, our home. We'll make four proper beds. And we'll each have our own place to sit in. And we'll arrange everything tidily on that big stone shelf there. It might have been made for us!'

'We'll leave Anne to play "houses" by herself,' said George, who was longing to stretch her legs again. 'We'll go and get some heather for beds. And oh! – what about one of us keeping a watch on the old wreck, to see who comes there?'

'Yes – that's important,' said Julian at once. 'I'll take first watch. The best place would be up on the cliff just above this cave. I can find a gorse bush that will hide me all right from anyone out at sea. You others get the heather. We will take two-hourly watches. We can read if we like, so long as we keep on looking up.'

Dick and George went to get the heather. Julian climbed up the knotted rope that still hung down through the hole, tied firmly to the great old root of an enormous gorse bush. He pulled himself out on the cliff and lay on the heather panting.

He could see nothing out to sea at all except for some big steamer miles out on the sky-line. He lay down in the sun, enjoying the warmth that poured in to every inch of his body. This look-out job was going to be very nice!

He could hear Anne singing down in the cave as she tidied up her 'house'. Her voice came up through the cave roof hole, rather muffled. Julian smiled. He knew Anne was enjoying herself thoroughly.

So she was. She had washed the few bits of crockery they had used for breakfast, in a most convenient little rain-pool outside the cave. Timmy used it for drinking-water too, but he didn't seem to mind Anne using it for washing-up water, though she apologised to him for doing so.

'I'm sorry if I spoil your drinking water, Timmy darling,' she said, 'but you are such a sensible dog that I know if it suddenly tastes nasty to you, you will go off and find another rain-pool.'

'Woof!' said Timmy, and ran off to meet George, who was just arriving back with Dick, armed with masses of soft, sweet-smelling heather for beds.

'Put the heather outside the cave, please, George', said Anne. 'I'll make the beds inside when I'm ready.'

'Right!' said George. 'We'll go and get some more. Aren't we having fun?'

'Julian's gone up the rope to the top of the cliff,' said Anne. 'He'll yell if he sees anything unusual. I hope he does, don't you?'

A DAY ON THE ISLAND

'It would be exciting,' agreed Dick, putting down his heather on top of Timmy, and nearly burying him. 'Oh sorry, Timmy – are you there? Bad luck!'

Anne had a very happy morning. She arranged everything beautifully on the shelf – crockery and knives and forks and spoons in one place – saucepan and kettle in another – tins of meat next, tins of soup together, tins of fruit neatly piled on top of one another. It really was a splendid larder and dresser!

She wrapped all the bread up in an old tablecloth they had brought, and put it at the back of the cave in the coolest place she could find. The containers of water went there too, and so did all the bottles of drinks.

Then the little girl set to work to make the beds. She decided to make two nice big ones, one on each side of the cave.

'George and I and Tim will have the one this side,' she thought, busy patting down the heather into the shape of a bed. 'And Julian and Dick can have the other side. I shall want lots more heather. Oh, is that you, Dick? You're just in time! I want more heather.'

Soon the beds were made beautifully, and each had an old rug for an under-blanket, and two better rugs for covers. Cushions made pillows.

'What a pity we didn't bring night-things,' thought Anne. 'I could have folded them neatly and put them under the cushions. There! It all looks lovely. We've got a beautiful house.'

Julian came sliding down the rope from the cliff to the cave. He looked round admiringly. 'My word, Anne – the cave does look fine! Everything in order and looking so tidy. You are a good little girl.'

Anne was pleased to hear Julian's praise, though she didn't like him calling her a little girl.

'Yes, it does look nice, doesn't it?' she said. 'But why aren't you watching up on the cliff, Ju?'

'It's Dick's turn now,' said Julian. 'The two hours are up. Did we bring any biscuits? I feel as if I could do with one or two, and I bet the others could too. Let's all go up to the cliff-top and have some. George and Timmy are there with Dick.'

Anne knew exactly where to put her hand on the tin of biscuits. She took out ten and climbed up to the cliff-top. Julian went up the rope. Soon all five were sitting by the big gorse-bush, nibbling at biscuits, Timmy too. At least, he didn't nibble. He just swallowed.

The day passed very pleasantly and rather lazily. They took turns at being look-out, though Anne was severely scolded by Julian in the afternoon for falling asleep during her watch. She was very ashamed of herself and cried.

'You're too little to be a look-out, that's what it is,' said Julian. 'We three and Timmy had better do it.'

'Oh, no, do let me too,' begged poor Anne. 'I never, never will fall asleep again. But the sun was so hot and . . .'

'Don't make excuses,' said Julian. 'It only makes things worse if you do. All right – we'll give you another chance,

116

Anne, and see if you are really big enough to do the things we do.'

But though they all took their turns, and kept a watch on the sea for any strange vessel, none appeared. The children were disappointed. They did so badly want to know who had put that trunk on the wreck and why, and what it contained.

'Better go to bed now,' said Julian, when the sun sank low. 'It's about nine o'clock. Come on! I'm really looking forward to a sleep on those lovely heathery beds that Anne has made so nicely!'

CHAPTER FOURTEEN

Disturbance in the night

IT WAS dark in the cave, not really quite dark enough to light a candle, but the cave looked so nice by candlelight that it was fun to light one. So Anne took down the candle-stick and lit the candle. At once strange shadows jumped all round the cave, and it became a rather exciting place, not at all like the cave they knew by daylight!

'I wish we could have a fire,' said Anne.

'We'd be far too hot,' said Julian. 'And it would smoke us out. You can't have a fire in a cave like this. There's no chimney.'

'Yes, there is,' said Anne, pointing to the hole in the roof. 'If we lit a fire just under that hole, it would act as a chimney, wouldn't it?'

'It might,' said Dick, thoughtfully. 'But I don't think so. We'd simply get the cave full of stifling smoke, and we wouldn't be able to sleep for choking.'

'Well, couldn't we light a fire at the cave entrance then?' said Anne who felt that a real home ought to have a fire somewhere. 'Just to keep away wild beasts, say! That's what the people of old times did. It says so in my history book. They lit fires at the cave entrance at night to keep away any wild animal that might be prowling around.'

DISTURBANCE IN THE NIGHT

'Well, what wild beasts do you think are likely to come and peep into this cave?' asked Julian, lazily, finishing up a cup of cocoa. 'Lions? Tigers? Or perhaps you are afraid of an elephant or two.'

Everyone laughed. 'No – I don't really think animals like that would come,' said Anne. 'Only – it would be nice to have a red, glowing fire to watch when we go to sleep.'

'Perhaps Anne thinks the rabbits might come in and nibble our toes or something,' said Dick.

'Woof!' said Tim, pricking up his ears as he always did at the mention of rabbits.

'I don't think we ought to have a fire,' said Julian, 'because it might be seen out at sea and give a warning to anyone thinking of coming to the island to do a bit of smuggling.'

'Oh no, Julian – the entrance to this cave is so well-hidden that I'm sure no one could see a fire out to sea,' said George, at once. 'There's that line of high rocks in front, which must hide it completely. I think it would be rather fun to have a fire. It would light up the cave so strangely and excitingly.'

'Oh good, George!' said Anne, delighted to find some-one agreeing with her.

'Well, we can't possibly trek out and get sticks for it now,' said Dick, who was far too comfortable to move.

'You don't need to,' said Anne, eagerly. 'I got plenty myself today, and stored them at the back of the cave, in case we wanted a fire.'

119

'Isn't she a good housewife!' said Julian, in great admiration. 'She may go to sleep when she's look-out, but she's wide-awake enough when it comes to making a house for us out of a cave! All right, Anne – we'll make a fire for you!'

They all got up and fetched the sticks from the back of the cave. Anne had been to the jackdaw tower and had picked up armfuls that the birds had dropped when making their nests in the tower. They built them up to make a nice little fire. Julian got some dried seaweed too, to drop into it.

They lit the fire at the cave entrance, and the dry sticks blazed up at once. The children went back to their heather-beds, and lay down on them, watching the red flames leaping and crackling. The red glow lit up the cave and made it very weird and exciting.

'This is lovely,' said Anne, half-asleep. 'Really lovely. Oh Timmy, move a bit, do. You're so heavy on my feet. Here, George, pull Timothy over to your side. You're used to him lying on you.'

'Goodnight,' said Dick, sleepily. 'The fire is dying down, but I can't be bothered to put any more wood on it. I'm sure all the lions and tigers and bears and elephants have been frightened away.'

'Silly!' said Anne. 'You needn't tease me about it – you've enjoyed it as much as I have! Goodnight.'

They all fell asleep and dreamed peacefully of many things. Julian awoke with a jump. Some strange noise had awakened him. He lay still, listening.

DISTURBANCE IN THE NIGHT

Timothy was growling deeply, right down in his throat.
'R-r-r-r-r-r-r,' he went. 'Gr-r-r-r-r-r-r-r-r!'

George awoke too, and put out her hand sleepily.
'What's the matter, Tim?' she said.

'He's heard something, George,' said Julian, in a low
voice from his bed on the other side of the cave.

George sat up cautiously. Timmy was still growling. 'Sh!' said George and he stopped. He was sitting up straight, his ears well cocked.

'Perhaps it's the smugglers come in the night,' whispered George, and a funny prickly feeling ran down her back. Somehow smugglers in the day time were rather exciting and quite welcome – but at night they seemed different. George didn't at all want to meet any just then!

'I'm going out to see if I can spy anything,' said Julian, getting off his bed quietly, so as not to wake Dick. 'I'll go up the rope to the top of the cliff. I can see better from there.'

'Take my torch,' said George. But Julian didn't want it.

'No, thanks. I can feel the way up that knotted rope quite well, whether I can see or not,' he said.

He went up the rope in the dark, his body twisting round as the rope turned. He climbed up on to the cliff and looked out to sea. It was a very dark night, and he could see no ship at all, not even the wreck. It was far too dark.

'Pity there's no moon,' thought Julian. 'I might be able to see something then.'

He watched for a few minutes, and then George's voice came through the hole in the roof, coming out strangely at his feet.

'Julian! Is there anything to see? Shall I come up?'

'Nothing at all,' said Julian. 'Is Timmy still growling?'

'Yes, when I take my hand off his collar,' said George. 'I can't imagine what's upset him.'

DISTURBANCE IN THE NIGHT

Suddenly Julian caught sight of something. It was a light, a good way beyond the line of rocks. He watched in excitement. That would be just about where the wreck was! Yes – it must be someone on the wreck with a lantern!

'George! Come up!' he said, putting his head inside the hole.

George came up, hand over hand, like a monkey, leaving Timothy growling below. She sat by Julian on the cliff-top. 'See the wreck – look, over there!' said Julian. 'At least, you can't see the wreck itself, it's too dark – but you can see a lantern that someone has put there.'

'Yes – that's someone on our wreck, with a lantern!' said George, feeling excited. 'Oh, I wonder if it's the smugglers – coming to bring more things.'

'Or somebody fetching that trunk,' said Julian. 'Well, we'll know tomorrow, for we'll go and see. Look! – whoever is there is moving off now – the light of the lantern is going lower – they must be getting into a boat by the side of the wreck. And now the light's gone out.'

The children strained their ears to hear if they could discover the splash of oars or the sound of voices over the water. They both thought they could hear voices.

'The boat must have gone off to join a ship or something,' said Julian. 'I believe I can see a faint light right out there – out to sea, look! Maybe the boat is going to it.'

There was nothing more to see or hear, and soon the two of them slid down the knotted rope back to the cave. They didn't wake the others, who were still sleeping peacefully. Timothy leapt up and licked Julian and George, whining joyfully. He did not growl any more.

'You're a good dog, aren't you?' said Julian, patting him. 'Nothing ever escapes *your* sharp ears, does it?'

Timothy settled down on George's feet again. It was plain that whatever it was that had disturbed him had gone. It must have been the presence of the stranger or strangers on the old wreck. Well, they would go there in the morning and see if they could discover what had been taken away or brought there in the night.

Anne and Dick were most indignant the next morning when they heard Julian's tale. 'You *might* have woken us!' said Dick, crossly.

'We would have if there had been anything much to see,' said George. 'But there was only just the light from a lantern, and nothing else except that we thought we heard the sound of voices.'

When the tide was low enough the children and Timothy set off over the rocks to the wreck. They clambered up and stood on the slanting, slippery deck. They looked towards the locker where the little trunk had stood. The door of the locker was shut this time.

Julian slid down towards it and tried to pull it open. Someone had stuffed a piece of wood in to keep the locker from swinging open. Julian pulled it out. Then the door opened easily.

'Anything else in there?' said George, stepping carefully over the slimy deck to Julian.

DISTURBANCE IN THE NIGHT

'Yes,' said Julian. 'Look! Tins of food! And cups and plates and things – just as if someone was going to come and live on the island too! Isn't it funny? The trunk is still here too, locked as before. And here are some candles – and a little lamp – and a bundle of rags. Whatever *are* they here for?'

It really was a puzzle. Julian frowned for a few minutes, trying to think it out.

'It looks as if someone is going to come and stay on the island for a bit – probably to wait here and take in whatever goods are going to be smuggled. Well – we shall be on the look-out for them, day or night!'

They left the wreck, feeling excited. They had a fine hiding-place in their cave – no one could possibly find them there. And, from their hiding-place, they could watch anyone coming to and from the wreck, and from the wreck to the island.

'What about our cove, where we put our boat?' said George, suddenly. 'They might use that cove, you know – if they came in a boat. It's rather dangerous to reach the island from the wreck, if anyone tried to get to the rocky beach nearby.'

'Well – if anyone came to our cove, they'd see our boat,' said Dick, in alarm. 'We'd better hide it, hadn't we?'

'How?' said Anne, thinking that it would be a difficult thing to hide a boat as big as theirs.

'Don't know,' said Julian. 'We'll go and have a look.'

All four and Timmy went off to the cove into which they

had rowed their boat. The boat was pulled high up, out of reach of the waves. George explored the cove well, and then had an idea. 'Do you think we could pull the boat round this big rock? It would just about hide it, though anyone going round the rock would see it at once.'

The others thought it would be worthwhile trying, anyway. So, with much panting and puffing, they hauled the boat round the rock, which almost completely hid her.

'Good!' said George, going down into the cove to see if very much of the boat showed. 'A bit of her does show still. Let's drape it with seaweed!'

So they draped the prow of the boat with all the seaweed they could find at hand, and after that, unless anyone went deliberately round the big rock, the boat really was not noticeable at all.

'Good!' said Julian, looking at his watch. 'I say – it's long past tea-time – and, you know, while we've been doing all this with the boat, we quite forgot to have someone on the look-out post on the cliff-top. What idiots we are!'

'Well, I don't expect anything has happened since we've been away from the cave,' said Dick, putting a fine big bit of seaweed on the prow of the boat, as a last touch. 'I bet the smugglers will only come at night.'

'I dare say you're right,' said Julian. 'I think we'd better keep a look-out at night, too. The look-out could take rugs up to the cliff-top and curl up there.'

'Timmy could be with whoever is keeping watch,' said Anne. 'Then if the look-out goes to sleep by mistake, Timmy would growl and wake them up if he saw anything.'

'You mean, when *you* go to sleep,' said Dick, grinning. 'Come on – let's get back to the cave and have some tea.'

And then Timothy suddenly began to growl again!

CHAPTER FIFTEEN

Who is on the island?

'SH!' SAID Julian, at once. 'Get down behind this bush, quick, everyone!'

They had left the cove and were walking towards the castle when Timmy growled. Now they all crouched behind a mass of brambles, their hearts beating fast.

'Don't growl, Timmy,' said George, in Timothy's nearest ear. He stopped at once, but he stood stiff and quivering, on the watch.

Julian peeped through the bush, parting the brambles and scratching his hands. He could just see somebody in the courtyard – one person – two persons – maybe three. He strained his eyes to try and see, but even as he looked, they disappeared.

'I believe they've moved those big stones over the entrance to the dungeons, and have gone down there,' he whispered. 'Stay here, and I'll creep out a bit and see. I won't let anyone spot me.'

He came back and nodded. 'Yes – they've gone down the dungeons. Do you think they can be the smugglers? Do you suppose they are storing their smuggled goods down there? It would be a marvellous place, of course.'

'Let's get back to the cave while they are underground,'

said George. 'I'm so afraid Timmy will give the game away by barking. He's just bursting himself trying not to make some sort of noise.'

'Come on, then!' said Julian. 'Don't go across the courtyard – make for the shore and we'll scramble round it till we get to the cave. Then one of us can pop up through the hole and hide behind that big gorse-bush there to see who the smugglers are. They must have come in by boat either from the wreck, or by rowing cleverly through the rocks off-shore.'

They got to the cave at last and went in. But no sooner had Julian shinned up the rope, helped by the others, than Timothy disappeared! He ran out of the cave while the others' backs were turned, and when George turned round there was no Timmy to be seen!

'Timmy!' she called in a low voice. 'Timmy! Where are you?'

But no answer came! Timmy had gone off on his own. If only the smugglers didn't see him! What a bad dog he was to do that!

But Timmy had smelt something exciting – he had smelt a smell he knew – a dog-smell – and he meant to find the owner of it and bite off his ears and tail! 'Gr-r-r-r-r!' Timmy was not going to allow dogs on *his* island!

Julian sat close beside the gorse-bush, watching all round. There was nothing to be seen on the wreck, and there was no ship out to sea. Probably the boat that had brought the strangers to the island was hidden down below among the rocks. Julian looked behind him, towards the castle – and even as he looked, he saw an astonishing sight!

A dog was sniffing about the bushes not far away – and creeping up behind him, all his hackles up, was Timothy! Timothy was stalking the dog as if he were a cat stalking a rabbit! The other dog suddenly heard him and leapt round, facing Timothy. Timmy flung himself on the dog with a blood-curdling howl, and the dog howled in fright.

Julian watched in horror, not knowing what to do. The two dogs made a fearful noise, especially the other dog whose howls of terror and yelps of rage resounded everywhere.

'This will bring the smugglers up, and they will see Timmy and know there's someone on the island,' thought Julian. 'Oh, blow you, Timmy! – why didn't you stay with George and keep quiet?'

From the walls of the ruined castle came three figures, running pell-mell to see what was happening to their dog – and Julian stared at them in the very greatest amazement – for the three people were no other than Mr Stick, Mrs Stick and Edgar!

'Golly!' said Julian, crawling round the bush to get to the hole quickly. 'They've come after us! They've guessed we've gone here and they've come to look for us, the beasts, to make us go back! Well, they won't find us! But oh, what a pity Timmy's given the show away!'

130

There came a shrill whistle from down below him. It was
George, who, hearing the row from the dogs, was feeling
worried, and had sent out her piercing whistle for Timmy.
It was a whistle the dog always obeyed, and he let go his

hold on the dog and shot off to the cliff-top at once, just as the three Sticks arrived on the scene, and picked up their bleeding, whining mongrel.

Edgar tore after Timmy, up to the cliff-top. Julian dropped down to the cave when he spotted Edgar appearing. Timmy ran to the hole and dropped bodily down, landing almost on top of Julian. He flung himself on George.

'Shut up, shut up!' said George, in an urgent whisper to the excited dog. 'Do you want to give our hiding-place away, you idiot?'

Edgar, panting and puffing, arrived on the cliff-top, and was completely amazed to see Timothy apparently disappear into the solid earth. He hunted about for a bit, but it was clear that the dog was no longer on the cliff.

Mr and Mrs Stick came up too. 'Where did that dog go?' shouted Mrs Stick. 'What was he like?'

'He looked awfully like that horrible dog of the children's,' said Edgar. His voice could clearly be heard by everyone down in the cave. The children kept as quiet as mice.

'But it *couldn't* be!' came Mrs Stick's voice. 'The children have gone home – we saw them, *and* the dog too, making off towards the railway. It must be some sort of stray dog left here by a tripper.'

'Well, where is he, then?' said Mr Stick's hoarse voice. 'Can't see any dog anywhere about now.'

'He disappeared into the earth,' said Edgar, in a surprised voice.

WHO IS ON THE ISLAND?

Mr Stick made a rude and scornful noise. 'You tell lovely tales, you do,' he said. 'Disappeared into the earth! What next? Fell over the cliff, I should think. Well, he got his teeth into poor Tinker good and proper. My word, if I see that dog, I'll shoot him!'

'He might have some hiding-place about this cliff,' said Mrs Stick. 'Let's have a look!'

The children sat as quiet as mice, George with a warning hand on Timmy's collar. They could hear that the Sticks were really very near. Julian expected one of them to fall down the hole at any moment!

But mercifully they didn't happen on the hole that led down to the cave. They stood quite near to it, though, while they were discussing the problem.

'If it's the children's dog, then those tiresome kids must have come to this island, instead of going home,' said Mrs Stick. 'That would upset our plan all right! We shall have to find out. I'll have no peace till I know.'

'We can soon find out,' said Mr Stick. 'No need to worry about that. Their boat will be here somewhere – and they'll all be about, too! It's impossible for four children, a dog and a boat to be hidden on this small island once anyone starts hunting for them! Edgar, you go round that way. Clara, you get along round about the castle. They may be hiding somewhere in the ruins. I'll have a look about here.'

The children crouched together in the cave. How they hoped that their boat would not be found! How they hoped that no one would find any traces of them at all! Timmy growled softly, wishing that he could go and find that Stinker-dog again! It had been lovely to bite his ears hard.

Edgar was half-scared of finding the children, and a good deal more scared of coming up against Timmy somewhere. So he did not make much of a search for either the children or the boat. He went into the cove where the boat had been pulled up, and although he saw traces where the vessel had been hauled up, barely smoothed out by the sea-water at high-tide, he did not notice the seaweedy prow of the boat sticking out round the rock behind which it was hidden.

'Nothing here!' he called to his mother, who was going round and about the ruins, looking into every likely nook. But she found nothing either, and neither did Mr Stick.

'Couldn't have been the children's dog,' said Mr Stick, at last. 'They'd be here if he was, and so would their boat, but there's no sign of them at all. That dog must have been some wild stray. Have to look out for him, no doubt about it. Gone wild, I should think.'

The children relaxed after about an hour, thinking that the Sticks must have given up looking for them. They boiled the kettle to make some tea, and Anne began to cut some sandwiches. Timmy was tied up in case he wandered out again to look for Stinker.

They ate their tea quietly, not speaking above a whisper.

WHO IS ON THE ISLAND?

'The Sticks haven't come here to look for us, after all,' said Julian. 'It's quite plain from what they said that they thought we had gone to catch the train home, taking George and Timmy with us.'

'Then what are they here for?' demanded George, fiercely. 'It's *our* island! They've no right here. Let's go and turn them off! They're scared of Timmy. We'll take him with us and say we'll set him on to them if they don't clear out.'

'No, George,' said Julian. 'Do be sensible. We don't want them rushing off and telling your father we are here, or he may lose his temper and come flying home to order us back. And – there's another thing I've thought of.'

'What?' asked the others, seeing Julian's eyes gleam in the way they did when he had an idea.

'Well,' said Julian, 'don't you think it's possible that the Sticks are something to do with the smugglers? Don't you think they may come here to take off smuggled goods, or to hide them till they can take them off in safety? Mr Stick is a sailor, isn't he? He would know all about smuggling. I bet he's in the pay of the smugglers all right.'

'I believe you're right!' said George, in excitement. 'Well – we'll wait till the Sticks have gone, and then we'll go down into the dungeons and see if they've hidden anything there! We'll find out their little game and stop it! It will be terribly thrilling, won't it?'

CHAPTER SIXTEEN

The Sticks get a fright

BUT THE Sticks didn't go! The children peeped out of the
spy-hole at the top of the cave-roof every now and again,
and saw one or other of the Sticks. The evening went on
and it began to be dark. Still the Sticks didn't go. Julian
ran down to the nearby shore and discovered a small boat
there. So the Sticks had managed to find their way round
the island, rowed near the wreck, maybe landed on it too,
and then came to the shore, cleverly avoiding the rocks
they might strike against.

'It looks as if the Sticks have come to stay for the night,'
said Julian, gloomily. 'This is going to spoil our stay here,
isn't it? We rush away here to escape from the Sticks – and
lo and behold! the Sticks are on top of us again. It's too
bad.'

'Let's frighten them,' said George, her eyes shining by
the light of the one candle in the cave.

'What do you mean?' said Dick, cheering up. He always
liked George's ideas, mad as they sometimes were.

'Well, I suppose they must be living down in one of the
dungeon rooms, mustn't they?' said George. 'There is no
place in the ruins to live in proper shelter, or we'd be there
ourselves – and the only other place is down in the

136

dungeons. I wouldn't care to sleep there myself, but I don't suppose the Sticks would mind.'

'Well, what about it?' said Dick. 'What's your idea?'

'Couldn't we creep down, and do a bit of shouting, so that the echoes start up all round?' said George. 'You know how frightening we found the echoes when we first went down into the dungeons. We only had to say one or two words, and the echoes began saying them over and over again shouting them back at us.'

'Oh yes, I remember,' said Anne. 'And wasn't Timmy frightened when he barked! The echoes barked back at him, and he thought there were thousands of dogs hiding down there! He was awfully frightened.'

'It's a good idea,' said Julian. 'Serve the Sticks right for coming to our island like this! If we can frighten them away, that would be one up to us! Let's do it.'

'What about Timothy?' said Anne. 'Hadn't we better leave him behind?'

'No. He can come and stand at the dungeon entrance to guard it for us,' said George. 'Then if any of the real smugglers happened to come, Timmy could give us warning. I'm not going to leave him behind.'

'Come on, then, let's go now!' said Julian. 'It would be a fine trick to play. It's quite dark, but I've got my torch, and as soon as we are certain that the Sticks are down in the dungeons, we can start to play our joke.'

There was no sign or sound of the Sticks anywhere about. No light of fire or candle was to be seen, no sound of voices to be heard. Either they had gone, or they were below in the dungeons. The stones had been taken from the entrance, so the children felt sure they were down there.

'Now Timmy, you stay quite still and quiet here,' whispered George to Timmy. 'Bark if anyone comes, but not unless. We're going down into the dungeons.'

'I think perhaps I'll stay up here with Timothy,' said Anne, suddenly. She didn't like the dark look of the dungeon entrance. 'You see, George – Timmy might be frightened or lonely up here by himself.'

The others chuckled. They knew Anne was frightened. Julian squeezed her arm. 'You stay here, then,' he said, kindly. 'You keep old Timmy company.'

Then Julian, George and Dick went down the long flight of steps that led into the deep old dungeons of Kirrin Castle. They had been there the summer before, when they had been seeking for lost treasure; now here they were again!

They crept down the steps and came to the many cellars or dungeons cut out of the rock below the castle. There were scores of those, some big and some small, weird, damp underground rooms in which, maybe, unhappy prisoners had been kept in the olden days.

The children crept down the dark passages. Julian had a piece of white chalk with him, and drew a chalk line here and there on the rocky walls as he went, so that he might easily find the way back.

Suddenly they heard voices and saw a light. They stopped and whispered softly together in each other's ears.

THE STICKS GET A FRIGHT

'They're in that room where we found the treasure last year! That's where they're camping out! What noises shall we make?'

'I'll be a cow,' said Dick. 'I can moo awfully like a cow. I'll be a cow.'

'I'll be a sheep,' said Julian. 'George, you be a horse. You can whinny and hrrrumph just like a horse. Dick, you begin!'

So Dick began. Hidden behind a rocky pillar, he opened his mouth and mooed dolefully, like a cow in pain. At once the echoes took up the mooing, magnified it, sent it along all the underground passages, till it seemed as if a thousand cows had wandered there and were mooing together.

'Moo – oo – oo – oooooooo, ooo – oo – moooooooo!'

The Sticks listened in amazement and fright at the sudden awful noise.

'What is it, Ma?' said Edgar, almost in tears. Stinker crouched at the back of the cave, terrified.

'It's cows,' said Mr Stick, amazed. 'I think it's cows. Can't you hear the moos? But how did cows get to be here?'

'Nonsense!' said Mrs Stick, recovering herself a little. 'Cows down these caves! You're mad! You'll be telling me there're sheep next!'

It was funny that she should have said that, for Julian chose that moment to begin baa-ing like a flock of sheep. His one long, bleating 'baa-baa-aa-aa' was taken up by the echoes at once, and it seemed suddenly as if hundreds of poor lost sheep were baa-ing their way down the dungeons!

Mr Stick jumped to his feet, as white as a sheet.

'Well, if it isn't sheep now!' he said. 'What's up? What's in these 'ere dungeons? I never did like them.'

'Baa-baa-baa-aa-AAAAAAAAAA!' went the mournful bleats all round and about. And then George started

140

her whinnying and neighing, just like an impatient horse. The little girl tossed her head in the darkness and hrrrumphed exactly like a horse and then she stamped with her foot, and at once the echoes stamped too, sending her whinnying and neighing and stamping into the Sticks's cave twenty times louder than George had made them.

Poor Stinker began to whine pitifully. He was frightened almost out of his life. He pressed himself against the floor as if he would like to disappear into it. Edgar clutched his mother's arm. 'Let's go up,' he said. 'I can't stay here. There're hundreds of sheep and horses and cows roaming these dungeons, you can hear them. They're not real, but they've got voices and hoofs, and I'm scared of them.'

Mr Stick went to the door of the room they were in, and shouted loudly.

'Get out, you! Clear out! Whoever you are!'

George giggled. Then she shouted out in a very deep, hoarse voice.

'BE-WARE!' And the echoes thundered out all round. ''WARE! 'WARE! 'WARE-ARE-ARE!'

Mr Stick went back quickly into the cave-room, and lit another candle. He shut the big wooden door that led into the room. His hands were shaking.

'Peculiar goings-on,' he said. 'Shan't stay here much longer if we get this kind of thing happening every night.'

Julian, Dick and George were now in such a state of giggles that they could not imitate any more cows, horses or sheep. George did begin to be a pig, and gave such a

141

realistic snort and grunt that Dick nearly died of laughing. The snorts and grunts were echoed everywhere.

'Come out,' gasped Julian, at last. 'I shall burst with trying not to laugh. Come out!'

'Come out!' whispered the echoes. 'Come out, out, out!'

They stumbled out, stuffing hankies into their mouths as they went, following Julian's chalk marks easily by the light of his torch. It was impossible to take the wrong passage if they followed his guiding lines.

They sat on the dungeon steps with Anne and Timmy, and choked with laughter as they related all they had done. 'We heard old Stick yelling to us to clear out,' said George, 'and he sounded scared stiff. As for Stinker, we never heard even the smallest growl from him. I bet the Sticks will clear off tomorrow after this! It must have given them a most terrible fright.'

'Oh, that was grand!' said Julian. 'It was a pity I began to laugh. I was just feeling I might trumpet like an elephant next. The echoes would like that!'

'Funny the Sticks all staying on the island like this,' said Dick, thoughtfully. 'They've left Kirrin Cottage – but they're not looking for us. They must be in league with the smugglers all right. Perhaps that's why Mrs Stick took the job with your mother, George – to be near the island when the time came – when the smugglers wanted their help.'

'We could really go back to Kirrin Cottage, couldn't we?' said Anne, who, much as she loved the island, was not nearly so keen on it now that the Sticks were there.

142

THE STICKS GET A FRIGHT

'Go back! Leave an adventure just when it's beginning!' said George, scornfully. 'How silly you are, Anne. Go back if you want to – but I'm sure nobody will go with you.'

'Oh, Anne will stay with us all right,' said Julian, knowing that Anne would feel hurt at the suggestion she should leave them. 'It will be the Sticks who have to go, don't worry!'

'Let's go back to the cave,' said Anne, thinking longingly of its safety and bright little candle. They got up and made their way across the courtyard to the little wall that ran round the castle. They climbed over it and turned their steps to the cliff. Julian switched on his torch when he thought it was safe, for it was impossible to see clearly in the dark, and he did not want any of them to fall down the hole, instead of climbing down properly by the rope.

Julian stood by the hole at last, shining his torch so that the others might climb down the rope in safety, one by one. He glanced up, looking over the dark sea as he stood there, and then stared intently.

There was a light out to sea, and it was signalling. It must have seen his torchlight! Julian watched, wondering if it was a ship that was signalling, and how far out it was, and why it was signalling.

'Perhaps they're going to put more stuff into the old wreck for the Sticks to find,' he thought. 'I wonder if they are. How I'd like to find out – but it would be dangerous to go there in daylight in case the Sticks see us.'

The signalling went on for a long time, as if a message was being flashed. Julian could not for the life of him make out what it was. It simply looked like the flash-flash-flash of a lantern to him. But it must mean a signal or message of some sort to the Sticks.

'Well, they won't get it tonight!' thought Julian, with a chuckle, when at last the signalling stopped. 'I rather think the Stick family will stay where they are tonight, too scared of sheep and cows and horses rushing about in those dungeons!'

Julian was quite right – the Sticks did stay where they were! Nothing would get them out of their underground room till morning.

CHAPTER SEVENTEEN

A shock for Edgar

THE CHILDREN slept well that night, and as Timothy did not growl at all, they were sure that nothing important could have happened. They had a fine breakfast of tongue, tinned peaches, bread and butter, golden syrup and ginger-beer.

'That's the end of the ginger-beer, I'm afraid,' said Julian, regretfully. 'I must say ginger-beer is a gorgeous drink – seems to go with simply everything.'

'That was the nicest meal I've ever had,' said Anne. 'It really was. We do have lovely meals on Kirrin Island. I wonder if the Sticks are having nice meals too.'

'You bet they are!' said Dick. 'I expect they have ransacked Aunt Fanny's cupboards and taken the best they can find.'

'Oh, the beasts!' said George, her eyes flashing. 'I never thought of that – they may have robbed the house and taken all kinds of things.'

'They probably have,' said Julian, and he frowned. 'I say, I never thought of that, somehow. How awful, George, if your mother came back, feeling ill and weak, and found half her belongings gone!'

'Oh dear!' said Anne, dismayed. 'George, wouldn't that be dreadful?'

'Yes,' said George, looking very angry. 'I would believe anything of those Sticks! If they have the cheek to come to our island and live here, they've the cheek to steal from my mother's house. I wish we could find out.'

'They could have brought quite a lot of things away in their boat,' said Julian. 'They must have come here by boat. If they did bring stolen goods, they must have put them somewhere – down in the dungeons, I suppose.'

'We might have a look round and see if we can spy anything, without the Sticks seeing us,' suggested Dick.

'Let's have a look round now,' said George, who always liked doing things at once. 'Anne, you do the washing-up and tidy our cave-house for us, will you?'

Anne was torn between wanting to go with the others, and longing to play 'house' again. She did so love arranging everything and making the beds and tidying up the cave. In the end she said she would stay and the others could go.

So up the rope they went. Timothy stayed with Anne, because they were afraid he might bark. Anne tied him up, and he whined a little, but did not make a terrible noise.

The other three lay flat on the cliff-top, looking down on the ruined castle. There seemed to be no one about, but, even as they watched, the three Sticks appeared, apparently coming up from the dungeons. They seemed glad to be in the sunshine, and the children were not surprised, for the dungeons were so cold and dark.

A SHOCK FOR EDGAR

The Sticks looked all round. Stinker kept close to Mrs Stick, his tail well down.

'They're looking for the cows and sheep and horses they heard down in the dungeons last night!' whispered Dick to Julian.

The Sticks spoke together for a minute or two, and then went off in the direction of the shore that faced the wreck. Edgar went to the room in which the children had first planned to sleep – the one whose roof had fallen in.

'I'm going to stalk the two Sticks,' whispered Julian to the others. 'You two see what Edgar is up to.'

Julian disappeared, keeping behind bushes as he watched where the Sticks went, and followed them. George and Dick went cautiously and quietly over the cliff to the castle in the middle of the little island. They could hear Edgar whistling. Stinker was running about the courtyard of the castle.

Edgar appeared out of the ruined room, carrying a pile of cushions, which had evidently been stored there. George went red with rage and clutched Dick's arm fiercely.

'Mother's best cushions!' she whispered. 'Oh, the beasts!'

Dick felt angry too. It was quite plain that the Sticks had helped themselves to anything handy when they had left Kirrin Cottage. He picked up a clod of earth, took careful aim, and flung it into the air. It fell between Edgar and Stinker, breaking into a shower of earth.

A SHOCK FOR EDGAR

Edgar dropped the cushions, and looked up into the air in fright. It was plain that he thought something had fallen from the sky. George picked up another clod, took aim, and flung it higher into the air. It fell all over Stinker, and the dog gave a yelp, and scuttled down the hole that led into the dungeons.

Edgar looked up into the sky and then all around and about him, his mouth wide open. What could be happening? Dick waited until he was looking in the opposite direction, and then once more sent a big clod into the air. It fell into bits and scattered itself all over the startled Edgar.

Then Dick gave one of his realistic moos, exactly like a cow in pain, and Edgar stood rooted to the spot, almost frightened out of his skin. Those cows again! Where were they?

Dick mooed again, and Edgar gave a yell, found his feet, and almost fell down the dungeon steps. He disappeared with a dismal howl, leaving behind all the cushions on the ground.

'Quick!' said Dick, jumping to his feet. 'He won't be back for a few minutes, anyhow. He'll be too scared. Let's grab the cushions and bring them here. I don't see why the Sticks should use them down in those awful old dungeons.'

The two children raced to the courtyard, picked up the cushions and raced back to their hiding-place. Dick looked across to the room where Edgar had brought them from.

'What about slipping across there and seeing what else they've stored away?' he said. 'I don't see why they should be allowed to have anything that isn't theirs.'

'I'll go across, and you keep watch by the dungeon entrance,' said George. 'You've only got to moo again if you see Edgar, and he'll run for miles.'

'Right,' said Dick, with a grin, and went swiftly to the flight of steps that led underground to the dungeons. There was no sign of Edgar at all, nor of Stinker.

George went to the ruined room and gazed round in anger. Yes, the Sticks certainly *had* helped themselves to her mother's things, no doubt about that! There were blankets and silver and all kinds of food. Mrs Stick must have gone into the big cupboard under the stairs and taken out various things stored there for weekly use.

George ran to Dick. 'There are heaps of our things!' she said, in a fierce whisper. 'Come and help me to get them. We'll see if we can take them all before Edgar appears, or the Sticks come back.'

Just as they were whispering together, they heard a low whistle. They looked round, and saw Julian coming along. He joined them.

'The Sticks have rowed off to the wreck,' he said. 'They've got an old boat somewhere down among those rocks. Old Pa Stick must be a good sailor to be able to take the boat in and out of those awful hidden rocks.'

'Oh, then we've got time to do what we want to do,' said

A SHOCK FOR EDGAR

Dick, pleased. He hurriedly told Julian of the things George had seen in the ruined room.

'Awful thieves!' said Julian, indignantly. 'They don't mean to go back to Kirrin Cottage, that's plain. They've got some business on with the smugglers here – and when that is done they'll go off with all their stolen goods, join a ship somewhere, and get off scot-free.'

'No, they won't,' said George at once. 'We are going to get everything and take it to the cave! Dick's going to keep watch for Edgar at the cave entrance, and you and I, Julian, can quickly carry the things away. We can drop them down the hole into the cave.'

'Hurry then!' said Julian. 'We must do it before the Sticks return, and I don't expect they'll be long. They've probably gone to fetch the trunk and anything else in the wreck. You know I saw a light out to sea last night – maybe that's a signal that the smugglers were leaving something in the wreck for the Sticks to fetch.'

George and Julian ran to the ruined room, piled their arms with the goods there, and then ran to hide them on the cliff, ready to take them to the hole when they had time. It looked as if the Sticks had just taken whatever was easiest to lay their hands on. They had even got the kitchen clock!

Edgar did not appear at all, so Dick had nothing to do but sit by the steps of the dungeon and watch the others. After some time Julian and George gave a sigh of relief and beckoned to Dick. He left his place and went to join them.

151

'We've got everything now,' said Julian. 'I'm just going to the cliff-edge to see if the Sticks are returning yet. If they're not we'll all carry the things to the hole in the roof of the cave.'

He soon returned. 'I can see their boat tied to the wreck,' he said. 'We're safe for some while yet. Come on, let's get the things to safety! This really is a bit of luck.'

They carried the things to the hole and called down it to Anne. 'Anne! We've got tons of things to put down the hole. Stand by to catch!'

Soon all kinds of things came down the hole into the cave! Anne was most astonished. The silver and anything that might be hurt by a fall was first wrapped up in the blankets, and then let down by a rope.

'My goodness!' said Anne. 'This cave will *really* look like a house soon, when I have arranged all these things too!'

Just as they were finishing their job the children heard voices in the distance.

'The Sticks are back!' said Julian, and looked cautiously over the cliff-top. He was right. They had returned to their boat, and were even now on their way back to the castle, carrying the trunk from the wreck.

'Let's follow them, and see what happens when they find everything gone,' grinned Julian. 'Come on, everyone!'

They wriggled over the cliff on their tummies, and came to a clump of bushes behind which they could hide and watch. The Sticks put the trunk down, and looked round for Edgar. But Edgar was nowhere to be seen.

A SHOCK FOR EDGAR

'Where's that boy?' said Mrs Stick, impatiently. 'He's had plenty of time to do everything. Edgar! Edgar! Edgar!'

Mr Stick went to the ruined room and peeped inside. He came back to Mrs Stick.

'He's taken everything down,' he said. 'He must be down in the dungeon. That room's quite empty.'

'I told him to come up and sit in the sun when he'd finished,' said Mrs Stick. 'It isn't healthy down in those dungeons. EDGAR!'

This time Edgar heard, and his head appeared, looking out of the entrance to the dungeon. He looked extremely scared.

'Come on up!' said Mrs Stick. 'You've got all the

153

things down, and you'd better stay up here in the sunshine now.'

'I'm scared,' said Edgar. 'I'm not staying up here alone.'

'Why not?' said Mr Stick, astonished.

'It's those cows again!' said poor Edgar. 'Hundreds of them, Pa, all a-mooing round me, and throwing things at me. They're dangerous animals, they are, and I'm not coming up here alone!'

CHAPTER EIGHTEEN

An unexpected prisoner

THE STICKS stared at Edgar as if he was mad.

'Cows throwing things?' said Mrs Stick at last. 'What do you mean by that? Cows don't throw anything.'

'These ones did,' said Edgar, and then began to exaggerate in order to make his parents sympathise with him. 'They were dreadful cows, they were – hundreds of them, with horns as long as reindeer, and awful mooing voices. And they threw things at me and Tinker. He was really scared, and so was I. I dropped the cushions I was taking down, and rushed away to hide.'

'Where are the cushions?' said Mr Stick, looking round. 'I can't see any cushions. I suppose you'll tell us the cows ate them.'

'Didn't you take everything down into the dungeons?' demanded Mrs Stick. 'Because that room's empty now. There's not a thing in it.'

'I didn't take anything down at all,' said Edgar, coming cautiously out of the dungeon entrance. 'I dropped the cushions just about where you're standing. What's happened to them?'

'Look 'ere!' said Mr Stick, in amazement. 'Who's been 'ere since we've been gone? Someone's taken the cushions and everything else too. Where have they put them?'

'Pa, it was the cows,' said Edgar, looking all round as if he expected to see cows walking off with cushions and silver and blankets.

'Shut up about the cows,' said Mrs Stick, suddenly losing her temper. 'For one thing there aren't any cows on this island, and that we do know, for we looked all over it this morning. What we heard last night must have been strange sort of echoes rumbling round. No, my boy – there's something funny about all this. Looks as if there *is* somebody on the island!'

A dismal howl came echoing up from below the ground. It was Stinker, terrified at being alone below, and not daring to come up.

'Poor lamb!' said Mrs Stick, who seemed much fonder of Stinker than of anyone else.

'What's up with him?'

Stinker let out an even more doleful howl, and Mrs Stick hurried down the steps to go to him. Mr Stick followed her, and Edgar lost no time in going after them.

'Quick!' said Julian, standing up. 'Come with me, Dick. We may just have time to get that trunk! Run!'

The two boys ran quickly down to the courtyard of the ruined castle. Each took a handle of the small trunk, and lifted it between them. They staggered back to George with it.

'We'll take it to the cave,' whispered Julian. 'You stay here a few minutes and see what happens.'

AN UNEXPECTED PRISONER

The boys went over the cliff with the trunk. George flattened herself behind her bush and watched. Mr Stick appeared again in a few minutes, and looked round for the trunk. His mouth fell open in astonishment when he saw that it was gone. He yelled down the entrance to the dungeon.

'Clara! The trunk's gone!'

Mrs Stick was already on her way up, with Stinker close beside her and Edgar just behind. She climbed out and stared round.

'Gone?' she said, in enormous surprise. 'Gone! Where's it gone?'

'That's what *I'd* like to know!' said Mr Stick. 'We leave it here a few minutes – and then it goes. Walks off by itself – just like all the other things!'

'Look here! There's someone on this island,' said Mrs Stick. 'And I'm going to find out who it is. Got your gun, Pa?'

'I have,' said Mr Stick, slapping his belt. 'You get a good stout stick too, and we'll take Tinker. If we don't ferret out whoever's trying to spoil our plans, my name's not Stick!'

George slipped away quietly to warn the others. Before she slid down the rope into the cave, she pulled several bramble sprays across the hole. She dropped down to the floor of the cave, and told the others what had happened.

Julian had been trying to open the trunk, but it was

still locked. He looked up as George panted out her tale.

'We'll be all right here so long as no one falls down that hole in the roof!' he said. 'Now keep quiet everyone, and don't you dare to growl, Timmy!'

Nothing was heard for some time, and then Stinker's bark came in the distance. 'Quiet now,' said Julian. 'They are near here.'

The Sticks were up on the cliff once more, searching carefully behind every bush. They came to the great bush behind which the children often hid, and saw the flattened grass there.

'Someone's been here,' said Mr Stick. 'I wonder if they're in the middle of this bush – it's thick enough to hide half an army! I'll try and force my way in, Clara, while you stand by with my gun.'

Edgar wandered off by himself while this was happening, feeling certain that nobody would be foolish enough to live in the middle of such a prickly bush. He walked across the cliff – and then, to his awful horror, he found himself falling! His legs disappeared into a hole, he clutched at some thorny sprays but could not save himself. Down he went and down and down – and down – crash!

Edgar had fallen down the hole in the roof of the cave. He suddenly appeared before the children's startled eyes, and landed in a heap on the soft sand. Timmy at once pounced on him with a fearsome growl, but George pulled him off just in time.

Edgar was half-stunned with fright and his fall. He lay on the floor of the cave, groaning, his eyes shut. The children stared at him and then at one another. For a few moments they were completely taken aback and didn't know what to do or say. Timmy growled ferociously – so ferociously that Edgar opened his eyes in fright. He stared round at the four children and their dog in the utmost surprise and horror.

He opened his mouth to yell for help, but at once found Julian's large hand over it. 'Yell just once and Timmy shall have a bite out of any part of you he likes!' said Julian, in a voice as ferocious as Timothy's growl. 'See? Like to try it? Timmy's waiting to bite.'

'I shan't yell,' said Edgar, speaking in such a low whisper that the others could hardly hear him. 'Keep that dog off. I shan't yell.'

George spoke to Timothy. 'Now you listen, Timothy – if this boy shouts, you just go for him! Lie here by him and show him your big teeth. Bite him wherever you like if he yells.'

'Woof!' said Timmy, looking really pleased. He lay down by Edgar, and the boy tried to move away. But Timmy came nearer every time he moved.

Edgar looked round at the children. 'What are you doing on this island?' he said. 'We thought you'd gone home.'

'It's *our* island!' said George, in a very fierce voice. 'We've every right to be on it if we want to – but you have no right at all. None! What are you and your father and mother here for?'

'Don't know,' said Edgar, looking sulky.

'You'd better tell us,' said Julian. 'We know you're in league with smugglers.'

AN UNEXPECTED PRISONER

Edgar looked startled. 'Smugglers?' he said. 'I didn't know that. Pa and Ma don't tell me anything. I don't want anything to do with smugglers.'

'Don't you know *any*-thing?' said Dick. 'Don't you know why you've come to Kirrin Island?'

'I don't know anything,' said Edgar, in an injured tone. 'Pa and Ma are mean to me. They never tell me anything. I do as I'm told, that's all. I don't know anything about smugglers, I tell you that.'

It was quite plain to the children that Edgar really did not know anything of the reasons for his parents coming to the island. 'Well, I'm not surprised they don't let Spotty-Face into their secrets,' said Julian. 'He'd blab them if he could, I bet. Anyway, we know it's smuggling they're mixed up in.'

'You let me go,' said Edgar, sullenly. 'You've got no right to keep me here.'

'We're not going to let you go,' said George at once.

'You're our prisoner now. If we let you go back to your parents, you'd tell them all about us, and we don't want them to know we're here. We're going to spoil their pretty plans, you see.'

Edgar saw. He saw quite a lot of things. He felt rather sick. 'Was it you that took the cushions and things?'

'Oh no, dear Edgar,' said Dick. 'It was the cows, wasn't it? Don't you remember how you told your mother about the hundreds of cows that mooed at you and threw things and stole the cushions you dropped? Surely you haven't

161

forgotten your cows already?'

'Funny, aren't you?' said Edgar, sulkily. 'What you going to do with me? I won't stay here, that's flat.'

'But you will, Spotty-Face,' said Julian. 'You will stay here till we let you go – and that won't be till we've cleared up this little smuggling mystery. And let me warn you that any nonsense on your part will be punished by Timmy.'

'Lot of beasts you are,' said Edgar, seeing that he could do nothing but obey the four children. 'My pa and ma won't half be furious with you.'

His ma and pa were feeling extremely astonished. There had, of course, been nobody hiding in the big thick bush, and when Mr Stick had wriggled out, scratched and bleeding, he had looked round for Edgar. And Edgar was not to be seen.

'Where's that dratted boy?' he said, and shouted for him. 'Edgar! ED-GAR!'

But Edgar did not answer. The Sticks spent a very long time looking for Edgar, both above ground and underground. Mrs Stick was convinced that poor Edgar was lost in the dungeons, and she tried to send Stinker to find him. But Stinker only went as far as the first cave. He remembered the peculiar noises of the night before and was not at all keen on exploring the dungeons.

Julian turned his attention to the little trunk, once Edgar had been dealt with. 'I'm going to open this somehow,' he said. 'I'm sure it's got smuggled goods in, though goodness knows what.'

AN UNEXPECTED PRISONER

'You'll have to smash the locks then,' said Dick. Julian got a small rock and tried to smash the two locks. He managed to wrench one open after a while, and then the other gave way too. The children threw back the lid.

On the top was a child's blanket, embroidered with white rabbits. Julian pulled it off, expecting to see the smuggled goods below. But to his astonishment there were a child's clothes!

He pulled them out. There were two blue jerseys, a blue skirt, some vests and knickers and a warm coat. At the bottom of the trunk were some dolls and a teddy bear!

'Golly!' said Julian, in amazement. 'What are all these for? Why did the Sticks bring these to the island – and why did the smugglers hide them in the wreck? It's a puzzler!'

Edgar appeared to be as astonished as the rest. He too had expected valuable goods of some kind. George and Anne pulled out the dolls. They were lovely ones. Anne cuddled them up to her. She loved dolls, though George scorned them.

'Who do they belong to?' she said. 'Oh won't they be sad not to have them! Julian, isn't it funny? *Why* should anyone bring a trunk full of clothes and dolls to Kirrin Island?

CHAPTER NINETEEN

A scream in the night

NOBODY COULD even guess the answers to Anne's surprised questions. The children stared into the trunk and puzzled over it. It seemed such a funny thing to smuggle. They remembered the other things in the wreck too – the tins of food. They were peculiar things to smuggle on to the island. There didn't seem any point in it.

'Funny,' said Dick, at last. 'It beats me. There's no doubt that strange things are afoot here, or the Sticks wouldn't be hanging around our island. And we've seen signals from a ship out to sea. Something's going on. We thought if we opened this trunk it might help us – but it's only made the mystery deeper.'

Just then the voices of the two parent Sticks could be heard shouting for Edgar. But Edgar did not dare to shout back. Timmy's nose was poked against his leg. He might be nipped at any time. Timmy growled every now and again to remind Edgar that he was still there.

'Do you know anything about the ship that signals to this island at night?' asked Julian, turning to Edgar.

The boy shook his head. 'Never heard of any signals,' he said. 'I just heard my mother saying that she expected the *Roamer* tonight, but I don't know what she meant.'

'The *Roamer*?' said George, at once. 'What's that – a man – or a boat – or what?'

'I don't know,' said Edgar. 'I'd only have got a clip on the ear if I'd asked. Find out yourself.'

'We will,' said Julian, grimly. 'We'll watch out for the *Roamer* tonight! Thanks for the information.'

The children spent a quiet and rather boring day in the cave – all but Anne, who had plenty of things to arrange again. Really, the cave looked most home-like when she had finished! She put the blankets on the bed, and used the rugs as carpets. So the cave really looked most imposing!

Edgar was not allowed to go out of the cave, and Timothy didn't leave him for a moment. He slept most of the time, complaining that 'those cows and things' had frightened him so much the night before that he'd not been able to sleep a wink.

The others discussed their plans in low voices. They decided to keep watch on the cliff-top, two and two together, that night. They would wait and see what happened. If the *Roamer* came, they would hurriedly make fresh plans then.

The sun sank. The night came up dark over the sea. Edgar snored softly, after a very good supper of sardines, corned beef sandwiches, tinned apricots and tinned milk. Anne and Dick went up to keep the first watch. It was about half-past ten.

At half-past twelve Julian and George climbed up the

knotted rope and joined the other two. They had nothing to report. They went down into the cave, got into their comfortable beds and went to sleep. Edgar was snoring away in his corner, Timmy still on guard.

Julian and George looked out to sea, watching for any sign of a ship. The moon was up that night, and things were not quite so dark. Suddenly they heard low voices, and saw shadowy figures down by the rocks below.

'The two Sticks,' whispered Julian. 'Going to row out to the wreck again, I suppose.'

There was the splash of oars, and the children saw a boat move out over the water. At the same time George nudged Julian violently and pointed out to sea. A light was being shown a good way out, from a ship that the children could barely see. Then the moon went behind a cloud, and they could see nothing for some time.

They watched breathlessly. Was that shadowy ship a good way out the *Roamer*? Or was the owner of it the 'Roamer'? Were the smugglers at work tonight?

'There's another boat coming – look!' said George. 'It must be coming from that ship out to sea. Now the moon has come out again, you can just see it. It is going to the old wreck. It must be a meeting-place, I should think.'

Then, most irritatingly, the moon went behind a cloud again, and remained there so long that the children grew impatient. At last it sailed out again and lit up the water.

'Both boats are leaving the wreck now,' said Julian
excitedly. 'They've had their meeting – and passed over
the smuggled goods, I suppose – and now one boat is

returning to the ship, and the other, the Sticks' boat, is coming back here with the goods. We'll follow the Sticks when they get back and see where they put the goods.'

After a long time the Sticks' boat came to shore again. The children could not see anything then, but presently they saw the Sticks going back towards the castle. Mr Stick carried what looked like a large bundle, flung over his shoulder. They could not see if Mrs Stick carried anything.

The Sticks went into the courtyard of the castle, and came to the dungeon entrance. 'They're taking the smuggled goods down there,' whispered Julian to George. The children were now watching from behind a nearby wall. 'We'll go back and tell the others, and make some more plans. We must somehow or other get those goods ourselves, and take them back to the mainland and get in touch with the police!'

Just then a scream rang out in the night. It was a high-pitched, terrified scream, and frightened the watching children very much. They had no idea where it came from.

'Quick! It must be Anne!' said Julian, and the two ran as fast as they could to the hole that led down to the cave. They dropped down the rope and Julian looked round the quiet cave anxiously. What had happened to Anne to make her scream like that?

But Anne was peacefully asleep on her bed, and so was Dick. Edgar still snored and Timmy watched, his eyes gleaming green.

'Funny,' said Julian, still startled. 'Awfully funny. Who

screamed like that? It couldn't possibly have been Anne – because if she had screamed in her sleep like that, she would have woken the others.'

'Well, who screamed, then?' said George, feeling rather scared. 'Wasn't it weird, Julian? I didn't like it. It was somebody who was awfully frightened. But who could it be?'

They woke Dick and Anne and told them about the strange scream. Anne was very startled. Dick was interested to hear that two boats had met at the wreck, and that the Sticks had brought back smuggled goods of some sort, and taken them down in the dungeons.

'We'll get those tomorrow, somehow!' he said, cheerfully. 'We'll have good fun.'

'Why did you think it was me screaming?' asked Anne. 'Did you think it was a girl screaming?'

'Yes. It sounded like the scream you give when one of us jumps out at you suddenly,' said Julian.

'It's funny,' said Anne. She cuddled down into her bed again, and George got in beside her.

'Oh Anne!' said George, in disgust. 'You've got our bed simply *full* of those dolls – and that teddy bear is here too! You really are a baby!'

'No, I'm not,' said Anne. 'The dolls and the bear are babies – they are frightened and lonely because they're not with the little girl they belong to. So I had them in bed with me instead! I'm sure the little girl would be glad.'

'The little girl!' said Julian, slowly. 'We thought we

heard a little girl scream tonight – we found a small trunk full of a little girl's clothes, and a little girl's dolls. What does it all mean?'

There was a silence – and then Anne spoke excitedly. 'I know! The smuggled goods are a little girl! They've stolen a little girl away – and these are her dolls, and those over there are her clothes that were stolen at the same time, for her to dress in and play with. The little girl's here, on this island now – you heard her scream tonight when those horrid Sticks carried her down into the dungeons!'

'Well – I do believe Anne has hit on the right idea,' said Julian. 'Clever girl, Anne! I think you're right. It isn't smugglers who are using this island – it's kidnappers!'

'What are kidnappers?' said Anne.

'People who steal away children or grown-ups and hide them somewhere till a large sum of money is paid out for them,' explained Julian. 'It's called a ransom. Till the ransom is paid, the prisoner is held by the captors.'

'Well, that's what's happened here then!' said George.

'I bet it has! Some poor little rich girl has been stolen away – and brought to the wreck by boat from some ship – and taken over by those horrible Sticks. Wicked creatures!'

'And we heard the poor little thing scream just as she was taken down underground,' said George. 'Julian, we've got to rescue her.'

'Yes, of course,' said Julian. 'We will, never fear! We'll rescue her tomorrow.'

Edgar woke up and joined in the conversation suddenly. 'What you talking about?' he said. 'Rescue who?'

'Never you mind,' said Julian.

George nudged him and whispered.

'All I hope is that Mrs Stick is feeling as upset about losing her dear Edgar as the mother of the little girl,' she said.

'Tomorrow we find the little girl somehow, and take her away,' said Julian. 'I expect the Sticks will be on guard, but we'll find a way.'

'I'm tired now,' said George, lying down. 'Let's go to sleep. We'll wake up nice and fresh. Oh Anne, do put these dolls your side. I'm lying on at least three.'

Anne took the dolls and the bear and arranged them on her side of the bed. 'Don't feel lonely,' George heard her say. 'I'll look after you all right till you go back to your own mistress. Sleep tight!'

Soon they all slept – all but Timothy, who lay with one eye open all night long. There was no need to put anyone on guard while Timmy was there. He was the best guardian they could have.

CHAPTER TWENTY

A rescue – and a new prisoner!

THE NEXT day Julian was awake early and went up the rope to the cliff-top to see if the Sticks were about. He saw them coming up the steps that led from the dungeons. Mrs Stick looked pale and worried.

'We've got to find our Edgar,' she kept saying to Mr Stick. 'I tell you we've got to find our Edgar. He's not down in the dungeons. That I do know. We've yelled ourselves hoarse down there.'

'And he's not on the island,' said Mr Stick. 'We hunted all over it yesterday. I think whoever was here then, took our goods, caught Edgar, and made off with him and everything else in their boat. That's what I think.'

'Well, they've taken him to the mainland then,' said Mrs Stick. 'We'd better take our boat and go back there and ask a few questions. What I'd like to know is – who is it messing about here and interfering with our plans? It makes me scared. Just when things are going nicely too!'

'Is it all right to leave here just now?' said Mr Stick, doubtfully. 'Suppose whoever was here yesterday is still here – they might pop down into the dungeons when we're gone.'

'Well, they're not here,' said Mrs Stick, firmly. 'Use

your common sense, if you've got any – wouldn't our Edgar yell the place down if he was being kept prisoner on this little island – and wouldn't we hear him? I tell you he must have been taken off in a boat, together with all the other things that are gone. And I don't like it.'

'All right, all right!' said Mr Stick, in a grumbling tone. 'That boy's always a nuisance – always in silly trouble of some sort.'

'How can you talk of poor Edgar like that?' cried Mrs Stick. 'Do you think the poor child *likes* being captured! Goodness knows what he's going through – feeling frightened and lonely without me.'

Julian felt disgusted. Here was Mrs Stick talking like that about old Spotty-Face – and yet she had a little girl down in the dungeons – a child much younger than Edgar! What a beast she was.

'What about Tinker?' said Mr Stick, in a sulky tone. 'Better leave him here, hadn't we, to guard the entrance to the dungeons? Not that there will be anyone here, if what you say is right.'

'Oh, we'll leave Tinker,' said Mrs Stick, setting off to the boat. Julian saw them embark, leaving the dog behind. Tinker watched them rowing away, his tail well down between his legs. Then he turned and ran back to the courtyard, and lay down dolefully in the sun. He was very uneasy. His ears were cocked and he kept looking this way and that. He didn't like this strange island and its unexpected noises.

A RESCUE – AND A NEW PRISONER!

Julian tore back to the cave and dropped down the rope, startling Edgar very much. 'Come outside the cave and I'll tell you my plans,' said Julian to the others. He didn't want Edgar to hear them. They all went outside. Anne had got breakfast ready while Julian had been gone, and the kettle was boiling away merrily on the little stove.

'Listen!' said Julian. 'The Sticks have gone off in their boat back to the mainland to see if they can find their precious little darling Edgar. Mrs Stick is all hot and bothered because she thinks someone's gone off with him and she's afraid the poor boy will be feeling frightened and lonely!'

'Well!' said George. 'Doesn't she think that the little kidnapped girl must be feeling much worse? What a horrid woman she is!'

'You're right,' said Julian. 'Well, what I propose to do is this – we'll go down into the dungeons now and rescue the little girl – and bring her here to our cave for breakfast. Then we'll take her off in our boat, go to the police, find out where her parents are, and telephone to them that she is safe.'

'What shall we do with Edgar?' said Anne.

'I know!' said George at once. 'We'll put Edgar into the dungeon instead of the little girl! Think how astonished the Sticks will be to find the little girl gone and their dear Edgar shut up in the dungeon instead!'

'Oooh! – that *is* a good idea,' said Anne, and all the others laughed and agreed.

'You stay here, Anne, and cut some more bread and

butter for the little girl,' said Julian. He knew that Anne hated going down into the dungeons.

Anne nodded, pleased.

'All right, I will. I'll just take the kettle off for a bit too, or else the water will boil away.'

'They all went back into the cave. 'Come with us, Edgar,' said Julian. 'You come too, Timmy.'

'Where're you going to take me?' said Edgar, suspiciously.

'A nice cosy, comfortable place, where cows can't get at you,' said Julian. 'Come on! Buck up.'

'Gr-r-r-r-r-r,' said Timmy, his nose against Edgar's leg. Edgar got up in a hurry.

They all went up the rope, one after another, though Edgar was terribly scared, and was sure he couldn't. But with Timmy snapping at his ankles below, he climbed up the rope remarkably quickly, and was hauled out at the top by Julian.

'Now, quick march!' said Julian, who wanted to get everything over before the Sticks thought of returning. And quick march it was, over the cliffs, over the low wall of the castle, and down into the courtyard.

'I'm not going down into those dungeons with you,' said Edgar, in alarm.

'You are, Spotty-Face,' said Julian, amiably.

'Where's my Pa and Ma?' said Edgar, looking anxiously all round.

'Those cows have got them, I expect,' said George. 'The ones that came and mooed at you and threw things, you know.'

Everyone giggled, except Edgar, who looked worried and pale. He did not like this kind of adventure at all. The children came to the dungeon entrance, and found that the Sticks had not only closed down the stone that opened the way to the dungeons, but had also dragged heavy rocks across it.

'Blow your parents!' said Julian, to Edgar. 'Making a lot of trouble for everybody. Come on, stir yourself all hands to these stones. Edgar, pull when we pull. Go on! You'll get into trouble if you don't.'

Edgar pulled with the rest, and one by one the rocks were moved away. Then the heavy trapdoor stone was hauled up too, and the flight of steps was exposed leading down into darkness.

'There's Tinker!' suddenly cried Edgar, pointing to a bush some distance away. Tinker was there, hiding, quite terrified at seeing Timothy again.

'Fat lot of good Stinker is,' said Julian. 'No, Timmy you're not to eat him. Stay here! He wouldn't taste nice if you did eat him!'

Timothy was sorry not to be able to chase Stinker round and round the island. If he couldn't chase rabbits, he might at least be allowed to chase Stinker!

They all went down into the dungeons. Julian's white chalk-marks were still on the rocky walls, so it was easy to find the way to the cave-like room where the children, last summer, had found piles of golden ingots. They felt sure that the little kidnapped girl had been put there, for this cave had a big wooden door that could be bolted on the outside.

They came to the door. It was well and truly bolted. There was no sound from inside. Everyone halted outside and Timmy scratched at the door, whining gently. He knew there was someone inside.

'Hallo, there!' shouted Julian, in a loud and cheerful voice. 'Are you all right? We've come to rescue you.'

There was a scrambling noise, as if someone had got up from a stool. Then a small voice sounded from the cave.

'Hallo! Who are you? Oh, do please rescue me! I'm so lonely and frightened!'

'Just undoing the door!' called back Julian, cheerfully. 'We're all children out here, so don't be afraid. You'll soon be safe.'

A RESCUE – AND A NEW PRISONER!

He shot back the bolts, and flung open the door. Inside the cave, which was lit by a lantern, stood a small girl, with a scared little white face, and large dark eyes. Dark red hair tumbled round her cheeks, and she had evidently been crying bitterly, for her face was dirty and tear-stained.

Dick went to her and put his arm round her. 'Everything's all right now,' he said. 'You're safe. We'll take you back to your mother.'

'I do want her, I do, I do,' said the little girl, and tears ran down her cheeks again. 'Why am I here? I don't like being here.'

'Oh, it's just an adventure you've had,' said Julian. 'It's over now – at least, nearly over. There's still a bit of it left – a nice bit, though. We want you to come and have breakfast with us in our cave. We've a lovely cave.'

'Oh, have you?' said the little girl, rubbing her eyes. 'I want to go with you, I like you, but I didn't like those other people.'

'Of course you didn't,' said George. 'Look! This is Timothy, our dog. He wants to be friends with you.'

'What a simply lovely dog!' said the little girl, and flung her arms around Timmy's neck. He licked her in delight. George was pleased. She put her arm round the little girl.

'What's your name?' she said.

'Jennifer Mary Armstrong,' said the little girl. 'What's yours?'

'George,' said George, and the little girl nodded, thinking that George was a boy, not a girl, for she was dressed in jeans just like Julian and Dick, and her hair was short, too, though very curly.

The others told her their names – and then she looked at Edgar, who had said nothing.

'This is Spotty-Face,' said Julian. 'He isn't a friend of

ours. It was his father and mother who put you here, Jennifer. Now we are going to leave him here in your place. It will be such a pleasant surprise for them, won't it?'

Edgar gave a yell of dismay and tried to back away – but Julian gave him a strong shove that sent him flying into the cave.

'There's only one way to teach people like you and your parents that wickedness doesn't pay!' said the boy, grimly. 'And that is to punish you hard. People like you don't understand kindness. You think it's just being soft and silly. All right – you can have a taste of what Jennifer has had. It will do you good, and do your parents a lot of good too! Goodbye!'

Edgar began to howl dismally as Julian bolted the big wooden door top and bottom. 'I shall starve!' he wailed.

'Oh no, you won't,' said Julian. 'There's plenty of food and water in there, so help yourself. It would do you good to go hungry for a while, all the same.'

'Mind the cows don't get you!' called Dick, and he gave a realistic moo that startled Jennifer very much, for the echoes came mooing round too.

'It's all right – only the echoes,' said George, smiling at her in the torch-light. Edgar howled away in the cave, sobbing like a baby.

'Little coward, isn't he?' said Julian. 'Come on – let's get back. I'm awfully hungry for my breakfast.'

'So am I,' said Jennifer, slipping her small hand into

Julian's. 'I wasn't hungry at all in that cave – but now I am. Thank you for rescuing me.'

'Don't mention it,' said Julian, grinning at her. 'It's a real pleasure – and an even greater one to put old Spotty-Face there instead of you. Nice to give the Sticks a dose of their own medicine.'

Jennifer didn't know what he meant, but the others did, and they chuckled. They made their way back through the dark, musty passages of the dungeons, passing many caves, big and small, on the way. They came at last to the flight of steps and went up them into the dazzling sunlight.

'Oh!' said Jennifer, breathing in great gulps of the fresh, sea-smelling air. 'Oh! This is lovely! Where am I?'

'On our island,' said George. 'And this is our ruined castle. You were brought here last night in a boat. We heard you scream, and that's how we guessed you were being made a prisoner.'

They walked to the cliff, and Jennifer was amazed at the way they disappeared down the knotted rope. She was eager to try too, and soon slid down into the cave.

'Nice kid, isn't she?' said Julian to George. 'My word, she's had even more of an adventure than we have!'

CHAPTER TWENTY-ONE

A visit to the police station

ANNE LIKED Jennifer very much, and gave her a hug and a kiss. Jennifer looked round the well-furnished cave in amazement and wonder – and then she gave a scream of surprise and joy. She pointed to Anne's neatly-made bed, on which sat a number of beautiful dolls, and a large teddy-bear.

'My dolls!' she said. 'Oh, and Teddy, too! Oh, oh, where did you get them? I've missed them so! Oh Josephine and Angela and Rosebud and Marigold, have you missed me?'

She flung herself on the dolls. Anne was very interested to hear their names. 'I've looked after them well,' she told Jennifer. 'They're quite all right.'

'Oh, thank you,' said the little girl, happily. 'I do think you're all nice. Oh, I say – what a lovely breakfast!'

It was. Anne had opened a tin of salmon, two tins of peaches, a tin of milk, cut some bread and butter, and made a big jug of cocoa. Jennifer sat down and began to eat. She was very hungry, and as she ate, she began to lose her paleness and look rosy and happy.

The children talked busily as they ate. Jennifer told them about herself.

'I was playing in the garden with my nanny,' she said,

183

'and suddenly, when nanny had gone indoors to fetch something, a man climbed over the wall, threw a shawl round my head, and took me away. We live by the sea, you know, and I soon heard the sound of the waves splashing on the shore, and I knew I was being put into a boat. I was taken to a big ship, and locked down in a cabin for two days. Then I suppose I was brought here one night. I was so frightened that I screamed.'

'That was the scream we heard,' said George. 'It was lucky we heard it. We had thought there was smuggling going on here, in our island – we didn't guess it was a case of kidnapping, till we heard you scream – though we had found your trunk with your clothes and toys.'

'I don't know how the man got those,' said Jennifer. 'Maybe one of our maids helped him. There was one I didn't like at all. She was called Sarah Stick.'

'Ah!' said Julian, at once. 'That's the one, then! It was Mr and Mrs Stick who brought you here. Sarah Stick, your maid, must be some relation of theirs. They must have been in the pay of someone else, I should think – someone who had a ship, and could bring you here to hide you.'

'Jolly good hiding-place, too,' said George. 'No one but us would ever have found it out.'

They ate all their breakfast, made some more cocoa, and discussed their future plans.

'We'll take our boat and go to the mainland this morning,' said Julian. 'We'll go straight to the police station with Jennifer. I expect the newspapers are full of her disappearance, and the police will recognise her at once.'

'I hope they catch the Sticks,' said George. 'I hope they won't disappear into thin air as soon as they hear that Jennifer is found.'

'Yes – we must warn the police of that,' said Julian, thoughtfully. 'Better not spread the news abroad till the Sticks are caught. I wonder where they are?'

'Let's get the boat now,' said Dick. 'There's no point in waiting about. Jennifer's parents will be thrilled to know she is safe.'

'I don't really want to leave this lovely cave,' said Jennifer, who was thoroughly enjoying herself now. I wish I lived here, too. Are you going to come back to the island and live here, Julian?'

'Well, we shall come back for a few days more, I expect,' said Julian. 'You see, our aunt's home is empty at the moment because she is away ill and our uncle is with her. So we might as well stay on our island till they come back.'

'Oh, *could* I come back with you?' begged Jennifer, her small round face alight with joy at the thought of living in a cave on an island with these nice children and their lovely dog. 'Oh, do let me! I would so like it. And I do so love Timmy.'

'I don't expect your parents would let you, especially after you've just been kidnapped,' said Julian. 'But you can ask them, if you like.'

They all went to the boat and got in. Julian pushed off. George steered the boat in and out of the rocks. They saw the wreck, which interested Jenny very much indeed. She badly wanted to stop, but the others thought they ought to get to land as quickly as possible.

Soon they were near the beach. Alf, the fisher-boy was there. He saw them and waved. He ran to help them to pull in their boat.

'I was coming out in my boat this morning,' he said. 'Your father's back, Master George. But not your mother. She's getting better, they say, and will be back in a week's time.'

'Well, what's my father come back for?' demanded George, in surprise.

'He got worried because nobody answered the telephone,' explained Alf. 'He came down and asked me where you all were. I didn't tell him, of course. I kept your secret. But I was just coming out to warn you this morning. He got back last night – and wasn't he wild? No one there to give him any food – all the house upside down and half the things gone! He's at the police station now.'

'Golly!' said George. 'That's just where *we* are going too! We shall meet him there. Oh dear, I do hope he won't be in an awful temper. You just can't do anything with my father when he's cross.'

'Come on!' said Julian. 'It's a good thing, in a way, that your father is here, George – we can explain everything to him and to the police at the same time.'

A VISIT TO THE POLICE STATION

They left Alf, who looked very surprised to see Jennifer with the others. He couldn't make out where she had come from. Certainly she had not started out to the island with them – but she had come back in their boat. How was that? It seemed very mysterious to Alf.

The children arrived at the police station and marched in, much to the surprise of the policeman there.

'Hallo!' he said. 'What's the matter? Been doing a burglary, or something, and come to own up?'

'Listen!' said George, suddenly, hearing a loud voice in the room next to theirs. 'That's Father's voice!'

She darted to the door. The policeman called to her, shocked. 'Now don't you go in there. The Inspector's in there. Come over here special, he has, and mustn't be interrupted.'

But George had flung open the door and gone inside. Her father turned and saw her. He rose to his feet. 'George! Where have you been? How dare you go away like this and leave the house and everything! It's been robbed right and left! I've just been telling the Inspector about all the things that have been stolen.'

'Don't worry, Father,' said George. 'Really don't worry. We've found them all. How's Mother?'

'Better, much better,' said her father, still looking amazed and angry. 'Thank goodness I can go back and tell her where you are. She kept asking me about you all, and I had to keep saying you were all right, so as not to worry her – but I hadn't any idea what was happening to you or where you had gone. I feel very displeased with you. Where were you?'

'On the island,' said George, looking rather sulky, as she often did when her father was angry with her. 'Julian will tell you all about it.'

Julian came in, followed by Dick, Anne, Jennifer and Timothy. The Inspector, a big, clever-looking man with dark eyes under shaggy eyebrows, looked at them all closely. When he saw Jennifer, he stared hard – and then suddenly rose to his feet.

'What's your name, little girl?' he said.

'Jennifer Mary Armstrong,' said Jenny, in a surprised voice.

'Bless us all!' said the Inspector, in a startled voice. 'Here's the child the whole country is looking for – and she walks in here as cool as a cucumber! Lands sakes, where did she come from?'

'What do you mean?' said George's father, looking surprised. 'What child is the whole country looking for? I haven't read the papers for some days.'

'Then you don't know about little Jenny Armstrong being kidnapped?' said the Inspector, sitting down and pulling Jenny near him. 'She's the daughter of Harry Armstrong, the millionaire, you know. Well, somebody kidnapped her and wants a hundred thousand pounds ransom for her. My word, we've combed the country for her – and here she is, as merry as you please. Well, I'm blessed – this is the strangest thing I ever knew. Where have you been, little Missy?'

'On the island,' said Jenny. 'Julian – you tell it all.'

So Julian told the whole story from beginning to end. The policeman from outside came in, and took notes down as he spoke. Everyone listened in amazement. As for George's father, his eyes nearly fell out of his head. What adventures these children did have to be sure, and how well they managed everything!

'And do you happen to know who was the owner of the ship that brought little Miss Jenny along – the one that sent a boat off to the wreck and put her there for the Sticks to take?' asked the Inspector.

'No,' said Julian. 'All we heard was that the *Roamer* was coming that night.'

'A-HA!' said the Inspector, with great satisfaction in his voice. 'Aha and oho! We know the *Roamer* all right – a ship we've been watching for some time – owned by somebody we're very, very suspicious of – we think he's dabbling in a whole lot of shady deals. Now this is very good news indeed. The thing is – where are the Sticks – and how can we catch them red-handed, now you've got Miss Jenny out of their clutches? They'll probably deny everything.'

'I know how we could catch them,' said Julian quickly. 'We've left their nasty son, Edgar, locked in the same dungeon where they put Jenny. If only one of us could pass the word to the Sticks, that that is where Edgar is, they'd go back to the island all right, and go right in to the dungeons – so if you found them there, it wouldn't be much good them denying that they don't know anything about the island, and have never been there.'

'That would certainly make things a lot easier,' said the Inspector. He pressed a bell and another policeman came into the room. The Inspector gave him a full description of Mr and Mrs Stick, and told him to watch the countryside round about, and report when they were found.

A VISIT TO THE POLICE STATION

'Then, Julian, you might like to go and have a little conversation with them about their son, Edgar,' said the Inspector, smiling. 'If they do go back to the island, we shall follow them, and get all the evidence we want. Thank you for your very great help. Now we must telephone to Jenny's parents and tell them she is safe.'

'She can come back to Kirrin Cottage with us,' said George's father, still looking rather dazed at all that had happened. 'I've got Joanna, our old cook, to come back for a while to put things straight, so there will be someone there to see to the children. They must all come back.'

'Well, Father,' said George, firmly, 'we will come back just for today, but we plan to spend another week on Kirrin Island till Mother comes back. She said we could, and we are having such a fine time there. Let Joanna stay at Kirrin Cottage and keep it in order and get it ready for Mother when she comes home – she won't want the bother of looking after us too. We can look after ourselves on the island.'

'I certainly think these children deserve a reward for the good work they have done,' remarked the Inspector, and that settled the matter.

'Very well,' said George's father, 'you can all go off to the island again – but you must be back when your mother returns, George.'

'Of course I will,' said George. 'I badly want to see Mother. But home isn't nice without her. I would rather be on our island.'

'And I want to be there, too,' said Jenny, unexpectedly. 'Ask my parents to come to Kirrin, please – so that I can ask them if I can go with the other children.'

'I'll do my best,' said the Inspector, grinning at the five children. They liked him very much. George's father stood up.

'Come along!' he said. 'I want my lunch. All this has made me feel hungry. We'll go and see if Joanna has got anything for us.'

Off they all went, talking nineteen to the dozen, making George's poor father feel quite bewildered. He always seemed to get into the middle of some adventure when these children were about!

CHAPTER TWENTY-TWO

Back to Kirrin Island!

SOON EVERYONE was at Kirrin Cottage. Joanna, the old cook they had had before, gave them a good welcome, and listened to their adventures in astonishment, getting the lunch ready all the while.

It was while they were having lunch that Julian, looking out of the window, suddenly caught sight of a figure he knew very well – someone skulking along behind the hedge.

'Old Pa Stick!' he said, and jumped up. 'I'll go after him. Stay here, everyone.'

He went out of the house, ran round a corner and came face to face with Mr Stick.

'Do you want to know where Edgar is?' said Julian mysteriously.

Mr Stick looked startled. He stared at Julian not knowing what to say.

'He's down in the dungeons, locked in that cave,' said Julian, even more mysteriously.

'You don't know anything about Edgar,' said Mr Stick. 'Where have you been? Didn't you go home?'

'Never you mind,' said Julian. 'But if you want to find Edgar – look in that cave!'

FIVE RUN AWAY TOGETHER

Mr Stick gave the boy a glare and left him. Julian hurried indoors and rang up the police station. He felt sure that Mr Stick would tell Mrs Stick what he had said, and that Mrs Stick would insist on going back to the island to see if what he had said was true. So all that needed to be done was for the police to keep a watch on the boats along the shore and see when the Sticks left.

The children finished their dinner, and Uncle Quentin announced that he must return to his wife, who would want to know his news. 'I'll tell her you are having a fine time on the island,' he said, 'and we can tell her all the extraordinary details when she returns home, better.'

He left in a car, and the children wondered whether they

194

might now return to their island or not. But they decided to wait a little, for they did not know what to do with Jennifer.

Very soon a large car drove up and stopped outside the gate of Kirrin Cottage. Out jumped a tall man with dark red hair, and a pretty woman. 'They must be your father and mother, Jenny,' said Julian.

They were – and Jennifer got so many hugs and kisses that she quite lost her breath. She had to tell her story again and again, and her father could not thank Julian and the others enough for all they had done.

'Ask me for any reward you like,' he said, 'and you can have it. I shall never, never be able to tell you how grateful I am to you for rescuing our little Jenny.'

'Oh – we don't want anything, thank you,' said Julian, politely. 'We enjoyed it all very much. We like adventures.'

'Ah, but you *must* tell me something you want!' said Jenny's father.

Julian glanced round at the others. He knew that none of them wanted a reward. Jenny nudged him hard and nodded her head vigorously. Julian laughed.

'Well,' he said, 'there *is* one thing we'd all like very much.'

'It's granted before you ask it!' said Jenny's father.

'Will you let Jenny come and spend a week with us on our island?' said Julian. Jenny gave a squeal and pressed Julian's arm very hard between her two small hands.

Jenny's parents looked rather taken-aback. 'Well,' said

her father, 'well – she's just been kidnapped, you know – and we don't feel inclined to let her out of our sight at the moment – and . . .'

'You promised Julian you'd grant what he asked, you promised, Daddy,' said Jenny, urgently. 'Oh please do let me. I've always wanted to live on an island. And this one has got a perfectly marvellous cave, and a wonderful ruined castle, and the dungeons where I was kept, and—'

'And we take Timothy, our dog, with us,' said Julian. 'See what a big powerful fellow he is – nobody could come to much harm with Timmy about – could they, Tim?'

'Woof!' said Timothy, in his deepest voice.

'Well, you can go, Jenny, on one condition,' said the little girl's father at last, 'and that is that your mother and I come over tomorrow and spend the day on the island, to see that everything is all right for you.'

'Oh, thank you, thank you, Daddy!' cried Jenny, and danced round the room in delight. A whole week on the island with these new friends of hers, and Timmy the dog! What could be lovelier?

'Jenny can stay here the night, can't she?' said George. 'You'll be staying at the hotel, I suppose?'

Soon Jenny's parents left and went to the police station to get all the details of the kidnapping. The children went to see if Joanna was going to make cakes for tea.

Just about tea-time there came a knocking at the door. A large policeman stood outside.

BACK TO KIRRIN ISLAND!

'Is Julian here?' he said. 'Oh, you're the boy we want. The Sticks have just left for the island in their boat, and we've got ours on the beach to follow. But we don't think we know the way in and out of those hidden rocks that lie all round Kirrin Island. Could you or Miss Georgina guide us, do you think?'

'I'm Master George, not Miss Georgina,' said George in a cold voice.

'Sorry,' said the policeman, with a grin. 'Well, could you come too?'

'We'll all come!' said Dick, jumping up. 'I want to go back to the dear old island and sleep in our cave again tonight. Why should we miss a single night? We can fetch Jenny's people tomorrow in our own boat. We'll all come.'

The policeman was a little doubtful about the arrangement, but the children insisted, and as there was no time to waste, they all ended in crowding into the two boats, with three big policemen, George and Julian leading the way in their own boat. Timmy lay down at George's feet as usual.

George guided the boat as cleverly as ever, and soon they landed in the usual little sandy cove. The Sticks had evidently gone round by the wreck as usual, and landed on the rockier part.

'Now, no noise,' said Julian, warningly. They all went quietly towards the ruin, and came into the courtyard. There was no sign of the Sticks.

'We'll go down underground,' said Julian. 'I've got my torch. I expect the Sticks are down there already, letting out dear Edgar.'

They went down the steps into the dark dungeons.

Anne went too, this time, holding on to the hand of one of the big policemen. They moved quietly through the long, dark, winding passages.

They came at last to the door of the cave in which they had imprisoned Edgar. It was still bolted at the top and bottom!

'Look!' said Julian, in a whisper, shining his torch on to the door. 'The Sticks haven't been down here yet.'

'Sh!' said George, as Timmy growled softly. 'There's someone coming. Hide! It's the Sticks, I expect.'

They all hid behind the wall that ran nearby. They could hear footsteps coming nearer, and then the voice of Mrs Stick raised in anger.

'If my Edgar's locked in there, I'll have something to say about it! Locking up a poor innocent boy like that. I don't understand it. If he's there, where's the girl? You answer me that. Where's the girl? It's my belief that the boss has done some double-crossing to do us out of our share of the money. Didn't he say that he'd give us two thousand pounds if we kept Jenny Armstrong for a week? Now I think he must have sent someone to this island, played tricks on us, taken the girl himself and locked up our Edgar.'

'You may be right, Clara,' said Mr Stick, his voice

coming nearer and nearer. 'But how did this boy Julian know where Edgar was? There's a lot I don't understand about all this.'

Now the Sticks were right at the door of the cave, with Stinker at their heels. Stinker smelt the others in hiding and whined in fear. Mr Stick kicked him.

'Stop it! It's enough to hear our own voices echoing away all round without your whines too!'

Mrs Stick was calling out loudly: 'Edgar! Are you there? Edgar!'

'Ma! Yes, I'm here!' yelled Edgar. 'Let me out, quick! I'm scared. Let me out!'

Mrs Stick undid the bolts at once and flung open the door. By the light of the lantern in the cave she saw Edgar. He ran to her, half-crying.

'Who put you here?' demanded Mrs Stick. 'You tell your Pa and he'll knock their heads off, won't you, Pa? Putting a poor frightened child into a dark cave like this. It's a wicked thing to do!'

Suddenly the Stick family had the fright of their lives – for a large policeman stepped out of the shadows, torch in one hand and notebook in the other!

'Ah!' said the policeman, in a deep voice. 'You're right, Clara Stick. To shut up a poor frightened child in that cave *is* a wicked thing to do – and that's what you did, isn't it? You put Jenny Armstrong there! She's only a little girl. This boy of yours knew he wasn't coming to any harm – but that little girl was scared to death!'

Mrs Stick stood there, opening and shutting her mouth like a goldfish, not finding a word to say. Mr Stick squealed like a rat caught in a corner.

'We're copped! It's a trap, that's it. We're copped!'

Edgar began to cry, sobbing like a four-year-old. The other children felt disgusted with him. The Sticks suddenly caught sight of all the children when Julian switched on his torch.

'Snakes alive, there's all the children – and there's Jenny Armstrong too!' said Mr Stick, in a tone of the greatest amazement. 'What's all this? What's happening? Who shut up Edgar?'

'We'll tell you the answers when we get to the police station,' said the big policeman. 'Now, are you coming quietly?'

The Sticks went quietly, Edgar sobbing away to himself. He imagined his mother and father in prison, and he himself sent to a hard and difficult school, not allowed to see his mother for years. Not that that would matter, for the Sticks, both mother and father, were no good to Edgar, and had taught him nothing but bad things. There might be a chance for the wretched boy if he were kept away from them, and set a good example instead of a bad one.

'We shan't be coming back with you,' said Julian, politely, to the policeman. 'We're staying here the night. You could go back in the Sticks's boat. They know the way all right. Take their dog with you. There he is – Stinker, we call him.' Then he added, 'I guess your colleagues could follow in the police boat!'

The Sticks's boat was found and the policeman, the two grown-up Sticks and Edgar got in. Stinker jumped in too, glad to get away from the glare of Timothy's green eyes.

Julian pushed the boat out. 'Goodbye!' he called, and

the other children waved goodbye, too. 'Goodbye, Mr Stick, don't go kidnapping any more children. Goodbye, Mrs Stick, look after Edgar better, in case *he* gets kidnapped again! Goodbye, Spotty-Face, try and be a better boy! Goodbye, Stinker, do get a bath as soon as possible. Goodbye!'

The policemen grinned and waved. The Sticks said not a word, nor did they wave. They sat sullen and angry, trying to work out in their minds what had happened to make things end up like this.

The boats rounded a high rock and were soon out of sight. 'Hurrah!' said Dick. 'They've gone – gone for ever! We've got our island to ourselves at last. Come on, Jenny, we'll show you all over it! What a lovely time we're going to have.'

They raced away, happy and carefree, five children and a dog, alone on an island they loved. And we will leave them there to enjoy their week's happiness. They really do deserve it!

FIVE GO TO SMUGGLER'S TOP

FIVE GO TO SMUGGLER'S TOP

ENID BLYTON

Illustrated by
Eileen A. Soper

Hodder
Children's
Books

a division of Hachette Children's Books

CONTENTS

CHAPTER ONE

Back to Kirrin Cottage

ONE FINE day, right at the beginning of the Easter holidays, four children and a dog travelled by train together.

'Soon be there now,' said Julian, a tall strong boy, with a determined face.

'Woof,' said Timothy the dog, getting excited, and trying to look out of the window too.

'Get down, Tim,' said Julian. 'Let Anne have a look.'

Anne was his younger sister. She put her head out of the window. 'We're coming into Kirrin Station!' she said. 'I do hope Aunt Fanny will be there to meet us.'

'Of course she will!' said Georgina, her cousin. She looked more like a boy than a girl, for she wore her hair very short, and it curled close about her head. She too had a determined face, like Julian. She pushed Anne away and looked out of the window.

'It's nice to be going home,' she said. 'I love school – but it will be fun to be at Kirrin Cottage and perhaps sail out to Kirrin Island and visit the castle there. We haven't been since last summer.'

'Dick's turn to look out now,' said Julian, turning to his younger brother, a boy with a pleasant face, sitting read-

1

ing in a corner. 'We're just coming into sight of Kirrin, Dick. Can't you stop reading for a second?'

'It's such an exciting book,' said Dick, and shut it with a clap. 'The most exciting adventure story I've ever read!'

'Pooh! I bet it's not as exciting as some of the adventures *we've* had!' said Anne, at once.

It was quite true that the five of them, counting in Timmy the dog, who always shared everything with them, had had the most amazing adventures together. But now it looked as if they were going to have nice quiet holidays, going for long walks over the cliffs, and perhaps sailing out in George's boat to their island of Kirrin.

'I've worked jolly hard at school this term,' said Julian. 'I could do with a holiday!'

'You've gone thin,' said Georgina. Nobody called her that. They all called her George. She would never answer to any other name. Julian grinned.

'Well, I'll soon get fat at Kirrin Cottage, don't you worry! Aunt Fanny will see to that. She's a great one for trying to fatten people up. It will be nice to see your mother again, George. She's an awfully good sort.'

'Yes. I hope Father will be in a good temper these hols,' said George. 'He ought to be because he has just finished some new experiments, Mother says, which have been quite successful.'

George's father was a scientist, always working out new ideas. He liked to be quiet, and sometimes he flew into a temper when he could not get the peace he needed or things did not go exactly as he wanted them to. The children often thought that hot-tempered Georgina was very like her father! She too could fly into fierce tempers when things did not go right for her.

Aunt Fanny was there to meet them. The four children jumped out on the platform and rushed to hug her. George got there first. She was very fond of her gentle mother, who had so often tried to shield her when her father got angry with her. Timmy pranced round, barking in delight. He adored George's mother.

She patted him, and he tried to stand up and lick her face. 'Timmy's bigger than ever!' she said, laughing. 'Down, old boy! You'll knock me over.'

Timmy was certainly a big dog. All the children loved him, for he was loyal, loving and faithful. His brown eyes looked from one to the other, enjoying the children's excitement. Timmy shared in it, as he shared in everything.

But the person he loved most, of course, was his mistress, George. She had had him since he was a small puppy. She took him to school with her each term, for she and Anne went to a boarding-school that allowed pets. Otherwise George would most certainly have refused to go!

They set off to Kirrin in the pony-trap. It was very windy and cold, and the children shivered and pulled their coats tightly round them.

'It's awfully cold,' said Anne, her teeth beginning to chatter. 'Colder than in the winter!'

3

'It's the wind,' said her aunt, and tucked a rug round her. 'It's been getting very strong the last day or two. The fishermen have pulled their boats high up the beach for fear of a big storm.'

The children saw the boats pulled right up as they passed the beach where they had bathed so often. They did not feel like bathing now. It made them shiver even to think of it.

The wind howled over the sea. Great scudding clouds raced overhead. The waves pounded on the beach and made a terrific noise. It excited Timmy, who began to bark.

'Be quiet, Tim,' said George, patting him. 'You will have to learn to be a good quiet dog now we are home again, or Father will be cross with you. Is Father very busy, Mother?'

'Very,' said her mother. 'But he's going to do very little work now you are coming home. He thought he would like to go for walks with you, or go out in the boat, if the weather calms down.'

The children looked at one another. Uncle Quentin was not the best of companions. He had no sense of humour, and when the children went off into fits of laughter, as they did twenty times a day or more, he could not see the joke at all.

'It looks as if these hols won't be quite so jolly if Uncle Quentin parks himself on us most of the time,' said Dick in a low voice to Julian.

4

BACK TO KIRRIN COTTAGE

'Sh,' said Julian, afraid that his aunt would hear, and be hurt. George frowned.

'Oh Mother! Father will be bored stiff if he comes with us – and we'll be bored too.'

George was very outspoken, and could never learn to keep a guard on her tongue. Her mother sighed. 'Don't talk like that, dear. I daresay your father will get tired of going with you after a bit. But it does him good to have a bit of young life about him.'

'Here we are!' said Julian, as the trap stopped outside an old house. 'Kirrin Cottage! My word, how the wind is howling round it, Aunt Fanny!'

'Yes. It made a terrible noise last night,' said his aunt. 'You take the trap round to the back, Julian, when we've got the things out. Oh, here's your uncle to help!'

Uncle Quentin came out, a tall, clever-looking man, with rather frowning eyebrows. He smiled at the children and kissed George and Anne.

'Welcome to Kirrin Cottage!' he said. 'I'm quite glad your mother and father are away, Anne, because now we shall have you all here once again!'

Soon they were sitting round the table eating a big tea. Aunt Fanny always got ready a fine meal for their first one, for she knew they were very hungry after their long journey on the train.

Even George was satisfied at last, and leaned back in her chair, wishing she could manage just one more of her mother's delicious new-made buns.

Timmy sat close to her. He was not supposed to be fed at meal-times but it was really surprising how many titbits found their way to him under the table!

The wind howled round the house. The windows rattled, the doors shook, and the mats lifted themselves up and down as the draught got under them.

'They look as if they've got snakes wriggling underneath them,' said Anne. Timmy watched them and growled. He was a clever dog, but he did not know why the mats wriggled in such a strange way.

'I hope the wind will die down tonight,' said Aunt Fanny. 'It kept me awake last night. Julian dear, you look rather thin. Have you been working hard? I must fatten you up.'

The children laughed. 'Just what we thought you'd say, Mother!' said George. 'Goodness, what's that?'

They all sat still, startled. There was a loud bumping noise on the roof, and Timmy put up his ears and growled fiercely.

'A tile off the roof,' said Uncle Quentin. 'How tiresome! We shall have to get the loose tiles seen to, Fanny, when the storm is over, or the rain will come in.'

The children rather hoped that their uncle would retire to his study after tea, as he usually did, but this time he didn't. They wanted to play a game, but it wasn't much good with Uncle Quentin there. He really wasn't any good at all, not even at such a simple game as snap.

'Do you know a boy called Pierre Lenoir?' Uncle

Quentin suddenly asked, taking a letter from his pocket. 'I believe he goes to your school and Dick's, Julian.'

'Pierre Lenoir – oh you mean old Sooty,' said Julian. 'Yes – he's in Dick's form. Mad as a hatter.'

'Sooty! Now why do you call him that?' said Uncle Quentin. 'It seems a silly name for a boy.'

'If you saw him you wouldn't think so,' said Dick, with a laugh. 'He's awfully dark! Hair as black as soot, eyes like bits of coal, eyebrows that look as if they've been put in with charcoal. And his name means "The black one", doesn't it? Le-noir – that's French for black.'

'Yes. Quite true. But what a name to give anyone – *Sooty*!' said Uncle Quentin. 'Well, I've been having quite a lot of correspondence with this boy's father. He and I are interested in the same scientific matters. In fact, I've asked him whether he wouldn't like to come and stay with me a few days – and bring his boy, Pierre.'

'Oh really!' said Dick, looking quite pleased. 'Well it wouldn't be bad sport to have old Sooty here, Uncle. But he's quite mad. He never does as he's told, he climbs like a monkey, and he can be awfully cheeky. I don't know if you'd like him much.'

Uncle Quentin looked sorry he had asked Sooty after he had heard what Dick had to say. He didn't like cheeky boys. Nor did he like mad ones.

'Hm,' he said, putting the letter away. 'I wish I'd asked you about the boy first, before suggesting to his father that

7

he might bring him with him. But perhaps I can prevent him coming.'

'No, don't, Father,' said George, who rather liked the sound of Sooty Lenoir. 'Let's have him. He could come out with us and liven things up!'

'We'll see,' said her father, who had already made up his mind on no account to have the boy at Kirrin Cottage, if he was mad, climbed everywhere, and was cheeky. George was enough of a handful without a devil of a boy egging her on!

Much to the children's relief Uncle Quentin retired to read by himself about eight o'clock. Aunt Fanny looked at the clock.

'Time for Anne to go to bed,' she said. 'And you too, George.'

'Just one good game of Slap-Down Patience, all of us playing it together, Mother!' said George. 'Come on – you play it too. It's our first evening at home. Anyway, I shan't sleep for ages, with this gale howling round! Come on, Mother – one good game, then we'll go to bed. Julian's been yawning like anything already!'

CHAPTER TWO

A shock in the night

IT WAS nice to climb up the steep stairs to their familiar bedrooms that night. All the children were yawning widely. Their long train journey had tired them.

'If only this awful wind would stop!' said Anne, pulling the curtain aside and looking out into the night. 'There's a little moon, George. It keeps bobbing out between the scurrying clouds.'

'Let it bob!' said George, scrambling into bed. 'I'm jolly cold. Hurry, Anne, or you'll catch a chill at that window.'

'Don't the waves make a noise?' said Anne, still at the window. 'And the gale in the old ash tree is making a whistling, howling sound, and bending it right over.'

'Timmy, hurry up and get on my bed,' commanded George, screwing up her cold toes. 'That's one good thing about being at home, Anne. I can have Timmy on my bed! He's far better than a hot water bottle.'

'You're not supposed to have him on your bed at home, any more than you're supposed to at school,' said Anne, curling up in bed. 'Aunt Fanny thinks he sleeps in his basket over there.'

'Well, I can't stop him coming on my bed at night, can I, if he doesn't want to sleep in his basket?' said George.

'That's right, Timmy darling. Make my feet warm. Where's your nose? Let me pat it. Goodnight, Tim. Goodnight, Anne.'

'Goodnight,' said Anne, sleepily. 'I hope that Sooty boy comes, don't you? He does sound fun.'

'Yes. And anyway Father would stay in with Mr Lenoir, the boy's father, and not come out with us,' said George. 'Father doesn't mean to, but he does spoil things somehow.'

'He's not very good at laughing,' said Anne. 'He's too serious.'

A loud bang made both girls jump. 'That's the bathroom door!' said George, with a groan. 'One of the boys must have left it open. That's the sort of noise that drives Father mad! There it goes again!'

'Well, let Julian or Dick shut it,' said Anne, who was now beginning to feel nice and warm. But Julian and Dick were thinking that George or Anne might shut it, so nobody got out of bed to see to the banging door.

Very soon Uncle Quentin's voice roared up the stairs, louder than the gale.

'Shut that door, one of you! How can I work with that noise going on?'

All four children jumped out of bed like a shot. Timmy leapt off George's bed. Everyone fell over him as they rushed to the bathroom door. There was a lot of giggling and scuffling. Then Uncle Quentin's footsteps were heard on the stairs and the five fled silently to their rooms.

The gale still roared. Uncle Quentin and Aunt Fanny

came up to bed. The bedroom door flew out of Uncle Quentin's hand and slammed itself shut so violently that a vase leapt off a nearby shelf.

Uncle Quentin leapt too, startled. 'This wretched gale!' he said, fiercely. 'Never known one like it all the time we've been here. If it gets much worse the fishermen's boats will be smashed up, even though they've pulled them as high up the beach as possible.'

'It will blow itself out soon, dear,' said Aunt Fanny, soothingly. 'Probably by the time morning comes it will be quite calm.'

But she was wrong. The gale did not blow itself out that night. Instead it raged round the house even more fiercely, shrieking and howling like a live thing. Nobody could sleep. Timmy kept up a continuous low growling, for he did not like the shakes and rattles and howls.

Towards dawn the wind seemed in a fury. Anne thought it sounded as if it was in a horrible temper, out to do all the harm it could. She lay and trembled, half-frightened.

Suddenly there was a strange noise. It was a loud and woeful groaning and creaking, like someone in great pain. The two girls sat up, terrified. What could it be?

The boys heard it too. Julian leapt out of bed and ran to the window. Outside stood the old ash tree, tall and black in the fitful moonlight. It was gradually bending over!

'It's the ash! It's falling!' yelled Julian, almost startling Dick out of his wits. 'It's falling, I tell you. It'll crash on the house! Quick, warn the girls!'

Shouting at the top of his voice, Julian raced out of his door on to the landing. 'Uncle! Aunt! George and Anne! Come downstairs quickly. The ash tree is falling!'

George jumped out of bed, snatched at her dressing-gown, and raced to the door, yelling to Anne. The little girl was soon with her. Timmy ran in front. At the door of Aunt Fanny's bedroom Uncle Quentin appeared, tall and amazed, wrapping his dressing-gown round him.

'What's all this noise? Julian, what's—?'

'Aunt Fanny! Come downstairs – the ash tree is falling! Listen to its terrible groans and creaks!' yelled Julian, almost beside himself with impatience. 'It'll smash in the roof and the bedrooms! Listen, here it comes!'

Everyone fled downstairs as, with an appalling wail, the great ash tree hauled up its roots and fell heavily on to Kirrin Cottage. There was a terrible crash, and the sound of tiles slipping to the ground everywhere.

'Oh dear!' said poor Aunt Fanny, covering her eyes. 'I knew something would happen! Quentin, we ought to have had that ash tree topped. I knew it would fall in a great gale like this. What has it done to the roof?'

After the great crash there had come other smaller noises, sounds of things falling, thuds and little smashing noises. The children could not imagine what was happening. Timmy was thoroughly angry, and barked loudly. Uncle Quentin slapped his hand angrily on the table, and made everyone jump.

'Stop that dog barking! I'll turn him out!' But nothing would stop Timmy barking or growling that night, and George at last pushed him into the warm kitchen, and shut the door on him.

'I feel like barking or growling myself,' said Anne, who

knew exactly what Timmy felt like. 'Julian, has the tree broken in the roof?'

Uncle Quentin took a powerful torch and went carefully up the stairs to the landing to see what damage had been done. He came down looking rather pale.

'The tree has crashed through the attic, smashed the roof in, and wrecked the girls' bedroom,' he said. 'A big branch has penetrated the boys' room too, but not badly. But the girls' room is ruined! They would have been killed if they had been in their beds.'

Everyone was silent. It was an awful thought that George and Anne had had such a narrow escape.

'Good thing I yelled my head off to warn them then,' said Julian, cheerfully, seeing how white Anne had gone. 'Cheer up, Anne – think what a tale you'll have to tell at school next term.'

'I think some hot cocoa would do us all good,' said Aunt Fanny, pulling herself together, though she felt very shaken. 'I'll go and make some. Quentin, see if the fire is still alight in your study. We want a little warmth!'

The fire was still alight. Everyone crowded round it. They welcomed Aunt Fanny when she came in with some steaming milk-cocoa.

Anne looked curiously round the room as she sat sipping her drink. This was where her uncle did his work, his very clever work. He wrote his difficult books here, books which Anne could not understand at all. He drew his weird diagrams here, and made many strange experiments.

A SHOCK IN THE NIGHT

But just at the moment Uncle Quentin did not look very clever. He looked rather ashamed, somehow. Anne soon knew why.

'Quentin, it is a mercy none of us was hurt or killed,' said Aunt Fanny, looking at him rather sternly. 'I told you a dozen times you should get that ash tree topped. I knew it was too big and heavy to withstand a great gale. I was always afraid it would blow down on the house.'

'Yes, I know, my dear,' said Uncle Quentin, stirring his cup of cocoa very vigorously. 'But I was so busy these last months.'

'You always make that an excuse for not doing urgent things,' said Aunt Fanny, with a sigh. 'I shall have to manage things myself in the future. I can't risk our lives like this!'

'Well, a thing like this would only happen once in a blue moon!' cried Uncle Quentin, getting angry. Then he calmed down, seeing that Aunt Fanny was really shocked and upset, very near to tears. He put down his cocoa and slipped his arm round her.

'You've had a terrible shock,' he said. 'Don't you worry about things. Maybe they won't be so bad when morning comes.'

'Oh, Quentin – they'll be much worse!' said his wife. 'Where shall we sleep tonight, all of us, and what shall we do till the roof and upstairs rooms are repaired? The children have only just come home. The house will be full of workmen for weeks! I don't know how

I'm going to manage.'

'Leave it all to me!' said Uncle Quentin. 'I'll settle everything. Don't worry. I'm sorry about this, very sorry, particularly as it's my fault. But I'll straighten things out for everyone, you just see!'

Aunt Fanny didn't really believe him, but she was grateful for his comforting. The children listened in silence, drinking their hot cocoa. Uncle Quentin was so very clever, and knew so many things – but it was so like him to neglect something urgent like cutting off the top of the old ash tree. Sometimes he didn't seem to live in this world at all!

It was no use going up to bed! The rooms upstairs were either completely ruined, or so messed up with bits and pieces, and clouds of dust, that it was impossible to sleep there. Aunt Fanny began to pile rugs on sofas. There was one in the study, a big one in the sitting-room and a smaller one in the dining-room. She found a camp bed in a cupboard and, with Julian's help, put that up too.

'We'll just have to do the best we can,' she said. 'There isn't much left of the night, but we'll get a little sleep if we can! The gale is not nearly so wild now.'

'No – it's done all the damage it can, so it's satisfied,' said Uncle Quentin, grimly. 'Well, we'll talk things over in the morning.'

The children found it very difficult to go to sleep after such an excitement, tired though they were. Anne felt worried. How could they all stay at Kirrin Cottage now? It wouldn't be fair on Aunt Fanny. But they couldn't go home because her father and mother were both away and the house was shut up for a month.

'I hope we shan't be sent back to school,' thought Anne, trying to get comfortable on the sofa. 'It would be too awful, after having left there, and starting off so cheerfully for the holidays.'

George was afraid of that, too. She felt sure that they would all be packed back to their schools the next morning. That would mean that she and Anne wouldn't see Julian and Dick any more these holidays, for the boys, of course, went to a different school.

Timmy was the only one who didn't worry about things. He lay on George's feet, snoring a little, quite happy. So long as he was with George he didn't really mind *where* he went!

CHAPTER THREE

Uncle Quentin has an idea

NEXT MORNING the wind was still high, but the fury of the gale was gone. The fishermen on the beach were relieved to find that their boats had suffered very little damage. But word soon went round about the accident to Kirrin Cottage, and a few sightseers came up to marvel at the sight of the great, uprooted tree, lying heavily on the little house.

UNCLE QUENTIN HAS AN IDEA

The children rather enjoyed the importance of relating how nearly they had escaped with their lives. In the light of day it was surprising what damage the big tree had done. It had cracked the roof of the house like an eggshell, and the rooms upstairs were in a terrible mess.

The woman who came up from the village to help Aunt Fanny during the day exclaimed at the sight: 'Why, it'll take weeks to set that right!' she said. 'Have you got on to the builders? I'd get them up here right away and let them see what's to be done.'

'*I'm* seeing to things, Mrs Daly,' said Uncle Quentin. 'My wife has had a great shock. She is not fit to see to things herself. The first thing to do is to decide what is to happen to the children. They can't remain here while there are no usable bedrooms.'

'They had better go back to school, poor things,' said Aunt Fanny.

'No. I've a better idea than that,' said Uncle Quentin, fishing a letter out of his pocket. 'Much better. I've had a letter from that fellow Lenoir this morning – you know, the one who's interested in the same kind of experiments as I am. He says – er, wait a minute, I'll read you the bit. Yes here it is.'

Uncle Quentin read it out: 'It is most kind of you to suggest my coming to stay with you and bringing my boy Pierre. Allow me to extend hospitality to you and your children also. I do not know how many you have, but all are welcome here in this big house. My Pierre will be glad of company, and so will his sister, Marybelle.'

19

Uncle Quentin looked up triumphantly at his wife. 'There you are! I call that a most generous invitation! It couldn't have come at a better time. We'll pack the whole of the children off to this fellow's house.'

'But Quentin – you can't possibly do that! Why, we don't know anything about him or his family!' said Aunt Fanny.

'His boy goes to the same school as Julian and Dick, and I know Lenoir is a remarkable, clever fellow,' said Uncle Quentin, as if that was all that really mattered. 'I'll telephone him now. What's his number?'

Aunt Fanny felt helpless in the face of her husband's sudden determination to settle everything himself. He was ashamed because it was his forgetfulness that had brought on the accident to the house. Now he was going to show that he *could* see to things if he liked. She heard him telephoning, and frowned. How could they possibly send off the children to a strange place like that?

Uncle Quentin put down the receiver, and went to find his wife, looking jubilant and very pleased with himself.

'It's all settled,' he said. 'Lenoir is delighted, most delighted. Says he loves children about the place, and so does his wife, and his two will be thrilled to have them. If we can hire a car today, they can go at once.'

'But Quentin – we *can't* let them go off like that to strange people! They'll hate it! I shouldn't be surprised if George refuses to go,' said his wife.

20

'Oh – that reminds me. She's not to take Timothy,' said Uncle Quentin. 'Apparently Lenoir doesn't like dogs.'

'Well, then, you know George won't go!' said his wife. 'That's foolish, Quentin. George won't go anywhere without Timmy.'

'She'll have to, this time,' said Uncle Quentin, quite determined that George should not upset all his marvellous plans. 'Here are the children. I'll ask them what *they* feel about going, and see what they say!'

He called them into his study. They came in, feeling sure that they were to hear bad news – probably they were all to return to school!

'You remember that boy I spoke to you about last night?' began Uncle Quentin. 'Pierre Lenoir. You had some absurd name for him.'

'Sooty,' said Dick and Julian together.

'Ah yes, Sooty. Well, his father has kindly invited you all to go and stay with him at Smuggler's Top,' said Uncle Quentin.

The children were astonished.

'*Smuggler's Top!*' said Dick, his fancy caught by the peculiar name. 'What's Smuggler's Top?'

'The name of his house,' said Uncle Quentin. 'It's very old, built on the top of a strange hill surrounded by marshes over which the sea once flowed. The hill was once an island, but now it's just a tall hill rising up from the marsh. Smuggling went on there in the old days. It's a very peculiar place, so I've heard.'

All this made the children feel excited. Also Julian and Dick had always liked Sooty Lenoir. He was quite mad, but awfully good fun. They might have a first-rate time with him.

'Well – would you like to go? Or would you rather go back to school for the holidays?' asked Uncle Quentin impatiently.

'Oh *no* – not back to school!' said everyone at once.

'I'd *love* to go to Smuggler's Top,' said Dick. 'It sounds a thrilling place. And I always liked old Sooty, especially since he sawed half-way through one of the legs of our form-master's chair. It gave way at once when Mr Toms sat down!'

'Hm. I don't see that a trick like that is any reason for liking someone,' said Uncle Quentin, beginning to feel a little doubtful about Master Lenoir. 'Perhaps, on the whole, school would be best for you.'

'Oh no, no!' cried everyone. 'Let's go to Smuggler's Top! Do, do let's!'

'Very well,' said Uncle Quentin, pleased at their eagerness to follow his plan. 'As a matter of fact, I have already settled it. I telephoned a few minutes ago. Mr Lenoir was very kind about it all.'

'Can I take Timmy?' asked George, suddenly.

'No,' said her father. 'I'm afraid not. Mr Lenoir doesn't like dogs.'

'Then I shan't like *him*,' said George, sulkily. 'I won't go without Timmy.'

'You'll have to go back to school, then,' said her father, sharply. 'And take off that sulky expression, George. You know how I dislike it.'

But George wouldn't. She turned away. The others looked at her in dismay. Surely old George wasn't going to get into one of her moods, and spoil everything! It would be fun to go to Smuggler's Top. But, of course, it certainly wouldn't be so much fun without Timmy. Still – they couldn't all go back to school just because George wouldn't go anywhere without her dog.

They all went into the sitting-room. Anne put her arm through George's. George shook it off.

'George! You simply *must* come with us,' said Anne. 'I can't bear to go without you – it would be awful to see you going back to school all alone.'

'I shouldn't be all alone,' said George. 'I should have Timmy.'

The others pressed her to change her mind, but she shook them off. 'Leave me alone,' she said. 'I want to think. How are we supposed to get to Smuggler's Top, and where is it? Which road do we take?'

'We're going by car, and it's right up the coast some-where, so I expect we'll take the coast-road,' said Julian. 'Why, George?'

'Don't ask questions,' said George. She went out with Timmy. The others didn't follow her. George was not very nice when she was cross.

Aunt Fanny began to pack for them, though it was

impossible to get some of the things from the girls' room. After a time George came back, but Timmy was not with her. She looked more cheerful.

'Where's Tim?' asked Anne, at once.

'Out somewhere,' said George.

'Are you coming with us, George?' asked Julian, looking at her.

'Yes. I've made up my mind to,' said George, but for some reason she wouldn't look Julian in the eyes. He wondered why.

Aunt Fanny gave them all an early lunch, and then a big car came for them. They packed themselves inside. Uncle Quentin gave them all sorts of messages for Mr Lenoir, and Aunt Fanny kissed them goodbye. 'I do hope you have a nice time at Smuggler's Top,' she said. 'Mind you write at once and tell me all about it.'

'Aren't we going to say goodbye to Timmy?' said Anne, her eyes opening wide in amazement at George, forgetting. 'George, surely you're not going without saying goodbye to old Timmy!'

'Can't stop now,' said Uncle Quentin, afraid that George might suddenly become awkward again. 'Right, driver! You can go off now. Don't drive too fast, please.'

Waving and shouting the children drove away from Kirrin Cottage, sad when they looked back and saw the smashed roof under the fallen tree. Never mind – they had not been sent back to school. That was the main thing.

Their spirits rose as they thought of Sooty and his oddly-named home, Smuggler's Top.

'Smuggler's Top! It sounds too exciting for words!' said Anne. 'I can picture it, an old house right on the top of a hill. Fancy being an island once. I wonder why the sea went back and left marshes instead.'

George said nothing for a while, and the car sped on. The others glanced at her once or twice, but came to the conclusion that she was grieving about Timmy. Still she didn't look very sad!

The car went over a hill and sped down to the bottom. When they got there George leaned forward and touched the driver's arm.

'Would you stop a moment, please? We have to pick somebody up here.'

Julian, Dick and Anne stared at George in surprise. The driver, also rather surprised, drew the car to a standstill. George opened the car door and gave a loud whistle.

Something shot out of the hedge and hurled itself joyfully into the car. It was Timmy! He licked everyone, trod on everyone's toes, and gave the little short barks that showed he was excited and happy.

'Well,' said the driver, doubtfully, 'I don't know if you're supposed to take that dog in. Your father didn't say anything about him.'

'It's all right,' said George, her face red with joy. 'Quite all right. You needn't worry. Start the car again, please.'

'You *are* a monkey!' said Julian, half-annoyed with George, and half-pleased because Timmy was with them after all. 'Mr Lenoir may send him back, you know.'

'Well, he'll have to send *me* back too,' said George, defiantly. 'Anyhow, the main thing is, we've got Timmy after all, and I am coming with you.'

'Yes – that's fine,' said Anne, and gave first George and then Timmy a hug. 'I didn't like going without Tim either.'

'On to Smuggler's Top!' said Dick, as the car started off again. 'On to Smuggler's Top. I wonder if we shall have any adventures there!'

26

CHAPTER FOUR

Smuggler's Top

THE CAR sped on, mostly along the coast, though it sometimes went inland for a few miles. But sooner or later it was in sight of the sea again. The children enjoyed the long drive. They were to stop somewhere for lunch, and the driver told them he knew of a good inn.

At half past twelve he drew up outside an old inn, and they all trooped in. Julian took charge, and ordered lunch. It was a very good one, and all the children enjoyed it. So did Timmy. The innkeeper liked dogs, and put down such a piled-up plate for Timmy that the dog hardly liked to begin on his meal in case it was not for him!

He looked up at George and she nodded to him. 'It's your dinner, Timmy. Eat it up.'

So he ate it, hoping that if they were going to stay anywhere they might be staying at the inn. Meals like this did not arrive every day for a hungry dog!

But after lunch the children got up. They went to find the driver, who was having his lunch in the kitchen with the innkeeper and his wife. They were old friends of his.

'Well, I hear you're going to Castaway,' said the innkeeper, getting up. 'You be careful there!'

27

'Castaway!' said Julian. 'Is that what the hill is called, where Smuggler's Top is?'

'That's its name,' said the innkeeper.

'Why is it called that?' said Anne. 'What a funny name! Were people cast away on it once, when it was an island?'

'Oh no. The old story goes that the hill was once joined to the mainland,' said the innkeeper. 'But it was the haunt of bad people, and one of the saints became angry with the place, and cast it away into the sea, where it became an island.'

'And so it was called Castaway,' said Dick. 'But perhaps it has got good again, because the sea has gone away from it, and you can walk from the mainland to the hill, can't you?'

'Yes. There's one good road you can take,' said the innkeeper. 'But you be careful of wandering away from it, if you go walking on it! The marsh will suck you down in no time if you set foot on it!'

'It does sound a most exciting place,' said George. 'Smuggler's Top on Castaway Hill! Only one road to it!'

'Time to get on,' said the driver, looking at the clock. 'You've got to be there before tea, your uncle said.'

They got into the car again, Timmy clambering over legs and feet to a comfortable place on George's lap. He was far too big and heavy to lie there but just occasionally he seemed to want to, and George never had the heart to refuse him.

They drove off once more. Anne fell asleep, and the

others felt drowsy too. The car purred on and on. It began to rain, and the countryside looked rather dreary.

The driver turned round after a while and spoke to Julian. 'We're coming near to Castaway Hill. We'll soon be leaving the mainland, and taking the road across the marsh.'

Julian woke Anne. They all sat up expectantly. But it was very disappointing after all! The marshes were full of mist! The children could not pierce through it with their eyes, and could only see the flat road they were on, raised a little higher than the surrounding flat marsh. When the mist shifted a little now and again the children saw a dreary space of flat marsh on either side.

'Stop a minute,' said Julian. 'I'd like to see what the marsh is like.'

'Well, don't step off the road,' warned the driver stopping the car. 'And don't you let that dog out. Once he runs off the road and gets into the marsh he'll be gone for good.'

'What do you mean – gone for good?' said Anne, her eyes wide.

'He means the marsh will suck down Timmy at once,' said Julian. 'Shut him in the car, George.'

So Timmy, much to his disgust, was shut safely in the car. He pawed at the door, and tried to look out of the window. The driver turned and spoke to him. 'It's all right. They'll be back soon, old fellow!'

But Timmy whined all the time the others were out of

29

the car. He saw them go to the edge of the road. He saw Julian jump down the couple of feet that raised the road above the marsh.

There was a line of raised stones running in the marsh alongside the road. Julian stood on one of these peering at the flat marsh.

'It's mud,' he said. 'Loose, squelchy mud! Look, when I touch it with my foot it moves! It would soon suck me down if I trod heavily on it.'

Anne didn't like it. She called to Julian. 'Come up on the road again. I'm afraid you'll fall in.'

Mists were wreathing and swirling over the salty marshes. It was a weird place, cold and damp. None of the children liked it. Timmy began to bark in the car.

'Tim will scratch the car to bits if we don't get back,' said George. So they all went back, rather silent. Julian wondered how many travellers had been lost in that strange sea-marsh.

'Oh, there're many that've never been heard of again,' said the driver, when they asked him. 'They say there're one or two winding paths that go to the hill from the mainland, that were used before the road was built. But unless you know every inch of them you're off them in a second, and find your feet sinking in the mud.'

'It's horrid to think about,' said Anne. 'Don't let's talk about it any more. Can we see Castaway Hill yet?'

'Yes. There it is, looming up in the mist,' said the driver. 'The top of it is out of the mist, see? Strange place, isn't it?'

The children looked in silence. Out of the slowly moving mists rose a tall, steep hill, whose rocky sides were as steep as cliffs. The hill seemed to swim in the mists, and to have no roots in the earth. It was covered with buildings which even at that distance looked old and quaint. Some of them had towers.

'That must be Smuggler's Top, right at the summit,' said Julian, pointing. 'It's like an old building of centuries ago – probably is! Look at the tower it has. What a wonderful view you'd get from it.'

The children gazed at the place where they were to stay. It looked exciting and picturesque, certainly – but it also looked rather forbidding.

'It's sort of – sort of *secret*, somehow,' said Anne, putting into words what the others were thinking. 'I mean – it looks as if it had kept all kinds of strange secrets down the centuries. I guess it could tell plenty of tales!'

The car drove on again, quite slowly, because the mists came down thickly. The road had a line of sparkling round buttons set all along the middle, and when the driver switched on his fog-lamp, they shone brightly and guided him well. Then as they neared Castaway Hill the road began to slope upwards.

'We go through a big archway soon,' said the driver. 'That used to be where the city gate once was. The whole town is surrounded by wall still, just as it used to be in olden times. It's wide enough to walk on, and if you start at a certain place, and walk long enough, you'll come round to the place you started at!'

All the children made up their minds to do this without fail. What a view they would have all round the hill, if they chose a fine day!

The road became steeper, and the driver put the engine into a lower gear. It groaned up the hill. Then it came to an archway, from which old gates were fastened back. It passed through, and the children were in Castaway.

'It's almost as if we've gone back through the centuries, and come to somewhere that existed ages ago!' said Julian, peering at the old houses and shops, with their cobbled streets, their diamond-paned windows, and stout old doors.

They went up the winding high street, and came at last to a big gateway, set with wrought-iron gates. The driver hooted and they opened. They swept into a steep drive, and at last stopped before Smuggler's Top.

They got out, feeling suddenly shy. The big old house seemed to frown down at them. It was built of brick and timber, and its front door was as massive as that of a castle.

Weird gables jutted here and there over the diamond-paned windows. The house's one tower stood sturdily at the east side of the house, with windows all round. It was not a square tower, but a rounded one, and ended in a point.

'Smuggler's Top!' said Julian. 'It's a good name for it somehow. I suppose lots of smuggling went on here in the old days.'

33

Dick rang the bell. To do this he had to pull down an iron handle, and a jangling at once made itself heard in the house.

There was the sound of running feet, and the door was opened. It opened slowly, for it was heavy.

Beyond it stood two children, one a girl of about Anne's age, and the other a boy of Dick's age.

'Here you are at last!' cried the boy, his dark eyes dancing. 'I thought you were never coming!'

'This is Sooty,' said Dick to the girls, who had not met him before. They stared at him.

He was certainly very, very dark. Black hair, black eyes, black eyebrows, and a brown face. In contrast to him the girl beside him looked pale and delicate. She had golden hair, blue eyes and her eyebrows were so faint they could hardly be seen.

'This is Marybelle, my sister,' said Sooty. 'I always think we look like Beauty and the Beast!'

Sooty was nice. Everyone liked him at once. George found herself twinkling at him in a way quite strange to her, for usually she was shy of strangers, and would not make friends for some time. But who could help liking Sooty with his dancing black eyes and his really wicked grin?

'Come in,' said Sooty. 'Driver, you can take the car round to the next door, and Block will take in the luggage for you and give you tea.'

Suddenly Sooty's face lost its smile and grew very solemn. He had seen Timmy!

34

'I say! I say – that's not your dog, is it?' he said.

'He's mine,' said George, and she laid a protecting hand on Timmy's head. 'I had to bring him. I can't go anywhere without him.'

'Yes, but – no dog's allowed at Smuggler's Top,' said Sooty, still looking very worried, and glancing behind him as if he was afraid someone might come along and see Timmy. 'My stepfather won't allow any dogs here. Once I brought in a stray one and he licked me till I couldn't sit down – my stepfather licked me, I mean, not the dog.'

Anne gave a frightened little smile at the poor joke. George looked stubborn and sulky.

'I thought – I thought maybe we could hide him somewhere while we were here,' she said. 'But if that's how you feel, I'll go back home with the car. Goodbye.'

She turned and went after the car, which was backing away. Timmy went with her. Sooty stared, and then he yelled after her. 'Come back, stupid! We'll think of *some*thing!'

CHAPTER FIVE

Sooty Lenoir

SOOTY RAN down the steps that led to the front door, and tore after George. The others followed. Marybelle went too, shutting the big front door behind her carefully.

There was a small door in the wall just where George was. Sooty caught hold of her and pushed her roughly through the door, holding it open for the others.

'Don't shove me like that,' began George, angrily. 'Timmy will bite you if you push me about.'

'No, he won't,' said Sooty, with a cheerful grin. 'Dogs like me. Even if I boxed your ears your dog would only wag his tail at me.'

The children found themselves in a dark passage. There was a door at the farther end. 'Wait here a minute and I'll see if the coast is clear,' said Sooty. 'I know my stepfather is in, and I tell you, if he sees that dog he'll pack you all into the car again, and send you back! And I don't want him to do that because I can't tell you how I've looked forward to having you all!'

He grinned at them, and their hearts warmed towards him again, even George's, though she still felt angry at being so roughly pushed. She kept Timmy close beside her.

SOOTY LENOIR

All the same everyone felt a bit scared of Mr Lenoir. He sounded rather a fierce sort of person!

Sooty tiptoed to the door at the end of the passage and opened it. He peeped into the room there, and then came back to the others.

'All clear,' he said. 'We'll take the secret passage to my bedroom. No one will see us then, and once we're there we can make plans to hide the dog. Ready?'

A secret passage sounded thrilling. Feeling rather as if they were in an adventure story, the children went quietly to the door and into the room beyond. It was a dark, oak-panelled room, evidently a study of some sort, for there was a big desk there, and the walls were lined with books. There was no one there.

Sooty went to one of the oak panels in the wall, felt along it deftly, and pressed in a certain place. The panel slid softly aside. Sooty put in his hand and pulled at something. A much larger panel below slid into the wall, and left an opening big enough for the children to pass through.

'Come on,' said Sooty in a low voice. 'Don't make a noise.'

Feeling excited, the children all passed through the opening. Sooty came last, and did something that shut the opening and slid the first panel back into its place again.

He switched on a small torch, for it was pitch dark where the children were standing.

They were in a narrow stone passage, so narrow that two people could not possibly have passed one another unless both were as thin as rakes. Sooty passed his torch along to Julian, who was in front.

'Keep straight on till you come to stone steps,' he said. 'Go up them, turn to the right at the top, and keep straight on till you come to a blank wall, then I'll tell you what to do.'

Julian led the way, holding up the torch for the others. The narrow passage ran straight, and came to some stone steps. It was not only very narrow but rather low, so that Anne and Marybelle were the only ones who did not have to bend their heads.

Anne didn't like it very much. She never liked being in a very narrow enclosed space. It reminded her of dreams she sometimes had of being somewhere she couldn't get away from. She was glad when Julian spoke. 'The steps are here. Up we go, everyone.'

'Don't make a noise,' said Sooty, in a low voice. 'We're passing the dining-room now. There's a way into this passage from there too.'

Everyone fell silent, and tried to walk on tiptoe, though this was unexpectedly difficult when heads had to be bent and shoulders stooped.

They climbed up fourteen steps, which were quite steep, and curved round half-way. Julian turned to the right at the top. The passage ran upwards then, and was as narrow as before. Julian felt certain that a very fat person could not possibly get along it.

He went on until, with a start, he almost bumped into a blank stone wall! He flashed his torch up and down it. A low voice came from the back of the line of children.

'You've got to the blank wall, Julian. Shine your torch up to where the roof of the passage meets the wall. You will see an iron handle there. Press down on it hard.'

Julian flashed his torch up and saw the handle. He put his torch into his left hand, and grasped the thick iron handle with his right. He pressed down as hard as he could.

And, quite silently, the great stone in the middle of the wall slid forward and sideways, leaving a gaping hole.

Julian was astonished. He let go of the iron handle and flashed his torch into the hole. There was nothing but darkness there!

'It's all right. It leads into a big cupboard in my bedroom!' called Sooty from the back. 'Get through, Julian, and we'll follow. There won't be anyone in my room.'

Julian crawled through the hole and found himself in a spacious cupboard, hung with Sooty's clothes. He groped his way through them and bumped against a door. He opened it and at once daylight flooded into the cupboard, lighting up the way from the passage into the room.

One by one the others clambered through the hole, lost themselves in clothes for a moment and then went thankfully into the room through the cupboard door.

Timmy, puzzled and silent, followed close beside George. He had not liked the dark, narrow passage very much. He was glad to be in daylight again!

Sooty, coming last, carefully closed the opening into the

passage by pressing the stone back. It worked easily, though Julian could not imagine how. There must be some sort of pivot, he thought.

Sooty joined the others in his bedroom, grinning. George had her hand on Timmy's collar. 'It's all right George,' said Sooty. 'We're quite safe here. My room and Marybelle's are separate from the rest of the house. We're in a wing on our own, reached by a long passage!'

He opened the door and showed the others what he meant. There was a room next to his, which was Marybelle's. Beyond stretched a stone-floored, stone-walled passage, laid with mats. At the end of it a big window let in light. There was a door there, a great oak one, which was shut.

'See? We're quite safe here, all by ourselves,' said Sooty. 'Timmy could bark if he liked, and no one would know.'

'But doesn't anyone ever come?' said Anne surprised. 'Who keeps your rooms tidy, and cleans them?'

'Oh, Sarah comes and does that every morning,' said Sooty. 'But usually no one else comes. And anyway, I've got a way of knowing when anyone opens that door!'

He pointed to the door at the end of the passage. The others stared at him.

'How *do* you know?' said Dick.

'I've rigged up something that makes a buzzing noise here, in my room, as soon as that door is opened,' said Sooty, proudly. 'Look, I'll go along and open it, while you stay here and listen.'

He sped along the passage and opened the heavy door at the end. Immediately a low buzzing noise sounded somewhere in his room, and made everyone jump. Timmy was startled too, pricked up his ears, and growled fiercely.

Sooty shut the door and ran back. 'Did you hear the noise? It's a good idea, isn't it? I'm always thinking of things like that.'

The others thought they had come to rather a strange place! They stared round Sooty's bedroom, which was quite ordinary in its furnishings, and in its general untidiness. There was a big diamond-paned window, and Anne went to look out of it.

She gave a gasp. She had not expected to look down

42

such a precipice! Smuggler's Top was built at the summit of the hill, and, on the side where Sooty's bedroom was, the hill fell away steeply, down and down to the marsh below!

'Oh look!' she said. 'Look how steep it is! It really gives me a very funny feeling to look down there!'

The others crowded round and looked in silence, for it certainly was strange to gaze down such a long way.

The sun was shining up on the hill-summit, but all around, as far as they could see, mists hid the marsh and the far-off sea. The only bit of the marsh that could be seen was far down below, at the bottom of the steep hill.

'When the mists are away, you can see over the flat marshes to where the sea begins,' said Sooty. 'That's quite a fine sight. You can hardly tell where the marsh ends and sea begins except when the sea is very blue. Fancy, once upon a time, the sea came right up and around this hill, and it was an island.'

'Yes. The innkeeper told us that,' said George. 'Why did the sea go back and leave it?'

'I don't know,' said Sooty. 'People say it's going back farther and farther. There's a big scheme afoot to drain the marsh, and turn it into fields, but I don't know if that will ever happen.'

'I don't like that marsh,' said Anne, with a shiver. 'It looks wicked, somehow.'

Timmy whined. George remembered that they must hide him, and make plans for him. She turned to Sooty.

'Did you mean what you said about hiding Tim?' she asked. 'Where shall we put him? And can he be fed? And how can we exercise him? He's a big dog, you know.'

'We'll plan it all,' said Sooty. 'Don't you worry. I love dogs, and I shall be thrilled to have Timmy here. But I do warn you that if my stepfather ever finds out we shall probably all get a jolly good telling off, and you'll be sent home in disgrace.'

'But why doesn't your father like dogs?' said Anne puzzled. 'Is he afraid of them?'

'No, I don't think so. It's just that he won't have them here in the house,' said Sooty. 'I think he must have a reason for it, but I don't know what it is. He's an odd sort of man, my stepfather!'

'How is he odd?' asked Dick.

'Well – he seems full of secrets,' said Sooty. 'Strange people come here, and they come secretly without anyone knowing. I've seen lights shining in our tower on certain nights, but I don't know who puts them there or why. I've tried to find out, but I can't.'

'Do you think – do you think your father is a smuggler?' said Anne, suddenly.

'I don't think so,' said Sooty. 'We've got one smuggler here, and everyone knows him! See that house over there to the right, lower down the hill? Well, that's where he lives. He's as rich as can be. His name is Barling. Even the police know his goings-on, but they can't stop him! He is very rich and very powerful, so he does what he likes – and he won't let anyone play the same game as he plays! No one else would dare to do any smuggling in Castaway, while *he* does it!'

'This seems rather an exciting place,' said Julian. 'I have a kind of feeling there might be an adventure somewhere about!'

'Oh no,' said Sooty. 'Nothing happens, really. It's only just a feeling you get here, because the place is so old, so full of secret ways and pits and passages. Why, the whole hill is mined with passages in the rock, used by the smugglers of olden times!'

'Well,' began Julian, and stopped very suddenly. Everyone stared at Sooty. His secret buzzer had suddenly barked from its hidden corner! Someone had opened the door at the end of the passage!

CHAPTER SIX

Sooty's stepfather and mother

'SOMEONE'S COMING!' said George, in a panic. 'What shall we do with Tim? Quick!'

Sooty took Timmy by the collar and shoved him into the old cupboard, and shut the door on him. 'Keep quiet!' he commanded, and Timmy stood still in the darkness, the hairs at the back of his neck standing up, his ears cocked.

'Well,' began Sooty, in a bright voice, 'perhaps I'd better show you where your bedrooms are now!'

The door opened and a man came in. He was dressed in black trousers and a white linen coat. He had a peculiar face. 'It's a shut face,' thought Anne to herself. 'You can't tell a bit what he's like inside, because his face is all shut and secret.'

'Oh hallo, Block,' said Sooty, airily. He turned to the others. 'This is Block, my stepfather's man,' he said. 'He's deaf, so you can say what you like, but it's better not to, because though he doesn't hear he seems to sense what we say.'

'Anyway, I think it would be beastly to say things we wouldn't say in front of him if he wasn't deaf,' said George, who had very strict ideas about things of that sort.

Block spoke in a curiously monotonous voice. 'Your

stepfather and your mother want to know why you have not brought your friends to see them,' he said. 'Why did you rush up here like this?'

Block looked all round as he spoke – almost as if he knew there was a dog, and wondered where he had gone to, George thought, in alarm. She did hope the car-driver had not mentioned Timmy.

'Oh – I was so pleased to see them I took them straight up here!' said Sooty. 'All right, Block. We'll be down in a minute.'

The man went, his face quite impassive. Not a smile, not a frown! 'I don't like him,' said Anne. 'Has he been with you long?'

'No – only about a year,' said Sooty. 'He suddenly appeared one day. Even Mother didn't know he was coming! He just came, and, without a word, changed into that white linen coat, and went to do some work in my stepfather's room. I suppose my stepfather was expecting him – but he didn't say anything to my mother, I'm sure of that. She seemed so surprised.'

'Is she your real mother, or a stepmother, too?' asked Anne.

'You don't have a stepmother *and* a stepfather!' said Sooty, scornfully. 'You only have one or the other. My mother is my real mother, and she's Marybelle's mother, too. But Marybelle and I are only half-brother and sister, because my stepfather is her *real* father.'

'It's rather muddled,' said Anne, trying to sort it out.

'Come on – we'd better go down,' said Sooty, remembering. 'By the way, my stepfather is always being very affable, always smiling and joking – but it isn't real, somehow. He's quite likely to fly into a furious temper at any moment.'

'I hope we shan't see very much of him,' said Anne, uncomfortably. 'What's your mother like, Sooty?'

'Like a frightened mouse!' said Sooty. 'You'll like her, all right. She's a darling. But she doesn't like living here; she doesn't like this house, and she's terrified of my stepfather. She wouldn't say so herself, of course, but I know she is.'

Marybelle, who was too shy to have joined in any talking until then, nodded her head.

'I don't like living here, either,' she said. 'I shall be glad when I go to boarding-school, like Sooty. Except that I shall leave Mother all alone then.'

'Come on,' said Sooty, and led the way. 'We'd better leave Timmy in the cupboard till we come back, just in case Block does a bit of snooping. I'll lock the cupboard door and take the key.'

Feeling rather unhappy at leaving Timmy locked up in the cupboard, the children followed Sooty and Marybelle down the stone passage to the oak door. They went through, and found themselves at the top of a great flight of stairs, wide and shallow. They went down into a big hall.

At the right was a door, and Sooty opened it. He went in and spoke to someone.

'Here they all are,' he said. 'Sorry I rushed them off to

48

my bedroom like that, Father, but I was so excited to see them all!'

'Your manners still need a little polishing, Pierre,' said Mr Lenoir, in a deep voice. The children looked at him. He sat in a big oak chair, a neat, clever-looking man, with fair hair brushed upwards, and eyes as blue as Marybelle's. He smiled all the time, but with his mouth, not his eyes.

'What cold eyes!' thought Anne, when she went forward to shake hands with him. His hand was cold, too. He smiled at her, and patted her on the shoulder.

'What a nice little girl!' he said. 'You will be a good companion for Marybelle. Three boys for Sooty, and one girl for Marybelle. Ha ha!'

He evidently thought George was a boy, and she did look rather like one – she was wearing jeans and jersey as usual, and her curly hair was very short.

Nobody said that George wasn't a boy. Certainly George was not going to! She, Dick and Julian shook hands with Mr Lenoir. They had not even noticed Sooty's mother!

She was there, though, sitting lost in an armchair, a tiny woman like a doll, with mouse-coloured hair and grey eyes. Anne turned to her.

'Oh, how small you are!' she said, before she could stop herself.

Mr Lenoir laughed. He laughed no matter what anyone said. Mrs Lenoir got up and smiled. She was only as tall as Anne, and had the smallest hands and feet that Anne had ever seen on a grown-up. Anne liked her. She shook hands, and said, 'It's so nice of you to have us all here like this. You know, I expect, that a tree fell on the roof of our house and smashed it.'

Mr Lenoir's laugh came again. He made some kind of joke, and everyone smiled politely.

'Well, I hope you'll have a good time here,' he said. 'Pierre and Marybelle will show you the old town, and, if you promise to be careful, you can walk along the road to the mainland to go to the cinema there.'

'Thank you,' said everyone, and Mr Lenoir laughed his curious laugh again.

'Your father is a very clever man,' he said, suddenly

turning to Julian, who guessed that he had mistaken him for George. 'I am hoping he will come here to fetch you home again when you go, and then I shall have the pleasure of talking with him. He and I have been doing the same kind of experiments, but he has got further than I have.'

'Oh!' said Julian, politely. Then the doll-like Mrs Lenoir spoke in her soft voice.

'Block will give you all your meals in Marybelle's schoolroom, then you will not disturb my husband. He does not like talk at meal-times, and that would be rather hard on six children.'

Mr Lenoir laughed again. His cold blue eyes looked intently at all the children. 'By the way, Pierre,' he said suddenly, 'I forbid you to wander about the catacombs in this hill, as I have forbidden you before, and I also forbid you to do any of your dare-devil climbing, nor will I have you acting about on the city wall now that you have others here. I will not have them taking risks. Will you promise me this?'

'I don't act about on the city wall,' protested Sooty. 'I don't take risks, either.'

'You play the fools always,' said Mr Lenoir, and the tip of his nose turned quite white. Anne looked at it with interest. She did not know that it always did this when Mr Lenoir got angry.

'Oh, sir – I was top of my form last term,' said Sooty, in a most injured tone. The others felt certain that he was

51

trying to lead Mr Lenoir away from his request – he was not going to promise him what he had asked!

Mrs Lenoir now joined in. 'He really did do well last term,' she said. 'You must remember—'

'Enough!' snapped Mr Lenoir, and the smiles and laughs he had so freely lavished on everyone vanished, entirely. 'Get out, all of you!'

Rather scared, Julian, Dick, Anne and George hurried from the room, followed by Marybelle and Sooty. Sooty was grinning as he shut the door.

'I didn't promise!' he said. 'He wanted to take all our fun away. This place isn't any fun if you don't explore it. I can show you heaps of strange places.'

'What are catacombs?' asked Anne, with a vague picture of cats and combs in her head.

'Winding, secret tunnels in the hill,' said Sooty. 'Nobody knows them all. You can get lost in them easily, and never get out again. Lots of people have.'

'Why are there so many secret ways and things here?' wondered George.

'Easy!' said Julian. 'It was a haunt of smugglers, and there must have been many a time when they had to hide not only their goods, but themselves! And, according to old Sooty, there still *is* a smuggler here! What did you say his name was – Barling, wasn't it?'

'Yes,' said Sooty. 'Come on upstairs and I'll show you your rooms. You've got a good view over the town.'

He took them to two rooms set side by side, on the

opposite side of the big staircase from his bedroom and Marybelle's. They were small but well-furnished, and had, as Sooty said, a marvellous view over the quaint roofs and towers of Castaway Hill. They also had a remarkably good view of Mr Barling's house.

George and Anne were to sleep in one room, and Julian and Dick in the other. Evidently Mrs Lenoir had taken the trouble to remember that there were two girls and two boys, not one girl and three boys, as Mr Lenoir imagined!

'Nice cosy rooms,' said Anne. 'I like these dark oak panels. Are there any secret passages in our rooms, Sooty?'

'You wait and see!' grinned Sooty. 'Look, there are your things, all unpacked from your suitcases. I expect Sarah did that. You'll like Sarah. She's a good sort, fat and round and jolly – not a bit like Block!'

Sooty seemed to have forgotten all about Tim. George reminded him.

'What about Timmy? He'll have to be near me, you know. And we must arrange to feed him and exercise him. Oh, I do hope he'll be all right, Sooty. I'd rather leave straight away than have Timmy unhappy.'

'He'll be all right!' said Sooty. 'I'll give him the free run of that narrow passage we came up to my bedroom by, and we'll smuggle him out by a secret tunnel that opens half-way down the town, and give him plenty of exercise each morning. Oh, we'll have a grand time with Timmy!'

George wasn't so sure. 'Can he sleep with me at night?' she asked. 'He'll howl the place down if he can't.'

'Well – we'll try and manage it,' said Sooty, rather doubtfully. 'You've got to be jolly careful, you know. We don't want to land in serious trouble. You don't know what my stepfather can be like!'

They could guess, though. Julian looked curiously at Sooty. 'Was your own father's name Lenoir, too?' he asked.

Sooty nodded. 'Yes. He was my stepfather's cousin, and was as dark as all the Lenoirs usually are. My stepfather is an exception – he's fair. People say the fair Lenoirs are no good – but don't tell my stepfather that!'

'As if we should!' said George. 'Gracious, he'd cut off our heads or something! Come on – let's go back to Tim.'

CHAPTER SEVEN

The hidden pit

THE CHILDREN were all very glad to think that they were
going to have meals by themselves in the old schoolroom.
Nobody wanted to have much to do with Mr Lenoir! They
felt sorry for Marybelle because she had such a peculiar
father.

They soon settled down at Smuggler's Top. Once
George was satisfied that Timmy was safe and happy,
though rather puzzled about everything, she settled down
too. The only difficulty was getting Timmy to her room at
night. This had to be done in darkness. Block had a most
tiresome way of appearing silently and suddenly, and
George was terrified of him catching a glimpse of the
big dog.

Timmy had a strange sort of life the next few days!
While the children were indoors, he had to stay in the
narrow secret passage, where he wandered about, puzzled
and lonely, pricking his ears for a sound of the whistle that
meant he was to come to the cupboard and be let out.

He was fed very well, for Sooty raided the larder every
night. Sarah, the cook, was amazed at the way things like
soup-bones disappeared. She could not understand it. But
Timmy devoured everything that was given to him.

Each morning he was given good exercise by the children. The first morning this had been really very exciting!

George had reminded Sooty of his promise to take Timmy for walks each day. 'He simply must have exercise, or he'll be terribly miserable!' she said. 'But how can we manage it? We can't possibly take him through the house and out of the front door! We'd be certain to walk into your father!'

'I told you I knew a way that came out half-way down the hill, silly,' said Sooty. 'I'll show you. We shall be quite safe once we are down there, because even if we met Block or anyone else that knew us, they wouldn't know it was our dog. They would think it was just a stray we had picked up.'

'Well – show us the way,' said George, impatiently. They were all in Sooty's bedroom, and Timmy was lying on the mat beside George. They felt really safe in Sooty's room because of the buzzer that warned them when anyone opened the door at the end of the long passage.

'We'll have to go into Marybelle's room,' said Sooty. 'You'll get a shock when you see the way that leads down the hill, I can tell you!'

He looked out of the door. The door at the end of the passage was shut. 'Marybelle, slip along and peep through the passage door,' said Sooty. 'Warn us if anyone is coming up the stairs. If not, we'll all slip quickly into your room.'

Marybelle ran to the door at the end of the passage. She

56

opened it, and at once the warning buzzer sounded in Sooty's room, making Timmy growl fiercely. Marybelle looked through the doorway to the stair. Then she signalled to the others that no one was coming.

They all rushed out of Sooty's room into Marybelle's, and Marybelle came to join them. She was a funny little mouse of a girl, shy and timid. Anne liked her, and once or twice teased her for being so shy.

But Marybelle did not like being teased. Her eyes filled with tears at once, and she turned away. 'She'll be better when she goes to school,' Sooty said. 'She can't help being shy, shut up all the year round in this strange house. She hardly ever sees anyone of her own age.'

They crowded into the little girl's bedroom and shut the door. Sooty turned the key in the lock. 'Just in case friend Block comes snooping,' he said with a grin.

Sooty began to move the furniture in the room to the sides, near the walls. The others watched in surprise and then helped. 'What's the idea of the furniture removal?' asked Dick, struggling with a heavy chest.

'Got to get this heavy carpet up,' panted Sooty. 'It's put there to hide the trap-door below. At least, that's what I've always thought.'

Once the furniture stood by the walls, it was easy to drag up the heavy carpet. There was a felt lining under it too, and that had to be pulled aside as well. Then the children saw a trap-door, let flat into the floor, with a ring-handle to pull it up.

They felt excited. Another secret way! This house seemed full of them. Sooty pulled at the ring and the heavy door came up quite easily. The children peered down, but they could see nothing. It was pitch-dark.

'Are there steps down?' asked Julian, holding Anne back in case she fell.

'No,' said Sooty, reaching out for a big torch he had brought in with him. 'Look!'

He switched on his torch, and the children gave a gasp. The trap-door led down to a pit, far, far below!

'Why! It's miles below the foundations of the house, surely!' said Julian, surprised. 'It's just a hole down to a big pit. What's it for?'

'Oh, it was probably used to hide people – or to get rid of them!' said Sooty. 'Nice little place, isn't it? If you fell down there you'd land with an awful bump!'

'But – how in the world could we get Timmy down there – or get down ourselves?' said George. '*I'm* not going to fall down it, that's certain!'

Sooty laughed. 'You won't have to,' he said. 'Look here.' He opened a cupboard and reached up to a wide shelf. He pulled something down, and the children saw that it was a rope-ladder, fine but very strong.

'There you are! We can all get down by that,' he said.

'Timmy can't,' said George at once. 'He couldn't possibly climb up or down a ladder.'

'Oh, couldn't he?' said Sooty. 'He seems such a clever

dog – I should have thought he could easily have done a thing like that.'

'Well, he can't,' said George, decidedly. 'That's a silly idea.'

'I know,' said Marybelle, suddenly, going red at her boldness in breaking in on the conversation. 'I think I know! We could get the laundry basket and shut Timmy in it. And we would tie it with ropes, and let him down – and pull him up the same way!'

The others stared at her. 'Now that really *is* a brainwave!' said Julian, warmly. 'Good for you, Marybelle. Timmy would be quite safe in a basket. But it would have to be a big one.'

'There's a very big one in the kitchen,' said Marybelle. 'It's never used except when we have lots of people to stay, like now. We could borrow it.'

'Oh *yes*!' said Sooty. 'Of course we could. I'll go and get it now.'

'But what excuse will you give?' shouted Julian after him. Sooty had already unlocked the door and shot out! He was a most impatient person, and could never put off anything for a single minute.

Sooty didn't answer. He sped down the passage. Julian locked the door after him. He didn't want anyone coming in and seeing the carpet up and the yawning hole!

Sooty was back in two minutes, carrying a very heavy wicker laundry basket on his head. He banged on the door, and Julian unlocked it.

'Good!' said Julian. 'How did you get it? Did anyone mind?'

'Didn't ask them,' grinned Sooty. 'Nobody there to ask. Block's with Father, and Sarah has gone out shopping. I can always put it back if any awkward questions are asked.'

The rope-ladder was shaken out down the hole. It slipped like an uncoiling snake, down and down, and reached the pit at the bottom. Then Timmy was fetched from Sooty's room. He came in wagging his tail overjoyed at being with everyone again. George hugged him.

'Darling Timmy! I hate you being hidden away like this. But never mind, we're all going out together this morning!'

'I'll go down first,' said Sooty. 'Then you'd better let Timmy down. I'll tie his basket round with this rope. It's nice and strong, and there's plenty to let down. Better tie the other end to the end of the bed, then when we come up again we can easily pull him up.'

Timmy was made to get inside the big basket and lie down. He was surprised and barked a little. But George put her hand over his mouth.

'Sh! You mustn't say a word, Timmy,' she said. 'I know all this is very astonishing. But never mind, you'll have a marvellous walk at the end of it.'

Timmy heard the word 'Walk' and was glad. That was what he wanted – a really nice long walk in the open air and sunshine!

He didn't at all like having the lid shut down on him, but

as George seemed to think he must put up with all these strange happenings, Timmy did so, with a very good grace.

'He's really a marvellous dog,' said Marybelle. 'Sooty, get down the hole now, and be ready for when we let him down.'

Sooty disappeared down the dark hole, holding his torch between his teeth. Down and down he went, down and down. At last he stood safely at the bottom, and flashed his torch upwards. His voice came to them, sounding rather strange and far away.

'Come on! Lower Timmy down!'

The laundry basket, feeling extraordinarily heavy now, was pushed to the edge of the hole. Then down it went, knocking against the sides here and there. Timmy growled. He didn't like this game!

Dick and Julian had hold of the rope between them. They lowered Timmy as smoothly as they could. He reached the bottom with a slight bump, and Sooty undid the basket. Out leapt Timmy, barking! But his bark sounded very small and distant to the watchers at the top.

'Now come on down, one by one!' shouted up Sooty, waving his torch. 'Is the door locked, Julian?'

'Yes,' said Julian. 'Look out for Anne. She's coming now.'

Anne climbed down, a little frightened at first, but as her feet grew used to searching for and finding the rungs of the rope-ladder, she went down quite quickly.

Then the others followed, and soon they were all standing together at the bottom of the hole, in the enormous pit. They looked round curiously. It had a musty smell, and its walls were damp and greenish. Sooty swung his torch round, and the children saw various passages leading off here and there.

'Where do they all lead to?' asked Julian, in amazement.

'Well, I told you this hill was full of tunnels,' said Sooty. 'This pit is down in the hill and these tunnels lead into the catacombs. There are miles and miles of them. No one explores them now, because so many people have been lost in them and never heard of again. There used to be an old map of them, but it's lost.'

'It's weird!' said Anne, and shivered. 'I wouldn't like to be down here alone.'

'What a place to hide smuggled goods in,' said Dick. 'No one would ever find them here.'

'I guess the old-time smugglers knew every inch of these passages,' said Sooty. 'Come on! We'll take the one that leads out of the hillside. We'll have to do a bit of climbing when we get there. I hope you don't mind.'

'Not a bit,' said Julian. 'We're all good climbers. But I say, Sooty – you're sure you know the way? We don't want to be lost for ever down here!'

''Course I know the way! Come on!' said Sooty, and, flashing his torch in front of him, he led the way into the dark and narrow tunnel.

CHAPTER EIGHT

An exciting walk

THE TUNNEL ran slightly downwards, and smelt nasty in places. Sometimes it opened out into pits like the one they themselves had come from. Sooty flashed his torch up them.

'That one goes into Barling's house somewhere,' he said. 'Most of the old houses hereabouts have openings into pits, like ours. Jolly well hidden some of them are, too!'

'There's daylight or something in front!' said Anne, suddenly. 'Oh good! I hate this tunnel.'

Sure enough, it was daylight, creeping in through a kind of cave-entrance in the hillside. The children crowded there, and looked out.

They were outside the hill, and outside the town, somewhere on the steep cliff-side that ran down to the marsh. Sooty climbed out on to a ledge. He put his torch into his pocket.

'We've got to get to that path down there,' he said, pointing. 'That will lead us to a place where the city wall is fairly low, and we can climb over it. Is Timmy sure-footed? We don't want him tumbling into the marsh down there!'

The marsh lay a good way below, looking ugly and flat. George sincerely hoped Timmy would never fall into it.

Still, he was very sure-footed, and she didn't think he would slip. The path was steep and rocky, but quite passable.

They all went down it, clambering over rocks now and again. The path led them to the city wall, which, as Sooty had said, was fairly low just there. He climbed up to the top. He was like a cat for climbing!

'No wonder he's got such a name for climbing about everywhere at school!' said Dick to Julian. 'He's had good practice here. Do you remember how he climbed up to the roof of the school the term before last? Everyone was scared he'd slip and fall, but he didn't. He tied the Union Jack to one of the chimney-pots!'

'Come on!' called Sooty. 'The coast is clear. This is a lonely bit of the town, and no one will see us climbing up.'

Soon they were all over the wall, Timmy too. They set off for a good walk, swinging down the hill, enjoying themselves. The mist began to clear after a while, and the sun felt nice and warm.

The town was very old. Some of the houses seemed almost tumble-down, but there were people living in them, for smoke came from the chimneys. The shops were quaint, with their long narrow windows, and overhanging eaves. The children stopped to look into them.

'Look out – here's Block!' said Sooty suddenly in a low voice. 'Don't take any notice of Timmy at all. If he comes around licking us or jumping up, pretend to try and drive him off as if he were a stray.'

They all pretended not to see Block, but gazed earnestly into the window of a shop. Timmy, feeling rather out of it, ran up to George and pawed at her, trying to make her take notice of him.

'Go away, dog!' said Sooty, and flapped at the surprised Timmy. 'Go away! Following us about like this! Go home, can't you?'

Timmy thought this was some sort of a game. He barked happily, and ran round Sooty and George, giving them an occasional lick.

'Home, dog, home!' yelled Sooty, flapping hard again.

Then Block came up to them, no expression on his face

at all. 'The dog bothers you?' he said. 'I will throw a stone at him and make him go.'

'Don't you dare!' said George, immediately. 'You go home yourself! I don't mind the dog following us. He's quite a nice one.'

'Block's deaf, silly,' said Sooty. 'It's no good talking to him.' To George's horror Block picked up a big stone, meaning to throw it at Timmy. George flew at him, punched him hard on the arm, and made him drop the stone.

'How dare you throw stones at a dog!' yelled the little girl in a fury. 'I'll – I'll tell the police.'

'Now, now,' said a voice nearby. 'What's all this about? Pierre, what's the trouble?'

The children turned and saw a tall man standing near them, wearing his hair rather long. He had long, narrow eyes, a long nose and a long chin. 'He's long everywhere!' thought Anne, looking at his long thin legs and long narrow feet.

'Oh, Mr Barling! I didn't see you,' said Sooty, politely. 'Nothing's the matter, thanks. It's only that this dog is following us, and Block said he'd make it go away by chucking a stone at it. And George here is fond of dogs and got angry about that.'

'I see. And who are all these children?' said Mr Barling, looking at each one of them out of his long, narrow eyes.

'They've come to stay with us because their uncle's house has been damaged in a gale,' explained Sooty. 'George's father's house, I mean. At Kirrin.'

'Ah – at Kirrin?' said Mr Barling, and seemed to prick up his long ears. 'Surely that is where that very clever scientist friend of Mr Lenoir's lives?'

'Yes. He's my father,' said George. 'Why, do you know him?'

'I have heard of him – and of his very interesting experiments,' said Mr Barling. 'Mr Lenoir knows him well, I believe?'

'Not awfully well,' said George, puzzled. 'They just write to one another, I think. My father telephoned to Mr Lenoir to ask him if he could have us to stay while our own house is being mended.'

'And Mr Lenoir, of course, was only too delighted to have the whole company of you! said Mr Barling. '*Such* a good, generous fellow, your father, Pierre!'

The children stared at Mr Barling, thinking that it was strange of him to say nice things in such a nasty voice. They felt uncomfortable. It was plain that Mr Barling did not like Mr Lenoir at all. Well, neither did they, but they didn't like Mr Barling any better!

Timmy saw another dog and darted happily after him. Block had now disappeared, going up the steep high street with his basket. The children said goodbye to Mr Barling, not wanting to talk to him any more.

They went after Timmy, talking eagerly as soon as they had left Mr Barling behind.

'Goodness – that was a narrow escape from Block!' said Julian. 'Old beast – going to throw that enormous stone at

Timmy. No wonder you flew at him, George! But you very nearly gave the game away, though.'

'I don't care,' said George. 'I wasn't going to have Timmy's leg broken. It was a bit of bad luck meeting Block our very first morning out.'

'We'll probably never meet him again when we take Timmy out,' said Sooty, comfortingly. 'And if we do we'll simply say the dog always joins us when it meets us. Which is perfectly true.'

They enjoyed their walk. They went into a quaint old coffee shop and had steaming cups of delicious creamy coffee and jammy buns. Timmy had two of the buns and gobbled them greedily. George went off to buy some meat for him at the butcher's, choosing a shop that Sooty said Mrs Lenoir did not go to. She did not want any butcher telling Mrs Lenoir that the children had been buying dog-meat!

They went back the same way as they had come. They made their way up the steep cliff-path, and in at the tunnel-entrance, back through the winding tunnel to the pit, and there was the rope-ladder waiting for them. Julian and Dick went up first, while George packed the surprised Timmy into the basket again and tied the rope firmly round it. Then up went the whining Timmy, bumping against the sides of the hole, until the two panting boys pulled the basket into Marybelle's room and undid it.

It was ten minutes before the dinner-hour. 'Just time to shut the trap-door, pull back the carpet and wash our hands,' said Sooty. 'And I'll put old Timmy back into the secret passage behind the cupboard in my room, George. Where is that meat you bought? I'll put that in the passage too. He can eat it when he likes.'

'Did you put him a nice warm rug there, and a dish of fresh water?' asked George, anxiously, for the third or fourth time.

'You know I did. I keep telling you,' said Sooty. 'Look, we won't put back all the furniture except the chairs. We can say we want it left back because we like to play a game on the carpet. It'll be an awful bore if we have to move chests and things every time we exercise Tim.'

They were just in time for their dinner. Block was there to serve it, and so was Sarah. The children sat down hungrily, in spite of having had coffee and buns. Block and Sarah ladled out hot soup on to their plates.

'I hope you got rid of the unpleasant dog,' said Block in his monotonous voice. He gave George a rather nasty look. Evidently he had not forgotten how she had flown at him.

Sooty nodded. It was no good speaking an answer, for Block would not hear. Sarah bustled round, taking away the soup-plates and preparing to give them their second course.

The food was very good at Smuggler's Top. There was plenty of it, and the hungry visitors and Sooty ate everything put before them. Marybelle hadn't much appetite, but she was the only one. George tried to secrete titbits and bones whenever she could, for Timmy.

AN EXCITING WALK

Two or three days went by, and the children fell into their new life quite happily. Timmy was taken out each morning for a long walk. The children soon got used to slipping down the rope-ladder, and making their way with Timmy to the cliff-side.

In the afternoons they went to either Sooty's room or Marybelle's, and played games or read. They could have Timmy there, because the buzzer always warned them if anyone was coming.

At night it was always an excitement to get Timmy to George's room without being seen. This was usually done when Mr and Mrs Lenoir were sitting at their dinner, and Block and Sarah were serving them. The children had a light supper first, and Mr and Mrs Lenoir had their dinner an hour later. It was quite the best time to smuggle Timmy along to George's room.

Timmy seemed to enjoy the smuggling. He ran silently beside George and Sooty, stopped at every corner, and scampered gladly into George's room as soon as he got there. He lay quietly under the bed till George was in bed herself, and then he came out to lie on her feet.

George always locked their door at night. She didn't want Sarah or Mrs Lenoir coming in and finding Timmy there! But nobody came, and as night after night went by, George grew more easy about Timmy.

Taking him back to Sooty's room in the morning was a bit of a nuisance, because it had to be done early, before anyone was up. But George could always wake herself at any time she chose, and each morning about half past six the little girl slipped through the house with Timmy. She went in at Sooty's door, and he jumped out of bed to deal with Timmy. He was always awakened by the buzzer that sounded when George opened the door at the end of the passage.

'I hope you are all enjoying yourselves,' Mr Lenoir said to the children, whenever they met him in the hall or on the stairs. And they always replied politely. 'Oh yes, Mr Lenoir, thank you.'

'It's quite a peaceful holiday after all,' said Julian. 'Nothing happens at all!'

And then things *did* begin to happen and once they had begun they never stopped!

CHAPTER NINE

Who is in the tower?

ONE NIGHT Julian was awakened by someone opening his door. He sat up at once. 'Who is it?' he said.

'Me, Sooty,' said Sooty's voice, very low. 'I say, I want you to come and see something.'

Julian woke Dick, and the two of them put on their dressing-gowns. Sooty led them quietly out of the room and took them to a peculiar little room, tucked away in an odd wing of the house. All kinds of things were kept here, trunks and boxes, old toys, chests of old clothes, broken vases that had never been mended, and many other worthless things.

'Look,' said Sooty, taking them to the window. They saw that the little room had a view of the tower belonging to the house. It was the only room in the house that did, for it was built at a strange angle.

The boys looked – and Julian gave an exclamation. Someone was signalling from the tower! A light there flashed every now and again. In and out – pause – flash, flash, in and out – pause. The light went regularly on and off in a certain rhythm.

'Now – who's doing that?' whispered Sooty.

'Your father?' wondered Julian.

'Don't think so,' said Sooty. 'I think I heard him snoring away in his room. We could go and find out though – see if he really is in his bedroom.'

WHO IS IN THE TOWER?

'Well – for goodness' sake don't let's get caught,' said Julian, not at all liking the idea of prying about in his host's house.

They made their way to where Mr Lenoir had his room. It was quite plain he was there, for a regular low snoring came from behind the closed door.

'It may be Block up in the tower,' said Dick. 'He looks full of secrets. I wouldn't trust him an inch. I bet it's Block.'

'Well – shall we go to his room and see if it's empty?' whispered Sooty. 'Come on. If it's Block signalling, he's doing it without Father knowing.'

'Oh, your father might have told him to,' said Julian, who felt that he wouldn't trust Mr Lenoir much further than he would trust Block.

They went up the back-stairs to the wing where the staff slept. Sarah slept in a room there with Harriet the kitchen-maid. Block slept alone.

Sooty pushed open Block's door very softly and slowly. When he had enough room to put in his head, he did so. The room was full of moonlight. By the window was Block's bed. And Block was there! Sooty could see the humpy shape of his body, and the black round patch that was his head.

He listened, but he could not catch Block's breathing. He must sleep very quietly.

He withdrew his head, and pushed the other two boys quietly down the back-stairs.

'Was he there?' whispered Julian.

'Yes. So it can't be him, signalling up in our tower,' said Sooty. 'Well – who can it be then? I don't like it. It couldn't possibly be Mother or Sarah or Harriet. Is there a stranger in our house, someone we don't know, living here in secret?'

'Can't be!' said Julian, a little shiver running down his back. 'Look here – what about us going up to the tower and trying to peep through the door or something? We'd soon find out who it was then. Perhaps we ought to tell your father.'

'No. Not yet. I want to find out a whole lot more before I say anything to anyone,' said Sooty, sounding obstinate. 'Let's creep up to the tower. We shall have to be jolly careful though. You get to it by a spiral staircase, rather narrow. There's nowhere much to hide if anyone suddenly came down out of the tower.

'What's in the tower?' whispered Dick, as they made their way through the dark and silent house, thin streaks of moonlight coming in here and there between the crack of the closed curtains.

'Nothing much. Just a table and a chair or two, and a bookcase of books,' said Sooty. 'We use it on hot summer days when the breeze gets in strongly through the windows there, and we can see a long way all round us.'

They came to a little landing. From this a winding, narrow stairway of stone went up to the rounded tower. The boys looked up. Moonlight fell on the stairway from a slit-like window in the wall.

76

WHO IS IN THE TOWER?

'We'd better not all go up,' said Sooty. 'We should find it so difficult to hurry down, three of us, if the person in the tower suddenly came out. I'll go. You stay down here and wait. I'll see if I can spy anything through the crack in the door or the key-hole.'

He crept softly up the stairway, soon lost to view as he rounded the first spiral. Julian and Dick waited in the shadows at the bottom. There was a thick curtain over one of the windows there, and they got behind it, wrapping its folds round them for warmth.

Sooty crept up to the top. The tower-room had a stout oak door, studded and barred. It was shut! It was no use trying to look through the crack, because there wasn't one. He bent down to peer through the key-hole.

But that was stuffed up with something, so he could not see through that either. He pressed his ear to it and listened.

He heard a series of little clicks. Click – click – click – click – click. Nothing else at all.

'That's the click of the light they're using,' thought Sooty. 'Still signalling like mad! What for? Who to? And who is in our tower-room, using it as a signalling-station? How I wish I knew!'

Suddenly the clicking stopped. There was the sound of someone walking across the stone floor of the tower. And almost at once the door opened!

Sooty had no time to hurry down the stairs. All he could do was to squeeze into a niche, and hope that the person would

77

not see him or touch him as he went by. The moon went behind a cloud at that moment, and Sooty was thankful to know he was hidden in black shadow. Someone came down the stairs and actually brushed against Sooty's arm.

Sooty jumped almost out of his skin, expecting to be hauled out of his niche. But the person did not seem to notice, and went on down the spiral stairway, walking softly.

Sooty did not dare to go down after him, for he was afraid the moon would come out, and cast his shadow down for the signaller to see.

So he stayed squeezed in his niche, hoping that Julian and Dick were well-hidden, and would not think it was he, Sooty, who was walking down the stairs!

Julian and Dick heard the soft footsteps coming, and thought at first it was Sooty. Then, not hearing his whisper, they stiffened behind the curtains, guessing that it was the signaller himself who was walking by!

'We'd better follow him!' whispered Julian to Dick. 'Come on. Quiet, now!'

But Julian got muddled up with the great curtains, and could not seem to find his way out. Dick, however, slipped out easily enough, and padded after the disappearing person. The moon was now out again, and Dick could catch glimpses of the signaller as he went past the moonlight streaks. Keeping well in the shadows himself, he darted quietly after him. Where was he going?

He followed him across the landing to a passage. Then across another landing and up the back-stairs! But those led to the staff bedrooms. Surely the man was not going there?

Dick, to his enormous surprise, saw the person disappear silently into Block's bedroom. He crept to the door, which had been left a little ajar. There was no light in the room except that of the moon. There was no sound of talking. Nothing at all except a creak which might have come from the bed.

Dick peeped in, full of the most intense curiosity. Would he see the man waking up Block? Would he see him climbing out of the window?

He stared round the room. There was no one there at all, except Block lying in bed. The moonlight lit up the corners, and Dick could quite plainly see that the room was empty. Only Block lay there, and, as Dick watched, he heard him give a sigh and roll over in bed.

'Well! That's the strangest thing I ever saw,' thought Dick, puzzled. 'A man goes into a room and completely disappears, without a single sound! Where can he have gone?'

WHO IS IN THE TOWER?

He went back to find the others. Sooty by this time had crept down the spiral staircase and had found Julian, who had explained that Dick had gone to follow the peculiar signaller.

They went to find Dick, and suddenly bumped into him, creeping along quietly in the darkness. They all jumped violently, and Julian almost cried out, but stifled his voice just in time.

'Golly! You gave me a scare, Dick!' he whispered. 'Well, did you see who it was and where he went?'

Dick told them of his strange experience. 'He simply went into Block's room and vanished,' he said. 'Is there any secret passage leading out of Block's room, Sooty?'

'No, none,' said Sooty. 'That wing is much newer than the rest of the house, and hasn't any secrets in at all. I simply can't imagine what happened to the man. How very odd! Who is he, and why does he come, and where on earth does he go?'

'We really must find out,' said Julian. 'It's such a mystery! Sooty, how did you know there was signalling going on from the tower?'

'Well, some time ago I found it out, quite by accident,' said Sooty. 'I couldn't sleep, and I went along to that funny little box-room place, and ferreted about for an old book I thought I'd seen there. And suddenly I looked up at the tower, and saw a light flashing there.'

'Funny,' said Dick.

'Well, I went along there at night a good many times

81

after that, to see if I could see the signals again,' said Sooty, 'and at last I did. The first time I had seen them there was a good moon, and the second time there was, too. So, I thought, next time there's a moon, I'll creep along to that old box-room and see if the signaller is at work again. And sure enough he was!'

'Where does that window look out on, that we saw the light flashing from?' asked Julian, thoughtfully. 'The seaward side – or the landward?'

'Seaward,' said Sooty at once. 'There's something or someone out at sea that receives those signals. Goodness knows who.'

'Some kind of smugglers, I suppose,' said Dick. 'But it can't be anything to do with your father, Sooty. I say – let's go up into the tower, shall we? We might find something there – or see something.'

They went back to the spiral staircase and climbed up to the tower-room. It was dark, for the moon was behind a cloud. But it came out after a while, and the boys looked out of the seaward window.

There was no mist at all that night. They could see the flat marshes stretching away to the sea. They gazed down in silence. Then the moon went in and darkness covered the marsh.

Suddenly Julian clutched the others, making them jump. 'I can see something!' he whispered. 'Look beyond there. What is it?'

They all looked. It seemed like a tiny line of very small

dots of light. They were so far away that it was difficult to see if they stayed still or moved. Then the moon came out again, flooding everywhere with silvery light, and the boys could not see anything except the moonshine.

But when the moon went in again, there was the line of tiny, pricking lights again! 'A bit nearer, surely!' whispered Sooty. 'Smugglers – coming over a secret path from the sea to Castaway Hill! Smugglers!'

CHAPTER TEN

Timmy makes a noise

THE THREE girls were very excited the next day when the boys told them their adventure of the night before.

'Gracious!' said Anne, her eyes wide with surprise. 'Who can it be signalling like that? And wherever did he go to? Fancy him going into Block's room, with Block there in bed!'

'It's very peculiar,' said George. 'I wish you had come and told me and Anne.'

'There wasn't time – and anyway, we couldn't have Timmy about at night. He might have flown at the signaller,' said Dick.

'The man must have been signalling to the smugglers,' said Julian, thoughtfully. 'Let me see – probably they came over from France in a ship – came as near to the marsh as they could – waited for a signal to tell them that the coast was clear – probably the signal from the tower – and then waded across a path they knew through the marsh. Each man must have carried a torch to prevent himself from leaving the path and falling into the marsh. No doubt there was someone waiting to receive the goods they brought – someone at the edge of the marsh below the hill.'

'But who?' said Dick. 'It can't have been Mr Barling,

84

who, Sooty says, is known to be a smuggler. Because the signal lights came from *our* house, not his. It's all very puzzling.'

'Well, we'll do our best to solve the mystery,' said George. 'There's some peculiar game going on in this very house, without your father's knowledge, Sooty. We'll keep a jolly good lookout and see if we can find out what it is.'

They were at breakfast alone, when they discussed the night's adventure. Block came in to see if they had finished at that moment. Anne did not notice him.

'What does Mr Barling smuggle?' she asked Sooty. Immediately she got a hard kick on her ankle, and stared in pain and surprise. 'Why did you . . .?' she began, and got another kick, harder still. Then she saw Block.

'But he's deaf,' she said. 'He can't hear anything we say.'

Block began to clear away, his face as usual showing no expression. Sooty glared at Anne. She was upset and cross, but said no more. She rubbed her bruised ankle hard. As soon as Block went out of the room she turned on Sooty.

'You mean thing! You hurt my ankle like anything! Why shouldn't I say things in front of Block? He's quite deaf!' said Anne, her face very red.

'I know he's supposed to be,' said Sooty. 'And I think he is. But I saw a funny look come over his face when you asked me what Mr Barling smuggled – almost as if he had heard what you said, and was surprised.'

'You imagined it!' said Anne, crossly, still rubbing her

ankle. 'Anyway, don't kick me so hard again. A gentle push with your toe would have been enough. I won't talk in front of Block if you don't want me to, but it's quite plain he's as deaf as a post!'

'Yes, he's deaf all right,' said Dick. 'I dropped a plate off the table yesterday, by accident, just behind him, and it smashed to bits, if you remember. Well, he didn't jump or turn a hair, as he would have done if he could have heard.'

'All the same – I never trust Block, deaf or not,' said Sooty. 'I always feel he might read our lips or something. Deaf people can often do that, you know.'

They went off to take Timmy for his usual morning walk. Timmy was quite used to being shut in the laundry basket by now, and lowered into the pit. In fact, he always jumped straight into the basket as soon as the lid was opened, and lay down.

That morning they again met Block, who stared with great interest at the dog. He plainly recognised it as the same dog as before.

'There's Block,' said Julian, in a low voice. 'Don't drive Timmy off this time. We'll pretend he's a stray who always meets us each morning.'

So they let Timmy run round them, and when Block came up, they nodded to him, and made as if to go on their way. But the man stopped them.

'That dog seems to be a friend of yours,' he said, in his curious monotone of a voice.

'Oh yes. He goes with us each morning now,' said

Julian, politely. 'He quite thinks he's our dog! Nice fellow, isn't he?'

Block stared at Timmy, who growled. 'Mind you do not bring that dog into the house,' said Block. 'If you do, Mr Lenoir will have him killed.'

Julian saw George's face beginning to turn red with fury. He spoke hurriedly. 'Why should we bring him to the house, Block? Don't be silly!'

Block, however, did not appear to hear. He gave Timmy a nasty look, and went on his way, occasionally turning round to look at the little company of children.

'Horrid fellow!' said George, angrily. 'How dare he say things like that?'

When they got back to Marybelle's bedroom that morning, they pulled Timmy up from the pit, and let him out of the basket. 'We'll put him into the secret passage as usual,' said George, 'and I'll put some biscuits in with him. I got some nice ones for him this morning, the sort he likes, all big and crunchy.'

She went to the door – but just as she was about to unlock it and take Timmy into Sooty's room next door, Timmy gave a small growl.

George took her hand away from the door at once. She turned to look at Timmy. He was standing stiffly, the hackles on his neck rising up, and he was staring fixedly at the door. George put her hand to her lips warningly, and whispered: 'Someone's outside. Timmy knows. He's smelt them. Will you all talk loudly, and pretend to be playing a game? I'll pop Timmy into the cupboard where the rope-ladder is kept.'

At once the others began to talk to one another, while George swiftly dragged Timmy to the cupboard, patted him to make him understand he was to be quiet, and shut him in.

'My turn to deal,' said Julian loudly, and took a pack of snap cards from the top of the chest. 'You won last time, Dick. Bet I'll win this time.'

He dealt swiftly. The others, still talking loudly, saying anything that came into their heads, began to play snap. They yelled 'snap' nearly all the time, pretending to be very jolly and hilarious. Anyone listening outside the door would never guess it was all pretence.

George, who was watching the door closely, saw that the handle was gradually turning, very slowly indeed. Someone meant to open the door without being heard, and come in unexpectedly. But the door was locked!

Soon the person outside, whoever it was, realised that the door was locked, and the handle slowly turned the other way again. Then it was still. There came no other sound. It was impossible to know if anyone was still outside the door or not.

But Timmy would know! Signing to the others to carry on with their shouting and laughing, George let Timmy out of the cupboard. He ran to the door of the room, and stood there, sniffing quietly. Then he turned and looked at George, his tail wagging.

TIMMY MAKES A NOISE

'It's all right,' said George to the others. 'There's no one there now. Timmy always knows. We'd better quickly take him into your room, Sooty, while the coast is clear. Who could it have been, do you think, snooping outside?'

'Block, I should say,' said Sooty. He unlocked the door and peered out. There was no one in the passage. Sooty tiptoed to the door at the end and looked out there also. He waved to George to tell her it was all right to take Timmy into his room.

Soon Timmy was safely in the secret passage, crunching up his favourite biscuits. He had got quite used to his peculiar life now, and did not mind at all. He knew his way about the passage, and had explored other passages that led from it. He was quite at home in the maze of secret ways!

'Better go and have our dinner now,' said Dick. 'And mind, Anne – don't go and say anything silly in front of that horrid Block, in case he reads your lips.'

'Of course I shan't,' said Anne, indignantly. 'I wouldn't have before, but I never thought of him reading my lips. If he does, he's very clever.'

Soon they were all sitting down to lunch. Block was there, waiting to serve them. Sarah was out for the day and did not appear. Block served them with soup, and then went out.

Suddenly, to the children's intense surprise and fright, they heard Timmy barking loudly! They jumped violently.

'Listen! That's Timmy!' said Julian. 'He must be somewhere near here, in that secret passage. How weird it sounds, his bark coming muffled and distant like that. But anyone would know it was a dog barking.'

'Don't say anything at all about it in front of Block,' said Sooty. 'Not a word. Pretend not to hear at all, if Timmy barks again. What on earth is he barking for?'

'It's the bark he uses when he's excited and pleased,' said George. 'I expect he's chasing a rat. He always goes right off his head when he sees a rat or a rabbit. There he goes again. Oh, dear, I hope he catches the rat quickly and settles down!'

Block came back at that moment. Timmy had again just stopped barking. But, in a moment or two, his doggy voice could be heard once more, very muffled. 'Woof! Woof-woof!'

Julian was watching Block closely. The man went on serving the meat. He said nothing, but looked round at the children intently, as if he wanted to see each child's expression, or see if they said anything.

'Jolly good soup that was today,' said Julian, cheerfully, looking round at the others. 'I must say Sarah is a wonderful cook.'

'I think her ginger buns are gorgeous,' said Anne. 'Especially when they are all hot from the oven.'

'Woof-woof,' said Timmy's voice from far away behind the walls.

'George, your mother makes the most heavenly fruit cake I ever tasted,' said Dick to George, wishing Timmy would be quiet. 'I do wonder how they're all getting on at Kirrin Cottage, and if they've started mending the roof yet.'

'Woof!' said Timmy, joyfully chasing his rat down another bit of passage.

Block served everyone and then silently disappeared. Julian went to the door to make sure he had gone and was not outside.

'I hope old Block *is* as deaf as a post!' he said. 'I could have sworn I saw a surprised look come into those cold eyes of his, when Timmy barked.'

'Well, if he *could* hear him, which I don't believe,' said George, 'he must have been jolly surprised to see us talking away and not paying any attention to a dog's barking at all!'

The others giggled. They kept a sharp ear for Block's return. They heard footsteps after a time, and began to pile their plates together for him to take away.

The schoolroom door opened. But it was not Block who came in. It was Mr Lenoir! He came in, smiling as usual, and looked round at the surprised children.

'Ah! So you are enjoying your dinner, and eating it all up, like good children,' he said. He always irritated the children because he spoke to them as if they were very small. 'Does Block wait on you properly?'

'Oh yes, thank you,' said Julian, standing up politely. 'We are having a very nice time here. We think Sarah is a wonderful cook!'

'Ah, that's good, that's good,' said Mr Lenoir. The children waited impatiently for him to go. They were so afraid that Timmy would bark again. But Mr Lenoir seemed in no hurry.

And then Timmy barked again! 'Woof, woof, woof!'

CHAPTER ELEVEN

George is worried

MR LENOIR cocked his head on one side almost like a startled dog, when he heard the muffled barking. He looked at the children. But they made no sign of having heard anything. Mr Lenoir listened a little while, saying nothing. Then he turned to a drawing-book, belonging to Julian, and began to look at the sketches there.

The children felt somehow that he was doing it for the sake of staying in the schoolroom a little longer. Into Julian's mind came the quick suspicion that somehow Mr Lenoir must have been told of Timmy's barking and come to investigate it for himself. It was the first time he had ever come to the schoolroom!

Timmy barked again, a little more distantly. Mr Lenoir's nose grew white at the tip. Sooty and Marybelle knew the danger-sign, and glanced at one another. That white-tipped nose usually meant a storm of temper!

'Do you hear that noise?' said Mr Lenoir, snapping out the words.

'What noise?' asked Julian, politely.

Timmy barked again.

'Don't be foolish! There's the noise again!' said Mr

Lenoir. At that moment a gull called outside the window, circling in the sea-breeze.

'Oh – that gull? Yes, we often hear the gulls,' said Dick, brightly. 'Sometimes they seem to mew like a cat.'

'Pah!' said Mr Lenoir, almost spitting out the word. 'I suppose you will say they also bark like a dog?'

'Well, they might, I suppose,' agreed Dick, looking faintly surprised. 'After all, if they can mew like cats, there's no reason why they shouldn't bark like dogs.'

Timmy barked again very joyfully. Mr Lenoir faced the children, in a very bad temper indeed now.

'Can't you hear that? Tell me what *that* noise is!'

The children all put their heads on one side, and pretended to listen very carefully. 'I can't hear anything,' said Dick. 'Not a thing.'

'I can hear the wind,' said Anne.

'I can hear the gulls again,' said Julian, putting his hand behind one ear.

'I can hear a door banging. Perhaps that's the noise you mean,' said Sooty, with a most innocent expression. His stepfather gave him a poisonous look. He could really be very unpleasant.

'And there's a window rattling,' said Marybelle, eager to do her bit too, though she felt very frightened of her father, for she knew his sudden rages very well.

'I tell you, it's a dog, and you know it!' snapped Mr Lenoir, the tip of his nose so white now that it looked very strange indeed. 'Where's the dog? Whose is he?'

GEORGE IS WORRIED

'What dog?' began Julian, frowning as if he were very puzzled indeed. 'There's no dog here that I can see.'

Mr Lenoir glared at him, and clenched his fingers. It was quite clear that he would have liked to box Julian's ears. 'Then listen!' he hissed. 'Listen and say what you think could make that barking, if not a dog?'

They were all forced to listen, for by now they felt scared of the angry man. But fortunately Timmy made no sound at all. Either he had let the rat escape, or was now gobbling it up. Anyway, there was not a single sound from him!

'Sorry, but *really* I can't hear a dog barking,' said Julian, in rather an injured tone.

'Nor can I!' said Dick, and the others joined in, saying the same. Mr Lenoir knew that this time they were speaking the truth, for he too could not hear anything.

'When I catch that dog I will have him poisoned,' he said, very slowly and clearly. 'I will not have dogs in my house.'

He turned on his heel and went out quickly, which was a very good thing, for George was quite ready to fly into one of *her* rages, and then there would have been a real battle! Anne put her hand on George's arm to stop her shouting after Mr Lenoir.

'Don't give the game away!' she whispered. 'Don't say anything, George!'

George bit her lip. She had gone first red with rage and then white. She stamped her foot.

'How dare he, how dare he?' she burst out.

'Shut up, silly,' said Julian. 'Block will be back in a minute. We must all pretend to be awfully surprised that Mr Lenoir thought there was a dog, because, if Block can read our lips, he mustn't know the truth.'

Block came in with the pudding at that moment, his face as blank as ever. It was the most curious face the children had ever seen, for there was never any change of expression on it at all. As Anne said, it might have been a wax mask!

'Funny how Mr Lenoir thought there was a dog barking!' began Julian, and the others backed him up valiantly. If Block could indeed read their lips he would be

96

puzzled to know whether there had been a dog barking or not!

The children escaped to Sooty's room afterwards, and held a council of war. 'What are we to do about Timmy?' said George. 'Does your stepfather know the secret way behind the walls of Smuggler's Top, Sooty? Could he possibly get in and find Timmy? Timmy might fly at him, you know.'

'Yes, he might,' said Sooty, thoughtfully. 'I don't know if Father does know about the secret passages. I mean, I expect he knows, but I don't know if he guessed where the entrances are. I found them out quite by accident.'

'I'm going home,' said George, suddenly. 'I'm not going to risk Timmy being poisoned.'

'You can't go home alone,' said Julian. 'It would look funny. If you do, we'll all have to, and then we won't have a chance to solve this mystery with Sooty.'

'No, for goodness' sake don't go and leave me just now,' said Sooty, looking quite alarmed. 'It would make my father furious, simply furious.'

George hesitated. She didn't want to make trouble for Sooty, whom she liked very much. But, on the other hand, she certainly was not going to risk danger to Timmy.

'Well – I'll telephone my father and say I'm homesick and want to go back,' said George. 'I'll say I miss Mother. It's quite true. I do miss her. You others can stay on here and solve the mystery. It wouldn't be fair of you to try and keep me and Timmy here when you know I'd worry every moment in case someone got into the secret passage and put down poisoned meat for him to eat.'

The others hadn't thought of this. That would be terrible. Julian sighed. He would have to let George have her own way after all.

'All right. You telephone to your father,' he said. 'There's a phone downstairs. Do it now if you like. There won't be anyone about now, I don't suppose.'

George slipped down the passage, out of the door there, and down the stairs to where the telephone was enclosed in a dark little cupboard. She dialled the number she wanted.

There was a long wait. Then she heard the buzzing noise – brr – brr – brr – that told her that the telephone bell at Kirrin Cottage was ringing. She began to plan what she should say to her father. She must, she really must go home with Timmy. She didn't know how she was going to explain about Timmy – perhaps she needn't explain at all. But she meant to go home that day or the next!

'Brr – brr – brr – brr' said the bell at the other end. It went on and on, and nobody answered it. She did not hear her father's familiar voice – only the bell that went on ringing. Why did nobody answer?

The operator at the exchange spoke to her. 'I'm sorry, there's no reply.'

George put down the receiver miserably. Perhaps her parents were out? She would have to try again later on.

Poor George tried three times, but each time with the

same result. No reply. As she was coming out of the telephone cupboard for the third time, Mrs Lenoir saw her.

'Have you been trying to telephone to your home?' she said. 'Haven't you heard any news?'

'I haven't had a letter yet,' said George. 'I've tried three times to telephone Kirrin Cottage but each time there is no reply.'

'Well, we heard this morning that it is impossible to live in Kirrin Cottage while the men are hammering and knocking everywhere,' said Mrs Lenoir, in her gentle voice. 'We heard from your mother. She said that the noise was driving your father mad, and they were going away for a week or so, till things were better. But Mr Lenoir at once wrote and asked them here. We shall know tomorrow, because we have asked them to telephone a reply. We could not get them on the telephone today, of course, any more than you could, because they have gone away already.'

'Oh,' said George, surprised at all this news, and wondered why her mother had not written to tell her too.

'Your mother said she had written to you,' said Mrs Lenoir. 'Maybe the letter will come by the next post. The posts are often most peculiar here. It will be a pleasure to have your parents if they can come. Mr Lenoir particularly wants to meet your clever father. He thinks he is quite a genius.'

George said no more but went back to the others, her

face serious. She opened Sooty's door, and the others saw at once that she had had news of some sort.

'I can't go home with Timothy,' said George. 'Mother and Father can't stand the noise the workmen make, and they have both gone away!'

'Bad luck!' said Sooty. 'All the same, I'm glad you'll have to stay here, George. I should hate to lose you or Timmy.'

'Your father has written to ask my mother and father to come and stay here too,' said George. 'What I shall do about Timmy I don't know! And they are sure to ask questions about him too. I can't tell a downright lie and say I left him with Alf the fisher-boy, or anything like that. I can't think *what* to do!'

'We'll think of something,' promised Sooty. 'Perhaps I can get one of the villagers to look after him for us. That would be a very good idea.'

'Oh yes!' said George, cheering up. 'Why didn't I think of that before? Let's ask someone quickly, Sooty.'

But it was impossible to do anything that day because Mrs Lenoir asked them to go down into the drawing-room after tea, and have a game with her. So none of them could go out to find someone to look after Timmy. 'Never mind,' thought George. 'He'll be safe tonight on my bed! To-morrow will be soon enough.'

It was the first time that Mrs Lenoir had asked them down to be with her. 'You see, Mr Lenoir is out tonight on important business,' she explained. 'He has had to go to the mainland with the car. He doesn't like his evenings disturbed when he is at home, so I haven't been able to see as much of you all as I should have liked. But tonight I can.'

Julian wondered if Mr Lenoir had gone to the mainland on smuggling business! Somehow the smuggled goods must be taken across to the mainland and if all that signalling business the other night had to do with Mr Lenoir's smuggling then maybe he had now gone to dispose of the goods!

The telephone bell rang shrilly. Mrs Lenoir got up. 'I expect that is your mother or father on the phone,' she said to George. 'Maybe I shall have news for you! Perhaps your parents will be arriving here tomorrow.'

She went out into the hall. The children waited anxiously. Would George's parents come or not?

CHAPTER TWELVE

Block gets a surprise

MRS LENOIR came back after a time. She smiled at George.

'That was your father,' she said. 'He is coming tomorrow, but not your mother. They went to your aunt's, and your mother says she thinks she must stay and help her, because your aunt is not very well. But your father would like to come, because he wants to discuss his latest experiments with Mr Lenoir, who is very interested in them. It will be very nice to have him.'

The children would very much rather have had Aunt Fanny instead of Uncle Quentin, who could be very difficult at times. But still, he would probably be talking with Mr Lenoir most of the time, so that would be all right!

They finished their game with Mrs Lenoir and went up to bed. George was to get Timmy to take him to her room. Sooty went to see that the coast was clear. He could not see Block anywhere. His stepfather was still away from the house. Sarah was singing in the kitchen and the little kitchen-maid, Harriet, was knitting there in a corner.

'Block must be out,' thought Sooty, and went to tell George that the coast was clear. As he went across the landing to the long passage that led to his own room, the boy noticed two black lumps sticking out at the bottom of the thick curtains drawn across the landing window. He looked at them in surprise, and then recognised them. He grinned.

'So old Block suspects we have a dog, and he thinks it sleeps in George's room or Julian's, and he's posted himself there to watch!' he thought. 'Aha! I'll give friend Block a nasty shock!'

He ran to tell the others. George listened, alarmed. But Sooty, as usual, had a plan.

'We'll give Block an awful shock!' he said. 'I'll get a rope, and we'll all go down to the landing. I'll suddenly yell out that there's a robber hiding behind the curtains and I'll pounce on Block, and give him a few good punches. Then, with your help, Julian and Dick, I'll fold him up well in the curtains – a good jerk will bring them down on top of him as well!'

The others began to laugh. It would be fun to play a trick on Block. He really was such an unpleasant fellow. A good lesson would do him no harm.

'While all the excitement is beginning I'll slip by with Timmy,' said George. 'I only hope he won't want to join in! He might give Block a good nip!'

'Well, hold on to Timmy firmly,' said Julian. 'Get him into your room quickly. Now – are we ready?'

They were. Feeling excited they crept down the long passage that led to the door which opened out on to the landing where Block was hiding. They saw the curtains move very slightly as they came along. Block was watching.

George waited with Timmy at the passage door, not showing herself at all. Then, with a yell from Sooty, a really blood-curdling yell that made both George and Timmy jump, things began to happen!

Sooty flung himself on the hidden Block with all his might. 'A robber! Help, a robber hiding here!' he shouted.

Block jumped, and began to struggle. Sooty got in two or three well-aimed punches. Block had often got him into trouble with his father, and now Sooty was getting a bit of his own back! Julian and Dick rushed to help.

A violent tug at the curtains brought them down on Block's head! Not only that, the curtain pole descended on him too, and knocked him sideways. Poor Block – he was completely taken by surprise, and could do nothing against the three determined boys. Even Anne gave a hand, though Marybelle stood apart, enjoying the fun though not daring to take part in it.

Just as it all began George slipped by with Timmy. But Timmy could not bear to miss the fun. He dragged behind George, and would not go with her.

She tried to force him, her hand on his collar. But Timmy had seen a nice fat leg waving about near him, protruding from the curtain. He pounced on it.

There was an agonised yell from Block. Certainly Timmy could nip hard with his sharp white teeth. He worried at the kicking leg for a few seconds, and then had a sharp slap from George. Shocked, Timmy let go of the leg and humbly followed his mistress. She never slapped him! She must indeed be angry with him. With tail well down Timmy followed her into the bedroom and got under the bed at once. He poked his head out and looked beseechingly at George with big brown eyes.

'Oh, Timmy – I *had* to slap you!' said George, and she knelt down by the big dog and patted his head. 'You see, you might have spoilt everything if you'd been seen. As it is I'm sure you bit Block and I don't know how we're going to explain that! Lie quietly now, old fellow. I'm going out to join the others.'

Timmy's tail thumped softly on the floor. George ran out of the room and joined the others on the landing. They were having a fine game with Block, who was yelling and wriggling and struggling for all he was worth. He was wrapped up in the curtains like a caterpillar inside a cocoon. His head was completely covered and he could see nothing.

Suddenly Mr Lenoir appeared in the hall below, with a very scared Mrs Lenoir beside him. 'What's all this?' thundered Sooty's stepfather. 'Have you gone mad? How dare you behave like this at this time of night?'

'We've caught a robber and tied him up,' panted Sooty.

Mr Lenoir ran up the stairs two steps at a time, amazed. He saw the kicking figure on the ground well-tied up in the heavy curtains. 'A robber! Do you mean a burglar? Where did you find him?'

'He was hiding behind the curtains!' said Julian. 'We managed to get hold of him and tie him up before he could escape. Could you call the police?'

An anguished voice came from inside of the curtains.

BLOCK GETS A SURPRISE

'Let me go! I've been bitten! Let me go!'

'Good heavens! You've got Block tied up there!' said Mr Lenoir, in amazement and anger. 'Untie him, quickly.'

'But – it can't be Block. He was hiding behind those curtains at the window,' protested Sooty.

'Do as you're told,' commanded Mr Lenoir, getting angry. Anne looked at the tip of his nose. Yes, it was turning white, as usual!

The boys reluctantly undid the ropes. Block angrily parted the curtains that enfolded him, and looked out, his usually blank face crimson with rage and fright.

'I won't stand this sort of thing!' he raged. 'Look here, at my leg, sir! I've been bitten. Only a dog could have done that. See my leg?'

Sure enough there were the marks of teeth on his leg, slowly turning purple. Timmy had taken a good nip, and almost gone through the skin.

'There's no dog here,' said Mrs Lenoir, coming timidly up the stairs at last. 'You couldn't have been bitten by a dog, Block.'

'Who bit him, then?' demanded Mr Lenoir, turning fiercely on poor Mrs Lenoir.

'Do you think *I* could have bitten him, in my excitement?' suddenly said Sooty, to the enormous surprise of the others, and to their immense amusement. He spoke very seriously with a worried look on his face. 'When I lose my temper, I hardly know what I do. Do you think I bit him?'

'Pah!' said Mr Lenoir, in disgust. 'Don't talk nonsense, boy! I'll have you punished if I think you go about biting people. Get up, Block. You're not badly hurt.'

'My teeth do feel a bit funny, now I come to think of it,' said Sooty, opening and shutting his mouth as if to see if they were all right. 'I think I'd better go and clean them. I feel as if I've got the taste of Block's ankle in my mouth. And it isn't nice.'

Mr Lenoir, driven to fury by Sooty's impudence, reached out swiftly to box the boy's ears. But Sooty dodged and ran back up the passage. 'Just going to clean my teeth!' he called, and the others tried to keep from laughing. The idea of Sooty biting anyone was absurd. It was quite obvious, however, that neither Mr nor Mrs Lenoir guessed what had bitten Block.

'Go to bed, all of you,' ordered Mr Lenoir. 'I hope I shall not have to complain about you to your father tomorrow when he comes – or your uncle, as it may be. I don't know which of you are his children, and which not. I'm surprised at you making such a nuisance of yourselves in somebody else's house. Tying up my servant! If he leaves, it will be your fault!'

The children hoped fervently that Block would leave. It would be marvellous to have the deaf blank-faced fellow out of the house. He was on the watch for Timmy, they felt sure. He would snoop about till he got Timmy or one of them into trouble.

But Block was still there next morning. He came into the

schoolroom with the breakfast, his face almost as blank as usual. He gave Sooty an evil look.

'You look out for yourself,' he said, in a curiously soft voice. 'You look out. Something's going to happen to you one of these days. Yes – and that dog too! I know you've got a dog, see? You can't deceive *me*.'

The children said nothing, but looked at one another. Sooty grinned, and rapped out a cheerful little tune on the table with his spoon.

'Dark, dire, dreadful threats!' he said. 'You look out for yourself too, Block. Any more snooping about, and you'll find yourself tied up again – yes, and I might bite you again too. You never know. My teeth feel quite ready for it this morning.'

He bared his teeth at Block, who made no reply at all, but merely looked as if he had not heard a word. The man went out, and closed the door softly behind him.

'Nasty bit of work, isn't he?' said Sooty. But George felt rather alarmed. She feared Block. There was something cold and clever and bad about those narrow eyes of his. She longed with all her heart to get Timmy out of the house.

She got a terrible shock that morning! Sooty came to her, looking agitated. 'I say! What do you think? Your father's going to have *my* room. I've got to sleep with Julian and Dick. Block is taking all my things from my room to theirs this very minute, with Sarah. I hope we shall have a chance to get him out all right, before your father comes!'

109

'Oh Sooty!' said George, in despair. 'I'll go and see if I can get him at once.'

She went off, pretending to go to Marybelle's room for something. But Block was still in Sooty's room. And there he stayed, cleaning it all morning!

George was very worried about Timmy. He would wonder why she hadn't fetched him. He would miss his walk. She hovered about the passage all morning, getting into Sarah's way as she carried clothes from Sooty's old room to Julian's.

Block gave George some curious looks. He walked with a limp to show that his leg was bad from the bite. He left the room at last and George darted in. But Block returned almost at once and she dashed into Marybelle's room. Again Block left and went down the passage, and again the desperate little girl rushed into Sooty's room.

But Block was back before she could even open the cupboard door. 'What are you doing in this room?' he said, roughly. 'I haven't cleaned it all morning to have children in here messing it up again! Clear out of it!'

George went – and then once more waited for Block to go. He would have to see to the luncheon soon! He went at last. George rushed to the door of Sooty's room, eager to get poor Timmy.

But she couldn't open the door. It was locked – and Block had taken the key!

CHAPTER THIRTEEN

Poor George!

BY NOW George was in despair. She felt as if she was in a nightmare. She went to find Sooty. He was in Julian's room, next to hers, washing his hands ready for lunch.

'Sooty! I shall have to get into the secret passage the way you first took us in,' she said. 'Through that little study-room of your father's – you know, where the sliding panels are.'

'We can't,' said Sooty, looking rather alarmed. 'He uses it now, and he'd half-kill anyone who went in there. He's got the records of all his experiments there, and he's put them ready to show your father.'

'I don't care,' said George, desperately. 'I've got to get in there somehow. Timmy may starve!'

'Not Timmy! He'll live on the rats in the passages!' said Sooty. 'Timmy could always look after himself, I bet!'

'Well, he'd die of thirst then,' said George, obstinately. 'There's no water in those secret passages. You know that!'

George could hardly eat any lunch because she was so worried. She made up her mind somehow to get into that little study-room, and see if she could open the entrance into the wall behind the panels. Then she would slip in and get Timmy. She didn't care what happened; she was going to get Timmy.

'I shan't tell the others, though,' she thought. 'They would only try and stop me, or offer to do it themselves, and I don't trust anyone but myself to do this. Timmy's my dog, and *I'm* going to save him!'

After lunch, everyone went to Julian's room to discuss things. George went with them. But after a few minutes she left them. 'Back in a minute,' she said. They took no notice and went on discussing how to rescue Timmy. It really did seem as if the only way was to raid the study, and try and get into the secret passage without being seen.

'But my stepfather works there now,' said Sooty. 'And I shouldn't be surprised if he locks the door when he leaves the room.'

George didn't come back. After about ten minutes Anne grew puzzled.

'What can George be doing? It must be about ten minutes since she went.'

'Oh, she's probably gone to see if my old room is unlocked yet,' said Sooty, getting up. 'I'll peep out and see if she's about.'

She wasn't. She didn't seem to be anywhere! She wasn't in the passage that led to Sooty's old room; she couldn't be in that room because it was still locked, and she wasn't in Marybelle's room.

Sooty peeped in George's own room, the one she shared

with Anne. But that was empty too. He went downstairs and snooped around a bit. No George!

He went back to the others, puzzled.

'I can't find her anywhere,' he said. 'Where can she be?'

Anne looked alarmed. This was such a strange house, with strange happenings. She wished George would come.

'She's not gone into that little study-room, has she?' said Julian, suddenly. 'It would be just like George to try and get into the lion's den!'

'I didn't think of that,' said Sooty. 'Silly of me. I'll go and see.'

He went down the stairs. He made his way cautiously to his father's study. He stood quietly outside the shut door. There was no sound from inside. Was his father there or not?

Sooty debated whether to open the door and peep in or whether to knock. He decided to knock. Then, if his father answered he could rush back upstairs before the door could be opened, and his father would not know whom to scold for the interruption.

So he knocked, very smartly, rap-rap.

'Who's that?' came his stepfather's irritable voice. 'Come in! Am I to have no peace?'

Sooty fled upstairs at once. He went to the others. 'George can't be in the study,' he said. 'My stepfather's there, and he didn't sound in too good a temper either.'

'Then *where* can she be?' said Julian, looking worried. 'I do wish she wouldn't go off without telling us where she's going. She must be somewhere about. She wouldn't go very far from Timmy.'

They all had a good hunt over the house, even going into the kitchen. Block was there, reading a paper. 'What do you want?' he said. 'You won't get it, whatever it is.'

'We don't want anything from *you*,' said Sooty. 'How's your poor bad bitten leg?'

Block looked so unpleasantly at them that they all retreated from the kitchen in a hurry. Sooty put Julian and Dick on guard, and went up to the staff bedrooms to see if by any chance George had gone there. A silly idea, he knew, but George must be somewhere!

She wasn't there, of course. The children went back gloomily to Julian's room. 'This beastly house!' said Julian. 'I can't say I like it. Sorry to say so, Sooty, but it's a weird place with a funny feeling about it.'

Sooty was not hurt at all. 'Oh, I agree with you,' he said. 'I've always thought the same myself. So has Mother, and so has Marybelle. It's my stepfather that likes it.'

'Where *is* George?' said Anne. 'I keep on and on trying to think. There's only one place I'm certain she's not in – and that's your stepfather's study, Sooty. Even George wouldn't dare to go there while your stepfather was there.'

But Anne was wrong. The study was the very place where George was at that very moment!

The little girl had made up her mind that it was best to try and get in there, and wait for a chance to open the sliding panel. So she had slipped downstairs, gone across the hall, and tried the door of the study. It was locked.

'Blow!' said George, desperately. 'Everything is against me and Timmy. How can I get in? I must, I must!'

She slipped out of the side-door near the study and went into the little yard on to which the study-window looked. Could she get in there?

But the window was barred! So that was no good either. She went back again, wishing she could find the key to unlock the door. But it was nowhere to be seen.

Suddenly she heard Mr Lenoir's voice in the room across the hall. In a panic George lifted up the lid of a big wooden chest nearby, and climbed hurriedly into it. She closed the lid over her, and knelt there, waiting, heart beating fast.

Mr Lenoir came across the hall. He was going to his study. 'I shall get everything ready to show my visitor when he comes,' he called to his wife. 'Don't disturb me at all. I shall be very busy indeed.'

George heard the sound of a key being put into the study door. It turned. The door opened and shut with a click.

But it was not locked again from the inside. George knelt in the dark chest and considered matters. She meant to get into that study. She meant to get through the entrance into the secret passage, where Tim was. That passage led from the study to Sooty's old bedroom, and somewhere in that passage was Timmy.

What she was going to do once she had Timmy she didn't quite know. Perhaps Sooty would take him to someone who could look after him for her, someone on Castaway Hill.

She heard the sound of Mr Lenoir coughing. She heard the shuffling of papers. Then she heard the click of a cupboard being opened and shut. Mr Lenoir was evidently busy!

Then he gave an exclamation of annoyance. He said something in an irritable voice that sounded like 'Now where did I put that?'

Then the door opened very suddenly and Mr Lenoir came out. George had just time to close down the lid, which she had opened to let in fresh air. She knelt in the chest, trembling, as Mr Lenoir passed there and went on across the hall.

George suddenly knew that this was her chance. Mr Lenoir might be gone for a few minutes and give her time to open that panel in the wall! She lifted the lid of the chest, and jumped out quickly. She ran into the study, and went to the place where Sooty had pressed the panelling.

But before she could even run her fingers over the smooth brown oak, she heard returning footsteps! Mr Lenoir had hardly been half a minute. He was coming back at once.

In a panic poor George looked round for somewhere to hide. There was a large sofa against one wall. George crawled behind it, finding just room to crouch there without being seen. She was hardly there before Mr Lenoir entered the room, shut the door, and sat down at his desk. He switched on a big lamp over it, and bent to look at some documents.

George hardly dared to breathe. Her heart bumped against her ribs and seemed to make a terrible noise. It was very uncomfortable behind the sofa, but she did not dare to move.

She could not think what in the world to do. It would be terrible to be there for hours! What would the others think? They would soon be looking for her.

They were. Even at that moment Sooty was outside the study door, pondering whether to go in or to knock. He knocked smartly – rap-rap – and George almost jumped out of her skin!

She heard Mr Lenoir's impatient voice. 'Who's that? Come in! Am I to have no peace?'

There was no answer. No one came in. Mr Lenoir called again. 'Come in, I say!'

Still no answer. He strode to the door and flung it open angrily. No one was there. Sooty had fled upstairs at once.

'Those tiresome children, I suppose,' muttered Mr Lenoir. 'Well, if any of them comes and knocks again and goes away, I'll punish them properly. Bed and bread and water for them!'

He sounded fierce. George wished she was anywhere but in his study. What would he say if he knew she was only three or four feet away from him?

Mr Lenoir worked for about half an hour, and poor George got stiffer and stiffer, and more and more un-

118

POOR GEORGE!

comfortable. Then she heard Mr Lenoir yawn, and her heart felt lighter. Perhaps he would have a nap! That would be good luck. She might creep out then, and try to get into the secret passage.

Mr Lenoir yawned again. Then he pushed his papers aside and went to the sofa. He lay down on it and pulled the rug there over his knees. He settled himself down as if for a good sleep.

The sofa creaked under him. George tried to hold her breath again, afraid that now he was so near to her he would certainly hear her.

Soon a small snore came to her ears. Then another and another. Mr Lenoir was asleep! George waited for a few minutes. The snores went on, a little louder. Surely it would be safe now to creep from her hiding-place?

George began to move, very cautiously and quietly. She crept to the end of the sofa. She squeezed out from behind it. Still the snores went on.

She stood upright and went on tiptoe to the panel that had slid aside. She began to press here and there with her fingers, trying to find the spot that would move the panel to one side.

She couldn't seem to find it. She grew red with anxiety. She cast a glance at the sleeping Mr Lenoir, and worked feverishly at the panel. Where was the spot to press, oh, where was it?

Then a stern voice came from behind her, making her jump almost out of her skin.

'And what exactly do you think you are doing, my boy?
How dare you come into my study and mess about like
this?'

George turned round and faced Mr Lenoir. He always
thought she was a boy! She didn't know what to say. He
looked very angry indeed, and the tip of his nose was
already white.

POOR GEORGE!

George was frightened. She ran to the door, but Mr Lenoir caught her before she opened it. He shook her hard.

'What were you doing in my study? Was it you who knocked and ran away? Do you think it is funny to play tricks like that? I'll soon teach you that it isn't!'

He opened the door and called loudly. 'Block! Come here! Sarah, tell Block I want him.'

Block appeared from the kitchen, his face as blank as usual. Mr Lenoir wrote something down quickly on a piece of paper and gave it to him to read. Block nodded.

'I've told him to take you to your room, lock you in, and give you nothing but bread and water for the rest of the day,' said Mr Lenoir, fiercely. 'That will teach you to behave yourself in the future. Any more nonsense and I'll whip you myself.'

'My father won't be very pleased when he hears you're punishing me like this,' began George in a trembling voice. But Mr Lenoir sneered.

'Pah! Wait till he hears from me how you have misbehaved yourself, and I am sure he will agree with me. Now go, and you will not be allowed out of your room till tomorrow. I will make your excuses to your father, when he comes.'

Poor George was propelled upstairs by Block, who was only too delighted to be punishing one of the children. As she came to the door of the room George shouted to the others who were in Julian's room next door.

'Julian! Dick! Help me! Quick, help me!'

121

CHAPTER FOURTEEN

A very puzzling thing

JULIAN, DICK, and the others rushed out at once, just in time to see Block shove George roughly into her room and shut the door. There was a click as he locked it.

'Here! What are you doing?' cried Julian, indignantly.

Block took no notice, but turned to go. Julian caught hold of his arm, and yelled loudly in his ear. 'Unlock that door at once! Do you hear?'

Block gave no sign whether he had or not. He shook off Julian's hand, but the boy put it back again at once, getting angry.

'Mr Lenoir gave me orders to punish that girl,' said Block, looking at Julian out of his cold, narrow eyes.

'Well, you jolly well unlock that door,' commanded Julian, and he tried to snatch the key from Block. With sudden vicious strength the man lifted his hand and struck Julian, sending him half across the landing. Then he went swiftly downstairs to the kitchen.

Julian looked after him, a little scared. 'The brute!' he said. 'He's as strong as a horse. George, George, whatever's happened?'

George answered angrily from the locked bedroom. She told the others everything, and they listened in silence.

A VERY PUZZLING THING

'Bad luck, George,' said Dick. 'Poor old girl! Just as you were feeling for the opening to the passage too!'

'I must apologise for my stepfather,' said Sooty. 'He has such a terrible temper. He wouldn't have punished you like this if he had thought you were a girl. But he keeps thinking you're a boy.'

'I don't care,' said George. 'I don't care about any punishment. It's only that I'm so worried about Timmy. Well, I suppose I'll have to stay here now, till I'm let out tomorrow. I shan't eat anything that Block brings me, you can tell him. I don't want to see his horrid face again!'

'How shall I go to bed tonight?' wailed Anne. 'All my things are in your room, George.'

123

'You'll have to sleep with me,' said little Marybelle, who looked very frightened. 'I can lend you a nightie. Oh dear – what will George's father say when he comes? I hope he will say that George is to be set free at once.'

'Well, he won't,' said George, from behind the locked door. 'He'll just think I've been in one of my bad moods, and he won't mind my being punished at all. Oh dear – I wish Mother was coming too.'

The others were very upset about George, as well as about Timmy. Things seemed to be going very wrong indeed. At tea-time they went to the schoolroom to have tea, wishing they could take George some of the chocolate cake set ready for them.

George felt lonely when the others had gone to tea. It was five o'clock. She was hungry. She wanted Timmy. She was angry and miserable, and longed to escape. She went to the window and looked out.

Her room looked straight down the cliff-side, just as Sooty's old room did. Below was the city wall that ran round the town, going unevenly up and down as it followed the contours of the hillside.

George knew that she could not jump down to the wall. She might roll off it and fall straight down to the marsh below. That would be horrible. Then she suddenly remembered the rope-ladder that they used when they got down into the pit each day.

It had at first been kept in Marybelle's room, on the shelf in the cupboard, but since the children had been scared by knowing that someone had tried the handle of the door one morning, they had decided to keep the ladder in George's room for safety. They were afraid that perhaps Block might go snooping round Marybelle's room and find it. So George had smuggled it to her own room, and hidden it in her suitcase, which she had locked.

Now, her hands shaking a little with excitement, she unlocked her suitcase and took out the rope-ladder. She might perhaps escape out of the window with it. She looked out again, the rope in her hands.

But windows overlooked the city wall just there. The kitchen too must be just below, and maybe Block would see her climbing down. That would never do. She must wait till it was twilight.

When the others came back she told them what she was going to do, speaking in a low voice through the door.

'I'll get down on the wall, walk along it for some way, and then jump down and creep back,' she said. 'You get some food for me somehow, and I'll have it. Then tonight, when everyone has gone to bed I'll get into the study again and find the way through to the secret passage. Sooty can help me. Then I can get Timmy.'

'Right,' said Sooty. 'Wait till it's fairly dark before you go down the ladder, though. Block has gone to his room with a bad headache, but Sarah and Harriet are in the kitchen, and you don't want to be seen.'

So, when the twilight hung like a soft purple curtain over the house, George slid down the rope-ladder out of the window. She only needed to let about a quarter of it out for it was far too long for such a short distance.

She fastened it to the legs of her heavy little oak bed. Then she climbed out of the window and slid quietly down the rope-ladder.

She passed the kitchen window, which fortunately had its blinds drawn down now. She landed squarely on the old wall. She had brought a torch with her so that she could see.

She debated with herself what to do. She did not want to run any risk of coming up against either Block or Mr Lenoir. Perhaps it would be best to walk along the wall till she came to some part of the town she knew. Then she could jump off and make her way cautiously back up the hill, looking out for the others.

So she began to walk along the broad top of the old wall. It was very rough and uneven in places, and many stones were missing. But her torch showed a steady light and she did not miss her footing.

The wall ran round some stables, then round the backs of some quaint old shops. Then it ran round a big yard belonging to some house, and then round the house itself. Then down it went, around some more houses.

George could look into those windows that were not curtained. Lights shone out from them now. It was strange being able to see into the windows without being seen. A little family sat at a meal in one room, their faces cheerful and happy. An old man sat alone in another, reading and smoking.

A VERY PUZZLING THING

A woman sat listening to a radio, knitting, as George silently walked on the wall outside her window. Nobody heard her. Nobody saw her.

Then she came to another house, a big one. The wall ran close against it, for it was built where the cliff ran steeply down to the marsh just there.

There was a lit window there. George glanced in as she passed. Then she stood still in great surprise.

Surely, surely that was Block in there! He had his back to her, but she could have sworn it was Block. The same head, the same ears, the same shoulders!

Who was he talking to? George tried to see – and all at once she knew. He was talking to Mr Barling, whom everyone said was a smuggler – *the* smuggler of Castaway Hill!

But wait a minute – could it be Block? Block was deaf, and this man evidently wasn't. He was listening to Mr Barling, that was plain, and was answering him, though George could not hear the words, of course.

'I oughtn't to be snooping like this,' said George to herself. 'But it's very strange, very puzzling and very interesting. If only the man would turn round I'd know at once if it was Block!'

But he didn't turn. He just sat in his chair, his back to George. Mr Barling, his long face lit up by the nearby lamp, was talking animatedly, and Block, if it *was* Block, was listening intently and nodding his head in agreement every now and again.

George felt puzzled. If she only knew for certain that it

was Block! But why should he be talking to Mr Barling – and wasn't he stone deaf after all then?

George jumped down from the wall into a dark little passage and made her way through the town, up to Smuggler's Top. Outside the front door, hiding in the shadows was Sooty. He laid his hand on George's arm, making her jump.

'Come on in. I've left the side door open. We've got a fine spread for you!'

A VERY PUZZLING THING

The two slipped in at the side door, tiptoed past the study, across the hall, and up to Julian's bedroom. Truly there was a spread there!

'I went and raided the larder,' said Sooty, with satisfaction. 'Harriet was out, and Sarah had run along to the post. Block has gone to bed for a rest, because, he said, he had such an awful headache.'

'Oh,' said George, 'then it couldn't have been Block I saw. And yet I'm as certain as certain can be that it was!'

'Whatever do you mean?' asked the others, in surprise. George sat down on the floor and began to gobble up cakes and tarts, for she was terribly hungry. Between her mouthfuls she told them how she had got out of the window, walked along the city wall, and found herself unexpectedly by Mr Barling's house.

'And I looked into a lit window there, and saw Block talking to Mr Barling – and listening to him and answering him!' she said.

The others could not believe this. 'Did you see his face?' asked Julian.

'No,' said George. 'But I'm *certain* it was Block. Go and peep into his room and see if he's there, Sooty. He wouldn't be back yet from Mr Barling's, because he had a glass full of something or other, which would take him some time to drink. Go and peep.'

Sooty vanished. He came back quickly. 'He's in bed!' he said. 'I could see the shape of his body and the dark patch of his head. Are there *two* Blocks then? Whatever does this mean?'

CHAPTER FIFTEEN

Strange happenings

IT CERTAINLY was very puzzling – most of all to George, who felt so certain it had been Block talking to the well-known smuggler. The others did not feel so certain, especially as George admitted that she had not seen his face.

'Is my father here yet?' asked George, suddenly, remembering that he was supposed to come that evening.

'Yes. Just arrived,' said Sooty. 'Just before you came. I nearly got run over by the car! Just hopped aside in time. I was out there waiting for you.'

'What are our plans?' asked George. 'I'll have to get Timmy tonight, or he'll be frantic. I think I'd better go and climb back through my window again now, in case Block comes along and finds I've disappeared. I'll wait till everyone is in bed and then I'll slip out of the window again, and you must let me into the house, Sooty, please. Then I'll go to the study with you and you must open the secret way for me. Then I'll find Timmy and everything will be all right.'

'I don't see that everything will be all right,' said Sooty, doubtfully. 'But anyway, your plan is the only one to follow. You'd better get back into your room now, if you've had enough to eat.'

'I'll take a few buns back with me,' said George, stuffing

them into her pocket. 'Sooty, come and knock at my door when everyone is in bed and I'll know then that it's safe for me to slip out of the window, and come into the house again.'

It wasn't long before George was back in her room once more – just in time too, for Block appeared a little while after with a plate of dry bread and a glass of water. He unlocked the door and put them on the table.

'Your supper,' he said. George looked at his blank face and disliked it so much that she felt she must do something about it. So she took up the water and threw it deftly at the back of his head. It dripped down his neck and made him jump. Block took a step towards her, his eyes gleaming – but Julian and Dick were by the door, and he did not dare to strike her.

'I'll pay you back for that,' he said. 'See? You will never get that dog of yours back again!'

He went out and locked the door. Julian called through as soon as he had gone.

'What did you do that for, you idiot? He's a bad enemy to make.'

'I know. I just couldn't help it somehow,' said George, forlornly. 'I wish I hadn't now.'

The others had to go down to see Mr Lenoir. They left George feeling lonely. It was horrid to be locked up like this, even though she could escape through the window whenever she wanted to. She listened for the others to come back.

They soon did, and reported their meeting with George's father.

'Uncle Quentin is awfully tired and a bit cross, and frightfully annoyed with you for misbehaving,' said Julian, through the door. 'He said you were to be locked up the whole of tomorrow too, if you don't apologise.'

George didn't mean to apologise. She couldn't bear Mr Lenoir, with his false smiles and laughter, and his sudden odd rages. She said nothing.

'We've got to go and have our supper now,' said Sooty. 'We'll save you some of it as soon as Block goes out of the room. Look out for a knocking on your door tonight. It'll be me, telling you everyone's in bed.'

George lay on her bed, thinking. Many things puzzled

her. She couldn't get them straight somehow. The signaller in the tower – the peculiar man, Block – Mr Barling's talk to a man who looked so like Block; but Block was all the time in his bed at home. As she lay thinking, her eyes closed, and she fell asleep.

Anne went up to bed with Marybelle, and came to whisper goodnight to her. The boys all went into the next room, for Sooty was now to share Julian's and Dick's bedroom. George woke up enough to say goodnight and then slept again.

At midnight she awoke with a jump. Someone was knocking softly and impatiently on her door. It was Sooty.

'Coming!' whispered George through the door, and took up her torch. She went to the window and was soon safely down the rope-ladder. She jumped down from the wall, and went to the side door of the house. Sooty was there. She slipped in thankfully.

'Everyone's gone to bed,' whispered Sooty. 'I thought your father and my stepfather were never going. They stayed talking in the study for ages!'

'Come on. Let's go there,' said George, impatiently. They went to the study door, and Sooty turned the handle.

It was locked again! He pushed hard, but it wasn't a bit of good. It was well and truly locked!

'We might have thought of that,' said George, in despair. 'Blow, blow, blow! What are we to do now?'

Sooty thought for a few moments. Then he spoke in a low voice, in George's ear.

'There's only one thing left to do, George. I must creep into your father's room – my old bedroom – when he is asleep – and I must get into the cupboard there, open the entrance to the secret passage, and slip in that way. I'll find Timmy and bring him back the same way, hoping that your father won't wake!'

'Oh! Would you really do that for me?' said George gratefully. 'You *are* a good friend, Sooty! Would you rather I did it?'

'No. I know the way up and down that passage better than you do,' said Sooty. 'It's a bit frightening to be all alone there at midnight too. I'll go.'

George went with Sooty up the stairs, across the wide landing, to the door at the end of the passage that led to Sooty's old room, where George's father was now sleeping. When they got there, George pulled his arm.

'Sooty! The buzzer will go as soon as you open the door – and it will wake my father and warn him.'

'Idiot! I disconnected it as soon as I knew my room was to be changed,' said Sooty, scornfully. 'As if I wouldn't think of that!'

He opened the door that led into the passage. He crept up to his old room. The door was shut. He and George listened intently.

'Your father sounds a bit restless,' said Sooty. 'I'll wait my chance to creep in, George, and then, as soon as possible, I'll slip into the cupboard and open the secret passage to find Tim. As soon as I've got Timmy I'll bring him along to you. You could wait in Marybelle's room if you liked. Anne's there too.'

George crept into the room next door, where Anne and Marybelle lay fast asleep. She left the door open, so that she might hear when Sooty returned. How lovely it would be to have dear old Timmy again! He would lick her and lick her.

Sooty crept into the room where George's father lay, half-asleep. He made no sound. He knew every creaking board and avoided them. He made his way quietly to a big chair, meaning to hide behind it till he was certain George's father was sound asleep.

For some time the man in the bed tossed and turned. He was tired with his long journey, and his mind was excited with his talk with Mr Lenoir. He muttered now and again, and Sooty began to feel he would never be sound asleep! He grew sleepy himself, and yawned silently.

At last George's father grew quiet and peaceful. No more creaks came from the bed. Sooty cautiously moved out from behind the chair.

Then suddenly something startled him. He heard a sound over by the window! But what could it be? It was a very small sound, like a tiny creak of a door.

The night was rather dark, but the window, its curtains pulled right back, could easily be seen as a square of grey. Sooty fixed his eyes on it. Was someone opening the window?

No. The window did not move. But something strange was happening under it, near the sill.

A big window-seat was built in under the window, wide and comfortable. Sooty knew it well! He had sat on it hundreds of times to look out of the window. Now, what was happening to it?

It looked as if the top, or lid, of the seat was slowly moving upwards, bit by bit. Sooty was puzzled. He had never known it could be opened like that. It had always been screwed down, and he had thought it was just a seat and nothing else. But now it looked as if someone had unscrewed the top, and had hidden himself inside, lifting up the top like a lid when he thought it was safe.

Sooty stared at the upward-moving lid, quite fascinated. Who was in there? Why had he hidden? It was rather frightening, seeing the lid move slowly, bit by bit.

At last the lid was wide open and rested against the window-pane. A big figure cautiously and slowly got out, not making the slightest sound. Sooty felt his hair rising up on his head. He was afraid, terribly afraid. He could not utter a sound.

The figure tiptoed over to the bed. He made a quick and sudden movement, and there was a stifled sound from George's father. Sooty guessed he had been gagged, so that he could not cry out. Still the boy could not move or speak. He had never been so scared in all his life.

The intruder lifted the limp body from the bed, and went to the window-seat. He put George's father into the darkness there. What he had done to make him unable to struggle Sooty didn't know. He only knew that poor

STRANGE HAPPENINGS

George's father was being put down in the window-seat, and couldn't seem to move a hand to help himself!

The boy suddenly found his voice. 'Hi!' he yelled. 'Hi! What are you doing? Who are you?'

He remembered his torch and switched it on. He saw a face he knew, and cried out in surprise. 'Mr Barling!'

Then someone hit him a hard blow on the head and he remembered nothing more at all. He did not know that he was lifted into the window-seat too. He did not know that the intruder followed after him. He knew nothing.

George, awake in the next room, suddenly heard Sooty's voice crying out. 'Hi!' she heard. 'Hi! What are you doing? Who are you?' And then, as she slipped off the couch, she heard the next cry. 'Mr Barling!'

George was extremely startled. What was going on next door? She fumbled about for her torch. Anne and Mary-belle were still asleep. George could not find her torch. She fell over a chair and banged her head.

When at last she had found her torch she tiptoed, trembling, to the door. She shone her torch and saw that the door next to hers was a little ajar, just as Sooty had left it, when he had crept inside. She listened. There was absolutely no sound at all now. She had heard a small bumping noise after Sooty's last cry, but she didn't know what it was.

She suddenly put her head round the door of her father's room, and shone her torch again. She stared in surprise. The bed was empty. The room was empty. There was no one there at all! She flashed her torch all round. She opened the cupboard door fearfully. She looked under the bed. She was, in fact, extremely brave.

At last she sank down on the window-seat, frightened and puzzled. Where was her father? Where was Sooty? Whatever had been happening here that night?

CHAPTER SIXTEEN

Next morning

AS GEORGE sat by the window, on the very seat into which everyone had unaccountably disappeared, though she did not know it, she heard a faint sound from the passage.

Quick as lightning the girl slipped under the bed. Someone was creeping down the long passage! George lay silently on the floor, lifting the valance a little to try and see who it was. What strange things were going on tonight!

Someone came in at the door. Someone stopped there, as if to look and listen. Then someone crept over to the window-seat.

George watched and listened, straining her eyes in the darkness. She dimly saw the someone outlined against the grey square of the window. He was bent over the window-seat.

He showed no light at all. But he made some curious little sounds. First came the sound of his fingers tapping about on the closed lid of the seat. Then came the clink of something metallic, and a very faint squeaking. George could not imagine what the man – if it was a man – was doing.

For about five minutes the somone worked away at his

task in the darkness. Then, as quietly as he had come, he
went away. George couldn't help thinking it was Block,
though his outline against the dark-grey of the window
was too dim to recognise. But he had once given a little

cough exactly like Block so often gave. It *must* be Block! But whatever was he doing in her father's room at night, on the window-seat?

George felt as if she was in a bad dream. The strangest things happened and kept on happening, and they didn't seem to make sense at all. Where was her father? Had he left his room and gone wandering over the house? Where was Sooty, and why had he called out? He wouldn't have shouted out like that, surely, if her father had been asleep in the room!

George lay under the bed, shivering, for a little while longer. Then she rolled out softly and went out of the door. She crept down the long passage to the end. She opened the door there and peeped out. The whole house was in darkness. Little sounds came to George's ears – a window rattling faintly, the creak of some bit of furniture – but nothing else.

She had only one thought in her mind, and that was to get to the boys' room and tell them the mysterious things that had happened. Soon she was across the landing, and had slipped through the door of Julian's bedroom. He and Dick were awake, of course, waiting for Sooty to come with Timmy and George.

But only George arrived. A scared George, with a very very curious story to tell. She wrapped herself in the eiderdown on Julian's bed, and told what had happened, in whispers.

They were amazed. Uncle Quentin gone! Sooty disappeared! Someone creeping into the room and fiddling about on the window-seat! What did it all mean?

'We'll come to Uncle Quentin's room with you, straight away now,' said Julian, pulling on a dressing-gown, and hunting about for his slippers. 'I've got a feeling that things are getting pretty serious.'

They all padded off to the other rooms. They went into Marybelle's room and woke her and Anne. Both little girls felt scared. Soon all five children were in the next room, from which George's father and Sooty had so strangely vanished.

Julian shut the door, drew the curtains and switched on the light. At once they all felt better. It was so horrid to grope about in the dark with torches.

They looked round the silent room. There was nothing there to show them how the others had disappeared. The bed was crumpled and empty. On the floor lay Sooty's torch, where it had fallen.

George repeated again what she had thought she had heard Sooty call out, but it made no sense to anyone. 'Why call out Mr Barling's name, when there was only your father in the room?' said Julian. 'Surely Mr Barling wasn't hiding here – that would be nonsense. He has nothing to do with your father, George.'

'I know. But I'm sure it *was* Mr Barling's name that I heard Sooty call out,' said George. 'Do you think – oh yes, do you think Mr Barling could possibly have crept through the secret opening in the cupboard, meaning to do some dirty work or other – and have gone back the same way, taking the others with him because they discovered him?'

This seemed a likely explanation, though not a very good one. They all went to the cupboard and opened it. They groped between the clothes for the secret opening. But the little iron handle set there to pull on the stone at the back was gone! Someone had removed it – and now the secret passage could not be entered, for there was no way of opening it just there!

'Look at that!' said Julian in astonishment. 'Someone's been tampering with that too. No, George, the midnight visitor, whoever he was, didn't go back that way.'

George looked pale. She had been hoping to go and fetch Timmy, by slipping through the secret opening in the cupboard. Now she couldn't. She longed for Timmy with all her heart, and felt that if only the big faithful dog were with her things would seem much brighter.

'I'm sure Mr Lenoir is at the bottom of all this!' said Dick. 'And Block too. I bet that *was* Block you saw in here tonight, doing something in the dark, George. I bet he and Mr Lenoir are hand in glove with each other over something.'

'Well, then – we can't possibly go and tell them what has happened!' said Julian. 'If they are at the bottom of all these weird happenings it would be foolish to go and tell them what we know. And we can't tell your mother, Marybelle, because she would naturally go to your father

143

about it. It's a puzzle to know what to do!'

Anne began to cry. Marybelle, frightened and puzzled, at once began to sob too. George felt tears pricking the backs of her eyelids, but she blinked them away. George never cried!

'I want Sooty,' wept Marybelle, who adored her cheeky, daring brother. 'Where's he gone? I'm sure he's in danger. I do want Sooty.'

'We'll rescue him tomorrow, don't you worry,' said Julian, kindly. 'We can't do anything tonight, though. There's nobody at Smuggler's Top we can possibly get advice or help from, as things are. I vote we go to bed, sleep on it, and make plans in the morning. By that time Sooty and Uncle Quentin may have turned up again. If they haven't, Mr Lenoir will have to be told by someone, and we'll see how he behaves! If he's surprised and upset, we'll soon know if he has had anything to do with this mystery or not. He'll have to do something – go to the police, or have the house turned upside down to find the missing people. We'll soon see what happens.'

Everyone felt a little comforted after this long speech. Julian sounded cheerful and firm, though he didn't feel at all happy, really. He knew, better than any of the others, that something very strange, and probably dangerous, was going on at Smuggler's Top. He wished the girls were not there.

'Now listen,' he said. 'George, you go and sleep with Anne and Marybelle next door. Lock your door and keep the light on. Dick and I will sleep here, in Sooty's old room, also with the light on, so you'll know we are quite nearby.'

It was comforting to know that the two boys were so near. The three girls went at last into Marybelle's room, tired out. Anne and Marybelle got into bed again, and George lay down again on the small but comfortable couch, pulling a thick rug over her. In spite of all the worry and excitement the girls were soon asleep, quite exhausted.

The boys talked a little, as they lay in Sooty's old bed, where their Uncle Quentin had been asleep some time before. Julian did not think anything more would happen that night. He and Dick fell asleep, but Julian was ready to wake at the slightest noise.

Next morning they were awakened by a most surprised Sarah, who had come in to draw the curtains and bring George's father a pot of early-morning tea. She could not believe her eyes when she saw the two boys in the visitor's bed – and no visitor!

'What's all this?' said Sarah, gaping. 'Where's your uncle? Why are you here?'

'Oh, we'll explain later,' said Julian, who did not want to enter into any details with Sarah, who was a bit of a chatterbox. 'You can leave the tea, Sarah. *We'd* like it!'

'Yes, but where's your uncle? Is he in *your* room?' said the puzzled Sarah. 'What's up?'

'You can go and look in our room if you like and see if he's there,' said Dick, wanting to get rid of the amazed woman. She disappeared, thinking that the household must be going mad. She left the hot tea behind, though, and the boys at once took it into the girls' room. George unlocked the door for them. They took it in turns to sip the hot tea from the one cup.

Presently Sarah came back, with Harriet and Block. Block's face was as blank as usual.

'There's nobody in your room, Julian,' began Sarah. Then Block gave a sudden exclamation and stared at George angrily. He had thought she was locked in her room – and here she was in Marybelle's room, drinking tea!

'How did you get out?' he demanded. 'I'll tell Mr Lenoir. You're in disgrace.'

'Shut up,' said Julian. 'Don't you dare to speak to my cousin like that. I believe you're mixed up in this curious business. Clear out, Block.'

Whether Block heard or not, he gave no sign of going. Julian got up, his face set.

'Clear out of this room,' he said, narrowing his eyes. 'Do you hear? I have a feeling that the police might be interested in you, Block. Now clear out!'

Harriet and Sarah gave little shrieks. The sudden mystery was too much for them. They gazed at Block and began to back out of the room. Fortunately Block went too, casting an evil look at the determined Julian.

'I shall go to Mr Lenoir,' said Block, and disappeared.

146

In a few minutes along came Mr and Mrs Lenoir to Marybelle's room. Mrs Lenoir looked scared out of her life. Mr Lenoir looked puzzled and upset.

'Now, what's all this?' he began. 'Block has been to me with a most curious tale. Says your father has disappeared, George, and . . .'

'And so has Sooty,' suddenly wailed Marybelle, burst-

147

ing into tears again. 'Sooty's gone. He's gone too.'

Mrs Lenoir gave a cry. 'What do you mean? How can he have gone? Marybelle, what do you mean?'

'Marybelle, I think I had better take charge of the telling,' said Julian, who was not going to let the little girl give away all the things they knew. After all, Mr Lenoir was probably at the bottom of everything, and it would be foolish to tell him what they suspected about him.

'Julian – tell me what has happened. Quickly!' begged Mrs Lenoir, looking really upset.

'Uncle Quentin disappeared from his bed last night, and Sooty has vanished too,' said Julian, shortly. 'They may turn up, of course.'

'Julian! You are keeping back something,' said Mr Lenoir, suddenly, watching the boy sharply. 'You will tell us *everything*, please. How dare you keep anything back at a moment like this?'

'Tell him, Julian, tell him,' wailed Marybelle. Julian looked obstinate, and glared at Marybelle.

The tip of Mr Lenoir's nose went white. 'I am going to the police,' he said. 'Perhaps you will talk to *them*, my boy. They will knock some sense into you!'

Julian was surprised. 'Why – I shouldn't have thought *you* would want to go to the police!' he blurted out. 'You've got too many secrets to hide!'

CHAPTER SEVENTEEN

More and more puzzling

MR LENOIR stared in the utmost amazement at Julian. There was a dead silence after this remark. Julian could have kicked himself for making it, but he couldn't unsay it now.

Mr Lenoir opened his mouth to say something at last, when footsteps came to the door. It was Block.

'Come in, Block!' said Mr Lenoir. 'There seem to have been peculiar happenings here.'

Block did not appear to hear, and remained outside the door. Mr Lenoir beckoned him in impatiently.

'No,' said Julian, firmly. 'What we have to say is not to be said in front of Block, Mr Lenoir. We don't like him and we don't trust him.'

'What do you mean?' cried Mr Lenoir, angrily. 'What do *you* know about my servants? I've known Block for years before he came into my service, and he's a most trustworthy fellow. He can't help being deaf, and that makes him irritable at times.'

Julian remained obstinate. He caught an angry gleam in Block's cold eyes, and glared back.

'Well, this is incredible!' said Mr Lenoir, trying not to lose his temper. 'I can't think what's come over everybody

– disappearing like this – and now you children talking to me as if I wasn't master in my own house. I insist that you tell me all you know.'

'I'd rather tell it to the police,' said Julian, his eye on Block. But Block showed no trace of expression on his face.

'Go away, Block,' said Mr Lenoir at last, seeing that there was no hope of getting anything out of Julian while the servant was there. 'You'd better all come down to my study. This is getting more and more mysterious. If the police have got to know, you may as well tell me first. I don't want to look a complete idiot in my own house in front of them.'

Julian couldn't help feeling a bit puzzled. Mr Lenoir was not behaving as he had thought he might behave. He seemed sincerely puzzled and upset, and he was evidently planning to get the police in himself. Surely he wouldn't do that if he had had a hand in the disappearances? Julian was lost in bewilderment again.

Mrs Lenoir was now crying quietly, with Marybelle sobbing beside her. Mr Lenoir put an arm round his wife and kissed Marybelle, suddenly appearing very much nicer than he had ever seemed before. 'Don't worry,' he said, in a gentle voice. 'We'll soon get to the bottom of this, if I have to get the whole of the police force in. I think I know who's at the bottom of it all!'

That surprised Julian even more. He and the others followed Mr Lenoir down to his study. It was still locked.

MORE AND MORE PUZZLING

Mr Lenoir opened it and pushed aside a great pile of papers that were on his desk.

'Now – what do you know?' he said to Julian quietly. The children noticed that the top of his nose was no longer white. Evidently he had got over his burst of temper.

'Well, I think this is a strange house, with a lot of strange things happening in it,' said Julian, not quite knowing how to begin. 'I'm afraid, you won't like me telling the police all I know.'

'Julian, don't speak in riddles!' said Mr Lenoir, impatiently. 'You act as if I were a criminal, in fear of the police. I'm not. What goes on in this house?'

'Well – the signalling from the tower, for instance,' said Julian, watching Mr Lenoir's face.

Mr Lenoir gaped. It was clear that he was immensely astonished. He stared at Julian, and Mrs Lenoir cried out suddenly: 'Signalling! What signalling?'

Julian explained. He told how Sooty had discovered the light-flashing first, and then how he and Dick had gone with him to the tower when they had seen the flashing again. He described the line of tiny, pricking lights across the marsh from the seaward side.

Mr Lenoir listened intently. He asked questions about dates and times. He heard how the boys had followed the signaller to Block's room, where he had disappeared.

'Got out of the window, I suppose,' said Mr Lenoir. 'Block's got nothing to do with this, you can rest assured of that. He is most faithful and loyal, and has been a great help to me while he has been here. I have an idea that Mr Barling is at the bottom of all this. He can't signal from his house to the sea because it's not quite high enough up the hill, and is in the wrong position. He must have been using *my* tower to signal from – coming himself to do it too! He knows all the secret ways of this house, better than I do! It would be easy for him to come here whenever he wanted to.'

The children thought at once that probably Mr Barling *had* been the signaller! They stared at Mr Lenoir. They were all beginning to think that he really and truly had nothing to do with the strange goings-on after all.

'I don't see why Block shouldn't know all this,' said Mr Lenoir, getting up. 'It's plain to me that Barling could explain a lot of the odd things that have been happening. I'll see if Block has ever suspected anything.'

Julian pursed his lips together. If Mr Lenoir was going to tell everything to Block, who certainly must be in the plot somehow, he wasn't going to tell him anything more!

'I'll see what Block thinks about everything, and then if we can't solve this mystery ourselves, we'll get in the police,' said Mr Lenoir, going out of the room.

Julian did not want to say anything much in front of Mrs Lenoir. So he changed the subject completely.

'What about breakfast?' he said. 'I'm feeling hungry!'

So they all went to have breakfast, though Marybelle could eat nothing at all, because she kept thinking of poor Sooty.

MORE AND MORE PUZZLING

'I think,' said Julian, when they were alone at the table, 'I rather think we'll do a little mystery-solving ourselves. I'd like a jolly good look round that room of your father's, George, to begin with. There must be some other way of getting out of there, besides the secret passage we know.'

'What do you think happened there last night?' said Dick.

'Well, I imagine that Sooty went there and hid, to wait until it was safe to try and get into the secret passage as soon as Uncle Quentin was asleep,' said Julian, thoughtfully. 'And while he was hiding, someone came into that room from somewhere, to kidnap Uncle Quentin. Why, I don't know, but that's what I think. Then Sooty yelled out in surprise, and got knocked on the head or something. Then he and Uncle Quentin were kidnapped together, and taken off through some secret way we don't know.'

'Yes,' said George. 'And it was Mr Barling who kidnapped them! I distinctly heard Sooty yell out "Mr Barling". He must have switched on his torch and seen him.'

'They are quite probably hidden somewhere in Mr Barling's house,' said Anne, suddenly.

'Yes!' said Julian. 'Why didn't I think of that? Why, that's just where they would be, of course. I've a jolly good mind to go down and have a look!'

'Oh, let me come too,' begged George.

'No,' said Julian. 'Certainly not. This is rather a dangerous adventure, and Mr Barling is a bad and

153

dangerous man. You and Marybelle are certainly not to come. I'll take Dick.'

'You are absolutely *mean*!' began George, her eyes flashing. 'Aren't I as good as a boy? I'm going to come.'

'Well, if you're as good as a boy, which I admit you are,' said Julian, 'can't you stay and keep an eye on Anne and Marybelle for us? We don't want them kidnapped too.'

'Oh, don't go, George,' said Anne. 'Stay here with us.'

'I think it's mad to go, anyhow,' said George. 'Mr Barling wouldn't let you in. And if you did get in you wouldn't be able to find all the secret places in his house. There must be as many, and more, as there are here.'

Julian couldn't help thinking George was right. Still, it was worth trying.

He and Dick set out after breakfast, and went down the hill to Mr Barling's. But when they got there they found the whole house shut up. Nobody answered their knocking and ringing. The curtains were drawn across the closed windows, and no smoke came from the chimney.

'Mr Barling's gone away for a holiday,' said the gardener who was working in the next door flower-beds. 'Went this morning, he did. In his car. All his servants have got a holiday too.'

'Oh!' said Julian, blankly. 'Was there anyone with him in the car – a man and a boy, for instance?'

The gardener looked surprised at this question, and shook his head.

'No. He was alone, and drove off himself.'

'Thanks,' said Julian, and walked back with Dick to Smuggler's Top. This was most odd. Mr Barling had shut up the house and gone off without his captives! Then what had he done with them? And why on earth had he kidnapped Uncle Quentin? Julian remembered that Mr Lenoir had not put forward any reason for that. Did he know one, and hadn't wanted to say what it was? It was all most puzzling.

Meantime George had been doing a little snooping round on her own. She had slipped into Uncle Quentin's

155

room, and had had a really good look round everywhere to see if by chance there was another secret passage Sooty hadn't known about.

She had tapped the walls. She had turned back the carpet and examined every inch of the floor. She had tried the cupboard again, and wished she could get through into the secret passage there and find Timmy. The study door downstairs was again locked, and she did not dare to tell Mr Lenoir about Timmy and ask his help.

George was just about to leave the quiet room when she noticed something on the floor near the window. She bent to pick it up. It was a small screw. She looked round. Where had it come from?

At first she couldn't see any screws of the same size at all. Then her eyes slid down to the window-seat. There were screws there, screwing down the top oaken plank to the under ones that supported it.

Had the screw come out of the window-seat? Why should it, anyway? The others there were all screwed down tightly. She examined one. Then she gave a low cry.

'One's missing. The one in the middle of this side. Now just let me think.'

She remembered last night. She remembered how someone had crept in, while she had hidden under the bed, and had fiddled about by the window, bending over the polished window-seat. She remembered the little noises – the metallic clinks and the tiny squeaks. It was screws being screwed into the seat!

'Someone screwed down the window-seat last night –
and in the darkness, dropped one of the little screws,'
thought George, beginning to feel excited. 'Why did he
screw it down? To hide something? What's in this window-
seat? It sounds hollow enough. It never lifted up. I know
that. It was always screwed down, because I remember
looking for a cupboard under it, like the one we have at
home, and there wasn't one.'

George began to feel certain there was some secret
about the window-seat. She rushed off to get a screwdriver. She found one and hurried back.

She shut the door and locked it behind her in case Block
should come snooping around. Then she set to work with
the screwdriver. What would she find in the window-seat?
She could hardly wait to see!

CHAPTER EIGHTEEN

Curious discoveries

JUST AS she had unscrewed almost the last screw there came a tapping at the door. George jumped and stiffened. She did not answer, afraid that it was Block, or Mr Lenoir.

Then, to her great relief, she heard Julian's voice. 'George! Are you in here?'

The little girl hurried across to the door and unlocked it. The boys came in, looking surprised, followed by Anne and Marybelle. George shut the door and locked it again.

'Mr Barling's gone away and shut up the house,' said Julian. 'So that's that. What on earth are you doing, George?'

'Unscrewing this window-seat,' said George, and told them about the screw she had found on the floor. They all crowded round her, excited.

'Good for you, George!' said Dick. 'Here, let me finish the unscrewing.'

'No, thanks. This is *my* job!' said George. She took out the last screw. Then she lifted the edge of the window-seat. It came up like a lid.

Everyone peered inside, rather scared. What would they see? To their great surprise and disappointment they saw nothing but an empty cupboard! It was as if the window-seat was a box, with the lid screwed down for people to sit on.

'Well – what a disappointment!' said Dick. He shut down the lid. 'I don't expect you heard anyone screwing down the lid, really, George. It might have been your imagination.'

'Well, it wasn't,' said George, shortly. She opened the lid again. She got right into the box-like window-seat and stamped, and pressed with her feet.

And quite suddenly, there came a small creaking noise, and the bottom of the empty window-seat fell downwards like a trap-door on a hinge!

George gasped and clutched at the side. She kicked about in air for a moment and then scrambled out. Everyone looked down in silence.

They looked down a straight yawning hole, which, however, came to an end only about eight feet down. There it appeared to widen out, and, no doubt, entered a secret passage which ran into one of the underground tunnels with which the whole hill was honeycombed. It might even run to Mr Barling's house.

'Look at that!' said Dick. 'Who would have thought of that? I bet even old Sooty didn't know about this.'

'Shall we go down?' said George. 'Shall we see where it goes to? We might find old Timmy.'

There came the noise of someone trying the handle of the door. It was locked. Then there was an impatient rapping, and a cross voice called out sharply:

'Why is this door locked? Open it at once! What are you doing in there?'

'It's Father!' whispered Marybelle, with wide eyes. 'I'd better unlock the door.'

George shut the lid of the window-seat down at once, quietly. She did not want Mr Lenoir to see their latest discovery. When the door was opened Mr Lenoir saw the children standing about, or sitting on the window-seat.

'I've had a good talk to Block,' he said, 'and, as I thought, he doesn't know a thing about all the goings-on here. He was most amazed to hear about the signalling from the tower. But he doesn't think it's Mr Barling. He thinks it may be a plot of some sort against *me*.'

'Oh!' said the children, who felt that *they* would not believe Block so readily as Mr Lenoir appeared to.

'It's quite upset Block,' said Mr Lenoir. 'He feels really sick, and I've told him to go and have a rest till we decide what to do next.'

The children felt that Block would not be so easily upset as all that. They all suspected at once that he would not really go to rest, but would probably sneak out on business of his own.

'I've some work to attend to for a little while,' said Mr Lenoir. 'I've rung up the police, but unluckily the Inspector is out. He will ring me directly he comes back. Now can you keep out of mischief till I've finished my work?'

The children thought that was a silly question. They

made no reply. Mr Lenoir gave one of his sudden smiles and little laughs, and went.

'I'm going to pop along to Block's room and see if he really *is* there,' said Julian, as soon as Mr Lenoir was out of sight.

He went to the wing where the staff bedrooms were, and stopped softly outside Block's. The door was a little ajar, and Julian could see through the crack. He saw the shape of Block's body in the bed, and the dark patch that was his head. The curtains were drawn across the window to keep out the light, but there was enough to see all this.

Julian sped back to the others. 'Yes, he's in bed all right,' he said. 'Well, he's safe for a bit. Shall we have a shot at getting down to the window-seat hole? I'd dearly like to see where it leads to!'

'Oh yes!' said everyone. But it was not an easy job to drop eight feet down without being terribly jolted! Julian went first and was very much jarred. He called up to Dick: 'We'll have to get a bit of rope and tie it to something up there, and let it hang down the hole – it's an awful business to let yourself drop down.'

But just as Dick went to find a rope, Julian called up again. 'Oh, it's all right! I've just seen something. There are niches carved into the sides of the hole – niches you can put foot or hand into. I didn't see them before. You can use them to help you down.'

So down went everyone, one after another, feeling for the niches and finding them. George missed one or two, clawed wildly at the air, and dropped down the last few feet, landing with rather a bump, but she was not hurt.

As they had thought, the hole led to another secret passage in the house, but this one went straight downwards by means of steps, so that very soon they went well below the level of the house. Then they came into the maze of tunnels that honeycombed the hill. They stopped.

'Look here – we can't possibly go any farther,' said Julian. 'We shall get lost. We haven't got Sooty with us now, and Marybelle isn't any good at finding the way. It would be dangerous to wander about.'

They could hear the hollow sound of footsteps coming from a tunnel to the left of them. They all shrank back into the shadows, and Julian switched off his torch.

'It's *two* people!' whispered Anne, as two figures came out of the nearby tunnel. One was very tall and long. The other – yes, surely the other was Block! If it wasn't Block it was someone the exact image of him.

The men were talking in low voices, answering one another. How could it be Block, though, if he could hear as well as that? Anyway, Block was asleep in bed. It was hardly ten minutes since Julian had seen him there. Were there two Blocks, then? thought George, as she had once thought before.

The men disappeared into another tunnel, and the bright light of their lanterns disappeared gradually. The muffled rumble of their voices echoed back.

'Shall we follow them?' said Dick.

'Of course not,' said Julian. 'We might lose them – and lose ourselves too! And supposing they suddenly turned back and found us following them? We should be in a horrid fix.'

'I'm sure the first man was Mr Barling,' said Anne,

suddenly. 'I couldn't see his face because the light of the lantern wasn't on it – but he seemed just like Mr Barling – awfully tall and long everywhere!'

'But Mr Barling's gone away,' said Marybelle.

'*Supposed* to have gone away!' said George. 'It looks as if he's come back, if it *was* him. I wonder where those two have gone – to see my father and Sooty, do you think?'

'Quite likely,' said Julian. 'Come on, let's get back. We simply *daren't* wander about by ourselves in these old tunnels. They run for miles, Sooty said, and cross one another, and go up and down and round about – even right down to the marsh. We should never, never find our way out if we got lost.'

They turned to go back. They came to the end of the steps they had been climbing, and found themselves at the bottom of the window-seat hole. It was quite easy to pull themselves up by the niches in the sides of the hole.

Soon they were all in the room again, glad to see the sunshine streaming in at the window. They looked out. The marshes were beginning to be wreathed in mist once more, though up here the hill was golden with sunlight.

'I'm going to put the screws back into the window-seat again,' said Julian, picking up the screwdriver and shutting down the lid. 'Then if Block comes here he won't guess we've found this new secret place. I'm pretty certain that he unscrewed the seat so that Mr Barling could get into this room, and then screwed it down again so that no one would guess what had happened.'

CURIOUS DISCOVERIES

He quickly put in the screws. Then he looked at his watch.

'Almost dinner-time, and I'm jolly hungry. I wish old Sooty was here – and Uncle Quentin. I do hope they're all right – and Timmy too,' said Julian. 'I wonder if Block is still in bed – or wandering about the tunnels. I'm going to have a peep again.'

He soon came back, puzzled. 'Yes, he's there all right, safe in bed. It's jolly funny.'

Block did not appear at lunch-time. Sarah said he had asked not to be disturbed, if he did not appear.

'He does get the most awful sick headaches,' she said. 'Maybe he'll be all right this afternoon.'

She badly wanted to talk about everything, but the children had decided not to tell her anything. She was very nice and they liked her, but somehow they didn't trust anyone at Smuggler's Top. So Sarah got nothing out of them at all, and retired in rather a huff.

Julian went down to speak to Mr Lenoir after the meal. He felt that even if the Inspector of Police was not at the police-station, somebody else must be informed. He was very worried about his uncle and Sooty. He couldn't help wondering if Mr Lenoir had made up the bit about the Inspector being away, to put off time.

Mr Lenoir was looking cross when Julian knocked at his study-door. 'Oh, it's you!' he said to Julian. 'I was expecting Block. I've rung and rung for him. The bell rings in his room and I can't imagine why he doesn't come. I want him to come to the police-station with me.'

'Good!' thought Julian. Then he spoke aloud. 'I'll go and hurry him up for you, Mr Lenoir. I know where his room is.'

Julian ran up the stairs and went to the little landing up which the back-stairs went to the staff bedrooms. He pushed open Block's door.

Block was apparently still asleep in bed! Julian called loudly, then remembered that Block was deaf. So he went over to the bed and put his hand rather roughly on the hump of the shoulder between the clothes.

But it was curiously soft! Julian drew his hand away, and looked down sharply. Then he got a real shock.

There was no Block in the bed! There was a big ball of some sort, painted black to look like a head almost under the sheets – and, when Julian threw back the covers, he saw instead of Block's body, a large lumpy bolster, cleverly moulded to look like a curved body!

'*That's* the trick Block plays when he wants to slip off anywhere, and yet pretend he's still here!' said Julian. 'So it *was* Block we saw in the tunnel this morning – and it *must* have been Block that George saw talking to Mr Barling yesterday, when she looked through the window. He's not deaf, either. He's a very clever – sly – double-faced – deceitful ROGUE!'

166

CHAPTER NINETEEN

Mr Barling talks

MEANTIME, WHAT was happening to Uncle Quentin and Sooty? Many strange things!

Uncle Quentin had been gagged, and drugged so that he could neither struggle nor make any noise, when Mr Barling had crept so unexpectedly into his room. It was easy to drop him down the hole in the window-seat. He fell with a thud that bruised him considerably.

Then poor Sooty had been dropped down too, and after them had come Mr Barling, climbing deftly down by the help of the niches in the sides.

Someone else was down there, to help Mr Barling. Not Block, who had been left to screw down the window-seat so that no one might guess where the victims had been taken, but a hard-faced servant belonging to Mr Barling.

'Had to bring this boy, too – it's Lenoir's son,' said Mr Barling. 'Snooping about in the room. Well, it will serve Lenoir right for working against me!'

The two were half-carried, half-dragged down the long flight of steps and taken into the tunnels below. Mr Barling stopped and took a ball of string from his pocket. He tossed it to his servant.

'Here you are. Tie the end to that nail over there, and let

the string unravel as we go. I know the way quite well, but Block doesn't, and he'll be coming along to bring food to our couple of prisoners tomorrow. Don't want him to lose his way! We can tie the string up again just before we get to the place I'm taking them to, so that they won't see it and use it to escape by.'

The servant tied the string to the nail that Mr Barling pointed out, and then as he went along he let the ball unravel. The string would then serve as a guide to anyone not knowing the way. Otherwise it would be very dangerous to wander about in the underground tunnels. For some of them ran for miles.

After about eight minutes the little company came to a kind of rounded cave, set in the side of a big, but rather low tunnel. Here had been put a bench with some rugs, a box to serve as a table, and a jug of water. Nothing else.

Sooty by now was coming round from his blow on the head. The other prisoner, however, still lay unconscious, breathing heavily.

'No good talking to him,' said Mr Barling. 'He won't be all right till tomorrow. We'll come and talk to him then. I'll bring Block.'

Sooty had been put on the floor. He suddenly sat up, and put his hand to his aching head. He couldn't imagine where he was.

He looked up and saw Mr Barling, and then suddenly he remembered everything. But how had he got there, in this dark cave?

MR BARLING TALKS

'Mr Barling!' he said. 'What's all this? What did you hit me for? Why have you brought me here?'

'Punishment for a small boy who can't keep his nose out of things that don't concern him!' said Mr Barling, in a horrid sarcastic voice. 'You'll be company for our friend on the bench there. He'll sleep till the morning, I'm afraid. You can tell him all about it, then, and say I'll be back to have a little heart-to-heart talk with him! And see here, Pierre – you do know, don't you, the foolishness of trying to wander about these old passages? I've brought you to a little-known one, and if you want to lose yourself and never be heard of again, well, try wandering about, that's all!'

Sooty looked pale. He did know the danger of wandering about those lost old tunnels. This one he was in he was sure he didn't know at all. He was about to ask a few more questions when Mr Barling turned quickly on his heel and went off with his servant. They took the lantern with them and left the boy in darkness. He yelled after them.

'Hi, you beasts! Leave me a light!'

But there was no answer. Sooty heard the footfalls going farther and farther away, and then there was silence and darkness.

The boy felt in his pocket for his torch, but it wasn't there. He had dropped it in his bedroom. He groped his way over to the bench, and felt about for George's father. He wished he would wake up. It was so horrid to be there in the darkness. It was cold, too.

Sooty crept under the rugs and cuddled close to the unconscious man. He longed with all his heart for him to wake up.

From somewhere there sounded the drip-drip-drip of water. After a time Sooty couldn't bear it. He knew it was only drops dripping off the roof of the tunnel in a damp place, but he felt he couldn't bear it. Drip-drip-drip. Drip-drip-drip. If only it would stop!

'I'll have to wake George's father up!' thought the boy, desperately. 'I *must* talk to someone!'

He began to shake the sleeping man, wondering what to call him, for he did not know his surname. He couldn't call him 'George's father'! Then he remembered that the others called him Uncle Quentin, and he began yelling the name in the drugged man's ear.

'Uncle Quentin! Uncle Quentin! Wake up! Do wake up! Oh, won't you please wake up!'

Uncle Quentin stirred at last. He opened his eyes in the darkness, and listened to the urgent voice in his ear, feeling faintly puzzled.

'Uncle Quentin! Wake up and speak to me. I'm scared!' said the voice. 'UNCLE QUENTIN!'

The man thought vaguely that it must be Julian or Dick. He put his arm round Sooty and dragged him close to him. 'It's all right. Go to sleep,' he said. 'What's the matter, Julian? Or is it Dick? Go to sleep.'

He fell asleep again himself, for he was still half-drugged. But Sooty felt comforted now. He shut his

eyes, feeling certain that he couldn't possibly go to sleep.
But he did, almost at once! He slept soundly all through
the night, and was only awakened by Uncle Quentin
moving on the bench.

The puzzled man was amazed to find his bed so
unexpectedly hard. He was even more amazed to find
someone in bed with him, for he remembered nothing at
all. He stretched out his hand to switch on the reading-
lamp which had been beside his bed the night before.

But it wasn't there! Strange! He felt about and touched
Sooty's face. What was this beside him? He began to feel
extremely puzzled. He felt ill, too. What *could* have
happened?

'Are you awake?' said Sooty's voice. 'Oh, Uncle Quentin, I'm so glad you're awake. I hope you don't mind me calling you that, but I don't know your surname. I only know you are George's father and Julian's uncle.'

'Well – who are you?' said Uncle Quentin, in wonder.

Sooty began to tell him everything. Uncle Quentin listened in the utmost amazement. 'But *why* have we been kidnapped like this?' he said, astonished and angry. 'I never heard of such a thing in my life!'

'I don't know why Mr Barling has kidnapped *you* but I know he took me because I happened to see what he was doing,' said Sooty. 'Anyway, he's coming back this morning, with Block, and he said he would have a heart-to-heart talk with you. We'll have to wait here, I'm afraid. We can't possibly find our way to safety in the darkness, through this maze of tunnels.'

So they waited – and in due course Mr Barling did come, bringing Block with him. Block carried some food, which was very welcome to the prisoners.

'You beast, Block!' said Sooty, at once, as he saw the servant in the light of the lantern. 'How dare you help in this? You wait till my stepfather hears about it! Unless he's in it too!'

'Hold your tongue!' said Block.

Sooty stared at him. 'So you *can* hear!' he said. 'All this time you've been pretending you can't! What a sly fellow you are! What a lot of secrets you must have learnt, pretending to be deaf, and overhearing all kinds of things

172

not meant for you. You're sly, Block, and you're worse things than that!'

'Whip him, Block, if you like,' said Mr Barling, sitting down on the box. 'I've no time for rude boys myself.'

'I will,' said Block, grimly, and he undid a length of rope from round his waist. 'I've often wanted to, cheeky little worm!'

Sooty felt alarmed. He leapt off the bench and put up his fists.

'Let me talk to our prisoner first,' said Mr Barling. 'Then you can give Pierre the hiding he deserves. It will be nice for him to wait for it.'

Uncle Quentin was listening quietly to all this. He looked at Mr Barling, and spoke sternly.

'You owe me an explanation for your strange behaviour. I demand to be taken to Smuggler's Top. You shall answer to the police for this!'

'Oh no, I shan't,' said Mr Barling, in a curiously soft voice. 'I have a very generous proposal to make to you. I know why you have come to Smuggler's Top. I know why you and Mr Lenoir are so interested in each other's experiments.'

'How do you know?' said Uncle Quentin. 'Spying, I suppose!'

'Yes – I bet Block's been spying and reading letters!' cried Sooty, indignantly.

Mr Barling took no notice of the interruption. 'Now, my dear sir,' he said to Uncle Quentin, 'I will tell you very shortly what I propose. I know you have heard that I am a smuggler. I am. I make a lot of money from it. It is easy to run a smuggling trade here, because no one can patrol the marshes, or stop men using the secret path that only I and a few others know. On favourable nights I send out a signal – or rather Block here does so, for me, using the convenient tower of Smuggler's Top . . .'

'Oh! So it *was* Block!' cried Sooty.

'Then when the goods arrive,' said Mr Barling, 'and again at a favourable moment I – er – dispose of them. I cover my tracks very carefully, so that no one can possibly accuse me because they never have any real proof.'

'Why are you telling me all this?' said Uncle Quentin scornfully. 'It's of no interest to me. I'm only interested in a plan for draining the marshes, not in smuggling goods across them!'

'Exactly, my dear fellow!' said Mr Barling, amiably. 'I know that. I have even seen your plans and read about your experiments and Mr Lenoir's. But the draining of the marsh means the end of my own business! Once the marsh is drained, once houses are built there, and roads made, once the mists have gone, my business goes too! A harbour may be built out there, at the edge of the marshes – my ships can no longer creep in unseen, bringing valuable cargoes! Not only will my money go, but all the excitement, which is more than life to me, will go too!'

'You're mad!' said Uncle Quentin, in disgust.

174

MR BARLING TALKS

Mr Barling *was* a little mad. He had always felt a great satisfaction in being a successful smuggler in days when smuggling was almost at an end. He loved the thrill of knowing that his little ships were creeping in the mist towards the treacherous marshes. He liked to know that men were making their way over a small and narrow path over the misty marsh to the appointed meeting-place, bringing smuggled goods.

'You should have lived a hundred years or more ago!' said Sooty, also feeling that Mr Barling was a little mad. 'You don't belong to nowadays.'

Mr Barling turned on Sooty, his eyes gleaming dangerously in the light of the lantern.

'Another word from you and I'll drop you in the marshes!' he said. Sooty felt a shiver go down his back. He suddenly knew that Mr Barling really did mean what he said. He was a dangerous man. Uncle Quentin sensed it too. He looked at Mr Barling warily.

'How do I come into this?' he asked. 'Why have you kidnapped me?'

'I know that Mr Lenoir is going to buy your plans from you,' said Mr Barling. 'I know he is going to drain the marsh by using your very excellent ideas. You see, I know all about them! I know, too, that Mr Lenoir hopes to make a lot of money by selling the land once it is drained. It is all his, that misty marsh – and no use to anyone now except to me! But that marsh is not going to be drained – I am going to buy your plans, not Mr Lenoir!'

'Do *you* want to drain the marsh, then?' said Uncle Quentin, in surprise.

Mr Barling laughed scornfully. 'No! Your plans, and the results of your experiments, will be burnt! They will be mine, but I shall not want to use them. I want the marsh left as it is, secret, covered with mist, and treacherous to all but me and my men. So, my dear sir, you will please name your price to me, instead of to Mr Lenoir, and sign this document, which I have had prepared, making over all your plans to me!'

He flourished a large piece of paper in front of Uncle Quentin. Sooty watched breathlessly.

Uncle Quentin picked up the paper. He tore it into small pieces. He threw them into Mr Barling's face and said, scornfully: 'I don't deal with madmen, nor with rogues, Mr Barling!'

CHAPTER TWENTY

Timmy to the rescue

MR BARLING went very pale. Sooty gave a loud crow of delight. 'Hurrah! Good for *you*, Uncle Quentin!'

Block gave a loud exclamation, and darted to the excited boy. He took him by the shoulder, and raised the rope to thrash him.

'That's right,' said Mr Barling, in a funny kind of hissing voice. 'Deal with him first, Block, and then with this – this – stubborn – obstinate – fool! We'll soon bring them to their senses. A good thrashing now and again, a few days here in the dark, without any food – ah, that will make them more biddable!'

Sooty yelled at the top of his voice. Uncle Quentin leapt to his feet. The rope came down and Sooty yelled again.

Then there suddenly came the pattering of quick feet, and something flung itself on Block. Block gave a scream of pain and turned. He knocked the lantern over by accident, and the light went out. There was a sound of fierce growling. Block staggered about trying to keep off the creature that had fastened itself on to him.

'Barling! Help me!' he shouted.

Mr Barling went to his aid, but was attacked in his turn. Uncle Quentin and Sooty listened in amazement and fear.

What creature was this that had suddenly arrived? Would it attack them next? Was it a giant rat – or some fierce wild animal that haunted these tunnels?

The fierce animal suddenly barked. Sooty cheered.

TIMMY TO THE RESCUE

'TIMMY! It's you, Timmy! Oh, good dog, good dog! Go for him, then, go for him! Bite him, Timmy, hard.'

The two frightened men could do nothing against the angry dog. Soon they were running down the tunnel as fast as they could go, feeling for the string for fear of being lost. Timmy chased them with much enjoyment, and then returned to Sooty and George's father, rather pleased with himself.

He had a tremendous welcome. George's father made a great fuss of him, and Sooty put his arms round the big dog's neck.

'How did you come here? Did you find your way out of the secret passage you've been in? Are you half-starved? Look, here's some food.'

Timmy ate heartily. He had managed to devour a few rats, but otherwise had had no food at all. He had licked the drops that here and there he had found dripping from the roof, so he had not been thirsty. But he had certainly been extremely puzzled and worried. He had never before been so long away from his beloved mistress!

'Uncle Quentin – Timmy could take us safely back to Smuggler's Top, couldn't he?' said Sooty, suddenly. He spoke to Timmy. 'Can you take us home, old boy? Home, to George?'

Timmy listened, with his ears cocked up. He ran down the passage a little way, but soon came back. He did not like the idea of going down there. He felt that enemies were waiting for them all. Mr Barling and Block were not likely to give in quite so easily!

But Timmy knew other ways about the tunnels that honeycombed the hillside. He knew, for instance, the way down to the marsh! So he set off in the darkness, with Uncle Quentin's hand on his collar, and Sooty following close behind, holding on to Uncle Quentin's coat.

It wasn't easy or pleasant. Uncle Quentin wondered at times if Timmy really did know where he was going. They went down and down, stumbling over uneven places, sometimes knocking their heads against an unexpected low piece of roof. It was not a pleasant journey for Uncle Quentin, for he had no shoes on his feet, and was dressed only in pyjamas and rugs.

After a long time they came out on the edge of the marsh itself, at the bottom of the hill! It was a desolate place, and the mists were over it, so that neither Sooty nor Uncle Quentin knew which way to turn!

'Never mind,' said Sooty, 'we can easily leave it to Timmy. He knows the way all right. He'll take us back to the town, and once there we'll know the way home ourselves!'

But suddenly, to their surprise and dismay, Timmy stopped dead, pricking up his ears, whined and would go no farther. He looked thoroughly miserable and unhappy. What could be the matter?

Then, with a bark, the big dog left the two by themselves, and galloped back into the tunnel they had just left.

He disappeared completely!

'Timmy!' yelled Sooty. 'Timmy! Come here! Don't leave us! TIMMY!'

But Timmy was gone; why, neither Sooty nor Uncle Quentin knew. They stared at one another.

'Well – I suppose we'd better try to make our way over this marshy bit,' said Uncle Quentin, doubtfully, putting a foot out to see if the ground was hard. It wasn't! He drew back his foot at once.

The mists were so thick that it was really impossible to see anything. Behind them was the opening to the tunnel. A steep rocky cliff rose up about it. There was no path that way, it was certain. Somehow they had to make their way round the foot of the hill to the main-road that entered the town – but the way lay over marshy ground!

'Let's sit down and wait for a bit to see if Timmy comes back,' said Sooty. So they sat down on a rock at the entrance to the tunnel and waited.

Sooty began to think of the others. He wondered what they had thought when they had discovered that both he and Uncle Quentin were missing. How astonished they must have been!

'I wonder what the others are doing?' he said, aloud. 'I'd love to know!'

The others, as we know, had been doing plenty. They had found the opening in the window-seat where Mr Barling had taken the captives, and they had gone down it and actually seen Mr Barling and Block on their way to talk to Uncle Quentin and Sooty!

They had found out, too, that Block hadn't been in his bed – he had left a dummy there instead. Now everyone was talking at once, and Mr Lenoir was suddenly convinced that Block had been a spy, put in his house by Mr Barling, and not the good servant he had appeared!

Once Julian felt that he was convinced of this he spoke to him more freely, and told him of the way through the window-seat, and of how they had seen Mr Barling and Block that very day, in the underground tunnels!

'Good heavens!' said Mr Lenoir, now looking thoroughly alarmed. 'Barling must be mad! I've always thought he was a bit strange – but he must be absolutely mad to kidnap people like this – and Block must be, too. This is a plot! They've heard what I've been planning with your uncle – and they've made up their minds to stop it because it will interfere with their smuggling. Goodness knows what they'll do now! This is serious!'

'If only we had Timmy!' suddenly said George.

Mr Lenoir looked astonished.

'Who's Timmy?'

'Well, you might as well know everything now,' said Julian, and he told Mr Lenoir about Timmy, and how they had hidden him.

'Very foolish of you,' said Mr Lenoir, shortly, looking displeased. 'If you'd told me I would have had someone in the town look after him. I can't help not liking dogs. I detest them, and never will have them in the house. But

TIMMY TO THE RESCUE

I would willingly have arranged for him to be boarded out, if I'd known you'd brought him.'

The children felt sorry and a little ashamed. Mr Lenoir was an odd, hot-tempered person, but he didn't seem nearly as horrid as they had thought he was.

'I'd like to go and see if I can find Timmy,' said George. 'You'll get the police in now, I suppose, Mr Lenoir, and perhaps we could go and find Timmy? We know the way into the secret passage from your study.'

'Oh – so *that's* why you were hiding there in the afternoon yesterday,' said Mr Lenoir. 'I thought you were a very bad boy. Well, go and try and find him if you like, but don't let him come anywhere near me. I really cannot bear dogs in the house.'

He went to telephone the police-station again. Mrs Lenoir, her eyes red with crying, stood by him. George slipped away to the study, followed by Dick and Julian and Anne. Marybelle stayed beside her mother.

'Come on – let's get into that secret passage and try and find old Timmy,' said George. 'If we all go, and whistle and shout and call, he's sure to hear us!'

They found the way into the passage, by doing the things they had done before. The panel slid back, and then another, larger opening came as before. They all squeezed through it, and found themselves in the very narrow passage that led from the study up to Sooty's bedroom.

But Timmy was not there! The children were surprised, but George soon thought why.

'Do you remember Sooty telling us there was a way into this passage from the dining-room, as well as from the study and Sooty's bedroom? Well, I believe I saw a door or something there, as we passed where the dining-room must be, and it's likely Timmy may have pushed through it, and gone into another passage somewhere.'

They went back, one by one. They came to the dining-room – or rather, they walked behind the dining-room wall. There they saw the door that George had noticed as they passed – a door, small and set quite flat to the wall, so that it was difficult to see. George pushed it. It opened easily, and then flapped shut, with a little click. It could be opened from one side but not from the other.

'That's where Timmy's gone!' said George, and she pushed the door open again. 'He pushed against the door and it opened – he went through, and the door fastened itself so that he couldn't get back. Come on, we must find him.'

They all went through the small door. It was so low that they had to bend their heads to go through, even Anne. They found themselves in a passage rather like the one they had just left, but not quite so narrow. It suddenly began to go downwards. Julian called back to the others.

'I believe it goes down to the passages where we used to take Timmy when we let him down into that pit to go for a walk! Yes, look – we've come to where the pit itself is!'

They went on, calling Timmy, and whistling loudly, but

no Timmy came. George began to feel worried.

'Hallo! – Surely this is where we came out when we climbed down all those steps from the window-seat passage!' said Dick, suddenly. 'Yes, it is. Look, there's the tunnel where we saw Block and Mr Barling going!'

'Oh – do you think they've done something to Timmy?' said George, in a frightened voice. 'I never thought of that!'

Everyone felt alarmed. It was strange that Block and Mr Barling could go about unmolested by Timmy if Timmy was somewhere near! Could they have harmed him in any way? They had no idea that Timmy was at that very minute with George's father and Sooty!

'Look at this!' said Julian, suddenly, and he shone his torch on to something to show the others. 'String! String going right down this tunnel. Why?'

'It's the tunnel that Mr Barling and Block took!' said George. 'I believe it leads to where they've taken my father and Sooty! They're keeping them prisoners down here! I'm going to follow the string and find them! Who's coming with me?'

CHAPTER TWENTY-ONE

A journey through the hill

'I'M COMING!' said everyone at once. As if they would let George go alone!

So down the dark tunnel they went, feeling the string and following it. Julian ran it through his fingers, and the others followed behind, holding hands. It would not do for anyone to get lost.

After about ten minutes they came to the rounded cave where Sooty and George's father had been the night before. They were not there now, of course – they were on their way down to the marsh!

'Hallo, look! This is where they must have been!' cried Julian, shining his torch round. 'A bench – with tumbled rugs – and an over-turned lamp. And look here, scraps of paper torn into bits! Something's been happening here!'

Quick-witted George pieced it together in her mind. 'Mr Barling took them here and left them. Then he came back with some sort of proposal to Father, who refused it! There must have been a struggle of some sort and the lamp got broken. Oh – I do hope Father and Sooty got away all right.'

Julian felt gloomy. 'I hope to goodness they haven't gone wandering about these awful tunnels. Even Sooty doesn't know a quarter of them. I wish I knew what's happened.'

'Someone's coming!' suddenly said Dick. 'Snap out the light, Ju.'

Julian snapped off the torch he carried. At once they were all in darkness. They crouched at the back of the cave, listening.

Yes – footsteps were coming. Rather cautious footsteps. 'Sound like two or three people,' whispered Dick. They came nearer. Whoever was coming was plainly following the tunnel where the string was.

'Mr Barling perhaps – and Block,' whispered George. 'Come to have another talk with Father! But he's gone!'

A brilliant light flashed suddenly round the cave – and picked out the huddled children. There was a loud exclamation of astonishment.

'Good heavens! Who's here? What's all this?'

It was Mr Barling's voice. Julian stood up, blinking in the bright light.

'We came to look for my uncle and Sooty,' he said. 'Where are they?'

'Aren't they here?' said Mr Barling, seeming surprised. 'And is that horrible brute of a dog gone?'

'Oh – was Timmy here?' cried George, joyfully. 'Where is he?'

There were two other men with Mr Barling. One was Block. The other was his servant. Mr Barling put down the lantern he was carrying.

'Do you mean to say you don't know where the others are?' he said, uneasily. 'If they've gone off on their own, they'll never come back.'

Anne gave a little scream. 'It's all your fault, you horrid man!'

'Shut up, Anne!' said Julian. 'Mr Barling,' he said, turning to the angry smuggler, 'I think you'd better come back with us and explain things. Mr Lenoir is now talking to the police.'

'Oh, *is* he?' said Mr Barling. 'Then I think it would be as well for us all to stay down here for a while! Yes, you too! I'll make Mr Lenoir squirm! I'll hold you all prisoners – and this time you shall be bound so that you don't go wandering off like the others! Got some rope, Block?'

Block stepped forward with the other man. They caught hold of George first, very roughly.

She screamed loudly. 'Timmy! Timmy! Where are you? Timmy, come and help! Oh, TIMMY!'

But no Timmy came. She was soon in a corner with her hands tied behind her. Then they turned to Julian.

'You're mad,' Julian said to Mr Barling, who was standing nearby, holding the lantern. 'You *must* be mad to do things like this.'

'Timmy!' shouted George, trying to free her hands. 'Timmy, Timmy, Timmy!'

Timmy didn't hear. He was too far away. But the dog suddenly felt uneasy. He was with George's father and Sooty at the edge of the marsh, about to lead them round the hill to safety. But he stopped and listened. He could hear nothing of course. But Timmy knew that George was in danger. He knew that his beloved little mistress needed him.

His ears did not tell him, nor did his nose. But his heart told him. George was in danger!

He turned and fled back into the tunnel. He tore up the winding passages at top speed, panting.

And, quite suddenly, just as Julian was angrily submitting to have his hands tied tightly together, a furry thunderbolt arrived! It was Timmy!

He smelt his enemy, Mr Barling, again! He smelt Block. Grrrrrrrrrr-rrrrrr!

'Here's that awful dog again!' yelled Block, and leapt away from Julian. 'Where's your gun, Barling?'

But Timmy didn't worry about guns. He leapt at Mr Barling and got him on the floor. He gave him a nip in the shoulder that made him yell. Then he leapt at Block, and got him down, too. The other man fled.

'Call your dog off. Call him off, or he'll kill us!' cried Mr Barling, struggling up, his shoulder paining him terribly. But nobody said a word. Let Timmy do what he liked!

It wasn't long before all three of the men had gone into the dark tunnel, staggering about without a light, trying to find their way back. But they missed the string, and went wandering away in the darkness, groaning and terrified.

Timmy came running back very pleased with himself.

189

He went to George and, whining with joy, he licked his little mistress from head to foot. And George, who never cried, was most astonished to find the tears pouring down her cheeks. 'But I'm glad, not sad!' she said. 'Oh, somebody undo my hands! I can't pat Timmy!'

Dick undid her hands and Julian's. Then they all had a marvellous time making a fuss of Timmy. And what a fuss he made of them too! He whined and barked, he rolled over and over, he licked them and butted them all with his head. He was wild with delight.

'Oh Timmy – it's lovely to have you again,' said George, happily. 'Now you can lead us to the others. I'm sure you know where Father is, Timmy, and Sooty.'

Timmy did, of course. He set off, his tail wagging, George's hand on his collar, and the others behind in a line, holding hands.

They had the lantern with them and two torches, so they could see the way easily. But they would never have taken the right tunnels if Timmy hadn't been with them. The dog had explored them all thoroughly, and his sense of smell enabled him to go the right way without mistake.

'He's a marvellous dog,' said Anne. 'I think he's the best dog in the world, George.'

'Of course he is,' said George, who had always thought that ever since she had had Timmy as a puppy. 'Darling Tim – wasn't it wonderful when he came racing up and jumped at Block just as he was tying Julian's hands? He must have known we needed him!'

A JOURNEY THROUGH THE HILL

'I suppose he's taking us to wherever your father and Sooty are,' said Dick. 'He seems certain of the way. We're going steadily downhill. I bet we'll be at the marshes soon!'

When they at last came to the bottom of the hill, and emerged from the tunnel in the mists, George gave a yell. 'Look! There's Father – and Sooty too!'

'Uncle Quentin!' shouted Julian, Dick and Anne. 'Sooty! Hallo, here we are!'

Uncle Quentin and Sooty turned in the greatest surprise. They jumped up and went to meet the dog and the excited children.

'How *did* you get here?' said George's father, giving her a hug. 'Did Timmy go back for you? He suddenly deserted us and fled back into the tunnel.'

'What's happened?' asked Sooty, eagerly, knowing that the others would have plenty of news to tell him.

'Heaps,' said George, her face glowing. It was so nice all to be together again, Timmy too. She and Julian and Dick began to tell everything in turn, and then her father told his tale, too, interrupted a little by Sooty.

'Well,' said Julian at last, 'I suppose we ought to be getting back, or the police will be sending out blood-hounds to trace us all! Mr Lenoir will be surprised to see us all turning up together.'

'I wish I wasn't in pyjamas,' said his uncle, drawing the rugs about him. 'I shall feel most peculiar walking the streets like this!'

'Never mind – it's awfully misty now,' said George, and

she shivered a little, for the air was damp. 'Timmy – show us the way out of this place. I'm sure you know it.'

Timmy had never been out of the tunnel before, but he seemed to know what to do. He set off round the foot of the hill, the rest following, marvelling at the way Timmy found a dry path to follow. In the mist it was almost impossible to see which place was safe to walk on and which was not. The treacherous marsh was all around them!

'Hurrah! There's the road!' cried Julian, suddenly, as they came in sight of the roadway built over the marsh, running up the hill from the salty stretches of mud. They picked their way to it, their feet soaked with wet mud. Timmy tried to take a flying leap on to it.

But somehow or other he slipped! He fell back into the marsh, tried to find a safe foothold and couldn't. He whined.

'Timmy! Oh look, he's in the mud – and he's sinking!' screamed George, in panic. 'Timmy, Timmy, I'm coming!'

She was about to step down into the marsh to rescue Tim, but her father pulled her back roughly. 'Do you want to sink in, too?' he cried. 'Timmy will get out all right.'

But he wasn't getting out. He was sinking. 'Do something, oh, do something!' shouted George, struggling to get away from her father's hold. 'Oh, save Timmy, quick!'

CHAPTER TWENTY-TWO

Things come right at last

BUT WHAT could anyone do? In despair they all gazed at poor Timmy, who was struggling with all his might in the sinking mud. 'He's going down!' wept Anne.

Suddenly there came the sound of rumbling wheels along the road to the hill. It was a lorry carrying a load of goods – coal, coke, planks, logs, sacks of various things. George yelled to it.

'Stop, stop! Help us! Our dog's in the marsh.'

The lorry came to a stop. George's father ran his eye over the things it carried. In a trice he and Julian were dragging out some planks from the load. They threw these into the marsh, and, using them as stepping-stones, the two reached poor sinking Timmy.

The lorry-driver jumped down to help. Into the marsh, crosswise on the other planks, went some more wood, to make a safe path. The first lot were already sinking in the mud.

'Uncle Quentin's got Timmy – he's pulling him up! He's got him!' squealed Anne.

George had sat down suddenly at the edge of the road, looking white. She saw that Timmy would now be rescued, and she felt sick with shock and relief.

It was a difficult business getting Timmy right out, for the mud was strong, and sucked him down as hard as it could. But at last he was out, and he staggered across the sinking planks, trying to wag a very muddy tail.

Muddy as he was, George flung her arms round him.

'Oh Timmy – what a fright you gave us all! Oh, how you smell – but I don't care a bit! I thought you were gone, poor, poor Timmy!'

The lorry-driver looked ruefully at his planks in the marsh. They were now out of sight beneath the mud. Uncle Quentin, feeling rather foolish in pyjamas and rugs, spoke to him.

'I've no money on me now, but if you'll call at Smuggler's Top sometime I'll pay you well for your lost planks and your help.'

'Well, I'm delivering some coal to the house next to Smuggler's Top,' said the man, eyeing Uncle Quentin's curious attire. 'Maybe you'd all like a lift? There's plenty of room at the back there.'

It was getting dark now, as well as being foggy, and everyone was tired. Thankfully they climbed up into the lorry, and it roared up the hill into Castaway. Soon they were at Smuggler's Top, and they all clambered down, suddenly feeling rather stiff.

'I'll be calling tomorrow, said the driver. 'Can't stop now. Good evening to you all!'

The little company rang the bell. Sarah came hurrying to the door. She almost fell over in surprise as she saw everyone standing there in the light of the hall-lamp.

'Lands' sakes!' she said. 'You're all back! My, Mr and Mrs Lenoir will be glad – they've got the police hunting everywhere for you! They've gone down secret passages, and they've been to Mr Barling's, and . . .'

Timmy bounced into the hall, the mud now drying on him, so that he looked most peculiar. Sarah gave a scream. 'What's that? Gracious, it can't be a dog!'

'Come here, Tim!' said George, suddenly remembering that Mr Lenoir detested dogs. 'Sarah, do you think you'd have poor Timmy in the kitchen with you? I really can't turn him out into the streets – you've no idea how brave he's been.'

'Come along, come along!' said her father, impatient with all this talk. 'Lenoir can put up with Timmy for a few minutes, surely!'

'Oh, *I'll* have him with pleasure!' said Sarah. 'I'll give him a bath. That's what he wants. Mr and Mrs Lenoir are in the sitting-room. Oh, shall I get you some clothes?'

The little party went in, and made their way to the sitting-room, while Timmy went docilely to the kitchen with the excited Sarah. Mr Lenoir heard the talking and flung open the sitting-room door.

Mrs Lenoir fell on Sooty, tears pouring down her cheeks. Marybelle pawed at him in delight, just as if she was a dog! Mr Lenoir rubbed his hands, clapped everyone on the back, and said: 'Well, well! Fine to see you all safe and sound. Well, well! What a tale you've got to tell, I'm sure!'

'It's a strange tale, Lenoir,' said George's father. 'Very strange. But I'll have to see to my feet before I tell it. I've walked miles in my bare feet, and they're very painful now!'

THINGS COME RIGHT AT LAST

So, with bits of tales pouring out from everyone, the household bustled round and got hot water for bathing Uncle Quentin's feet, a dressing-gown for him, food for everyone, and hot drinks. It was really a most exciting time, and now that the thrills were all over, the children felt rather important to be able to relate so much.

Then the police came in, of course, and the Inspector at once asked a lot of questions. Everyone wanted to answer them, but the Inspector said that only George's father, Sooty and George were to tell the tale. They knew most about everything.

Mr Lenoir was perhaps the most surprised person there. When he heard how Mr Barling had actually offered to buy the plans for draining the marsh, and how he had frankly admitted to being a smuggler, he sat back in his chair, unable to say a word.

'He's mad, of course!' said the Inspector of Police. 'Doesn't seem to live in this world at all!'

'That's just what I said to him,' said Sooty. 'I told him he ought to have lived a hundred years ago!'

'Well, we've tried to catch him in the smuggling business many and many a time,' said the Inspector, 'but he was too artful. Fancy him planting Block here as a spy, sir – that was a clever bit of work – and Block using your tower as a signalling place! Bit of nerve, that! And Block isn't deaf, after all? That was clever, too – sending him about, pretending he was stone-deaf, so that he could catch many a bit of knowledge not meant for his ears!'

'Do you think we ought to do something about Block and Mr Barling and the other man?' said Julian, suddenly. 'For all we know they're still wandering about in that maze of tunnels – and two of them are bitten by Timmy, we know.'

'Ah yes – that dog saved your lives, I should think,' said the Inspector. 'A bit of luck, that. Sorry you don't like dogs, Mr Lenoir, but I'm sure you'll admit it was a lucky thing for you all that he was wandering about!'

'Yes – yes, it was,' said Mr Lenoir. 'Of course, Block never wanted dogs here, either – he was afraid they might bark at his curious comings and goings, I suppose. By the way – where *is* this marvellous dog? I don't mind seeing him for a moment – though I do detest dogs, and always shall.'

'I'll get him,' said George. 'I only hope Sarah's done what she said, and bathed him. He was awfully muddy!'

She went out and came back with Timmy. But what a different Timmy! Sarah had given him a good hot bath, and had dried him well. He smelt sweet and fresh, his coat was springy and clean, and he had had a good meal. He was feeling very pleased with himself and everything.

'Timmy – meet a friend,' said George to him, solemnly. Timmy looked at Mr Lenoir out of his big brown eyes. He trotted straight up to him, and held up his right paw politely to shake hands, as George had taught him.

Mr Lenoir was rather taken aback. He was not used to good manners in dogs. He couldn't help putting out his hand to Timmy – and the two shook hands in a most friendly manner. Timmy didn't attempt to lick Mr Lenoir or jump up at him. He took away his paw, gave a little wuff as if to say 'How-do-you-do?' and then went back to George. He lay down quietly beside her. 'Well – he doesn't seem like a *dog*!' said Mr Lenoir, in surprise.

'Oh, he *is*,' said George, at once, very earnestly. 'He's a real, proper dog, Mr Lenoir – only much, much cleverer than most dogs are. Could I keep him, please, while we stay here, and get someone in the town to look after him?'

'Well – seeing he is such a very fine fellow – and seems so sensible – I'll let you have him here,' said Mr Lenoir, making a great effort to be generous. 'Only – please keep him out of my way. I'm sure a sensible boy like you will see to that.'

Everyone grinned when Mr Lenoir called George a boy. He never seemed to realise she was a girl. She grinned, too. She wasn't going to tell him she wasn't a boy!

'You'll never see him!' she said, joyfully. 'I'll keep him right out of your way. Thank you very much. It's awfully good of you.'

The Inspector liked Timmy, too. He looked at him and nodded across to George. 'When you want to get rid of him, sell him to me!' he said. 'We could do with a dog like that in our police force! Soon round up the smugglers for us!'

George didn't even bother to reply! As if she would ever sell Timmy, or let him go into the police force!

All the same, the Inspector had to call on Timmy for help before long. When the next day came, and no one had found Mr Barling and his companions in the maze of tunnels, and they hadn't turned up anywhere, the Inspector asked George if she would let Timmy go down into the tunnels and hunt them out.

'Can't leave them there, lost and starving,' he said. 'Bad as they are we'll have to rescue them! Timmy is the only one who can find them.'

That was true, of course. So Timmy once more went underground into the hill, and hunted for his enemies. He found them after a while, lost in the maze of passages, hungry and thirsty, in pain and frightened.

THINGS COME RIGHT AT LAST

He took them like sheep to where the police waited for them. And after that Mr Barling and his friends disappeared from public life for quite a long time!

'The police must be glad to have got them at last,' said Mr Lenoir. 'They have tried to stop this smuggling for a long time. They even suspected *me* at one time! Barling was a clever fellow, though I still think he was half mad. When Block found out my ideas about draining the marsh, Barling was afraid that once the mists and the marsh were gone, that would be the end of all his excitement – no more smuggling! No more waiting for his little ships to come creeping up in the fog – no more lines of men slipping across the secret ways of the marsh – no more signalling, no more hiding away of smuggled goods. Did you know that the police had found a cave full of them inside the hill?'

It was an exciting adventure to talk about, now that it was all over. The children felt sorry about one thing, though – they were sorry that they had thought Mr Lenoir so horrid. He was a strange man in many ways, but he could be kind and jolly too.

'Did you know we're leaving Smuggler's Top?' said Sooty. 'Mother was so terribly upset when I disappeared, that Father promised her he'd sell the place and leave Castaway, if I came back safe and sound. Mother's thrilled!'

'So am I,' said Marybelle. 'I don't like Smuggler's Top – it's so weird and secret and lonely!'

'Well, if it will make you all happy to leave it, I'm glad,' said Julian 'But *I* like it! I think it's a lovely place, set on a hill-top like this, with mists at its foot, and secret ways all about it. I'll be sorry never to come here again, if you leave.'

'So will I,' said Dick, and Anne and George nodded.

'It's an adventurous place!' said George, patting Timmy. 'Isn't it, Timmy? Do *you* like it, Timmy? Have *you* enjoyed your adventure here?'

'Woof!' said Timmy, and thumped his tail on the floor. Of course he had enjoyed himself. He always did, so long as George was anywhere about.

'Well – now perhaps we'll have a nice peaceful time!' said Marybelle. 'I don't want any more adventures.'

'Ah, but *we* do!' said the others. So no doubt they will get them. Adventures always come to the adventurous, there's no doubt about that!